THE FIRE

On an impulse Dryden reached forward and took the pistol from Nelferch's surprised grip. He broke open the weapon, trying desperately to remember how Adamson had shown him. He revolved the chamber and saw one cartridge in it. An idea developed rapidly in his mind, faster than he would work out the implications. Acting more on instinct than a true reasoning, he pushed the chamber with the bullet to the firing position, snapped the gun shut and drew back the safety catch.

'Nelferch seeks a demonstration of my calling. Thus shall I show her,' he said, raising the pistol towards the old woman.

Nelferch watched him snake-like with her bright blue unwinking eyes. She made no move.

Dryden raised the gun past Nelferch's thin figure until it pointed to the great window at the far end of the throne room. Then he pressed the trigger.

There was a bark from the pistol, a flash and then the window splintered into a million fragments.

For a moment no one moved; it took them several seconds before they recovered from the shock of the noise, the blast and disintegrating window. Then shouts and screams echoed round the hall.

Now Dryden lowered the pistol back to Nelferch and pointed it towards her unmoving form. For the first time her eyes left his face and became opaque with fear as they stared towards the smoking barrel . . .

*Also available in Magnum Books
by Peter Tremayne*

THE REVENGE OF DRACULA

PETER TREMAYNE

The Fires of Lan-Kern

MAGNUM BOOKS

Methuen Paperbacks Ltd

A Magnum Book

THE FIRES OF LAN-KERN
ISBN 0 417 04270 1

First published in Great Britain 1980
by Bailey Brothers & Swinfen Ltd
Magnum edition published 1980

Copyright © 1980 by Peter Tremayne

Magnum Books are published
by Methuen Paperbacks Ltd
11 New Fetter Lane, London EC4P 4EE

Made and printed in Great Britain
by Cox & Wyman Ltd, Reading

For Eleni Triantafillaki, a fellow Piscean voyager:
Round about what is, lies a whole mysterious world of what might be, a psychological romance of possibilities and things that do not happen.
A. W. Longfellow,
Tabletalk,
Driftwood, 1857.

VOLUME ONE

The further adventures of Dryden through the strange once and future world of Lan-Kern will be told in Peter Tremayne's second powerful book in the Lan-Kern trilogy.

PUBLISHER'S FOREWORD

Lan-Kern: A Myth For Our Times

A Twentieth-Century botanist, Frank Dryden, is propelled into the weird and spectacular world of Lan-Kern...a world that is equally of the past and the future. This is the setting for the first volume of Peter Tremayne's exciting and powerful 'swords and sorcery' fantasy trilogy. But *The Fires of Lan-Kern* is more than a mere escapist romance. As well as high adventure, tense drama, romance and mysticism, it offers a deep philosophical approach to life and contains many telling parallels of our own times. This is modern mythology in the making; a saga that is as gloriously rich in incident as it is in human understanding and meaning.

Peter Tremayne has based his saga firmly in the fantastic (and often misinterpreted) world of Celtic mythology and has reworked many of its themes into his drama with bold and imaginative strokes. In Dryden's quest for *An Kevryn* (The Mystery), which - to the people of Lan-Kern - contains the meaning of creation, we find a startling parallel to the Arthurian legend of the quest for the Holy Grail. This theme, the quest for a magic vessel, goes further back into antiquity - even to pre-Christian Celtic mythology as in the tale *The Spoils of Annwyn*. It is not by coincidence that the geographical location of Lan-Kern is placed in Cornwall whose Celtic culture has given the world the romance of Tristan and Iseult and the Arthurian sagas. Neither is it a coincidence that the language of Lan-Kern is, in reality, the Celtic language of Cornwall which ceased to be generally spoken in the Duchy in the 18th Century.

It is envisaged that a glossary of the words and names used in this trilogy will be contained in the last volume of the saga.

It will come, perhaps, as no surprise - and is revealing no secret - to point out that Peter Tremayne is a pseudonym of a writer who, under his own name, is considered something of an expert on Celtic history and culture and who is author of the definitive history of the

Cornish language and its literature. This expertise is reflected in the accuracy of detail in this novel. For example; one only has to compare Peter Tremayne's descriptions of Lan-Kern dwellings with the remains at the 2,000 year old village at Chysauster, Cornwall. Kesmur of Lan-Kern's fortress at Dynas Dor, Fawy, is easily identified as the romantic Castle Dore, by Fowey, where King Mark of Cornwall ruled in the 6th Century AD and where still stands the inscribed tombstone of Tristan himself. And could Nelferch's gigantic fortress of Dynas Drok (Fort of Evil) have really stood? The description is remarkably similar to the 4,000 year old hillfort of Maiden Castle, Dorset. And what of the *golghva a-whes,* the bath house where Dryden has a sweat bath, similar to a Turkish Bath? Such baths are mentioned in ancient Celtic writings and one still survives in the north of Ireland.

Using this expert knowledge of pre-Christian Celtic life, of Celtic philosophies, ideals and aspirations, Peter Tremayne has woven a magnificent tapestry of myth and magic, of pure adventure and romance, of the philosophical yearnings of man to understand himself and the ambiguity of his place and purpose in a universe seemingly governed by chance and change. Legend and reality combine in this persuasive and dramatic product of a keen imagination.

PART ONE
Resurrection

"The unknown is frequently considered miraculous and is often terrifying, causing people to fear it until it is explained. But to truly understand the great mysteries, the ego must die and be reborn; the mind has to become as a block of ice entering a blazing fire."

An Lyver Mur a Lan-Kern
The Great Book of Lan-Kern

CHAPTER ONE

The great Arctic Ocean was a wild tumult of leaping, frenzied water from horizon to horizon. The sky's brooding blackness was reflected in the angry seas beneath. Snow flurries, sudden and swift, kept obscuring the horizon where the dark lines of what might be land could scarcely be seen.

Across the choppy, bursting swell, a black, pencil-shaped object thrashed its way, nosing through the sprays which washed and foamed around it, crashing over so that it seemed in constant danger of being dragged down beneath the ferocious swell. It twisted and turned through the thunderous threatening seas, dipping and rolling with the scream of a rising gale singing around the tall centre-section which rose up, tower-like, at right angles to its long cylindrical shape. The wind moaned and cried through the high masts and antennae which thrust into the sky above it.

The discordant scream of the klaxon horn brought Frank Dryden awake with a jerk, his heart hammering wildly.

For several seconds he lay, half raised on his bunk, balancing on one elbow and wondering where he was. Gradually, as the grey and black fitments of the tiny cabin focussed in his vision, he became fully awake and aware, feeling the uncomfortable roll and pitch of the ship.

The klaxon was sounding angrily over the loudspeaker system. Behind the blare he could hear the reassuring pulsing throb of the engines, steady, almost monotonous and he discarded the idea that something was wrong. He swung his legs from the bunk and sat up, wondering how to respond to the shrilling call of the klaxon.

The green baize curtain separating the cabin from the passageway was pushed aside and a freckle-faced young man, wearing the single ring of a sub-lieutenant on his jacket sleeve, peered in.

'What's up?' asked Dryden thickly, still tasting the sleep in his mouth.

'We've reached the edge of the ice pack, Doctor. We're about to submerge.'

The sub-lieutenant, Harris by name, came into the cabin which he and Dryden shared and pulled off his navy jacket, replacing it with a warm Aran sweater. With a cheerful nod he was gone along the corridor which buzzed with crewmen hurrying to their diving stations.

Dryden sank back onto the bunk and tried to shake off the feeling of panic that had seized him at the prospect of being entombed in a steel hulk hundreds of feet below the polar ice cap.

There had been several times during the past week when he'd regretted agreeing to join this expedition to the Angara Basin in the Arctic. An American, from Bloomington, Indiana, he had been working for two years in Britain, an exchange lecturer on loan from the US Navy Department to the British Royal Navy in whose muster rolls he was officially credited as a senior civilian botanist. His main duties to date had been to give lectures to navy personnel on survival by the use of edible plants and to supervise the updating of service handbooks on the subject. Several times he had longed to return to his little research laboratory in the University of Indiana.

A week ago he had been engaged in one of his routine lectures at the Royal Navy station at Scapa Flow, in the Orkney Islands, when he had received a request to proceed to the British scientific research station on the Lomonsov Ridge in the Arctic because a strange plant had been discovered which the personnel there had been unable to classify. A request from the Admiralty, even to an American member of the civilian establishment, was an order and Dryden agreed to go.

He frankly admitted that he was intrigued by the discovery. The strange plant had been found growing in the Angara area during the Arctic summer when the top soil had thawed enough to allow the usual growth of moss, lichen and stumpy shrubs to raise themselves on the areas of land known as the tundra. But from the descriptions and rough sketches of the unknown plant, Dryden could only relate it to the *papilionacae* family - the common red clover of the English early autumn.

But what would red clover be doing in the Arctic? It was extremely unlikely that the plant had 'travelled' to the area, that its spores had been carried by the winds and, by accident, found a fertile spot on which to grow.

As a botanist Dryden was aware of the line of division which existed even between the Arctic flora of America and the Arctic flora of Greenland. That being so, he was hard pressed to suppress his excitement that he might be on the verge of identifying a new form of plant life.

The British nuclear submarine, HMS *Argo,* had been in Scapa Flow by coincidence, about to leave for sea trials under the Arctic ice cap. Such trials had become commonplace since the USS *Nautilus,* made the first polar transit from Point Barrow in Alaska to the Greenland Sea back in August, 1958. With the presentation of the magical passport of Admiralty orders, the captain of the *Argo* had reluctantly agreed to transport Dryden to his destination, heading by way of the Arctic Ocean with the intention of submerging under the ice cap and surfacing three days later in the Angara Basin, alongside the Lomonsov Ridge station.

In the few days since the submarine had put out from Scapa Flow, Dryden had mixed little with the officers and men. They all seemed terribly young to Dryden, who looked down at them with the superiority of his thirty-two years. Dryden's prematurely greying-sandy hair and his craggy, almost ugly features, added to an impression of age which seemed to cause a barrier between him and the boyish crew. They were polite but distant. The captain, a Commander Adamson, had added to his alienation by a distant superiority. At first Dryden thought that Adamson might be reacting against his American nationality. He soon found out that Adamson was merely reacting against being ordered to 'run a ferry service for government boffins,' as he let slip one day.

The only person to whom Dryden spoke for any length of time was the young sub-lieutenant, Harris, whose cabin he shared. From him Dryden learned that the reticence of the crew was not due to any unfriendliness but to the fact that the *Argo* was carrying classified equipment. The submarine had recently been fitted with a fairly new and complex inertial navigation system that provided information on the submarine's position independently of any outside sources except gravity and Earth rotation. Harris did not seem to excel in

3

security matters and Dryden smiled at his boyish enthusiasm as he prattled on about the new system. Dryden understood little about technical matters and told Harris so, but the young officer appeared to think all 'boffins' were capable of understanding such things even if they were botanists and not technologists.

On the third day out from Scapa Flow, Commander Adamson had unbent sufficiently towards Dryden to give him a brief inspection tour around the *Argo*. Adamson was the only man on board who was older then Dryden, about thirty-five, tall, dark-haired and with a permanently bored expression on his lean face. He seldom spoke and then only in answer to Dryden's direct questions - if they did not fall within the realms of security. From him Dryden learned that the *Argo* was 320 feet in length, displaced 3,500 tons of water, had a maximum speed of thirty-five knots, both on the surface and submerged, and had a crew of 125 men. She was fitted with twenty-one inch torpedos that fired from four forward tubes and four tubes amidships but she carried no nuclear missiles. And that was the sum total of digestible knowledge that Dryden gained on his tour.

The First Lieutenant, a red-faced, chubby man, Lt-Commander Roxy, was slightly more garrulous than his captain but his conversation was mainly limited to the public house in Cornwall which he was going to run when he left the navy in two years' time. However, on several occasions, Dryden found that he could engage Roxy in a fairly enjoyable conversation on the sport of sword fencing. Ever since his early teens Dryden had followed fencing as a 'keep-fit' hobby and sport, preferring sabres to foils. He had even won several amateur championships with the sabres. Roxy, on the other hand, did not practise the sport any more but was still a keen follower of it.

The klaxon suddenly wheezed and was silent, bringing Dryden out of his reverie. The fear still cramped his stomach as he visualised the submarine about to sink beneath the ice pack into the darkness of the sea.

He became aware of a denim-clad rating standing in the doorway grinning down at him.

'Doctor Dryden, sir? Captain's compliments and would you like to join him in the control room?'

Dryden fought down the feeling of claustrophobic unease and

4

followed the rating amidships.

Commander Adamson was checking a chart. He glanced up briefly as Dryden came into the control centre.

'Morning, Dryden,' he said in his usual offhand manner. 'We're about to dive under the ice now. We'll be down about three days before we break through the ice into the Angara Basin. I thought you might like to watch the procedure.'

'Thank you, captain,' muttered Dryden, feeling somewhat honoured.

The First Lieutenant came forward.

'If you'll just stand over here, doctor, you won't...you'll have a better view of everything.'

'And won't be in the way?' smiled Dryden wryly, continuing Roxy's interrupted sentence.

The first Lieutenant gave an embarrassed grin. 'Just so, doctor.'

There seemed little outward activity in the control room but that was superficial and misleading. Each man was alert at his station, eyes on his instruments, hands on switches and levers. All it needed was the briefest word from the captain to direct the great submarine on its course.

'All hatches secure?'

'All hatches aye, sir.'

'Take her down to periscope depth.'

Automatically Dryden braced himself, expecting to feel a sensation akin to going down in a lift. But there was no sensation whatever before a sailor called out: 'Forty feet it is, sir!'

'Up periscope!'

Adamson grasped the handles of the long column as it slid smoothly and silently from its well in the centre of the control room. Even as it sped upwards, Adamson crouched to meet it and, twisting himself around it, fastened his eyes to the rubber eyepieces. He swiftly described a full circle. Then, slowly and carefully, he examined each quarter of the compass before standing back.

'Like a look, doctor?' he asked.

Dryden moved forward, uttering his thanks.

His eyes focussed beyond the snow flurries and the choppy swell of the dark, threatening seas, on a breath-taking expanse of white plain, surmounted by what seemed to be precipitous white mountains

5

against a blackening sky. So this was the Arctic ice pack under which they were to travel for the next three days?

'It's spectacular,' he breathed.

Commander Adamson grunted as he stepped away. He obviously had no time for an appreciation of scenic beauty.

'Down periscope! Depth, one hundred metres. Steady as she goes.'

A sailor echoed his orders.

The First Lieutenant sighed.

'That's the last daylight we'll see for a couple of days.'

'How can you navigate under all that ice for so long?' Dryden asked, intrigued. 'I know it's routine to you fellows nowadays but how is it done? By radar?'

Lt-Commander Roxy glanced at his captain who nodded almost imperceptibly.

'Well, old boy,' smiled Roxy, steering Dryden to what looked like a bank of radar instruments and dials, 'radar needs an antenna to work, so it is used only for navigation in coastal waters and when we are near the surface. We have to have the antenna on a retractable mast. But to navigate under the ice we need sonar, which lets us know what obstructions are in range. What we call 'active' sonar sends out acoustic pulses which are deflected when they hit the ice. It's the same principle as a bat flies by. Here,' he pointed to the instruments, 'you can see...'

Just then the metalwork of the submarine seemed to groan and shudder. Dryden nearly lost his balance and collided with the First Lieutenant.

'What is it? he gasped, at the same time as the captain snapped out: 'Report, sonar!'

The young sonar operator sat hunched over his instruments.

'Melting iceberg, captain, bearing green one-twenty. Distance three kilometres.'

The First Lieutenant grinned at Dryden's worried face.

'Nothing to fret yourself about, doctor. Large chunks of ice are breaking off the melting iceberg and dropping into the sea. They create small tidal waves. At this distance we can feel the faint impact of the wave as it becomes spent. You see ...'

'Sir!'

The word was almost a yelp from the pale-faced operator.

'I'm getting a hazy reading on green one-twenty, sir. Object on that reading closing rapidly with us.'

The First Lieutenant leant over the sonar operator's shoulder, placing his ear close to the headset.

'Water disturbance, captain,' he sang out. 'It could be...my God! A gigantic tidal wave bearing fragments of ice!'

Commander Adamson acted quickly.

'Secure all watertight doors! Stand by reactor room, emergency shut-down imminent! Crew to depth-charge stations! Secure for impact!'

With the klaxon screaming like an insane banshee, voices began to shout confirmation of the captain's orders.

'Bulkheads secured, sir!'

'Reactor room ready, sir!'

'All stations report present and correct!'

And then the tidal wave hit the *Argo*. The great submarine was tossed about like a child's toy. The lights flickered as the massive ship bucked and pitched. Large chunks of ice, carried along at great speeds by the wave, pounded upon the steel hull. It seemed an age before the ship stopped pitching and began to descend at an acute angle towards the seabed.

Commander Adamson was casting his eyes along the line of gauges.

Royston, the Chief Petty Officer, pointed out the obvious.

'Tidal wave's passed, sir. But she's going down at a forty-five degree angle.'

The angle was so steep that everyone had to hang on to something to prevent themselves slithering down the deck plates.

Adamson nodded.

'Level her out, helmsman.'

A sailor swung at the wheel before him. Nothing happened.

'No response from the diving planes, sir.'

The voice was flat and emotionless. A product of good training.

The First Lieutenant crawled across the sloping deck and tried the controls. He shrugged as his efforts met with the same negative response.

'Depth gauge reading?' snapped Adamson.

'Five hundred metres, sir,' replied Royston. 'Going down by the head very rapidly.'

'Blow all main ballast.'

A pause.

'No response, sir,' the Chief Petty Officer's voice was hoarse with excitement. 'Seven-fifty metres and still down by the head.'

The captain passed a hand over his brow.

'Control systems check, Number One.'

As the First Lieutenant began a swift check on the control panels, Adamson turned and peered at the navigational chart before him.

He bit his lower lip.

'Harris,' he snapped to the ashen sub-lieutenant, 'order all crew to get their escape equipment ready.'

'But sir...' whispered Harris.

'Now!' the captain's voice shut off any objections. Adamson knew that Harris was going to point out that even if the crew did get out of the submarine, they would come up under the ice cap and even if, by some miracle, they broke through the ice, they would be dead from exposure within seconds in the fierce Arctic climate. Even Dryden, his mouth dry, only half-understanding the drama being played out, understood that.

The First Lieutenant had finished his check.

'Steering systems malfunctioning, sir. Negative response on ballast control. All other systems operational.'

'What about trying all ballast tanks?'

The First Lieutenant shook his head.

'I think we're going down at too steep an angle and too fast to start blowing now, sir. We'll have to wait until we reach the bottom.'

'Sir!'

The voice of the young sonar operator was now panic-stricken and caused heads to jerk round.

'Ice dead ahead!'

There was a silence. It lasted three long, eternal seconds.

Commander Adamson grabbed the intercom.

'Captain to reactor room, shut down! shut down! All crew, emergency, emergency! Prepare for collision!'

'Ice bearing dead ahead, sir! Closing rapidly! Closing...' the excited cry of the sonar operator rose to an almost hysterical pitch.   The

8

First Lieutenant had reached the boy's position and laid a reassuring hand on his shoulder.

'Okay, son. We heard you.'

'Must be the bottom of a 'berg,' whispered the Chief Petty Officer, breaking the tense silence.

'We're at a depth of a thousand metres!' gasped Sub-Lieutenant Harris. 'It must be some 'berg!'

'All hands! All hands!'

The captain's voice was tense but calm.

'Stand by for collision!'

'Ice closing... closing...!'

The cry of the sonar operator was the last thing that Dryden heard before the impact. But it was not the collision that ended his state of consciousness. As the bow of the *Argo* smashed against the ice wall, there came the scream of tearing metal and the shuddering impact of splintering ice; then the *Argo* seemed to pass through the wall of ice for its speed did not decrease significantly. The fact must have registered with Commander Adamson for he threw a startled glance towards his First Lieutenant and opened his mouth.

It was at that moment that a wave of coldness seemed to envelop the submarine as if the *Argo* had suddenly sailed through the door of a deep-freeze. Dryden had just time enough to register that sensation of extreme and sudden cold before he passed out... falling, falling, falling into a black, bottomless pit.

CHAPTER TWO

A voice was calling him from a long, long way away.

Dryden's eyelids felt heavy. It was several moments before he could force them open and when he did he experienced a momentary sensation of panic. He could not see anything. He tried to sit up but found his body was like lead and he was unable to move. It was then he became aware of the chill, clammy wetness that seemed to permeate the atmosphere about him. He also became aware of a violent headache, of a mouth so dry that every intake of breath was painful.

The voice still called to him, an urgency in its tone.

He strained his eyes once more and gradually made out some dark shapes at the end of what seemed an incredibly long tunnel.

It was several moments before the oddly pale face of the First Lieutenant swam into focus, seeming to float before him and fuse with the surrounding shadows.

'Are you alright, doctor?'

The First Lieutenant's voice was a harsh cackle as if the man had difficulty in speaking.

Dryden nodded and then felt ridiculous. Of course he was not alright! He felt as if he were dying.

But some degree of warmth seemed to be returning to his body. He grunted in pain as great spasms of cramp surged through him. He tried to mouth the word 'water' but only succeeded in groaning.

Then a bottle was placed against his lips. There was a harsh smell of alcohol and a liquid was poured down his throat. His mouth was so dry that it had no taste at all, only his nose detected the faint odour of brandy. The liquid hit his stomach with fiery intensity. He nearly bent double as he felt it surge backwards towards his mouth - his stomach muscles rejecting it. He fought for control and won.

Soon a warm feeling was spreading through his shuddering limbs.

The First Lieutenant helped him sit up and he sat for a while trying to flex and co-ordinate his limbs, feeling the power gradually returning to them.

It was a few more moments before he was aware of his surroundings and remembrance flooded into his mind.

The lights burned dimly in the control room of the submarine, so dimly that it was difficult to make out details in the gloom. The air smelt dank and musky - he had experienced a similar sort of smell during a pot-holing expedition in the Derbyshire Peak District when encountering an enclosed underground pool. There was also something else which he could not place for a time, a feeling of decay.

He registered that the submarine was on an even keel and that there was a strange, eerie silence within its steel hull. Figures moved like sleepwalkers around the control room. Dryden saw that he must have been the last to recover from the shock of the impact - or had there been an impact? He frowned, trying to remember. Most of the submariners seemed to be alright except the young sonar operator sprawled in his seat and holding his head in his hands, whimpering softly.

'Have you made the damage check yet, Mister Harris?'

Dryden swung his head to take in the dark form of Commander Adamson.

Sub-Lieutenant Harris answered in a cracked voice.

'All the intercommunications systems seem to be out, sir. It's this strange wetness everywhere; it's fouled up the electrics. It must have seeped into everything. I don't understand it, sir.'

'Alright! Alright!' grunted Adamson. 'Set up a series of runners to all stations. I want a complete damage check and casualty report.'

Harris disappeared, muttering in the gloom.

The First Lieutenant had moved off and Dryden became aware of Chief Petty Officer Royston at his side.

'What is this wetness,' he asked the sailor. 'Are we leaking?'

Royston grunted, It was an attempt to laugh.

'No way, doctor. It's just some sort of heavy condensation. We've already checked for structural damage and we're as dry as a bone. Why, it's not even seawater.'

Dryden dipped his finger into the wetness and licked at it. It was

11

bitter but not seawater.

'Number One!'

First Lieutenant Roxy was at Adamson's side.

'Sir,' answered Roxy, anticipating the captain's question. 'All control room crew and the doctor are okay now. We're running an instrument check and everything seems haywire at the moment. Nothing seems to be registering.'

'Send a man to the air-recycling plant. I want to know the reason for this stale air.'

Dryden stood up tentatively and, to his surprise, found his legs were able to support his aching body.

He moved forward a few steps and fought down a wave of dizzyness and nausea.

'Commander...' he said hesitantly, 'is there anything I can do?'

Adamson swung round and examined Dryden keenly for a few moments. His face was grave with anxiety.

'Nothing at the moment, doctor. Thanks,' the last word was an afterthought.

'Captain!'

A seaman struggled through a hatch into the control room.

'Mister Harris's compliments, sir ... seven of the men are badly concussed and being taken to sickbay. One of 'em's Petty Officer Williams. And fifteen men are missing, sir.'

'Missing?' snapped Adamson.

'Sir, they were in the for'ard compartments when we went down. The for'ard torpedo room and storage area are flooded, sir. Mister Harris says everyone else is fit for duty apart from minor cuts and bruises.'

Adamson bit his lip.

'Very well. Did Mister Harris give you a damage report?'

'No, sir. He's still checking, I believe, sir.'

Adamson sent the man back to his station and turned to peer at the dials and gauges.

Dryden followed his gaze but could not tell anything from the mass of instruments. He had no means of deciphering what they meant or, indeed, whether they meant anything at all. One thing that did catch his eye was the clock on the control panel. It seemed to have stopped because its hands stood at more or less the same

12

position as when Dryden had entered the control room to witness the dive. He glanced at his own wristwatch and found that, too, had stopped. He asked a few sailors if they knew the time but no one had a watch that was working. There was no telling how long the crew had been unconscious; one minute or one hour. It took several attempts before Dryden set his watch going again. He gave an involuntary shudder. Everywhere was the cloying dampness, cold and irritating.

As if reading his thoughts, Adamson barked to CPO Royston:

'Chief, get a fatigue party to swab down the instrument panels. Get this condensation cleaned up. Then I want a working party to check out the electrics and see if we can get anything working, especially the air and lighting systems.'

Dryden, feeling rather useless, offered to lend a hand in swabbing down the panels under the guidance of Royston.

An hour passed rapidly as small gangs of men came and went, stripping panels and checking circuits, sponging away the condensation and holding whispered conferences with the captain. Suddenly there was a slight hum and Royston, in answer to Dryden's look of surprise, laconically said: 'Nuclear reactor, mate. We should have normal power soon.' Certainly, after a little while, the lights began to shine with more brilliance and the air was beginning to get fresher.

'Reckon things will soon be ship-shape,' smiled Royston.

Dryden nodded absently, realising that now he had time to think his mind was letting loose a riot of panic imagery - claustrophobic visions of entombment - of never being able to reach the surface again. He had always had a slight fear of enclosed places, perhaps that was why he had tried potholing to overcome it. Dryden had grown afraid of his own fear and would rather force himself into situations of which he was afraid than accept his own shortcomings, never learning to recognise the difference between commonsense and cowardice. It had been so when he was a boy at school, when he fought many unnecessary fights because he was afraid to be afraid to fight them. He sighed and tried to concentrate on other things.

There was an abrupt crackle of static electricity. The officer in charge of communications and two of his men had managed to rig up a make-shift tannoy system throughout the ship.

13

Adamson's voice, sounding weird and unnatural, like some monster from another planet, cracked through the speakers.

'This is the captain speaking. You are all wondering what our situation is. Briefly, it could be worse. A tidal wave tilted us out of control and we seem to have scraped the underside of an iceberg. The two for'ard compartments are flooded. I regret to say that we cannot entertain any hopes for the fifteen men who were in them when we went down.'

There was a long pause.

The men around Dryden stirred uneasily.

'As for the rest, we have sustained only minor injuries,' continued Adamson's voice. 'We have only seven men in sickbay with concussion.'

Another pause.

'Now to the operational status of the ship. I can report that, apart from the flooded for'ard compartments, the ship is dry and sound. Our nuclear reactor is working at half-power and there is a twenty-five percent instability reading.'

A few excited voices rose in a babble. Dryden saw CPO Royston give a wry grimace.

'Now,' the harsh tone of Adamson drowned out the babble, 'twenty-five percent is an acceptable risk level. We can operate with a safety margin of forty percent and still circle the globe several times before we get into trouble.'

'What does it mean?' Dryden asked Royston.

The Chief Petty Officer scratched his nose.

'It means our nuclear reactor, the power plant, is unstable: not really working up to par, if you see what I mean, doctor. It's not really my field, but the ship can operate with complete safety to the crew with as much as a forty percent instability reading. If it gets higher, we just shut down. There's no chance of us turning into a nuclear bomb, if that's what's worrying you.'

Dryden hardly felt reassured.

Adamson's voice was continuing.

'I must emphasise to you men that there is absolutely no question of radiation leakage. Everything is under control. The reactor is merely weak and seems curiously drained of energy. But we *do* have enough power to operate. I say again, we do have enough power to

14

operate.'

The captain paused and let the muttering subside.

'As to our operational status, I have to tell you that most of our equipment seems to be malfunctioning, either because of the impact, or the condensation which has pervaded the ship and blown out most of the electrical circuits. The engineers have repaired what they could and we still have enough working to be able to get topsides. The flooded compartments are not sufficient to disrupt our buoyancy although it will make the ship less manoeuvrable than before.

'We have ascertained that we are lying on the seabed at about sixty fathoms...' his voice took on a lighter note, '... and that's not a great depth for the old *Argo,* eh?'

Dryden saw a curious frown pass across Royston's face.

'Only sixty fathoms? That's odd, doctor,' he whispered. 'We were far deeper than that before we scraped the 'berg.'

Adamson's voice continued.

'So let's get to our diving stations, men. We'll soon have the *Argo* on the surface.'

'Yeah, but what if there are 'bergs overhead?' muttered a weasel-faced seaman near Dryden.

'Then it won't much matter one way or the other will it, Randall?' barked Royston.

The seaman looked aggrieved but was silent.

'Diving stations! Diving stations!' came the cackle from the speaker.

The men bustled away and Dryden followed Royston back to the centre of the control room.

A degree of normality had returned to the heart of the submarine. The lights were brighter and needles on several gauges and dials were quivering once more.

Commander Adamson swept his gaze over the control room personnel.

'Stand by to raise her!'

The men tensed, bracing themselves expectantly.

'Slowly by her head then, helmsman.'

The helmsman placed his hands on a wheel, his eyes peering towards a depth gauge which registered at 350 feet.

15

'Standing by, sir.'

'Blow for'ard ballast tanks!' said Adamson calmly.

A series of levers clicked into position. There came a faint electrical whine and then... nothing. There was no perceptible movement.

'Negative response on for'ard tanks, sir,' came back the voice of a crewman.

'Blow stern ballast tanks,' Adamson's voice was cold.

Again a series of levers was moved. This time there was not even an electrical reaction.

The submarine lay quiet.

'Negative response on stern ballast,' the crewman's voice was pitched higher than before.

'Blow all main ballast tanks!' Adamson's voice was beginning to crack with emotion.

Dryden tensed as he heard the levers clicking. Then came the electrical whine and the submarine shuddered, began to stir... there was a faint cheer and Dryden felt relief surge through his body.

Then abruptly the motion stopped. The submarine seemed to give an almost human sigh, shuddered slightly and settled back on the sea bed.

There was a moment of complete and utter silence.

'Negative response on all main ballast tanks, sir!'

Adamson's voice, drained of all emotion, came slowly.

'Shut down all blowing gear.'

They all listened rather than watched as the crewmen clicked the levers back into the neutral position.

Then the frightened, hysteria-ridden voice of the young sonar operater echoed through the ship.

'Oh Jesus! Jesus! We're trapped, trapped!'

CHAPTER THREE

'Belay that!' snarled Royston.

Adamson ran his keen eyes over the instrument panels, his thin-lipped face taut with anxiety.

'Instrument check, Number One,' he muttered.

The First Lieutenant relayed the order. There was a pause. Dryden felt the sweat standing out oddly from his cold forehead, tiny icy beads of it were running down his neck, under the collar of his shirt.

'Instrument check completed, sir,' Roxy was saying. 'All ballast systems are registering as operable.'

Adamson chewed his lower lip.

'Very well. Repeat blowing procedures.'

The helmsman took a grip of his wheel and muttered a 'Standing by, sir.'

'Blow for'ard ballast tanks!'

Again the series of levers clicked into position. In the tense stillness of the control room there came the faint electrical whine and then... miraculously the whine increased and there was a faint movement of the great steel hulk and a soft gushing sound.

'For'ard tanks blowing, sir,' the voice of the helmsman almost broke in relief.

'Blow stern ballast tanks,' a new assurance was creeping into Adamson's voice.

Again they waited in silence as another series of levers was moved. This time the electrical response was loud and strong.

The submarine shuddered and began to drag itself from the ocean bed.

'For'ard and aft tanks blowing, sir.'

'Blow all main ballast tanks!'

The submarine shuddered and heaved.

'All tanks blowing, sir.'

'Surface! Surface!'

The warning klaxon wheezed weakly through the ship. It began to rise, groaning as if struggling against tremendous forces that were holding it down. A helmsman read off the depths in a strangled voice.

'Thirty... twenty-five... twenty... fifteen... surfacing...'

'Lookouts to bridge!'

The First Lieutenant moved forward with two sailors who emerged with life jackets and binoculars. Roxy scrambled up the ladder to the conning tower hatch but seemed to have great difficulty in drawing back the clips and operating the wheel. It took all three men, working with difficulty in the narrow confines, to draw them back and heave the hatch open. A cascade of water drenched them as they pushed into the airlock and then opened the main hatch which led directly onto the conning tower.

Dryden experienced a peculiarly light-headed sensation as a gust of cold air swept into the control room; it seemed extraordinary that mere air could taste and smell so sweet to the senses. He leant against some piping and drew in great lungfuls as the air permeated the ship.

'Alright, Harris,' Adamson was saying to the sub-lieutenant. 'I want the after and for'ard maindeck hatches open and I want the crew assembled into their watches taking fifteen minute breaks on the casing. Keep the hatches open unless we get a big swell, let the air circulate. Oh, and get damage control to check the outer casing while we are able. It feels as if we have a calm sea with us.'

'Aye, aye, sir.' Harris turned away to fulfil his orders.

Adamson looked at Dryden and his mouth quirked in what was meant to be a smile.

'Come on, doctor, let's go up to the con.'

The first peculiar thing that Dryden registered was the light. It had been almost black when the *Argo* started her near fatal dive. Now, on the western horizon a blood-red semi-circle of sun showed where it was sinking below the rim of the sea, sending out bright orange and golden rays which lit the sea's surface with a strange other-world quality. Roxy passed his glasses to the captain as they came onto the bridge.

'Must have been unconscious longer than we thought,' muttered

Adamson, sweeping the horizon.

He suddenly stiffened.

'Why,' he whispered incredulously. 'Why, there's no ice!'

Dryden peered into the early evening and realised the significance of this. Where were the great icebergs, the start of the Arctic ice pack?

Roxy gave him a nervous glance and then turned to his captain.

'Yes, sir,' he whispered. 'And have you noticed how warm it is?'

It was true; the evening air was soft and gentle.

Adamson peered up at the sky.

'When these clouds clear away, Number One, I want an astral navigational fix on our position. All our electrical navigational aids seem out of action.' He paused and frowned. 'It seems unlikely, but I must assume that during the brief time we were unconscious we were swept south off our original position.'

'Yes, sir,' answered Roxy, jerking his head towards the setting sun, 'but we couldn't have been swept so far south ...'

'Let's not speculate, Mister,' interrupted Adamson, sweeping the horizon through the glasses once again.

Roxy lapsed into silence.

The light was now fading fast.

'We'd best rig up some lights,' suggested Adamson. 'We might be able to undertake repairs during the night and get underway by morning.'

'I'll check with CPO Royston, sir,' replied Roxy, turning to go down the hatch.

Sub-Lieutenant Harris scrambled by him.

'Sir, damage control report.'

His voice was eager and excited.

'Report, Mister Harris.'

'Only superficial damage to the outer casing, although we can't be sure what's below the water line. We could send a diver down tomorrow at first light. Also, on the for'ard compartments the bow was stove in. A pretty nasty mess, sir. No hope of repairs to the for'ard torpedo room but we might be able to pump out the storage room. Both chambers are flooded.'

Adamson nodded.

'And the crewmen?'

'Not a chance of survival, I'm afraid, sir.'

'Very well. Do you have a list of their names?'

'Yes sir.'

'How about communications? Everything seems to be malfunctioning in that quarter, doesn't it.'

'I'm afraid so, sir. We can't send or receive. The communications officer reckons he could rig up a makeshift transmitter-receiver but it will take him some time.'

'Get him working on it right away.'

'Radar and sonar report a low operational status now their instruments have dried out.'

Adamson sighed.

'It's something that they can raise anything at all, I suppose. What about engine control?'

'Very poor power, sir. I suppose it's due to the reactor. Engineering want a word with you about that as soon as possible. I reckon our top speed will be about fifteen knots.'

'Very well. There's nothing else we can do until we get the astral fix on our position. I'll go and talk to engineering now.'

Dryden watched the captain disappear, followed by the sub-lieutenant.

Roxy re-emerged by his side.

'Pretty exciting for you, I suppose, doctor?' the First Lieutenant smiled offering some barley sugar to Dryden. Dryden took one. It made his mouth feel better.

'I can't think of better excitement,' he returned.

Roxy nodded towards the horizon.

'Rum business, eh? Let's hope those clouds clear so that we can get a fix soon.'

'I suppose we will have to turn back?'

Roxy shrugged.

'We'll have to put into a base pretty soon to effect repairs. Once our position is known, I suppose the Government will lift you off by 'copter so that you can continue up to Lomonsov Ridge station.'

Dryden had forgotten about the purpose of his trip.

The Arctic red clover didn't really seem important any more.

'Ah, look!' Roxy pointed skywards. 'There's a clear patch over there to the east. If it continues this way, I'll be able to get a rudimentary fix.'

A sudden sharp squeal made Dryden jump.

The First Lieutenant tried to suppress his smile of amusement as he reached for the voice pipe.

'Con.'

'Radar here. We are picking up a strange blip, surface vessel bearing green four-five. Green four-five, on a collision course. Our instruments still seem to be malfunctioning because it seems to be closing at a terrific speed. We've checked it several times.'

Roxy frowned.

'Keep me informed, radar.'

He clicked a switch on the voice tube.

'Captain to con. Captain to con.'

Then he turned to the lookouts. 'Watch out for a surface vessel closing with us on green four-five.' To a hovering warrant officer he asked: 'Are our navigation lights rigged fore and aft?'

'Yes, sir.'

Adamson was clambering back into the conning tower.

'What is it, Number One?'

'Radar reports a surface vessel closing with us on green four-five, sir.'

'Let's hope it's one of ours, we can do with some help,' muttered Adamson, swinging his night glasses in the direction stated. 'More likely it's a Soviet vessel, especially in these waters.'

The voice tube squealed again.

'Radar here. Surface vessel very close and closing, she's still going too fast.... on a collision course...'

Adamson bent forward.

'Con to helm. Port rudder.'

'Port rudder it is, sir,' came the response.

'There she is, sir!' yelled an excited lookout. 'Dead on green four-five...'

All eyes swung in the direction.

'Damn it,' snapped Adamson, 'something's wrong with these night glasses - I can't pick up anything. Ah... there's a black shape. But it's too small to be a ship in these waters.... she's showing no lights.... it's...'

'What is it, sir?' asked Roxy.

21

Adamson shook his head.

'Can you make out what ship it is?' he called to a lookout.

'Can't make her out, sir. She's closing too fast. Why... by God! She's going to ram us!'

'Con to helm! Con to helm! Hard a' starboard!'

Adamson's voice rose shrilly.

The bows of the submarine started to turn sluggishly.

'Signaller,' cried Adamson, 'for Christ's sake just signal something.'

The Aldiss lamp flashed into the night.

The strange black shape suddenly swerved, an astonishing swerve for a vessel, and then with a strange silence, it curved and smacked into the bow of the *Argo,*, causing the great steel ship to swing and shudder.

'What the hell?' gasped Adamson as he staggered against the conning tower rail.

Dryden was jerked backwards and nearly fell.

'Get a searchlight on that vessel,' cried Adamson.

There were several people talking at once.

'No response to visual signals, sir.'

'There's no sound of her engines.'

'She's showing no lights, dammit.'

'Is that searchlight ready?'

'She's swinging around in a circle: coming back toward us, still on a collision course!'

'What the hell is it?'

The long, low black shape swerved and smacked into the bow once again. This time the severe shock of impact shuddered through the *Argo,* causing nearly everyone on the bridge to lose his foothold. Dryden, gripping the rail, managed to save himself from falling. It was at that moment that the searchlight snapped on... it focussed for a split second before the shuddering jar of the collision sent it swinging wildly skywards. Dryden caught just a glimpse of a great grey hulk, the hulk not of some vessel but of a glistening, grey pulsating mass. He caught the red reflection of light, like the malignant gleam of some eye as the thing scraped down the side of the *Argo,* swerved again and suddenly raced away into the night.

He felt a sudden sickness.

22

There was a sharp intake of breath behind him.

Commander Adamson was looking past him with an ashen face.

'You saw it?' Dryden asked slowly, jerking his head into the black night.

Adamson swallowed slowly.

'I saw it,' he said.

The First Lieutenant was now on his feet.

The voice tube squealed.

'Radar here. The blip has disappeared on a course red one-one-two. Fantastic speed. What was it, sir?'

Roxy hesitated.

'Acknowledged, radar,' he said shortly. He turned and looked at the white face of the captain. Then he raised his eyebrows at Dryden's nausea-pinched face.

'What the hell was it?'

For a moment no one replied.

'It was a whale, Mister Roxy,' Adamson said curtly. 'A crazed whale, that's all.'

Dryden opened his mouth.

In the faint light he saw Adamson's face turned towards him, the expression in his eyes seeming to forbid him to say anything further.

'But, sir,' Roxy was saying incredulously, 'the size of that thing...'

'I said it was a whale, Mister,' replied Adamson coldly and then, with a softer voice. 'We couldn't get a light on it and you can't judge size by shadows. It was just a whale.'

The First Lieutenant gave a half shrug, began to open his mouth and then changed his mind.

'Very well, sir.'

Adamson turned and scrambled below.

The First Lieutenant watched him disappear with troubled eyes.

'What was it, doctor?' he asked softly.

Dryden looked into the black night and suppressed a shudder.

'What else could it have been but a whale?' he replied.

Roxy was silent. Then: 'I suppose you're right. What else?'

Half an hour later Dryden was sitting in the officers' mess with Commander Adamson drinking a mug of fairly warm cocoa liberally laced with rum. As if by mutual consent the affair of the whale had not been referred to again after Adamson had announced to the

23

crew that the submarine had been rammed by a crazed whale. Such an occurrence was not unknown and the crew accepted it. Even Dryden began to accept the idea, resolving that his nightmare image had been conjured up by a trick of the light.

The First Lieutenant entered. His face was pale and strained.

'I have that navigational fix, captain,' he said in an odd voice, looking at Dryden.

Adamson smiled, interpreting the look.

'Well, I guess Doctor Dryden is entitled to know where we are.' he replied, motioning Roxy to sit down with his chart.

Roxy hesitated, biting his lip.

'Well?' urged Adamson.

'Sir, I've checked my readings twice and also asked Mister Harris to do a further independent fix in order to confirm my findings...'

Adamson waved his hand.

'Don't make a meal out of it, Number One, where are we?'

'We have just surfaced south of the Norwegian island of Jan Mayen.'

A look of disbelief crossed Adamson's face.

'That's impossible!'

'That's why I checked it, sir. And double checked it.'

'But,' began Adamson, 'but that would place our position...'

The First Lieutenant nodded emphatically.

'Exactly, sir. Our current position, give or take a mile or two, is some one thousand and two hundred miles south of where we went down!'

CHAPTER FOUR

Dryden looked at the dark shape of the approaching islands with a feeling of relief and yet, curiously, he could not completely dismiss the underlying feeling of apprehension, of dread. Commander Adamson, who stood by his side in the *Argo's* conning tower, was smiling with satisfaction.

'A damned fine piece of astral navigation, Number One,' he was saying to the First Lieutenant. 'That's Stronsay Firth without a doubt.'

The First Lieutenant's voice had a querulous quality to it.

'If that's so, shouldn't we see Copinsay Light House by now?'

Adamson shrugged.

'So much has happened during the last week that I wouldn't be surprised if there were no light house,' he said easily. 'Anyway, we'll lie-to here until dawn and then we can take her down into Pentland Firth and Scapa Flow in daylight.'

Dryden found himself agreeing with Adamson. So much had happened during the past seven days. It seemed much longer than that. It had been a week of tensions; of inexplicable discoveries which, had it not been for the iron discipline and control of Adamson, would have caused near mutiny.

Firstly there had been the shock of discovering that in the brief few moments, or so they supposed, that they had been unconscious, the submarine had somehow been carried to a position over a thousnd miles to the south. That would have been enough to make the strongest person nervous and uncertain. Indeed, Lt-Commander Roxy was certainly showing increasing signs of nervous irritability; his face wore a haggard, almost haunted expression. But he continued to function, fulfilling his duties almost automatically.

From the outset, Commander Adamson had taken firm control. Before accepting the navigational fix from Roxy, he had taken his own reading. To a meeting of his officers, which Dryden was allowed to attend, he placed three alternatives. Firstly, both Iceland and Norway were within easy reach. The *Argo* could put into either country for repairs but, Adamson pointed out, the ship was carrying a top-secret inertial radar system. Therefore, as the communications officer had promised to fix up a transmitter and receiver within a few hours, the *Argo* could make its way on the surface towards their home base of Scapa Flow in the Orkney Islands which were some eight hundred miles due south. Adamson said he proposed to make for the home port.

The second shock came the following day.

One of the forward compartments had been pumped clear of water and a salvage team had entered. They found, to their horror, the bodies of several fellow crewmen who had been trapped in the compartment when the submarine went down and the for'ard torpedo room and storage area were flooded. The horror was not so much the finding of the bodies but the overpowering smell of putrification. As the surgeon-lieutenant bent to examine the bodies they started to decompose before his eyes. Suppressing their nausea, the men had to bundle the bodies in canvas bags and throw them over the side, with little pretext of burial ceremony. The vile smell of death lingered in the submarine for several days.

The third shock was when the communications officer had announced that he had completed his radio transmitter and receiver. All that could be raised on it was static. The communications officer disassembled it and reassembled it several times, swearing that he could find no fault with it at all. But there were no answers to the ship's distress calls. Only the eerie crackle of static.

The crew began to develop a nervousness and rumours became rife. There was reference back to the attack on the submarine by the whale and even some of the more level-headed crewmen were openly talking about sea monsters.

Then early one morning a lookout sighted something on the horizon and started yelling that he had seen a monster, a strange, great grey beast that was neither whale nor any creature he knew. It had dived beneath the surface as soon as the crewman had sighted it. Unfortunately no one else could confirm the crewman's story and the man was in such a state that Adamson had him relieved of duty and confined to the crew messroom.

The rumours continued. But perhaps the most terrifying aspect was that no officer would talk to the men about the time factor. The *Argo* had begun her dive under the ice pack just after sunset and she had re-surfaced *during* sunset. That, at least, pointed to the crew being unconscious for twenty-four hours except for one more far disturbing factor. The *Argo* had sailed on her mission to the Arctic in the cold, short days of early winter. Now, even in these northern latitudes, the days were longer and warmer and the star-charts seemed to indicate the month should have been June or July.

Dryden, democrat as he was and unused to the more rigid British naval discipline, was puzzled that Adamson did not simply give this information out to the crew and discuss the matter with them. Instead, he forbade speculation on what had happened until Scapa Flow was reached. That only served to increase the feelings of unease and many of the crew began to suspect that Adamson and his officers knew far more than they, in fact, did. There was one positive aspect of the common adversity and that was the fact that Adamson appeared to overcome his personal prejudice about 'civilian boffins' and accept Dryden almost as one of his officers.

And now, after a week of riding the surface, without seeing any other ships or even an occasional reconnaisance aircraft, the *Argo* had arrived off the cluster of islands which protected the great British naval base. On Adamson's orders, the *Argo* lay to in a sheltered bay off one of the islands until morning.

Dryden was awoken by cries from the deck. Scrambling into his clothes he hastened into the conning tower.

Adamson and his First Lieutenant were staring towards the coastline through their glasses in the first light of early dawn. On the for'ard casing of the submarine group of crewmen stood chattering wildly and waving their arms towards the shore. Sub-Lieutenant Harris leant over the conning tower rail and cried 'Stow that noise, you men!'

'What's the matter?' asked Dryden as he came on deck.

Silently, a grim faced Adamson handed Dryden his binoculars.

Dryden could not suppress a gasp of astonishment as he surveyed the shoreline.

The coastline of South Ronaldsay, which island he judged them to be facing, had been a bleak windswept vista of wild heather, tufts of green grassland which only sheep could use, and grey granite rocks. What lay before him was a riot of high grassland and strange twisted trees, trees bent double under the onset of the northern winds. But it was not the strange, contrasting vegetation that caused Dryden to gaze in helpless amazement but the colours of that vegetation. Colours that were bright, vivid and predominantly red as if the inhabitants of the islands had suddenly gone mad and started to toss vast vats of paint across the countryside.

'Where are we?' he whispered, not taking his eyes from the incredible exotic scene.

It was Roxy who answered, his voice edged with hysteria. 'The Orkney Islands.'

'Alright, Number One,' Adamson's voice was low but hard. 'Let's figure this out logically. Where are the position markings we took last night? We must have made a mistake somewhere. God knows where we are but it can't be the Orkneys. I've never seen such vegetation before, have you, doctor? You're a botanist so you can tell us what these plants and trees are.'

Dryden shook his head. Reluctantly he lowered his glasses and handed them back to the captain.

'I've never seen anything like them,' he said quietly. 'It looks almost like a tropical rain forest.'

'That's impossible,' said Adamson sharply. His eyes moved to the wide-eyed lookouts who were overhearing the conversation. 'Have you checked those positions, Number One?'

Roxy was pale. His mouth twitched slightly in a nervous tic.

'The figures put us off South Ronaldsay in the Orkney Islands, sir,' he said in a tremulous voice.

'I can't accept that,' began Adamson.

Roxy turned and swept the coastline with a forefinger.

'Damn it, sir, look there!' his voice quivered. 'Look at the shape of the coastline. I *know* the Orkneys! Forget about the coloured vegetation. Look to the north there - that's Grim Ness, up by Saint Margaret's Hope. I know the shape of that headland like the back of my hand. And look down to the south. If that isn't the Old Head of Brough Ness then.... and look beyond, aren't those rocks the Pentland

Skerries? Don't ask me how or why but I tell you these are the Orkney Islands!'

There was a long silence.

For some minutes the officers on the bridge studied the coastline carefully with their glasses.

Adamson suddenly sighed deeply.

'I want all officers in the officers' mess within ten minutes for a briefing. You too, doctor. Chief,' he turned to Royston, 'get some men you can trust and stand guard. I don't want anyone near the officers' mess without orders.'

Ten minutes later Adamson opened the briefing without preamble

'There is something abnormal going on. Speculation without facts is an idle pastime. I want facts. I want information. Astral navigation, whatever its faults, cannot lie about our position. We therefore have to assume that these are the Orkney Islands. Added to that we can recognise distinct and immovable geographical landmarks.'

A low muttering ran through the cabin.

Lieutenant Starr, the second officer, coughed nervously.

'What are we to make of this weird vegetation we can see on shore, sir?'

Adamson gave him a look of disapproval.

'Speculation without fact is, as I have just said, Starr, a useless exercise. I therefore propose to land a party on the island of Burray, or what I take to be the island of Burray. The party can cross to the far side of the island within sight of Scapa Flow and make a detailed examination of the base. Then we can find out what is going on here.'

The captain sat back and looked round.

'Roxy knows the islands well so he will be in command of the landing party. Harris will be his number two. CPO Royston will accompany them with two crewmen. All will be under arms, sidearms for the officers and some Three-oh-Threes for the crewmen. Understood?'

Dryden cleared his throat.

'Might I be allowed to accompany the shore party, captain? I am a botanist and will be able to see what these strange plants and trees are.'

29

'I can't accept responsibility for a civilian' began Adamson, shaking his head.

Dryden interrupted.

'Captain, you want information and you want it pretty quickly. I believe I am the only qualified person on board to give you the information you want about this strange vegetation, whether it is real or artificial and where it comes from.'

Adamson hesitated.

'I suppose you're right, doctor. Very well. You'll draw a sidearm with the officers.'

Dryden smiled.

'I wouldn't know what to do with it if I had it.'

Adamson's voice was hard.

'They are simple to operate, doctor. You merely pull the trigger, having pointed it in the right direction. The same goes for all of you, gentlemen. From now on until further orders all officers will appear with sidearms and a full ammunition pouch. Sidearms will be worn at all times. Understood? And I want a twenty-four hour guard on the armoury. A senior NCO and one officer. The situation is a strange one, gentlemen, and the crew are nervous. Until we get to the bottom of it, I want to be prepared for all contingencies.'

In less than an hour, Dryden found himself huddling in the stern of a rubber dinghy, seated next to Lt-Commander Roxy, as CPO Royston and two sailors bent over the oars while Sub-Lieutenant Harris stood guard in the bow. They had spent some fruitless time trying to get the outboard motor to start but had found it totally unusable because of corrosion. They approached the southern tip of the island of Burray but on Roxy's orders did not land. He directed the dinghy parallel with the exotic shoreline and headed along the channel which ran between Burray on the north and St. Margaret's Hope on the island of South Ronaldsay to the south.

'We'll soon meet the causeway that runs between the two islands,' said Roxy nervously to Dryden. 'It's where the A961 roadway crosses over the islands.' Dryden nodded absently. He recalled that Roxy's wife lived in married quarters at Scapa Flow and that Roxy knew the islands pretty well. He returned to examining the strange flora through his binoculars.

30

'Strange, aint it, sir?' piped up one of the sailors; a man with a weasel face whom Dryden had noticed before among the crew.

'Just keep on paddling, Randall,' grunted CPO Royston.

Dryden was puzzled by what he saw.

The vegetation certainly did not belong to Northern Europe nor could he honestly say from what country the weird plants came. The flowers were incredible shades of reds, blues and yellows, even the grass was more of a red, sandy tropical grass than anything he had seen north of the Tropic of Cancer. He had never encountered any of them before and this puzzled him. True, once or twice, he thought he saw some plant that was familiar to him but on closer inspection through the glasses it turned out not to be so. They seemed more like parodies of certain species of plant, even mutations.

He turned as he heard Roxy's surprised exhalation of breath. Peering at the First Lieutenant's strained and anxious face, Dryden felt apprehensive for the man's health.   The First Lieutenant was rubbing the back of his neck in bewilderment.

'I know these islands, Dryden,' he whispered, his voice almost hoarse with an indescribable fear. 'I know them. I've spent all my leave here and my wife and I have a cottage up at St. Mary's on the main island. You see that point there? Well, that's where the causeway should be - right across the channel from South Ronaldsay to Burray. But it just isn't there.'

Dryden placed a hand on his shoulder as he caught the catch in the man's voice.

'Steady, Roxy,' he urged, though he had to admit the information was unnerving enough. 'Are you sure?'

Roxy nodded unhappily.

'It's as if it never existed. As if we've been transported back in time, back before...'

Dryden interrupted his rising voice.

'Can we see Scapa Flow from here?'

Roxy looked at him for a second not understanding and then he shook his head and pointed.

'No, but you can see it from that headland there.'

'Very well,' Dryden answered, suddenly aware that he was in control. 'We'd best see what we can. I certainly can't make anything

31

out of the foliage. It's like being on another planet, I just can't get my bearings.'

'As if something's changed the face of the earth while we were under that iceberg,' muttered the First Lieutenant.

CPO Royston gave him a hard look and then turned to snarl at the two crewmen.

'Alright, sailors,' he snapped, 'no one told you to stop rowing. Put your backs into it.'

He turned to Roxy.

'Do we make for the headland, sir?'

Roxy merely stared shorewards.

Dryden nodded to Royston over the First Lieutenant's shoulder.

A few moments later the dinghy scraped on the pebble beach and they jumped out. Roxy made an effort to pull himself together.

'Harris, you and Randall and Jones: you stay here. Keep a close watch out. Royston and you, Dryden, come with me.'

He started up the beach towards a steep incline which led to a rocky outcrop of granite.

'We'll be able to see right across Scapa Flow from up there.'

Dryden, a little out of condition after the confines of the submarine, panted after the First Lieutenant and the Chief Petty Officer.

A quarter of an hour's swift climbing brought them to the point. It was a natural platform of granite giving them a commanding view of several miles in all directions.

Roxy was the first to reach it and to Dryden's horror he suddenly fell on his knees, his face working with horror.

'My God! It can't be! Rosie! Christ! Rosie!'

Dryden realised that Rosie was the name of Roxy's wife. He and Royston scrambled on to the top of the rock and stared about them.

Before them lay a huge sheltered inlet, a stretch of sea surrounded by islands, several square miles of empty sea.

Roxy was sobbing quietly.

Dryden looked at the sea in puzzlement.

'What is it?' he asked perplexed.

CPO Royston laughed a little nervously.

'It's a rum go and no mistake, sir. That's what it is. A rum go.'

It was Roxy who suddenly pointed a shaking hand to the expanse of sea before them.

'Scapa Flow, Dryden... that's Scapa Flow ... the biggest Royal Naval base... and now.... nothing! Not a jetty, not a ship, a wreck, a storage area... nothing...!'

CHAPTER FIVE

Dryden gazed about him. The area looked totally uncivilised, unpopulated since the dawn of time. There was no sign of man's presence at all. Yet, if Roxy was right and this was Scapa Flow, a few weeks ago Dryden had been here -among towering grey battleships, shipyards, buildings, towns - an area swarming with all manner of man's manifestations.

'Can't you be mistaken?' he asked.

Roxy had a paroxysm of laughter.

'Mistaken? Look to the south, there's the Sound of Hoxa. If I had a fiver for the times I navigated that water I'd be a millionaire. Look at the islands across there - there's Flotta, and Fara and Cava and behind them the big island of Hoy, there's the Brings Deeps, and there's the main island and see the hill there, yes that one, -that's Ward Hill where Rosie and I live - lived. How can I be mistaken?'

Royston, too, stood gazing in bewilderment.

'I'd say Mister Roxy is right, sir... this is where Scapa Flow was. But what in hell has happened to her? Where are our boats, the yards, the docks?'

Roxy turned pleading eyes to Dryden.

'Maybe this is all some mass hallucination?'

'Seems real enough to me,' muttered Royston.

Dryden swept the area with his binoculars. There was certainly no sign of human habitation, no sign of any civilisation at all. Everywhere he looked there was only the strange exotic flora whose vivid colours made the eyes ache.

'We'd better get back to the *Argo* and report,' he said uneasily.

'But what can we report?' pleaded Roxy. 'That we've crash-dived in one world and surfaced in another?'

Dryden plucked at his lower lip and frowned.

'We'd better not let any word of this get out until we report to

34

Adamson. He'll want to deal with the matter in his own way. Come on, Roxy. Best pull yourself together.'

Roxy clambered unwillingly to his feet.

'It is futile...'

He was cut off in mid-sentence by a snarling scream which could only have come from the throat of some beast.

The three men whirled round.

Below them, among the vivid undergrowth, a shadow was moving.

Before either Dryden or Royston could recover, Roxy, his face working in demonic fury, tore the pistol from his holster and sent shot after shot into the undergrowth.

There was a curious cry of pain and a further angry snarling.

Then came an abrupt crashing as if a large body were speeding through the undergrowth.

Dryden turned to Roxy whose pale face was still working, the gun wavering unsteadily in his trembling hand. It was obvious that Roxy had become totally unnerved by the strange experiences, especially the disappearance of Scapa Flow, his home and wife.

'Did you see it? Did you see it?' His voice was high-pitched.

'It's gone now,' Dryden reassured him. 'Whatever it was, it's gone. Let's get back to the submarine.'

There was a crashing in the undergrowth.

Roxy whirled and raised his pistol.

Dryden had to strike it out of the First Lieutenant's hand as Sub-Lieutenant Harris and the two seamen emerged at the foot of the outcrop.

'Alright up there?'

'We're alright, Harris,' shouted Dryden. 'Keep a watch out for animals though.' He turned to the shaking First Lieutenant. 'Come on, Roxy. Get a grip on yourself, man. Put the gun away. Don't let the men see you like this.'

Roxy looked at him.

'Where's Scapa Flow - where's Rosie - what's happened?'

The questions were jerked from his mouth.

'Never mind that now, Roxy. We're going back to the ship.'

The First Lieutenant was clearly incapable of command.

Dryden looked at Royston. He stood stoically by, his face a wooden mask.

'Not a word, Chief.'

The man nodded.

'We'd best be careful how we get him back to the ship, doctor.' Harris was starting to climb up the outcrop.

'What's happening?' he called.

'Stay there, Harris. We're coming down. Mister Roxy's had a bit of a shock. Some animal or other. Keep your eyes peeled.'

Dryden turned back to the First Lieutenant and gently took his pistol, thrusting it in his own waistband.

'Come on, Roxy,' he said coaxingly.

The three climbed down, Royston and Dryden guiding the broken officer. Harris stared at Roxy in bewilderment.

'Mister Roxy's had a nasty shock,' said Dryden. 'Some animal but it got away. We'll get back to the ship.'

Dryden suddenly realised how easy it was to give orders to these naval personnel.

'Very well, doctor,' said Harris.

'How were things in the old 'Flow, sir?' it was the weasel-faced seaman named Randall.

'Enough talk, my lad,' grunted Royston. 'Save your breath for rowing back to the ship.

'Aw,' Randall's voice was almost a whine, 'aw, come on, Chief, give us a break. What's happening in the 'Flow? Can we get into the docks?'

'You'll have to wait until we've made a report to the captain, Randall,' said Dryden, as he helped Roxy along the path back to the dinghy.

Behind him Randall muttered: 'Bloody civilian, gives 'imself an air. 'E aint even in the Navy. Why, 'e's just a Yank foreigner.'

It was a silent party which rowed back to the waiting black steel hulk of the *Argo*.

Dryden went straight to the conning tower to see Adamson while Royston helped Roxy straight down to the sick bay. Adamson stood silently as Dryden quickly outlined what he had seen. When he finished the submarine captain contacted the sick bay and enquired what state Roxy was in. The surgeon-lieutenant reported that Roxy appeared to be in some state of shock and seemed disorientated.

36

Adamson stood for a few moments with pursed lips.

'Come below, doctor,' he said, turning down the hatchway.

Dryden followed the naval officer to his cabin. Adamson motioned him to take a seat and, from a cabinet, produced a bottle of brandy and two glasses. He poured out two good measures and handed one to Dryden. Then he drained his own at one gulp.

'Doctor Dryden,' he began, slowly as if searching for the right words. 'I can talk to you on an equal footing because you are a civilian. As the captain of this ship, I cannot talk to my officers as I can with you. I cannot let them see any weakness otherwise they will lose their confidence in my ability to command. My command is undermined by the fact that my First Lieutenant seems to have gone to pieces.'

Dryden was surprised by the harshness in Adamson's voice.

'You can't blame Roxy for going to pieces. We're faced with a totally inexplicable situation; a situation which has something of a nightmare quality to it which could disorientate anyone. It's like going to sleep in your own bed, in your own home which you know well, and then waking up a few minutes later to discover yourself in an entirely different place.'

Adamson nodded.

'I can realise that, doctor. I also realise that what has happened to Roxy, a usually stable and trustworthy officer, can happen to any one of my officers and crew. That is, unless we can find some explanation for the phenomenon. Man to man, doctor, do you have any suggestions'

Dryden shifted uncomfortably in his seat.

'To be honest, no; I don't have any suggestions at all. Mass hallucinations, psychological warfare... your guess is as good as mine.'

Adamson thrust a pale, strained face forward.

'What in hell can I tell the men?'

Dryden considered, swallowing at his brandy.

'I am not a navy man, commander. I don't know about discipline and all that. But why not tell them the truth? Why not simply tell them that you just don't know? It might not make for good morale but at least it will stop the speculation that is going round the ship.'

'Speculation?'

'That the officers are keeping something from the men.'

Adamson inclined his head.

'In the final analysis, it is my decision.'

He sat for a moment gazing at his empty glass.

Then he glanced up and smiled wanly.

'Thanks for your time, doctor.'

Dryden stood up and nodded.

In the seclusion of his cabin he lay on his bunk with his mind whirling. What had happened? Where were they? It was as if they had gone to sleep in one world and woke up in another; a new world in which the land masses, judging by the Orkney Islands, were the same but in which the people had vanished and the vegetation had changed beyond recognition. Yet the stars were still constant in the heavens. There must be some explanation.

There was a sudden crackle of static from the makeshift tannoy system.

'Attention all crew. This is the captain. I have an important announcement.'

Dryden raised himself to one elbow on his bunk.

'Since we resurfaced the *Argo* after our crash dive we have encountered a few mysteries. The scuttlebutt around the ship has probably made every crewman aware of what those mysteries are. Of prime importance are the following:- firstly, during the time we were unconscious there seems to have been a change of seasons, from winter to summer, judging by the length of the days, temperature and star configurations. Could we have all been unconscious as long as six or seven months? Secondly, by astral navigation, which is pretty accurate, we have arrived off the island group estimated to be the Orkney Islands. The geographical shape and layout of the islands confirm this. Yet there are no people, no signs of civilisation or other familiar spots. It is, as someone has said, almost as if we have surfaced in a different world.'

Dryden felt his lips dry and licked them.

'Well, we all know that this cannot be true. There is obviously an explanation for what has happened to us. We can dispel the notion that we were unconscious for a long period for the simple reason that hair continues to grow when one is asleep or unconscious. As I have had to place no crew member on the carpet about the length of

38

his hair, I must conclude we were unconscious for a short period.'

There was a pause, presumably while Adamson hoped that the crew would raise a chuckle about hair-length regulations.

'Yet, men, something must have happened at the Orkneys while we were in the Arctic. That is a matter for speculation and, as you may know, I do not believe in speculation without facts.

'I have therefore decided that the best course of action is to head straight for the mainland, to make for one of the Scottish ports where we will be able to find out what has been happening. We shall be under way within the hour. In the meantime, I suggest the crew be better employed than indulging in unnecessary scuttlebutt. Let us wait until we get the facts before making deductions. That is all.'

Dryden sighed and lay back on his bunk.

It was good that Adamson had told the crew what they already knew by gossip; good that he showed them that the officers were at least being honest with them. But it was rather weak to suggest that something had happened at the Orkneys while the *Argo* had been in the Arctic. How could something have happened within the few weeks of their voyage? How could something have happened which had totally obliterated all signs of civilisations, destroyed all roadways, towns, villages and one of the biggest naval bases in Europe, replacing them with a thick, almost impenetrable, jungle coating of undergrowth and trees.

Dryden lay awake a long time turning the puzzle over in his mind until he finally fell into an exhausted sleep.

Adamson looked at Dryden with troubled eyes.

He and Dryden were breakfasting the next day in Adamson's cabin. 'And you still cannot hazard any guess to a possible explanation of the conditions of the islands, doctor? You can't even identify the flora you saw?'

Dryden shook his head.

'I couldn't imagine scenery like that in my wildest dreams, captain. Were it not for the proof of your astral navigation or the geographical landmarks, I'd simply say that we were in some semi-tropical island around South America. But even that would not explain the strange flora.'

Adamson pursed his lips.

'Geographically there is no way that these islands could be anything else but the Orkney islands -but where are the towns, the people?'

There was a movement at the green baize curtain which separated Adamson's cabin from the corridor.

'Enter!'

A young lieutenant, his gold braid of rank ringed in red to denote he was a surgeon, entered and sketched an informal salute with one hand

'I thought you would like a report on Mister Roxy, sir.'

Adamson nodded.

'Is he better?'

The surgeon-lieutenant adopted a 'stand easy' position and shook his head.

'Still in shock. I can't tell for sure how deep it is or what the precise cause is. At a guess I would say disorientation - the events of the past couple of days.'

'Disorientation? Roxy was a damned good officer...'

'Excuse me, sir,' interrupted the doctor, 'but to be plunged into inexplicable circumstances without a rational explanation can affect even the most mentally alert of men.'

Adamson waved the man to silence.

'I realise that, Bones. It's just that I didn't expect to find such an extreme reaction in Mister Roxy.'

'If I may say so, sir,' went on the surgeon-lieutenant, 'I suggest you should be prepared for a few more cases among the crew unless something is done to give them a satisfactory explanation.'

Adamson's face took on a wrathful expression.

'Are you questioning my command of this vessel, mister?'

He spoke softly but with the deadliness of a snake.

The surgeon-lieutenant bridled.

'I was advising you of the likely medical condition of your crew, captain. That is all.'

'This is a ship of the Royal Navy, mister. Not a debating society. When I have something to tell the crew, then I shall tell them.'

The surgeon-lieutenant shrugged.

'It is your decision, sir. There is a new rumour going round the ship, sir. It is that we are undergoing some new operational training scheme which involves disorientation - psychological warfare training.

40

I passed Leading Seaman Randall just now and he seems convinced that the officers know all about the training scheme and that all - ' he waved his hands expressively ' - all this is merely something dreamt up by the Admiralty.'

Adamson sat back and for a moment seemed lost in thought, drumming his fingers on the desk.

'Alright, Bones. You can go.'

To Dryden's surprise, Adamson looked at him with a grin.

'You know, I think Randall has handed us a rather reasonable idea. We can encourage the speculation of a disorientation training scheme.'

Dryden gazed at Adamson in concern.

'If I may say so, captain,' he said with heavy emphasis, 'I think you are going to bring down a whole load of trouble on yourself if you admit to the notion that this is merely some sort of weird military exercise. When your crew find out that you have been misleading them and if you can't provide a suitable explanation...'

Adamson got to his feet.

'How would they find out, doctor? As far as I am concerned, Randall's idea is the best explanation of what has happened to us that I have heard so far. Perhaps it *is* true and Admiralty orders have not informed me.'

'You don't believe that?' asked Dryden in astonishment.

'Why shouldn't I believe it? As far as I am concerned, this is just a disorientation exercise.'

'And how long can that deception last?'

Adamson's eyes flashed.

'As long as it has to. Until a better explanation presents itself. Now just see to it that there is no loose speculation on your part.'

Dryden felt the blood surge to his head.

'You may have no cause for concern on that score, captain. But just remember that I am not one of your crew.'

Adamson nodded.

'I have not forgotten that fact, doctor. Neither have I forgotten that you are not a subject of the British Crown but merely a guest on this ship for whose safety I am responsible.'

Dryden stood up and turned to leave the cabin.

Adamson stretched out a hand as if to detain him but let it fall back to his side.

'Listen, Dryden,' he earnestly and quietly. 'My job is not the easiest at the best of times. I am responsible for the safety of this ship and one hundred and twenty-five crewmen. What would you do in my place? Admit that I, their captain, haven't got one idea in hell of what has happened to us and asked for suggestions? How long do you think discipline would last? How long would this ship be run with any degree of efficiency?'

Dryden turned back and his gaze softened. Adamson was presumably trying the best he knew how in the circumstances.

'What will you do, captain? Sooner or later the men will start demanding explanations. Already there is unease and speculation about Roxy's collapse.'

Adamson scratched at his temple.

'I'm going to take the *Argo* south, we'll make for one of the naval stations on the mainland - Aberdeen, or Rosyth.'

'And what if they are gone? What if the country is just like the Orkney islands?'

Adamson shook his head slowly.

'Then God help us!'

CHAPTER SIX

Neither God nor any other deity would help them.

Lieutenant-Commander Roxy jumped overboard shortly after the *Argo* left the mouth of the Firth of Forth following a fruitless journey down the east coast of Scotland. No one saw him go. Shortly after midnight a lookout heard a splash from the stern of the vessel. A search revealed Roxy's jacket and cap lying discarded on the after-casing. Sickbay was searched. His bed was empty. There was a scrawled note on the pillow. 'Gone to find Rosie. Sorry.' A thorough search was made of the entire vessel, although the searchers knew the conclusion was an inevitable one. Adamson recorded in his log that Roxy, completely unnerved by the sights and events of the past week or more, had taken his own life. The incident put a strain on morale and discipline.

It was no good pretending that this was not Scotland. The geographical landmarks, the coastline itself, were far too obvious for them to deny it. This was Scotland.

From the decks of the *Argo* the crew peered through glasses, gazing in stupefication at the bleak deserted shores, the areas of tall red-leafed trees whose configurations and surrounding vegetation seemed to come out of the pages of some child's fairy tale book. Gone were the cities - like Peterhead, Aberdeen and Edinburgh - only the strange vegetation remained.

Once or twice, Commander Adamson had sent ashore landing parties who returned with the same tale - strange, inexplicable vegatation, and here and there masses of rubble, as if they had been the sites of cities long destroyed. But there was no human life; no familiar signs at all. Only now and again strange animals and birds were sighted; odd, wild creatures who bore no resemblance to anything that the crew had seen before. Closer inspection revealed weird parodies of animals, like malformed horses, cows and other beasts.

The rumour that the submarine was on a special training exercise whose purpose was to test the effects of disorientation quickly died.

After Roxy's death no one believed that story. But what could they believe?

Lieutenant Starr, the second officer, who had now taken over Roxy's duties as First Lieutenant, expressed his anxiety to Adamson that the situation was drastically affecting morale and discipline and a group of malcontents, led by Leading Seaman Randall, were creating problems and spreading alarums among the crew.

Adamson's answer was to invoke naval discipline against Randall with stoppage of pay and privileges and thus provide him with a degree of martyrdom in the eyes of his shipmates, giving more credence to the boiling discontent.

Privately, one evening Adamson admitted to Dryden that he was going to try to make for the naval ports on the east coast of England because, surely, this vegetation could not have penetrated so far down. Surely, there were some naval bases still open? Adamson was driven by a blind desire not to accept the reality of the situation. The entire world, as they knew it before their crash dive, could not have been entirely eradicated; things could not have been entirely changed, altered beyond recognition, beyond comprehension? Adamson insisted that he would take the *Argo* into London itself in an effort to find some part of the world they had known.

Dryden had not been entirely inactive as the submarine nosed its way down the coastline. He had endeavoured to gather samples of vegetation and tried, in the cramped conditions of the submarine, to analyse and classify them. What he found was puzzling. The plants all seemed to be hybrids, mutations of common plants of the region...but mutated almost out of all superficial recognition. At one stage Dryden, acting on a hunch, borrowed the submarine's only working geiger-counter and tried to measure the radioactive content in the plants. The count was certainly abnormal but there was no basic consistency; some plants had higher count levels than others.

A germ of an idea had started to grow in Dryden's mind. Every time some animal or bird was sighted from the submarine, Dryden made a point of running on deck to peer at it and, as often as he could, sketch its features. In this manner, he came to another significant point. Like the plant life, so vividly colourful and exotic, the animal life appeared to be mutants of life-forms which would normally be found in that region - cows, horses, dogs and other beasts. Certainly Darwin's evolutionary theory still applied - the animals would have evolved from the animals he had known but how could an entirely new wildlife evolve in a matter of a few days, weeks or even months?

The problem worried Dryden as it did all the members of the crew.

It came to Dryden one evening after they had passed Hull, once one of the biggest fishing ports on the Yorkshire coast and now just a mess of jungle-like undergrowth. Dryden was leaning against the railing of the conning tower, gazing unseeingly at the dark coastline and thinking, strangely enough, of his life in the town of Bloomington, Indiana, at the university there. He was especially thinking about Paul Whitby, a close friend who was a research bio-chemist. It was then that the seed of the idea hit him. At first it was too ridiculous. He tried to dismiss it but the idea kept coming back and growing in his consciousness so that he was unable to ignore it. It began to take on shape and form until it became a rational hypothesis.

How long had the *Argo* lain on the seabed? How long had its occupants been unconscious?

Surely this was the key to the whole question?

If it had been a few minutes, as they all thought, then what was happening to them was incredible, fantastic, and enough to send Roxy or any man out of his mind.

But what if it had been longer... far, far longer? Not just days or months or even years. What if it had been centuries? Time enough for new plant life to evolve; new fauna to come into existence?

No, it was not quite so silly as he had at first thought.

The spark had been provided by his remembering Paul Whitby, the research bio-chemist. Whitby had been engaged on trying to freeze and reanimate living tissue at sub-zero temperatures. Dryden had known many scientists who had been working in cryogenics, the branch of physics which is concerned with phenomena at very low temperatures. Why, in America, some doctors were working on the theory of suspending life forms by means of freezing and then being able to reanimate the body at a later stage; a form of suspended animation. And many people, believing in the inevitability of cryogenic suspended animation, were allowing their bodies to be frozen. People with incurable diseases were undergoing cryogenic suspension in the belief that at some later date, when a cure for their disease was found, they would be reanimated and cured. Dryden knew that many were gullible people falling foul of scientific gobbledygook.

But Dryden also knew that many serious scientists were doing research on the subject, especially in relationship to Space Travel research. If man was to move to the stars beyond his own solar system, travelling many thousands of light years, then a form of suspended animation would have to be employed and cryogenics seemed an obvious path of research.

But how had that affected the *Argo?*

The last thing he recalled was that the *Argo* was going down by her head at a steep angle straight into the bottom of an iceberg. Everyone had braced himself for the collision. But no collision had occurred. It seemed as if they had smashed through the wall of the 'berg and then there had been a numbing coldness and... oblivion. They had all awoken a few moments later, or so they thought, but they had been 1,200 miles away from their last position...

What if the submarine had smashed through the ice wall of the 'berg, entering the 'berg itself, where the cold was so intense that they had been suddenly frozen; frozen so completely in that moment that the years had passed, decades, centuries, while the 'berg drifted on its inevitable route southwards, slowly melting until it had finally freed the *Argo* and its crew on the seabed 1,200 miles south...and as the warm currents washed the *Argo,* the life and feeling had returned to the crew?

What if the *Argo* had undergone some accidental natural cryogenic suspended animation? What if the crew, like so many Rip Van Winkles, had awoken in a future world? A world decades or even centuries in advance of the world they had known?

Dryden shook himself.

How ridiculous! How could he, a scientist, even contemplate the theory for one moment?

But then, it would explain so much: not just the physical changes to the landscape but little things such as the condition of the *Argo* when they had surfaced; the putrefication in the flooded forward compartments, the condensation, the cold....

Dryden bit his lip. No, it was a theory that he must keep to himself until he could substantiate it.

CHAPTER SEVEN

Two weeks passed before the *Argo* edged up the broad mouth of the River Thames and finally hove-to at a bend of the river where Adamson estimated the brooding Tower of London had once stood. The men clustered on the deck casing of the submarine and stared in frozen silence at the vista before them.

It was Harris who articulated Dryden's first thought.

'It reminds me of the ruins of Pompeii.'

Before them stretched northwards and southwards a panorama of London or, rather, what had been London; a vista of rubble, here and there overgrown by strange yellow and red grasses, of blue coloured brambles pushing through the concrete. There were stately trees which, at first sight, seemed to be majestic oak until one considered the colouring of the blood-red leaves. Fragments of tall buildings still pointed like crooked fingers upwards to the sky, refusing to perish. There were no recognisable landmarks and, had Adamson not pointed out the sweep of the river and insisted on where the Tower of London had stood, they had little way of knowing where they were or on what they gazed.

'What could have happened, sir?' whispered Lieutenant Starr, as his eyes wandered over the strange landscape. 'A bomb?'

'How could it have been a bomb?' asked Harris. 'The area would have been covered in radiation and... well, the vegetation would not have grown so quickly. We've only been away a few weeks. Maybe this isn't London?'

Adamson shrugged.

'The stars are constant and do not lie, Harris,' he said quietly, the strain in his voice echoing their perplexity.

Dryden moved uncomfortably.

'I have a theory.'

He spoke softly so that only Adamson and the executive officers standing close by would hear him.

Adamson swung round, his eyes raised in question.

'I think we should go below,' Dryden ventured.

Adamson nodded and led the way to his cabin, dismissing all his officers except Starr, Harris and CPO Royston to stand guard.

'Well, Dryden?' asked Adamson when they were seated around the green baize table.

'I don't think you will like this idea, captain,' Dryden began, 'but it seems the only logical and fairly scientific explanation in these circumstances.'

'Proceed,' said Adamson.

Dryden slowly explained the latest developments in cryogenic suspended animation research. Then he put forward his theory that the *Argo* and its crew had undergone some natural form of cryogenics and had awoken, not a few moments later, but a considerable time later... time enough for the whole world to have altered.

The faces before him were in turn incredulous, disbelieving and then filled with ridicule.

'Is that supposed to be a scientific explanation, Doctor Dryden?' asked Starr, an amused grin twisting his features.

'As far as it lies in my power to give one,' returned Dryden, reddening under the amused gaze of the officers.

'It's a bit rum, ain't it, doctor?' said Royston, standing by the doorway.

Adamson snorted.

'Rum! I would have thought you had better things to occupy yourself with rather than indulge in cheap science fiction romance. Is this all you have to offer, Dryden?'

Dryden stood up. He had not really expected to be believed; indeed, he only half-heartedly believed the idea himself. But he had expected to be listened to with some respect for his knowledge of science. After all, it was only a theory - however far fetched.

'I told you this was a theory, captain,' he said icily. 'Whether you accept it or not isn't my concern. But what does concern you and me at this moment is the state of your crew's morale. After Roxy cracked-up your men have been on tenterhooks. They want an explanation - any explanation - to alleviate their fear. I suggest you think about that.'

Adamson's face creased in a cynical smile.

'And you think your preposterous explanation will alleviate their fears? You are a civilian on this ship. I am the captain and what I consider is best for the morale of my men is my concern, not yours. I would respectfully suggest that...'

'Captain! Captain!'

A red-faced yeoman burst into the cabin.

'What is it, Jenkins?' snapped Adamson.

'Lieutenant Green sent me; some of the men have broken into the armoury, seized Lieutenant Barton as hostage...'

The officers were on their feet.

Adamson swore.

'Where are these men now? Who is leading them?'

The questions were machine-gun fired at the sailor.

The yeoman spread his hands.

'Mister Green is up by the armoury, sir. I'll take you to him.'

Adamson glanced around.

'Check your side-arms and come with me.'

They followed the yeoman in single file through the control room and down past the NCO's quarters which led to the armoury. An engineering lieutenant was standing guard alongside two men armed with carbines.

'What's going on Green?' demanded Adamson.

The engineering lieutenant pointed to where a body lay across the door of the armoury.

'It's poor Williams, sir. Happened about ten minutes ago. Petty Officer Williams was standing guard with Mister Barton on the armoury when a dozen men jumped them. Williams got a knife in his guts and they seized Barton. They've taken a few carbines, machine-pistols and ammunition. Randall seems to be the leader.'

'Randall?' Adamson frowned. 'Where are they now.'

'Gone on deck, I think.'

'Is the mutiny confined to these dozen men?'

Green nodded.

'As far as I know, sir. They're the ones who have been a bit vocal about the current situation. They think the officers know what is happening but are trying to withhold information from them.'

Adamson caught Dryden's gaze and lowered his eyes.

'Was that a general feeling among them?'

'Yes, sir. In fact, among most of the men.'

'Very well. Let's go and round up these mutineers. Starr, you take Royston and a couple of men and go to the conning tower. The rest come with me, we'll go through the for'ard hatchway. There's not many places they can go.'

Adamson was wrong.

As they emerged cautiously onto the submarine's for'ard casing they could see one of the ship's inflatable life rafts being rowed away by a group of men towards the northern bank of the river.

A burst of machine pistol fire from the raft made them duck and lie prone on the deck plating. In the silence that followed the burst they could hear a stream of abuse from someone in the boat. It sounded like Randall's whining voice.

'Shall we return fire?' yelled Starr from the conning tower.

'No,' returned Adamson. 'We want to capture those beauties alive.'

There was another burst of rapid fire.

Harris raised his head.

'Just covering themselves as they land, sir. They're making off into the rubble.'

Adamson sprang to his feet.

'Inflate the other two life rafts. I want a shore party. A dozen men to each raft. Mister Starr will command one group and you, Green, take command of the other. I suggest you try to outflank them. Cut 'em off and bring them back.'

A klaxon was summoning the crew to their stations and the captain was issuing orders to the petty officers to collect names and find out who the deserters were.

Dryden stood undecided on the deck plates. He had warned Adamson of the possibility of what had just happened but he had been met with coldness and ridicule. Why should he put himself out to make any more constructive suggestions. It was the scientist in him which overcame his injured ego. He moved across to Green. The young engineering lieutenant smiled.

'Green, can I join your party?'

The young man shook his head.

'Sorry, doctor. You're not naval personnel. There's probably going to be a gunfight and this is a strictly military show.'

'Rubbish,' returned Dryden. 'This is an emergency and you're in strange circumstances. The captain told you to take a dozen men, he didn't stipulate who they were to be.'

Green raised his arms helplessly.

'Very well, doctor,' he sighed. 'But on your head be it. I'm just asking for volunteers.'

Dryden nodded and climbed into the life raft which was now inflated and being held close to the *Argo's* side while sailors, each armed with a carbine, climbed in. Green stood for a moment talking with Starr, whose own life raft was being similarly filled. Then the young lieutenant climbed in and gave the order to push off for the shore.

Dryden suddenly found himself sitting next to Royston. The Chief Petty Officer grinned at him.

'Can't you keep away from excitement, doctor?'

Dryden smiled.

'Any excuse to get on dry land,' he returned.

'Listen men,' called Green, as the boat was propelled towards the bank. 'Lieutenant Starr and his men are going to swing in an arc towards the east in an attempt to try to circle in front of the deserters. We shall go straight after them. Remember they are all well armed, so keep your heads down. No heroics.

'Don't forget to keep spread out and don't present them with a good target.'

There was silence as the life raft bumped against the embankment, near to the deserted dinghy of the mutineers. The sailors leapt out, four men forming a covering party while the others climbed out. It was neat and done with military precision.

'You'd better stick by me, doctor,' whispered Royston, 'And don't forget to keep your head down.'

The patrol fanned out across the rubble, keeping close behind what cover the ruins and terrain presented. Green led them off at a fairly quick pace in the direction in which Randall and his mutineers were last observed heading. Slightly to the east of them they could just see Lieutenant Starr and his party landing and heading slightly towards the east.

The thought that was uppermost in Dryden's mind, as he followed

the burly figure of Royston over the debris-strewn terrain, was:
'How unreal! How ridiculously unreal!'

CHAPTER EIGHT

It took them several hours to traverse great expanses of concrete debris, which here and there had given way to the relentless onslaught of nature, allowing strange shrubs and bushes to push through. Dryden and the sailors had become so used to the brilliantly coloured plants that they were no longer impressed by them.

Randall and his group seemed to have vanished for they marched for some hours without a sign of them. Dryden saw that Green was now casting anxious glances towards the lowering sun. They came to a long, slow-climbing hill and Green signalled a rest.

Royston peered round curiously.

'I'm not a Londoner, sir, but I reckon we must be in the vicinity of Camden Town.'

'That's right, Chief,' chimed in a sailor whose accent betrayed his North London origin. 'Lay a quid on it, sir. This is Haverstock Hill going up towards Hampstead.'

'Okay,' acknowledged Green. 'We'll make Hampstead our camping point. If we don't spot them in the morning, we'll turn back. We only have rations for two days.'

Royston ordered the men to their feet and the group moved upwards silently, eyes straining in the oncoming gloom of early evening, trying vainly to catch a sight of Randall and his men. At last they came to the crest of the hill and flung themselves down in the open shelter of a crumbling building whose walls still looked remarkably sturdy. While the men rested, Green made a quick reconnaisance with Royston and Dryden, surveying the terrain through night-glasses.

'We must be about five miles from the submarine,' he observed.

Royston nodded morosely.

'The land beyond here looks a bit more overgrown.'

'You're right, Chief. I think it's too unfamiliar to press on further.

54

I'm sure Starr will turn back tomorrow morning. Anyway, that's what I propose to do.'

Royston stood and surveyed the crumbling building.

'Pity we didn't bring full kit. We could do with some sleeping bags,' he said. Then he raised his voice. 'Alright lads, spread yourselves out. I want two sentries, two hour watches. One up by the window and the other over there by the door. The rest of you can snatch some shuteye. I'll tell you who relieves who.'

Dryden decided to take his advice and sank down gratefully against a pile of masonry.

'Christ, sir, look at this!' one of the sailors was on his hands and knees busy scraping dust away from a piece of board.

Dryden joined the group peering over the sailor's shoulder.

The colours on the board, which turned out to be a square piece of metal, were faded. In places it had been chipped but the colours were still discernible. On a yellowing white background was a faded red circle while, horizontally across the circle, was a blue bar with some letters standing out in white relief. The inscription was partially legible. It read: 'HAMPSTE..'

'Hampstead!' exclaimed the sailor from North London. 'So I was right.'

A shrill scream of agony ripped across the gloom of twilight.

Each man sprung to his weapon and peered nervously around.

'What in hell's that?' whispered one man.

Royston motioned him to silence.

Dryden moved up to where Green was crouching by the open doorway.

'That was a human cry, Chief,' he said unnecessarily.

'Could it be one of Starr's men in trouble?'

A second scream, more terrifying than the first, rose and ended abruptly. Its tone sent a chill through Dryden's bones.

'We need a recce,' whispered Green.

'I'll go with you,' whispered Dryden as Green started to move forward. Green paused, caught the light in Dryden's eyes and nodded.

'Cover us, Chief,' he snapped to Royston.

Crouching low, he made a sudden dash towards a pile of bricks which afforded some cover. Dryden followed swiftly. In his

55

excitement it did not even occur to him to take out the pistol which was strapped to his side. Indeed, Dryden had never bothered to handle the automatic pistol since the start of their strange adventures.

The screams seemed to come from a complex of ruins to their right and Dryden followed Green as the young lieutenant zig-zagged his way towards the grey stone, roofless edifice. Together they reached a doorway and stood on either side, panting. Then Green inclined his head towards Dryden, tensed his body and shot through the doorway, pistol at the ready. Dryden followed a split second later and copied Green who had dropped to a crouching position on the floor.

It was difficult to make anything out in the large clearing in which they found themselves. It had obviously been a large room once, but now it was more like a small, walled field. Dryden suddenly felt a coldness pricking at his scalp. He laid a hand on Green's shoulder and pointed to a far corner.

A dark shadow was moving stealthily in the dark recesses by the wall. Suddenly the two pin-pricks of light shone straight at them, two fiery, glistening eyes, like the eyes of a prowling night cat. They stared unwinkingly for a moment.

With his mouth dry, Dryden felt his hand close around a stone and, unable to bear the tense silence, he suddenly hurled it at the eyes. At the same time Green snapped on a flashlight. There was an angry snarl, an animal roar that seemed to Dryden to be like the growl of a lion. The shadow darted across the beam of Green's torch and was gone. They had just a brief glimpse of a grey, leather-like hide.

For a moment they could hear it, whatever it was, as it scrambled out of the ruins.

Dryden reached up to wipe his face and suddenly realised that he was sweating. Cautiously, the two men stood up.

The stabbing beam of Green's torch stopped at the spot where the beast had been crouching. A body lay in the circle of light. It was a mass of red and all that was distinguishable was blue seamen's denims.

Green swallowed.

'Stay here, doctor. Keep me covered.'

He moved carefully forward and Dryden could see him bending over the body. He removed something from the neck, examined it with his flashlight and then walked slowly back. Even in the faint light from the torch, Dryden could see the young lieutenant's face was pale.

'It was one of the deserters, poor sod,' said Green softly. 'Whatever it was, it chewed him up pretty thoroughly. We'd better post a double guard tonight.'

He thrust the identification disc which he had removed from the corpse, in his pocket and led the way back to the waiting men.

The sound of machine-gun fire awoke them at dawn.

Dryden was on his feet rubbing the sleep from his eyes while Green was trying to still the questions of the men.

'Which way do you make it, yeoman?' he snapped to one of the sailors on sentry duty.

'Over towards the east, maybe a quarter of a mile away,' replied the man. 'About two minutes ago I heard some shouting but the voices probably carry quite a distance in these conditions. I was coming to wake you when the machine gun opened up. There's also small arms fire, sir. It must be Mister Starr.'

Green acknowledged the man's information.

'We'll fan out in five-yard intervals and move up towards the firing. It's probably Starr and Randall.'

The sailors began to move forward. Dryden, keeping close by Royston, was surprised when, after a hundred yards or so, they left the rubble and moved into an area of dense vegetation; an area of wild plant life that looked like something out of an Amazonian jungle.

'Hampstead Heath', Royston commented.

Dryden shrugged. Of course that would explain the lack of debris and the denseness of the vegetation.

The machine-gunfire was spasmodic. They could clearly distinguish the crack of small arms and the whine of carbine bullets. The firing sounded very close.

It was Royston who saw them first.

The party emerged from a belt of tall trees on the brow of a hill which sloped gently down into a wide clearing, matted by yellowing grassland. To one side of the clearing were the remains of a brick building surrounded by concrete blocks. From their position, Dryden could see a number of men crouching in firing positions by this scant cover. They were firing at points on the far side of the valley. Looking in that direction, Dryden could see an occasional flash of gunfire.

Green ordered his men to drop to the ground. He wriggled forward and focussed his glasses on the men below. Even before he spoke Dryden had seen the officer's cap among the men and realised they must be Starr's party.

'Damn!' swore Green. 'Lieutenant Starr must have been sheltering there during the night and his party have been ambushed by Randall and his men from that ridge.'

He studied the wild terrain.

'Chief,' he turned to Royston. 'I want you to take six men and ease your way onto their left flank. I'll take the rest of the men and bear down on the right flank.'

Royston glanced to where Starr's men were defending their positions.

'Any chance of Mister Starr mistaking us for Randall's lot?' he asked anxiously.

Dryden had an idea.

'Perhaps I can help? As soon as you've drawn Randall's fire, I can get down to Starr and tell him where you are.'

'Good man,' smiled Green. Then, 'I can't order you to do that, doctor.'

'I'm volunteering.'

'Very well. As soon as you hear us open fire, you move off.'

Royston intervened.

'Better signal with your Very pistol, sir. There's too much firing already.'

Green grinned sheepishly.

'Damned right, Chief. Okay, doctor? Then, let's go!'

Dryden watched the two groups move out under cover of the ridge. He lay hugging the ground and watching the occasional exchange of gunfire between Starr's men and the mutineers on the far side of the valley. He could see that Starr had already suffered three casualties. One sailor lay in the open, obviously dead. He could see two other men from his vantage point, lying prone behind some boulders. His eyes swept the valley cautiously. He couldn't get over the feeling that he was watching a television adventure, that he would awake to find himself in his apartment which, ironically enough, must have been only a few hundred yards from this very spot; that is, if this was truly Hampstead Heath. But there was a grim reality to the blood-stained bodies below, to the echo of gunfire and to the terrible experience of the previous night.

Dryden strained to see the far side of the valley. Green and Royston must surely be closing in on Randall by now. He started to raise himself, to get ready to run down the slope towards Starr's fortified position.

'Well, well...'

The voice was cold.

'If it ain't the boffin from civvy street!'

Dryden swung round abruptly and found himself staring at the weasel face of Randall, his eyes glinting coldly in the early morning light. A machine pistol was held unwaveringly at Dryden's chest.

CHAPTER NINE

Behind Randall were two other sailors, both holding guns and grinning down at their captive. Dryden felt sick with apprehension.

'Now this ain't nice of you, is it, doctor?' smirked Randall, waving his machine pistol in an arc. 'Here you are, armed I see, chasing us poor matelots with the intention of putting us to 'arm? Why, you ain't even in the Navy, ain't even a British subject. Not nice, I call it. A guest on our soil, so to speak, and trying to kill us.'

In spite of the brave words, Dryden could sense the nervous tension in the man. One of the sailors moved forward and yanked Dryden's pistol from his belt.

'This won't help you any, Randall,' he said slowly, trying to keep his voice from trembling. 'You're in enough trouble already.'

Randall gave a rather high pitched laugh.

'Yeah! I've killed a couple of men these past couple of days. And just you remember that, Mister Boffin! It won't add to my troubles to kill another. Anyway, I ain't gonna kill you just yet. No, I'm taking you 'ostage, see. Ensure our safety, like.'

He jerked his head to the two grinning sailors behind him. They moved forward and took Dryden under the arms, hauling him to his feet and pushing him before them.

'You're coming with us, doctor.'

Dryden glanced quickly up the valley but Randall saw the movement and laughed.

'Don't fret about Mister Green. A few mates of mine saw 'em coming and so we outsmarted 'em. Just a simple out-flanking manoeuvre, like they taught us to do... Now, move!'

His voice was suddenly brittle and Dryden felt the muzzles of two pistols in his ribs. He was forced to march away from the valley, back through the trees.

'Just what do you think you're going to do, Randall?' he asked after a while. 'Where are you taking me?'

Randall turned and motioned with his pistol.

'We're taking you over in them buildings, doctor.'

'I don't mean right this moment. I mean, why did you jump ship and just where do you think you are going?'

It was one of the sailors who replied.

'Home, that's where, mister. Ain't that so, Randall?'

Randall nodded.

Dryden frowned, trying to understand.

'Home? What do you mean?'

'Home, England, that's where.' replied the sailor.

'And where do you think you are now?' asked Dryden.

'Can't be sure - Randy thinks it must be Russia.'

'Russia? Why Russia?'

'Randy reckons...' began the man.

'Stow your gab, Raikes,' snarled Randall.

'But I was just...'

'I said, shut up!' Randall's eyes were blazing.

Dryden's mind was working rapidly.

'Randall has told you that you are in Russia?' he pressed, addressing himself to the sailor called Raikes. 'But you were in the *Argo* when she want to the Orkneys and sailed down the east coast of Scotland and England. How can we be in Russia?'

The man shot a nervous glance at Randall.

'Randall says it's psycho... psychological warfare,' the sailor stumbled over the word.

Dryden shook his head slowly.

'That's a lot of nonsense and Randall knows it.'

Randall turned abruptly and hit Dryden across the face with his clenched fist.

'Shut up!'

Raikes looked on, slightly worried.

'Oughtn't we to listen, Randy?' he urged. 'He's a boffin. He might know.'

Randall spat disgustedly.

'Can't you see he's one of them? 'E'll only tell you a lot of lies, try to make out you're somewhere you're not just to get us back to the submarine. They'll 'ang us when we get back as soon as look at us.'

'Yeah, but...'

'But nothing! It's as I told you. The whole thing's a put-up job. Only Adamson knows what's going on. 'E said so. He's a Rusky spy; 'e's taken the submarine somewhere in Russia where,' he waved his hands towards the surrounding area, '...all this is just to fool us, to make us crack up like poor Roxy did. They want to make us crack up and talk. No, I tell you, the only chance is to stick with me, to escape and get back to England.'

Dryden lay where the force of Randall's blow had landed him and gazed at the sailor in amazement. Either Randall was completely insane or merely a fool.

'You can't believe what you're saying?' he gasped. 'Do you men really believe him?'

Randall aimed a vicious kick at Dryden.

'I told you to shut up, didn't I?'

The two sailors looked from Dryden to Randall, their pistols pointing at the ground.

'Are you really sure about this, Randy?' ventured Raikes.

'Yeah,' chimed in the second man. 'How do we know he ain't telling us the truth. What if this is really England?'

Randall laughed without amusement.

'Blimey! They've even got at you. Are you really off your chump? Ask yourself, 'ow the 'ell can this be England? Does it look like England? Christ, we've only been away a couple of weeks, so 'ow can things change so much, eh? Use your sense, if you've got any! It may fool you but it don't fool me. I'm not 'anging around to be brainwashed by the Ruskies, and you're damned fools if you do. Now pick 'im up and let's go. Starr and Green'll be after us in a moment.'

With some show of reluctance, the two sailors heaved Dryden to his feet. He raised a hand to wipe a smear of blood from the corner of his mouth.

'You're damned fools if you believe Randall,' he whispered. 'The man's round the bend. Of course we aren't in Russia.'

The two sailors exchanged glances but said nothing. Instead they pushed Dryden in front of them, though not too roughly this time. Randall walked in front, muttering to himself now and again.

It was then that Dryden began to realise that Randall was really insane. Like Roxy, the sailor had been unable to adapt to the fantastic change of surroundings, but he had come to an extraordinary rationalisation in order to protect himself. Unfortunately, Randall's reasoning had caused several lives to be lost. And, Dryden knew, the next life on the line was his.

'Come on,' growled Randall. 'We ain't got all day.'

They moved out of the forest and away from the undergrowth towards the rubble-strewn area.

'Where did you tell the others that we'd meet them?' asked Raikes.

'Near the building where Evans got it last night,' replied Randall.

'Poor sod,' muttered Raikes. 'I wonder what it was? Poor sod only went off for a ... heard him screaming for some time.'

Dryden realised that they were talking about the sailor who had been killed by the strange animal.

'Yeah,' Randall was saying. 'The Ruskies got him. Must have tortured the poor bastard.'

'It was an animal that killed your friend,' said Dryden quietly. 'There aren't any Russians here, this isn't Russia. It is - or was - London. Evans was attacked and killed by an animal.'

Randall turned with a snarl distorting his features.

'I've taken enough from you, you lousy Commie agent! 'Ostage or no, I've 'ad enough!'

Dryden took an involuntary step backwards as Randall moved towards him, his face contorted.

'Easy now, Randy,' said Raikes nervously.

'Easy nothing! You 'eard 'im say 'ow Evans died. 'Im and 'is Commie friends probably tortured the poor bastard to death. Well, 'e'll get what's coming to 'im now!'

Randall started to raise his machine pistol.

It was Raikes who stepped in front of Dryden.

'Now then, now then, Randy. You don't know what happened about Evans. We've seen enough strange beasts the past few days. He could have got himself killed, just like the boffin says.'

There was an abrupt roar from Randall's machine pistol.

Raikes' eyes rounded in amazement as he sank down before Dryden, blood saturating the front of his jersey.

The other sailor started to back away, not even bothering to raise his pistol. Dryden felt his mouth dry but, strangely, he felt no horror, no fear. There was just a feeling of detached coldness as he gazed into the eyes of the madman who now held a wavering machine pistol towards his chest.

'You damned Commie spy!' Randall screamed. 'You're gonna pay...'

Dryden was preparing to throw himself sideways to avoid the burst of gunfire, when a blur of grey and yellow hurtled through the air and fastened itself at Randall's throat. Randall fell to the ground screaming, with the animal snarling and growling at his shoulders. To call it a cat would not have been accurate. It was like a panther, but certainly no species of the great cat that Dryden had seen before. The beast was squat and muscular, the teeth were large and already tearing at Randall's flesh.

Raikes' companion gave a wild cry of terror, turned and fled into the forest.

Dryden dived for the gun which Raikes had been holding when Randall had viciously cut him down. Even as he felt the cold grip of its butt in his hand he knew he was too late to save the insane sailor. The great cat seemed oblivious of his presence and was now crouching on its prey, snarling and gnawing.

Dryden suppressed an urge to vomit. For months afterwards he would hear the terrible sound of those sharp gnawing teeth.

Slowly he raised the machine pistol to take aim.

Then the unholy yellow eyes of the beast were on him, gleaming like the fires of hell. Dryden felt himself turning to stone as he saw the great muscular hind legs of the beast moving up under its haunches, readying for the spring. He realised that even if he were a crack shot he could not possibly fend off the beast with the pistol before it reached his throat.

Hardly had the thought flashed through his mind before he felt the hot air of bullets and the staccato chatter of a machine gun.

As if in slow motion, Dryden saw the blood spots appear on the yellow fur of the beast, heard it scream in angry anguish and saw it suddenly turn and bound off into the forest. Weakly, he dropped to his knees as a group of sailors burst through the undergrowth. He saw Starr, Green and Royston at their head and a moment later Royston was offering him a brandy flask.

64

It gave him sufficient strength to tell what had happened.

Lieutenant Starr eyed Randall's mangled corpse dispassionately.

'Poor stupid bastard,' he said. 'Are you sure he went insane, Dryden?'

Dryden nodded. 'God knows how he fooled the others but the man was really gone.'

'Just like Roxy, eh?'

Dryden looked hard at Green.

'Different extreme reactions,' he agreed, 'but the same cause.'

'Where are the rest of Randall's men?' asked Starr. 'Did he say?'

'Nearby where we camped last night.'

'I can lead the way there,' volunteered Royston.

'Are you fit to come with us, doctor?' asked Starr.

'Yes. What's going to happen to them?'

'Them? Oh, the mutineers? Hopefully we can take them peacefully.'

He moved over to the corpses of Randall and Raikes and removed their identification discs.

'Let's go!'

They spent several hours exploring the ruins. There were signs in one building that the deserters had gathered there, a few cigarette butts and some torn scraps of paper. But the rest of the mutineers had obviously decided to press on. Starr finally called back his search parties.

'I'm officially calling off the search,' he told Green, Royston and Dryden. 'We've sustained two dead and one wounded. As far as we can count, they've lost five dead. Well, all I say, is God help the poor bastards now.'

It was a silent and morose party which made its way slowly back through the rubble and dust of the once great city towards the banks of the river where the *Argo* lay. The excited questions of the rest of the crewmen went unanswered. No one was really in the mood to speak.

Starr had gone to report to Adamson and Dryden had barely time to wash and change before Royston put his head into the cabin and told him that the Captain wanted to speak with him.

Adamson's face was haggard.

'So,' he said without preamble, 'Randall went mad and thought I was some sort of Communist agent who had led the ship to a disorientation centre in Russia so that the Russians could brainwash the crew?'

'Idiotic as it sounds, captain, that's substantially correct.'

Adamson bit his lip.

'Incredible.'

Not only did Adamson look haggard and ill, but he had obviously been through a severe emotional crisis and was doing his best to retain control of himself.

'I suppose you will say something like "I told you so", that I should have been honest with my crew about our lack of knowledge?'

Dryden shrugged.

'You're the captain. I've learned enough about your navy now to know you must do what you consider is the best for your ship and crew.'

It was too glib a reply. Dryden knew it. Adamson knew it. But the captain seized the excuse and nodded slowly.

'I've had time to think a bit about the past few days, especially looking out on the landscape hereabouts.'

He paused and his eyes sought Dryden's.

'When you put forward that theory of yours - the cry - cry?'

'Cryogenic suspended animation.'

'That's it. Were you being serious?'

'I was.'

'Is it feasible?'

'It's feasible. Nothing more.'

'Dryden, I apologise for what I said to you yesterday. Ridiculing your theory, that is. I should not have done so.'

Dryden made a gesture with his hand.

'I said it was a theory only, captain. Everyone's entitled to his own opinions.'

There was a pause.

'What do you mean to do now, captain?' asked Dryden.

Adamson reached for a chart.

'After we've carried out some repairs and filled up with fresh water, I will take the *Argo* back into the Channel.'

'I heard talk about the reactor becoming increasingly unstable.'

Green, the engineering officer, had told him as much.

'We still have some way to go before it gets into the danger level,' answered Adamson.

'And where will you take her?'

'My plan is to make for the naval base at Plymouth; there's a chance, just a chance, that someone has survived in this Godforsaken world.'

'And if not?' frowned Dryden.

'Well then, by that time the reactor will probably be totally unstable and the *Argo* worse than useless. Then I shall disband the ship's company and they can make their own choice as to what they want to do.'

'But captain, if civilisation has so totally vanished from the Orkney islands down to London, what chance would there be of survivors at Plymouth?'

'Damn it, mister,' Adamson suddenly snapped, 'don't talk logic to me. This whole situation is totally illogical. Why should we expect the Orkneys to be turned into a strange jungle? Where's the logic to these grey ruins of London? What's happened to the millions of people who inhabit this country? Where's the logic, eh?'

He paused and then his face crumbled for a moment.

'My wife lives at Plymouth - and that's where the *Argo* was launched and fitted. I'm taking her home....her home, my home.'

Dryden looked at the man with sympathy.

'Very well, captain.'

It was a sober crew that gathered on the *Argo's* for'ard casing two days later and looked expectantly up at the conning tower where Commander Adamson and his executive officers were gathered.

Dryden leaned moodily against the side of the conning tower, watching the sailors and wondering how they would react to Adamson's statement.

The captain cleared his throat.

'Men, there is little I can tell you. You know the facts as well as I do. We've made some temporary repairs to the flooded for'ard compartments of the ship. We now have some fresh water but very little consumable food. However, I must tell you that our reactor is becoming increasingly unstable. There is no immediate danger and we are working well within the safety margin.'

The sailors shuffled and muttered among themselves.

'Now, let us be clear on one point. My officers and I have no more information about the conditions in which we find ourselves than you. We have on board an Admiralty scientist, Doctor Dryden. He does have a theory which, so far, I have discounted. However, I feel that you should all be aware of any theories or information on our situation in order to avoid any further breakdowns of discipline and good order. For in discipline, men, lies our only hope for immediate survival. We are still a Royal Navy ship. I want you to remember that.

'So, commencing at eighteen hundred hours, or as near as dammit because our chronometers are not accurate, Doctor Dryden will hold discussions on his theory in the for'ard mess room. Seeing that only thirty-five men can attend each sitting, the Petty Officers will organise you into your watches.

'Our immediate sailing plan is to head to Plymouth - the home of the *Argo*. I, personally, feel that if we are likely to find anyone alive, or any remnant of our navy left, it will be in the west country. If we do not, then the entire crew will be gathered and the situation will be open to discussion.

'Now I know you have many questions. Would you please save them until the briefing sessions start with Doctor Dryden. I shall be in attendance. In the meantime, we shall be underway for Plymouth within the hour. That is all.'

The crew stood for a few moments as if uncertain as to how they should react. Dryden noticed that few of the men spoke to their neighbours, each man preferring to remain silent with his own thoughts and fears. The hardest hit would be the married men or those with close relatives on shore. Dryden was grateful that he had always been a solitary boy: growing up in an orphanage in Fort Wayne, Indiana, working his way through High School and then University in Bloomington.

He stood for a while on the deck casing until the klaxon sounded and the submarine began to pull slowly along the river, pushing backward towards the wide mouth of the Thames.

CHAPTER TEN

Five days later, painfully and slowly, the great hulk of the *Argo* pushed around the Great Mew Stone which guarded the entrance to the wide bay where the rivers Lynher, Tamar and Tavy emptied themselves into the sea. Most of the crew stood excited and voluble on the deck casing, eagerly watching the countryside. Ever since the submarine had passed within sight of the Bill of Portland, they had noticed that the strange vegetation was diminishing. They could see familiar green trees, flowers and even birds which were identifiable. And now, as they entered the bay and pushed towards Drake's Island which fronted the city of Plymouth all eyes were strained for a sight of their world, or normality, of buildings and people.

Even Dryden was beginning to hope that Adamson was right. Perhaps some survivors had made a new world for themselves here in the British west country.

But even as they strained shoreward, they saw no signs of life, no buildings, no people, just thick, matted vegetation and only the plaintive cry of seabirds. Sluggishly, the submarine turned towards the site of Devonport, a vast tangle of trees, and made fast opposite the headland which was once called Torpoint.

For over an hour Commander Adamson stood gazing across the verdant mass that had once been the city of Plymouth; his home. There his wife and two children had lived. Now it was no more. Even in his misery a tinge of guilt was stirring in him because he had used his position as captain to bring his vessel to his home to rest. No, Plymouth was the *Argo's* home, too. It was right she should come here. But now Plymouth was gone. Now there was nothing. Nothing to strive for, nothing to work for. Nothing.

'Well, sir?'

Lieutenant Starr was asking for orders.

Adamson shrugged. Dryden, who had been watching him, guessed at the emotions going through the man. Adamson turned and moved down the hatchway to his cabin. Dryden laid a restraining hand on Starr's arm and shook his head.

'What are we going to do now?' demanded the First Lieutenant.

'The captain was going to disband the ship's company.'

'But then what?' pressed Starr. 'Does each men fend for himself or what? What are we going to do?'

'At least Adamson has brought us to what seems the most normal and habitable part of the country,' Dryden said.

'But the cities, the towns, the people - they've gone,' interposed Harris, who had been listening to the conversation.

'Yes. But if my theory is correct, they haven't existed for some time. There must be a new society here somewhere.'

'You mean,' asked Green, coming into the bridge, 'you mean you believe that there are people out there like ourselves?'

'Perhaps,' said Dryden. 'You can see that the bird life has remained unchanged. Look at the trees and shrubbery through your glasses. Apart from one or two, they all seem fairly recognisable to me. So where plant life and some bird life have remained unchanged, I would say that it's an odds-on bet that the human species has survived as well. We must find them. And I think we've come to the best place in the whole of the island to do so.'

It was a very quiet and sober ship's company who ate a sparse evening meal and turned in. There were no jokes; no stories; each man appeared to want to be alone with his memories - for memories were now all they had of the world they had known.

Before turning in Dryden went for a stroll around the deck casing to watch the sun lowering itself gently over the western rim of the world. A cough caused him to turn. It was Lieutenant Green. For a while the two men stood at the stern of the submarine in silence.

'Strange, isn't it?' said Green after a while.

Dryden did not reply.

'Do you think that humanity, everyone, has been totally destroyed and we are all that's left?'

Dryden sighed.

'There's a good chance that people have survived somewhere.'

'Ah,' said Green soberly. 'But here?'

70

He suddenly pointed in the fading light towards the end of the bay in which the submarine lay.

'That's Cornwall,' he said, unnecessarily for Dryden had gone on vacation there during his time in Britain. 'Or *was* Cornwall. And see that point at the end of the bay? That used to be a little village called St. John. I spent most of my childhood there watching the ships come and go. Did you know that it was there that poor Roxy planned to open his pub? Now it's as if it never existed.'

He turned abruptly and walked off along the deck.

Dryden stood awhile longer, letting his thoughts run on all he had known. His university acquaintances; his colleagues at work. Well, there was none to mourn or be mourned by. The past belonged to the past. He must prepare himself for the present. With a final sigh he turned and made his way through the stillness of the submarine to his cabin.

He woke late in the morning. Already there were orders being shouted and men moving here and there. There was no one in the ward room, but a percolator of coffee still simmered and his breakfast had been placed on a hot plate. Dryden hurriedly ate the meal and was finishing his coffee when Harris thrust his face into the cabin.

'Thought you might be here. The captain wants a word with you in his cabin. Can you go at once?' Thoughtfully, Dryden made his way to Adamson's cabin.

Adamson shot him a brief smile.

'You've probably heard the rumour? I'm going to evacuate the *Argo*.'

Dryden raised his eyebrows.

'The reactor is well into the danger limit,' went on Adamson. 'To be truthful, it has been so for the past twenty-four hours but I wanted to get the ship here. The instability reading is well over forty-five percent. Anyway, our main problem is food. Our edible canned food is nearly gone and we shall have to start living off the land. That, I understand, was your speciality before...before...'

'I can't see any problem there, captain,' replied Dryden. 'At least the flora and fauna here are not outrageously different from what they should be. The trees and grasses seem pretty much the same.'

Adamson ran a hand through his hair.

'I would like some more precise information, though. You

obviously know what to look for - mushrooms, roots, vegetables and that sort of thing. I'd like you to take Chief Petty Officer Royston and have a look round the bay here. I think the Cornish side seems more hospitable. Don't go too far from shore but do see if you can get an idea of how rich this area is in edible plant life and game.'

Dryden nodded assent.

'After we've shut down the reactor,' said Adamson, 'I plan to beach the *Argo* and tow her onto the shore. At least that will save my immediate problem of shelter for the men.' Dryden turned to go. Adamson looked old and ill as he sat hunched over his papers. For the first time Dryden became aware of a cluster of greying hairs above the man's temples. Adamson suddenly peered up.

'If your theory is right, Dryden, and if we have gone through some sort of suspended animation and awoken in some future world, are there people in it? Has man totally destroyed himself? And if there are people, where are they?'

Dryden shrugged.

'Everyone seems to be asking the same question.'

'If we're the only human beings left in the world, what is there to survive for?'

'There's always something to survive for, captain,' replied Dryden, leaving the cabin.

Chief Petty Officer Royston's face was beaded with sweat as he and Dryden propelled the rubber dinghy up onto the sandy beach. Dryden stood for a moment, head thrown back.

'I'd almost forgotten what land and Nature feel like, Chief,' he said with a smile.

Royston cast a nervous glance about him.

'Well, doctor, I can't say that I'm very happy to be away from the *Argo* at this moment. Look around you. I always get the idea that people are lurking behind trees and - .' His eyes narrowed as he looked at Dryden's waist.

'Where is your sidearm, doctor?'

Dryden smiled.

'You don't expect me to take that business seriously? All that's over now. Anyway, I could never shoot the damned thing.'

'Nevertheless, doctor, it was an order from the captain.'

'A request, in my case, Royston. Remember I'm a civilian.'

A shout interrupted them.

They turned towards the *Argo*. Someone was on the for'ard casing of the submarine signalling wildly; waving his arms in circles.

'What is it, Royston?' asked Dryden.

'I don't know. Why doesn't the idiot use proper signal procedure? He seems a bit frantic, though. Look, doctor, I'd better push back and see what's up. Will you be okay here?'

'Of course.'

Dryden helped the burly Chief Petty Officer push the rubber dinghy into the surf and then he waded back to the beach as Royston bent over his paddle.

Dryden turned and walked up the sandy beach. He pushed his way into the edge of the wood and stood in a small clearing of beech trees. Around the beeches grew clusters of fungi, some of them as much as six inches across with brown caps, almost yellow to olive-brown. Dryden bent forward and broke one off. The stem was short and bulging, pale brown, streamed with white. He drew out his sheath knife and cut into it. The flesh was firm and white. It had a pleasant smell and he popped a little of it into his mouth.

'*Boletus edulis,*' he smiled to himself. 'Not bad for starters.'

He examined the surrounding wood. Apart from a few species here and there which were entirely unknown to him, and which, he began to suspect, were mutants, the flora seemed to be pretty much the same as it had been before - well, whenever it was. It was going to be fairly easy to find food here. But what had caused such a terrific change of flora in the Orkney islands while, down here, in Cornwall, the flora was relatively unchanged? There had to be a logical explanation.

From where he stood he felt the blast of warm air a split second before the roar of the explosion reached his ears.

A sudden coldness encased his body and then, with fear clawing at his heart, he turned and raced down to the shore. Where the *Argo* had been was a small cloud of rising steam and smoke, a patch of disturbed water, an oil slick and a few pieces of floating debris, a couple of them alight.

Like a sleep walker, with mouth opening and closing soundlessly, Dryden walked slowly into the surf until the waves washed over his

73

waist.

'Hey!' he shouted, helplessly. 'Hey!'

He looked up and down the shore line.

Apart from the squawking of gulls and other birds disturbed by the explosion, there was no sound, just the whisper of the waves on the sea shore. For how long Dryden stood there helplessly mesmerised by the spreading patch of oil and debris, he did not know.

Dryden now knew that he was alone. He was cast away in an alien new world, a strange new world that was not his; in a time that was not his. Cast away and utterly alone.

PART TWO
The Land of Bel

"Nothing is found only once in the world, for repetition is Nature's only form of permanence. In the society of Mankind the past is the architect of the present and the present predestines the future. Repetition becomes an inalienable law. Therefore, the dead always govern the living, tradition becomes a jailer not a guide and people remain what they are because they have come out of what was. The circle of existence is never broken. Who will dare change the circle into a spiral?"

An Lyver Mur a Lan-Kern
The Great Book of Lan-Kern

CHAPTER ONE

The first three days were the worst.

Each day Dryden wandered up and down the shore, giving way to black waves of despair and helplessness. Once, very early on, his heart beat a wild tattoo of hope when he heard a loud crack reverberate along the sea shore and for a while he was sure that it was the report of a pistol. He cried aloud several times but only the forest noises and the mocking cries of the gulls answered him. He spent most of that day trying to find the direction from which the noise had come, but by evening he gave up, deciding that the sound had merely been the snapping of a rotten tree and that he was truly alone. His sense of despair then gripped him anew.

But the instinct of survival is ever stronger than the emotion of despair. He had managed to find a small brook gushing down over a rock into the sea. The water was sweet and good. By this rockface, which was a small outcrop of limestone, was a grassy area in which grew a cluster of yellow flowering plants several feet tall. Dryden was able to pull some of these out, exposing the roots: they were wild parsnip. He washed them in the stream and gnawed at them, wishing he had the means of making a fire. The first two such meals he immediately vomited back but soon his digestive system had learned to cope with the new dietary regime.

On the fourth day a sense of purpose began to grow in his mind: if the fates had ordained he should survive, then survive he would. He whetted his knife on a stone, went to the stream and there, painfully and slowly, he shaved the beginnings of his beard and moustache. Then he took a swim in the sea and began to feel vastly refreshed.

He took stock of his situation, sitting on the sunbaked sand.

Survival was important but mere survival was not enough. It was ridiculous for him to contemplate a future of existence on roots and berries by the sea shore. He was certain that people must exist inland and, although the loss of the *Argo* and its crew had plunged him into a temporary depression, there was no reason to change his mind. But to venture inland he would need better protection for himself.

A spear was the weapon needed most; simple to make and easy to use as a means of immediate defence. He would also try his hand at making a bow and arrows. His one great prize was a long length of twine which he had discovered among the flotsam on the shore.

Dryden took his knife and wandered slowly through the woods, making sure to keep fairly near the open beaches, his eyes searching for the particular tree he wanted. He was not long in finding it. It was in a copse of large evergreen trees, covered in oval red berries whose shapes closely resembled acorns. Dryden had remembered from his youthful reading that in ancient times the best longbows were made from the branches of the yew. He examined the cluster of yew trees carefully and selected a branch which would suit his purpose. He seized the branch and cut it to size.

He spent some time searching for an ash tree, for under the grey bark was the white, hard wood from which arrows and a spear could be made. The embryonic arrows, of two foot lengths, were easily found and cut. Dryden collected two dozen such pieces. The search for a length of ash suitable for his spear took longer but it, too, was eventually found.

Finally he returned to the beach and commenced his most difficult task - making a fire. It was over an hour before he managed to start a smouldering glow among a pile of dried grass. His means of ignition were two flat flint stones. It was hardly the easy method mentioned in most popular adventure stories. This done, however, he started work on making his weapons.

The yew bough he stripped of bark and left drying in the sun. He did the same with the small lengths of ash, which he cut to a standard size and whittled to points at one end. These points he hardened, American Indian fashion, in the fire. The spear was also stripped and hardened - one end into a point. It took him several days to carry out this work. His final task was bending his bow and fitting the twine as a bowstring.

He awoke one morning, well over a week after the explosion had cast him alone on shore, feeling a ridiculous pride in his new weapons.

His first attempt to shoot with his bow was a disaster and at the end of two hours, in which he found he could not even hit a tree trunk at twenty paces, he threw it aside in disgust.

He had better luck with his spear but it became obvious to him that it was going to take him a long, long time to obtain any degree of proficiency. It was not until a week later that he was confident of hitting an immovable object with both spear and arrow. He felt a childish pleasure in the fact until he realised that when the time came to use his weapons in earnest, his targets would not be passively standing still.

However, he had spent nearly two weeks on the shore of this alien country, two weeks without seeing or hearing any signs of his fellow man. Now he felt a desperate urge to move inland, to begin his search whether he was fully prepared for it or not. After all, he could still live on roots and other plants. But he could certainly not stay in this lonely, depressing spot any longer.

That evening, sitting before his fire on the empty expanse of beach, Dryden made up his mind to start moving into the interior at first light.

CHAPTER TWO

The rising sun casting its warmth on his face awakened Dryden. For a few seconds he lay in the crotch of the tree smiling gently at the strange nightmare which he had been having. Then the angry snarl of some beast in pursuit of its prey caused his eyelids to spring open and his deep set blue eyes to search his surroundings rapidly for any sign of danger. Having ascertained that there was no immediate threat, he stretched his limbs and stood up.

A black depression caught him as he realised that the nightmare of the past few weeks was, in fact, reality. He was still alone. It was now three weeks since the *Argo* had blown up; three weeks of searching for survivors and trying to survive himself. Though pieces of odd wreckage, some pieces of clothing and even one or two tragically recognisable personal effects, had floated ashore, there was no sign of Adamson or his crew. It was not really knowing if anyone else had survived the explosion that depressed him. This past week he had tried not to think about it as he pushed further inland, following the wide river which had once separated Cornwall from Devon.

He descended cautiously from his perch, listening carefully all the time, head to one side. One of the first lessons, which he had learnt the hard way during his journey through the forest, was that those who descend from their trees first and look afterwards are the prey while those who look first and descend afterwards live to seek prey.

Dryden stood awhile, wondering what to do. He ate a snack of wild parsnip roots, gnawing at the dirty tubers with his teeth. For three weeks he had lived thus, thanking the powers for the botanical knowledge which helped him choose edible roots and berries, tubers and fungi by which he had been able to survive. But his stomach ached for meat. He would not even cavil at red raw meat. But try as he might he had been singularly unsuccessful as a hunter in spite of his weapons.

Today he was determined to bring down a rabbit at least.

He stopped to wash the earthy taste of the roots from his mouth by swallowing some evil smelling, brackish water from a nearby pool. Then he began to move northward again.

He had been an hour in the hunt without the slightest sign of beast nor fowl, although he could hear the grunt and occasional bark of animals in the thickets around him. He stopped to rest on a wooded rise, squatting down beside a small stream of clear, sweet water and drinking thirstily.

At first he thought it was a distortion of sound from the running water but for a second he swore he had heard a human cry.

He paused, listening intently.

He was about to curse his senses when he heard the sound again. It was a human cry! A hoarse cry!

He sprang up.

Survivors from the *Argo*!

He gave an answering yell. Invisible animals blundered this way and that through the undergrowth, alarmed by his strident voice.

A faint cry answered him.

Snatching his weapons, Dryden raced down the incline towards the shore of the river. He reached a clump of trees growing close to the river bank and halted, his breath coming in quick jerks.

He could hear several voices shouting now.

Looking across the river, he saw two strange craft skimming across the water. Something made him keep to the cover of the closely growing trees. His eyes widened with amazement. The craft were small coracle-like boats. In the first sat a young man, crouching low over his paddle, sending the coracle shooting forward as if his very life depended on it. In the second craft, a larger coracle than the first, were three men. Two of them worked at the paddles while the third stood, balanced precariously, urging his companions to greater efforts. In one hand he balanced a long javelin.

For some moments Dryden was awestruck by the sight of these strange figures. They were certainly not from the *Argo*. Indeed, they looked like figures from some history book. As they came closer to the bank, he could see a similarity in their dress - loose tunics fastened over breeches which came to just below the knee. The man in the first coracle was distinguished from his pursuers by a short multi-coloured cloak, similar to a tartan weave, fastened at one shoulder by a large brooch.

Suddenly the man standing in the pursuing coracle loosed his javelin. It flew with amazing accuracy and it was only by a desperate back-paddle on the part of the fugitive that the javelin struck the side of his craft and not his back. The pursuers laughed and Dryden saw the spearman readying another javelin.

He glanced at the men's quarry. There was a desperation on the young man's face. He was paddling rapidly towards the shore, now and then throwing back his head and crying something which sounded like 'Gweres! Dew Gweres!' It was the cry which Dryden had heard moments before. The youth was obviously calling for help.

The javelin thrower brought back his arm and steadied himself.

A strange animal fury seized Dryden as he watched the unequal race for life or death. Swiftly he set an arrow to his bowstring, stretched it back and aimed.

The arrow sped swiftly.

The man with the javelin clutched at his chest with a surprised look at the protruding wood. Slowly, ever so slowly, he toppled over the side of the coracle and floated face downward in midstream.

For a moment Dryden was as surprised as he was horrified. He had not thought to hit the man, let alone kill him. After his failures of the past week he was amazed that his arrow had reached its target. He had merely thought to frighten the pursuers. But events were moving too swiftly for him to entertain the remorse which welled up within him.

The young fugitive had glanced round, preparing to evade the next throw, and had seen his enemy disappear into the water. With a cry, halfway between triumph and desperation, he bent over his paddle again, striking out for the bank with renewed vigour.

The two men in the pursuing coracle sat back-paddling and looking in horror at the floating body of their dead companion.

Some instinct urged Dryden to follow up his advantage and he loosed off another arrow which embedded itself in the prow of their craft.

With cries of fear, the two men, now paddling furiously, turned their coracle and sent it racing back towards the far bank.

The young man had beached his craft and, grinning broadly, walked towards Dryden.

His was a broad, handsome face, with wide grey eyes, a pleasant mouth whose smile seemed a natural state. On his upper lip grew a long black moustache which, together with long raven black hair, hid the wearer's youth. He was obviously in his early twenties.

The youth stood a full foot taller than Dryden, who was not under average height. He wore a brightly-coloured, tartan, short cloak which was fastened over his left shoulder by a large brooch of roughly beaten metal. Dryden afterwards learnt that the metal was gold. This was inlaid with highly polished and colourful gem stones. His loose tunic was of a white material, fastened at the waist by a belt of broad leather from which hung a long double-edged sword and a knife. The trousers, like his cloak, were multi-coloured, similar, Dryden recalled, to Scottish tartan trews, and they came down to the calf. On his feet he wore rope sandals.

The two men stood awkwardly examining each other. Then the youth held up his palm in the age-old sign of peace among men. He spoke rapidly.

Dryden shook his head.

'I'm sure you're right,' he said, holding up his hand in imitation, 'but I wonder what language you speak?'

The youth gave a puzzled shake of his head.

He stood irresolutely for a moment and then he pointed towards the west.

'Lan-Kern,' he said slowly. *'Lan-Kern. Kerens! Kerens!'*

Dryden shook his head again.

'If I get your message, you're trying to tell me that your home lies westward.'

The young man bit his lower lip.

'Lan-Kern,' he said again. He turned and began to walk in the direction to which he had pointed. After a few steps he stopped and turned to see if Dryden was following. Seeing that Dryden still stood hesitantly by the river bank, he returned.

'Lan-Kern,' he repeated, pointing westward. 'Lan-Kern...*kerens!*'

Then he pointed eastward.

'Lan-Howlek. Lan-Howlek...*yskerens!*'

As he said the last word he drew a finger across his throat in an expressive gesture.

He pointed to the far bank of the river then to the beached coracle and made motions of someone rowing. Then he pointed to himself, to Dryden, and to the knife at his belt. Again he made a motion across his throat with his forefinger.

Dryden smiled and nodded.

'I get it. Your pursuers are from Lan-Howlek, over there. They are your enemies. They want to kill you. Your home is Lan-Kern where your friends are. You think your pursuers will return to kill us both, eh?'

At the sound of the words 'Lan-Kern' and 'Lan-Howlek' the young man nodded eagerly. He pointed westward again and repeated the words 'Lan-Kern' and gently pulled Dryden by the arm.

Dryden clapped him on the back and smiled.

'Very well. Lead on. I wasn't going anywhere else in particular. And at least I've found a fellow human being, even if I can't understand him.

The young man gave a puzzled, polite smile. Then shrugged and started to walk away.

Abruptly he stopped, turned and tapped his chest with a fore-finger

'*Hanow* - Pryderi. Pryderi,' he repeated slowly. Then he pointed to Dryden's chest and raised his eyebrows in interrogation. '*Why?*'

It did not need a linguist to translate.

Dryden tapped his chest, smiling.

'My name is Dryden. Dryden.' Then he pointed to the young man. 'Pryderi?'

The youth smiled broadly and nodded eagerly.

'Dri-dun?'

Dryden just recognised the pronunciation of his name and nodded.

For some days Dryden and his new companion travelled through the jungle-like forests of what had once, in Dryden's world, been Cornwall. They travelled due west for a while and then began to turn south-west. Pryderi proved to excel in woodcraft and hunting and Dryden's root diet was supplemented for the first time in weeks by fresh meat from several animals.

Each hour of the day as they travelled, Dryden tried to master some vocabulary of the language of Pryderi. It was a strange language, and yet it seemed to Dryden that he had heard its like before. It was oddly sing-song in inflection, like Welsh perhaps and yet it was not Welsh. Dryden was a quick linguist and was soon picking up words as they passed through the forests - he soon knew that an oak tree was *derowen,* a beech tree was *fawen* and an elm tree was *elowen.* He wondered whether the syllable *wen* stood for tree but found that *gwedhen* was the word. Soon he was remembering words for animals, items of clothing and anatomical parts of the body such as *pen* for head, *scovan* for ear, *luf* for hand, *lagas* for eye, and so forth.

Pryderi seemed amused and pleased in his role of tutor and by the end of the third day of travelling Dryden was even able to ask and answer simple questions.

Sometimes, however, Pryderi would lapse into long earnest questions and then shake his head and sigh. Dryden was sure that Pryderi was asking where he had materialised from. It was the same sort of question that Dryden wanted to ask Pryderi. But that would have to wait until Dryden had mastered some of the strange musical language of his companion.

There were so many questions that raced through Dryden's mind: there were so many mysteries to be sorted out.

On the morning of the fourth day, Pryderi and Dryden topped the brow of a rolling hill which marked the edge of the forest and gave an uninterrupted view stretching towards the horizon. Dryden could make out a blue pencil line of the sea to the south. Ahead of them, maybe two miles away, a series of undulating hills rose and were covered with thick woods.

Pryderi clapped him on the arm.

'There's Dynas Dor,' he said in his language, in a phrase simple enough for Dryden to understand. 'That is the capital of Lan-Kern.'

Dryden followed Pryderi's outstretched hand but could see nothing beyond the hills and the woods.

'Your home?' asked Dryden in the same tongue.

'By the blessing of Bel,' affirmed the other, invoking the name of what Dryden understood to be Pryderi's deity.

The two men started down the hill.

They had not gone far when the wild sound of a horn came to

their ears. Dryden stopped; he raised his bow and reached for an arrow. But Pryderi shook his head.

'*Kerens* - friends,' he said, pointing to where a knot of horsemen were bearing down upon them.

A dozen riders swept down from the woods, shouting and waving long swords above their heads, with cloaks billowing out behind them. Dryden stood uncertain whether to stand or flee, for the horsemen looked far from peaceful.

They spread out in a scythe-like formation and closed in a circle round the two men. Then, standing in their stirrups, they flashed their swords upwards in salute. Their leader leapt down with a cry of 'Pryderi!'

In an instant both man and youth were clasping each other and laughing.

The man was in his fifties. His dress was similar to Pryderi's and he wore the same tartan-like cloak. The elder man's features were curiously similar to Pryderi's own and in an instance the young man explained.

Quelling the older man's voluble speech, Pryderi turned and pointed to Dryden. The older man gave Dryden a swift, curious scrutiny from twinkling blue eyes.

'Dryden,' said Pryderi, speaking slowly and clearly, 'this is my father - Kesmur, high chieftain of all the tribes of Lan-Kern.'

CHAPTER THREE

Dryden had a sense of unreality as a burly warrior helped him to mount a horse. Pryderi had climbed up behind his father and then the small company of horsemen began to head through the hills. Looking round this unlikely group, it seemed to Dryden that he had suddenly been transported back in time, back to some pre-Christian European civilisation or even to some never-never period of mythology. It confused him for a while and he began to wonder whether the *Argo* had indeed been transported into the future or into the past. But then, had he not seen the ruins of London? Could history, civilisations, repeat themselves?

By the smell of salt in the air, and the gentle tugging of the breeze about him, Dryden knew they must be approaching the coast. He was aware that the warriors had kept up a laughing chatter between themselves and Pryderi, all speaking with great rapidity. Dryden felt an immense frustration because he could not understand them. They were certainly a colourful set of people, generally fair of skin; some were freckled, but all wore their hair long, to shoulder length, and had long moustaches, although all apparently shaved their beards. Their clothes were colourful with the tartan-wove material predominating. Most of them also wore bright jewellery, brooches and a bracelet here and a necklace there. Their weapons appeared to be of bronze and iron. To Dryden it all seemed vaguely familiar, as if they were a group out of some illustration. But he was uncomfortably aware that these warriors were real - that Pryderi was real - and his strange precipitation into this weird, alien world was real.

They stopped on a rise of a fairly steep hill and Dryden found himself looking at a long, low blue expanse of sea which could not have been more than two miles distant. Just below them was a large estuary into which a twisting, serpent-like river ran.

Kesmur edged his horse close to Dryden and Pryderi pointed downwards.

'Avon,' he said slowly, and Dryden recognised the word for river. 'Avon Fawy.'

Dryden followed the outstretched hand and found himself looking across the river at a cluster of what seemed to be small circular huts which were strung out around the foot of a small hill on which stood some sort of circular fortress.

'My home,' said Pryderi. 'Dynas Dor, capital of Lan-Kern.'

Dryden acknowledged that he understood, and then the group of horsemen went sweeping down the hillside and across a wooden bridge which spanned the river, uttering wild yells, with a speed that left Dryden breathless and made him cling tightly to the rider before him for fear of losing his balance.

As they came close to the start of the huts a crowd of people gathered to meet them. There were men, not much different from his companions, and women, some pretty, some old, and a crowd of yelling children.

The township was fascinating, although to Dryden's Twentieth-Century eyes it was flattering to call it a township. It was hardly more than a good-sized village, consisting of irregular rows of grey stone buildings, circular bee-hive shaped huts, some of which rose to several stories in height. They clustered in circular patterns around the hill on which stood the wooden stockades of the fortress. Before these wooden stockades were intricate ditches and banks excavated in the hill and which were obviously fortifications. Dynas Dor, as Dryden later discovered, meant the Fortress of Earth.

Inside the great wooden stockade was another group of stone beehive huts, large squat edifices which surrounded one gigantic building in the middle, a building which dwarfed all the others and was built of great stone slabs. This, Dryden later learnt, was the great hall in which the high chieftain held court.

The warriors began to dismount and were promptly surrounded by a group of men and women asking questions, smiling and helping to tend to the horses and their weary riders. Pryderi motioned for Dryden to follow him to a nearby hut. Dryden paused amazed on the threshold for it was belittling to call the structure a hut. There were several rooms in the beehive construction which centred round a main room and a central hearth. The walls were draped in fantastically woven tapestries, finely worked patterns and strange illustrations which seemed to carry a great deal of symbolism. The room was well furnished with carved wooden furniture on which stood beautiful pottery.

'This is guest house,' explained Pryderi, using simple words. 'You guest. Stay here. Wash. Refreshment come.'

Pryderi elaborated the simple words with motions of his hands to make Dryden understand.

'I go now.'

As Pryderi went, a smiling matron, a handsome woman in her fifties, entered with a man of her own age and began to heat water over a fire and lay out fresh clothes similar to those worn by Pryderi. They smiled shyly at him and spoke to him in their rapid speech, making signs that he should undress and bathe and then dress in the new clothes they had brought.

It was an age since Dryden had felt so relaxed and peaceful, sitting back in a chair, freshly bathed and in new, clean clothing. And now food was being brought before him, a roast of meat, some cakes made of an oaten meal and green vegetables, not unlike cabbage. The man brought a jug and a stoneware goblet and made motions for Dryden to drink, repeating several times the word 'Bragas .... bragas!' Dryden tried the beverage cautiously. It was definitely an alcoholic drink, very sweet and almost with a taste of honey in it. It was a very sweet mead, he decided.

Pryderi returned.

'Good?' he asked, pointing to the food and then to the hut.

'Good,' affirmed Dryden.

Pryderi smiled and seated himself.

'Must now teach you language,' he said slowly.

The first few weeks passed without Dryden noticing them go by. He hardly moved out of his guest hut and when he did it was in the company of Pryderi. He did not even notice his surroundings because Pryderi would seize each object to teach Dryden new words and so concentrate his mind that little of such walks could he remember except the new additions to his vocabulary. After the first week Dryden's brain rebelled against such impositions and he started to dream exhausting nightmares, mumbling gibberish in his sleep.

During the following week, however, Dryden started to progress with an amazing speed and soon possessed a working knowledge of the language. He found it difficult to grasp the grammar construction which was as precise and complex as Ancient Greek or Latin. What was confusing was the fact that the language had its changes at the beginning of the words, with eclipses and aspirations, whereas in English and a great many other European languages such changes occurred at the ending of a word. Thus *go* would be *kerdhes* in the language of Lan-Kern but the word *going* would be *gerdhes*.

Dryden also discovered that while writing was known among the people of Lan-Kern, it was seldom used and the people relied on a very sophisticated oral tradition for all their lore, poetry and religion. In fact, most of the older generation considered it wrong to commit any knowledge to writing. Pryderi explained that the younger people were breaking with the oral traditions and some were committing their philosophy into great vellum books. Dryden managed to obtain a slate and chalk and used it to transcribe words through English phonetics. He found this helped him with his grasp of the tongue.

It was three months before Dryden had adjusted to his new environment and was able to make his way in the township without linguistic problems. In answer to the many questions that were asked by Pryderi and the kindly Kesmur, the high chieftain, Dryden explained that he was a sailor, a voyager from a far country beyond the mighty oceans which bounded Lan-Kern, and that he had been shipwrecked on their shores. To have gone into further details would, Dryden felt, have given rise to unnecessary complications which it would do well to avoid until he knew more about this strange new world.

The people of Lan-Kern, he learnt, were basically an agricultural and pastoral society which was ruled over by Pryderi's father Kesmur. Dryden had translated the Lan-Kern term *gwelhevyn* as king. But later he found that this was not accurate. It seemed that the rank of chieftain was an elected role in society. Indeed, all offices in the society were filled by the election of the assembled tribesmen and women. There were no nobles or kings. Usually, the election of the *gwelhevyn*, or any other officer, was a lifetime appointment but should the person abuse his position he was thrown out and a new officer elected.

Dryden wondered about the choice of candidates and whether there was a law of primogeniture, a law of inheritance. Pryderi pointed out that some things in society, such as personal objects, were inherited but such inheritance was made through the mother and not the father.

'We trace our lineage back through the female line, Dryden,' he smiled observing Dryden's astonished face. 'A child grows in the belly of the mother and is of her flesh. Is that not so? One is always sure, therefore, who the mother of a child is, but never sure who the father is. The only true way to inherit is through the mother.'

Dryden discovered that there was no private property among the tribesmen and women and that all farming land was in the common ownership of the tribe. Its allotment and working was discussed in frequent tribal assemblies. The people seemed a close-knit group and were always in constant touch with each other throughout the villages and farming settlements from one end of the country to the other.

Pryderi, it seemed, had a special role in the society and not because he was the son of Kesmur, the high chieftain. Dryden learnt that he was a member of the religious order of the country called *drewyth*. The young man impressed upon Dryden that to be a fully qualified *drewyth* a candidate had to undergo many years of training in philosophy, natural science, the intricate laws of the society and in folklore. When Dryden asked how long he, Pryderi, had been studying for this priesthood, Pryderi replied, 'About five years'. But when Dryden had commented that he must surely be qualifying soon, Pryderi surprised him by replying: 'Oh no, it often takes twenty years of training to be accepted into the inner circle.'

For Dryden, the concept of a *drewyth*'s duties was difficult to grasp. It seemed that they were not just priests but the scientists and philosophers of society; the mystics and the artists; the lawgivers and judges; the storytellers and bards. They, it seemed, were the cornerstone of the cultural existence of the people.

Neither could Dryden grasp the concept of their religious belief. At first he thought they worshipped a single god called Bel, for he had frequently heard invocations to this deity. Later he discovered that Bel was the sun and then thought the people were primitive sun-worshippers. Again, he discovered that the sun was also called *howl* so what, then, was Bel? The philosophy was complex. Bel was not a god; more the life-force, that from which all creation had sprung; the essence of the mysteries of the great universe. Bel was the power of creation embodied in the sun - not merely the sun itself. Bel was also present in all things - not just living things - the plants, the animals and man, but in the earth, the stones and the sea.

In addition to this Dryden learnt that the people believed in a kind of immortality. They sometimes referred to the Otherworld and believed that a dual world existed. When a soul died in this world, it was reborn again in the other world; and when a soul died in that world, it was reborn in this one. Thus a constant interchange of souls took place.

Dryden also learnt more about his new friend. Pryderi's mother had died many years ago in childbirth and Pryderi could hardly recall her. His father had not married again. Now there were just Pryderi and his sister Kigva, a few years younger than himself. Dryden wondered why he had not met Kigva at Dynas Dor and Pryderi explained that for the past year his sister had been studying the ancient lore of the people with a female member of the *drewyth* order named Melyon at her retreat far to the west called Pen an Wlas, where the land cascaded in granite slopes into the sea. Melyon was approaching an age when any moment she could be called upon to make the journey to the Otherworld. His sister Kigva had gone to record Melyon's store of knowledge before the old woman passed on.

Dryden tried to press Pryderi for a history of the country but Pryderi started with such elaborate legends and myths that Dryden eventually gave up hope of finding out what had become of his world and its people. Instead he tried to press Pryderi about the nations which surrounded Lan-Kern and what, he asked, was the cause of the attempt on his life when Dryden had first encountered him.

Pryderi smiled sadly.

'The warriors who pursued me were from Lan-Howlek, the country from where the sun rises. Our relationship with Lan-Howlek is a great source of sadness to the people. Once, Lan-Kern and Lan-Howlek were one country, ruled by one chieftain. We spoke the same language, shared the same beliefs and customs. Then, it was three generations ago, the tribal assembly could not agree on who should be the high chieftain and rule us. Those of Lan-Howlek wanted a man called Talek while those of Lan-Kern wanted Kernewes. Eventually there was a split.'

Dryden frowned.

'Kernewes? Isn't that a woman's name? Are women allowed to become chieftains here?'

'Isn't it so in all lands?' asked Pryderi, surprised. 'Anyway,' he continued, 'in spite of our differences, Lan-Kern and Lan-Howlek existed side by side in mutual harmony, the only difference being that there were two separate chieftains ruling each country. Then twenty years ago the ruler of Lan-Howlek was overthrown by his wife. It is said that he was poisoned by her. She declared herself ruler.'

'But,' queried Dryden, 'I have noticed you set great weight by your system that each ruler must be elected.'

'The woman was strong and had powerful followers. The people of Lan-Howlek went down under her yoke. They counted without the power of Nelferch-an-Gwargh.'

'Nelferch the Witch?' asked Dryden, trying to translate the name.

'She has become known as Nelferch-an-Gwargh over the years,' agreed Pryderi. 'She has subverted all the institutions, customs and laws of Lan-Howlek and rules with a rod of iron. Whenever a man or woman stands up, strong enough to challenge her, they are blown away like chaff from the wheat. Her power is enormous. She is truly a witch.'

'So she still rules Lan-Howlek?'

'Older, more bitter, more hateful. Yet her power increases as what was abnormal in Lan-Howlek becomes normal. And now, for the past five years, she has tried to stir up insurrection against Kesmur, my father. But our people are wise and have resisted her. So now she attempts to overthrow the country by force.'

'For territorial gain?'

'For greed,' said Pryderi. 'Also, we hear that she fears for her rule in Lan-Howlek after she has gone. She wants her grandson Cador to take over and Cador is hated more than she is. She fears there might still be backbone enough among the people to rise up on her death and drive Cador out.'

'And who would replace her and Cador?'

'The talk is that the people would ask Kesmur to reinstitute the old dual high chieftainship and rule over Lan-Kern and Lan-Howlek. So several times she has sought to eliminate Kesmur and his family.'

Dryden frowned.

'I thought you didn't inherit your father's position? Why should she seek to eliminate his family?'

'Because a candidate for the office of high chieftain is usually chosen from among the family that has had practice of such office. A man or woman must firstly have the quality of good leadership but secondly they must know how to lead and be aware of the duties and obligations of chieftainship. Therefore it is likely that, on my father's death, a son - not necessarily the eldest - a daughter or some cousin may be elected to office. So Nelferch has tried to annihilate our family.

'During the last few years her despotic grandson Cador has led her warriors in countless raids on our country so that we have been driven to a state of siege warfare. A year ago my only brother Peredur was slain in a battle on the Plains of Keresk which must have pleased Nelferch greatly for it was said that he was greatly favoured as a successor to Kesmur.'

'And is that why the warriors of Lan-Howlek were chasing you when I first saw you?'

Pryderi inclined his head.

'This year I have forsaken many of my studies as a postulant of the *drewyth* and took up the sword with sorrow in my heart against the men of Lan-Howlek. It is not a *drewyth's* teaching to kill any animal, least of all a fellow human being. But we have to defend ourselves. Our people, as you have seen, are mostly farmers or shepherds or cowherds. Now they are forced to be warriors as well. I was on a visit to a border settlement when it was attacked and I was taken prisoner. They took me across the great river into Lan-Howlek. Knowing what my fate would be once Nelferch found out who I was, I seized the first opportunity to make good my escape. I was making the attempt when you saved my life.'

'Why don't the people of Lan-Kern raise an army and invade Lan-Howlek and drive Nelferch from the throne, or whatever it is called?' asked Dryden.

'It is plain to see that you are an *estrennek,* a stranger in our land. That is not the way of Bel which is a peaceful path. The *drewyth* will only consent to defence and not offence. Ours has been a great tradition of peace and our lives would become meaningless if we were to turn our backs on the peaceful path.'

'But surely you cannot leave your borders and people undefended from the raids made by this man Cador?'

Pryderi shook his head.

'Oh no. We have grown used to Cador's methods of raiding. The settlements close to the border are now well fortified and defended. We have, for the first time in our history, gathered a small army together, volunteers from all the tribes of Lan-Kern, who constantly travel the border to repel Cador's attacks. The warriors serve with this army for one moon or two moons and then they return to their farmsteads while others take their place.'

'That is a sensible idea,' agreed Dryden. 'So you always have a force guarding your borders.'

'Indeed. It is a necessary evil in these times. The tribal assemblies had even to make a special appointment of a man to command the army, a warlord.'

'Who is that?' asked Dryden with interest. 'Yourself?'

Pryderi laughed.

'I have not forsaken the way of the *drewyth* entirely, Dryden. I have transgressed enough of the teachings of Bel in that I have taken up the sword against my fellow man. No. My cousin, Teyrnon is warlord of Lan-Kern. He is an able warrior who is much admired by the people. In fact, now that Peredur is dead, it seems that he will be the choice to succeed Kesmur when he goes on his journey to the Otherworld. And you will meet him tomorrow. He is returning to Dynas Dor having spent four full moons in defence of our borders in the east.'

CHAPTER FOUR

At midday the following day a procession of twenty warriors rode wearily up to Dynas Dor. At their head sat a tall man. His dress, unlike the multi-coloured clothes of his companions, was completely black with little to create a relief. His face was striking. It was dark, saturnine. His hair was blue-black and his eyebrows rose together across his dark, flashing eyes in such a way that they almost met in the middle. The eyes gleamed with a fiery light and seemed never to cease looking this way and that, as if searching out hidden enemies. The face was handsome in a rather cruel way, for his lips were thin and set in a smile that had some malignant quality to it. A pale sword scar showed on his deeply tanned cheeks. Dryden put his age at about thirty years.

'That is Teyrnon, warlord of Lan-Kern,' whispered Pryderi, as the procession of horsemen came to a halt within the fortress of Kesmur.

The high chieftain was the first to greet Teyrnon and then Pryderi. Dryden noticed the warmth and affection in their embraces and he felt guilty that he could not, at first sight, like this austere warlord. Dryden had come to be immensely fond of Pryderi and have a profound respect for his insight into human nature. As for Kesmur, there was something of Pryderi's quality in him but he was a more practical man, a solid farmer, greatly concerned with the welfare of his people who were farmers like himself. That he was leader of their community was a good thing but for the war... that was different. Perhaps the people needed a harder man, cold as Teyrnon seemed to be.

Pryderi was beckoning Dryden forward.

'... and this is the stranger who saved my life, Teyrnon. This is the man called Dryden.'

Dryden found himself looking into the cold black eyes, which appraised him carefully. He felt a menacing strength in the hand-shake.

'So you are an *estrennek*, a stranger to our shore?'

Teyrnon's voice had a brittle quality to it; perhaps he was too used to giving orders in times of crisis for his voice to be soft and pleasant.

'I am,' replied Dryden.

'You are certainly not of Lan-Howlek,' agreed Teyrnon, as if this suspicion had been foremost in his thoughts. 'Where do you come from?'

Dryden frowned slightly.

'A country far beyond the ocean,' was his lame reply. 'My ship was wrecked just off the coast here. I was the only survivor.'

Kesmur interrupted, throwing an arm around the warlord's shoulders.

'Come, Teyrnon. There will be plenty of time to hear Dryden's tale at the evening feast. Already our bards have composed songs which tell of his coming and how he saved young Pryderi. Come now, I want to hear how our eastern borders stand. Have there been any raids since last we met?'

Teyrnon gave Dryden a close look and then turned and allowed Kesmur to lead him away.

Pryderi grinned as Dryden watched Teyrnon disappear.

'I see you do not have a ready liking for my cousin, Teyrnon?'

Dryden shrugged, his face reddening in guilt.

'No, I must confess it.'

'Behind the arrogant facade, he is basically a good man. I have known him all my life. He grew up with my sister, Kigva, and myself. He worries about the survival of our people and that is why he is suspicious of strangers. Years of seeking to stop Cador's raids and Nelferch's intrigues have made him so.'

Dryden rubbed the back of his neck thoughtfully.

'Yes; I suppose as warlord his concern must be for the people and naturally any stranger must be carefully scrutinised before accept-ance.

Pryderi clapped Dryden on the arm.

'Do not take offence, my friend. I accepted you from the first when you could not utter one syllable of our language. You will

95

get to know Teyrnon at the feast tonight. You'll soon see that you can be friends.'

That afternoon Dryden went by himself, along the wide path following the western bank of the river Fawy which was lined with countless beech trees and so gave the river its name. He walked along by the broadening estuary, along the wide, sand-covered shore for a distance, then sat down and stretched out, bathing in the warm rays of the sun.

Whatever the reason behind his mysterious arrival in this world, he would have to adjust totally to it because there was no path back. The people of this strange country were mostly friendly, and he had made a friend in young Pryderi at least. But what was he to do now? Be a farmer or...

There came a sudden thunderous pounding on the sand and, before he had time to glance up, a shrill scream echoed along the shore.

Dryden was on his feet in a second, the instinct of survival strong within him.

A black horse was bearing down on him, galloping wildly, while the slight figure of a girl clung frantically to its whipping mane. The reins streamed uselessly in the wind and Dryden realised that the beast was out of control.

The horse was almost upon him before it saw him and started to turn out of his path, snorting in its efforts to escape. But Dryden ran swiftly across the sand and leapt for the beast's bridle, throwing his full weight on the animal's head. The horse staggered, head down, and halted for a moment. Then, with a vicious swing of its forelegs, it reared frantically skyward, hooves pawing in the air.

The figure on its back gave a cry and slid backwards, hitting the sand of the beach with a loud thud, rolling over and lying still.

The horse reared again and this time sent Dryden crashing to the sand as well. Then the black beast was streaming down the beach.

Dryden lay stunned for a few moments and then rose carefully to his hands and knees.

The girl's figure lay where it had fallen.

Anxiously, Dryden crawled towards her and turned her over on her back.

For a moment something caught in his throat. The girl was

beautiful. Her hair was wispy, the colour of raven blackness, and surmounted a delicate heart-shaped face whose skin was pale, near white, with a gentle shade of red across the cheekbones. The mouth was full and naturally red. There was just a hint of freckles across the dainty nose. The girl could not have been more than twenty, clad in a multi-coloured cloak and a flared dress which did not hide her young, well-formed body. In repose, the girl was the most attractive being that Dryden considered he had ever seen.

A cursory examination indicated that the girl had only been knocked senseless by her awkward fall from her horse.

Suddenly the eyelids flickered and Dryden found himself peering into two puzzled grey eyes.

'What happened?' she whispered.

'Your horse threw you,' Dryden explained with a smile of reassurance. 'It was bolting. I tried to stop it and the beast threw you off.'

The girl frowned, trying to remember.

'Ah, yes...'

Abruptly her face contorted with fear. Before Dryden knew what she was doing, her hand had snaked to her belt and reappeared with a dagger that slashed at Dryden's chest. Dryden threw himself backwards in the sand, rolled over and scrambled awkwardly to his feet. The girl, too, had come to her feet in a crouching position, the knife held out before her.

'Try to harm me, man of Lan-Howlek, and I will kill you.'

The girl's voice was a whisper, but filled with so much vehemence that Dryden knew it was no idle boast.

He tried to force a smile to his lips.

'What makes you think I am from Lan-Howlek?' he asked.

The girl's eyes flashed.

'You are an *estrennek*, a stranger.'

'Are all strangers from Lan-Howlek?' parried Dryden.

'Yes,' came the uncompromising reply.

Dryden shrugged.

'Well, I am not of Lan-Howlek. I am a stranger from a land beyond the ocean who was shipwrecked on these shores.'

'What sort of trick is that?'

'No trick,' Dryden eagerly assured her. 'I am a shipwrecked stranger. Believe me. I live at Dynas Dor as a guest of Kesmur, the high chieftain. I am a friend of Pryderi.'

A tinge of uncertainty crept into the grey eyes of the girl.

'If you are Pryderi's friend, *estrennek*, you must know his family well.'

'I know Kesmur, his father,' replied Dryden.

'What of his mother?'

'I am told she died many years ago.'

'And does this Pryderi have any brothers or sisters?' pressed the girl. The dagger in her hand was wavering.

'His brother Peredur was slain and ...'

Dryden paused. He suddenly realised that he was staring into Pryderi's grey eyes and that the face before him bore a close resemblance to the young *drewyth*. Yes, in spite of the beauty of the face before him, Dryden could recognise something of Pryderi in it. He smiled and stretched out his hands, palm outwards.

'He also has a sister named Kigva. But he did not prepare me to meet such beauty in her.'

The girl coloured and bit her lower lip in confusion.

'How... how do you know that I am Kigva?'

'Who could know Pryderi and not recognise a little of him in you?'

The girl slowly lowered her knife.

'You must know my brother. And you are not of Lan-Howlek?'

'I am not.'

The girl sheathed her knife with a self-conscious air.

'You must forgive me, *estrennek*. But if you have been a guest in Dynas Dor you will know why I fear the men of Lan-Howlek. Nevertheless, you must also know that I have transgressed our ancient law of hospitality.'

She spoke contritely but Dryden shook his head.

'I understand the reason for your transgression,' he replied. 'There is nothing to forgive. But please believe that I am not your enemy. My name is Dryden.'

'Dri-dun?' the girl smiled awkwardly, trying to echo the name. 'That surely is an *estrennek* name.'

Dryden smiled sheepishly, aware of how attractive the girl was when she smiled.

'What happened to my horse?' she asked, peering round the deserted sands.

Dryden gave a rueful shrug.

'I tried to hold him but he threw me off and galloped on along the beach.'

Kigva pursed her lips.

'He'll be safe in Dynas Dor by now. I was returning home today from Pen-an-Wlas... a place in the west. I have been there transcribing tales from old Melyon. Some animal startled my horse and he bolted. I must have been daydreaming because I lost the reins.'

'I'll escort you back to Dynas Dor.'

'I would like that,' the girl turned with an open smile towards him. 'You can tell me all about yourself, *estrennek*. I am sure I will never be able to pronounce your name, Dri-dun.'

Dryden fell in step with the girl and found to his self-conscious annoyance, that his heart was beating more quickly than usual and a stupid boyish feeling of pleasure swept through him as the two of them walked along the shore.

But they had not gone far when the sound of hooves came to their ears. Two riders appeared along the shore and quickly bore down upon them.

Kigva screwed up her eyes.

'Why...' she cried excitedly. 'Why, here come my brother and Teyrnon!'

She shouted and waved towards the oncoming riders while Dryden tried to suppress his scowl of annoyance at being deprived of his walk with her.

The dark horse of Lan-Kern's warlord was the first to reach them, shuddering to a halt beside the girl, sand spurting from its hooves. The saturnine man, his every feature expressing concern, leapt from his horse. To Dryden's surprise, the girl flung herself into his arms and kissed him.

'Teyrnon!' she cried delightedly, holding him at arm's length. 'After a full year - it is so good to see you.'

Pryderi had dismounted and was standing by, laughing.

'And have you no greeting for your brother, Kigva?'

The girl gave an answering laugh and threw herself into his arms.

Teyrnon's face still expressed concern and he looked suspiciously at Dryden.

'Your horse came riderless into Dynas Dor. It was lathering. We were worried about you, Kigva. Pryderi and I mounted immediately and rode in search of you.'

Pryderi nodded.

'Are you hurt? What happened?'

The girl shrugged.

'I might have been hurt had it not been for Dri-dun, who is your friend,' she replied.

Pryderi smiled at Dryden.

'And what did Dryden do?' asked Teyrnon.

'Well, I was on my way home, daydreaming a little, when some animal startled my horse. I lost control, let go the reins, and the animal bolted. Then suddenly Dri-dun arose from the sand, leapt for the beast, held him for a moment while I fell off, and then the beast sped on. For saving me, I promptly tried to kill Dri-dun because I thought he was a man of Lan-Howlek.'

Teyrnon turned thoughtful eyes upon Dryden.

'He seems to have convinced you that is not the case,' he said quietly.

Pryderi clasped Dryden by the arm.

'Well, well, Dryden. It seems that you make a habit of saving the lives of the children of Kesmur.'

The girl turned sharply.

'What's that?'

Pryderi shrugged.

'The tale will be told this evening, doubtless. We are holding a feast to welcome Teyrnon from his patrols against Lan-Howlek. Now we can welcome Kigva as well.'

The girl smiled shyly at Dryden, making his mouth go dry.

'The feast can also be made in thanksgiving for my rescue.'

Teyrnon glowered. Dryden wondered whether the man was truly suspicious of him or whether he entertained some strange dislike for him. Perhaps it was a reaction to Dryden's own dislike? It was then that Dryden noticed the way that Teyrnon looked at Kigva and suddenly he realised that Teyrnon was jealous of Kigva's attention

100

to him.

The dour warlord swung himself up on his horse.

'Come, Kigva,' he said shortly. 'I'll take you back to Dynas Dor.'

To Dryden's surprise the girl obeyed, leaping up behind Teyrnon with an amazing agility.

'Until tonight, Dri-dun,' she cried, as Teyrnon spurred away.

Dryden stared a long time after their vanishing forms and when he turned he found Pryderi regarding him with a sympathetic look.

'So, Dryden? You are also human?'

'What do you mean?' asked Dryden shortly.

'Kigva always affects men like that.'

'Including Teyrnon, I see,' returned Dryden.

Pryderi sighed.

'Ah, but with Teyrnon it is different.'

'Different?'

'Yes. Kigva is to marry Teyrnon next year.'

Dryden felt a heavy weight fall into the pit of his stomach.

He shook himself fiercely. What right had he to have any feelings on the subject. He didn't know the girl.

Pryderi watched Dryden's face with a sympathetic smile.

'Come on, Dryden. I'll walk you back to Dynas Dor.'

The young *drewyth* turned and began to lead his horse along the edge of the pounding surf. 'Next week,' he suddenly began without preamble, 'I am to go to the eastern settlements again. I have to inspect our defences for the coming winter. Would you like to come with me?'

Dryden tried to take his mind away from its contemplation of Kigva's pretty, smiling face.

'Yes. I think I'd like that very much, Pryderi. But isn't it dangerous?'

The young man laughed.

'Not really. Cador usually gives up raiding when the autumn is far advanced and he does not begin again until the spring. Of course, it is always best to be on guard against raids. One must never underestimate Nelferch and the greed of Cador. She would exploit any weakness that arises - spring or winter.'

'Well, I would certainly like to come with you.'

The young man clapped Dryden on the back.

'Bel was kind when your arrow found the breast of the spearman of Lan-Howlek, Dryden.'

CHAPTER FIVE

Pryderi pointed across the river where the green trees mingled with tall reddish-leafed monstrosities which Dryden remembered seeing in profusion in the unpopulated eastern part of the country.

'There, across the river, begins the territory of Lan-Howlek,' said Pryderi.

It was over two weeks since Dryden had accepted Pryderi's offer to go with him to the eastern settlements of Lan-Kern. The two men sat at ease astride their horses.

'Can you explain why the vegetation is so different across the river?' asked Dryden.

'Different? You mean, why is it that certain plants and trees do not grow in Lan-Kern and yet flourish in Lan-Howlek? And in the country beyond Lan-Howlek, of which I have heard only rumours, there lies a vast wilderness of strange jungle?'

Dryden nodded solemnly.

'Well,' said Pryderi, easing his horse along the pathway by the river, 'Life differs from country to country as language differs. Once, many years ago, when Lan-Kern and Lan-Howlek were one country, long before the rise of Nelferch-an-Gwargh, there were many among the people who wanted to go beyond the oceans and explore the world that Bel had created for them. Many intrepid souls set forth in their coracles, small as they were, and journeyed across the waters. Some returned with tales of strange peoples, speaking many different tongues, and inhabiting countries where the trees and plants grow wild and differently. One man, who crossed the great sea to the south, came across a great land full of nothing but blackened earth. Not long after he returned, he died. So did all his crew. A strange vomiting sickness. There was a panic among the people because they thought the explorer had brought back a disease which would kill everyone. But only the explorer and his crew died. The high chieftain of the time took it as a warning that no more expeditions must cross the oceans. That happened many years ago, maybe as many as several centuries. The tale is handed down by our bards.'

Dryden pondered on the story. It seemed to fit in with a theory of some nuclear holocaust which had wiped out civilisation as he knew it. But how had Cornwall, or Lan-Kern as its inhabitants called it, become an oasis in the maelstrom of nuclear destruction? And how had a new civilisation grown up? How many centuries had passed?

Pryderi was leading the way over the undulating green hills towards the settlement they had come to see. Dryden found himself falling a little way behind and so he dug his heels into his mount and came abreast of the young *drewyth*.

'Do your people have any tales about the creation of the world?' he asked, trying a different tack.

'Of course,' replied Pryderi. 'We have many such tales.'

'Then how was your world created?'

'Ah, now you speak of the eternal mysteries. In the beginning was Bel the creator; Bel the life-force of the universe. Bel the eternal. One day Bel spat and each burning goblet of his spit formed a star like the sun. Even in that speck of waste from the creator's fiery mouth was enough of the life-force to create whole planets and life to cover them. Thus came about the world of man, of plants, of trees, animals. And yet man often thinks he is superior to Bel and all the other worlds of Bel's creation. Yet man's stature is not even a speck of dust in that one gob of spit from Bel's mouth.'

Dryden smiled wistfully.

'But how did your people come into existence?'

'There are many stories, Dryden,' said Pryderi, guiding his horse up a hill. 'It is said that the world is so old that countless civilisations have risen and fallen upon its surface. There are stories that each civilisation has come to an Age of Destruction. Then life had to be reborn.'

'An Age of Destruction?' Dryden's face took on a look of intense interest.

'Yes. Many of our wisest men teach that a great civilisation once spread across the face of the earth. In that civilisation were men who could grasp at the heavens, could attain to all sorts of magical things. But at the same time, they had discovered great powers of destruction. Instead of using the advances of their knowledge for the benefit of their fellows, they used the terrifying weapons of destruction to threaten them. Their minds were bent in greed, bent on conquest, domination, of creating a world after their own image. Each state upon the earth warred against its fellow, envy, greed and bitterness were the guiding factors. Eventually, inevitably, man unleashed the Age of Destruction and few survived the holocaust.'

Dryden realised that the tale was vaguely similar to the myth of Noah's Flood.

'How long ago was this Age of Destruction, Pryderi?'

Pryderi shrugged.

'It is only a story. If it really happened then it must have been countless generations ago. Ah, look! There is the settlement of Morvran.'

Before them in a small valley stood a circle of stone beehive huts, surrounded by a tall wooden stockade. The land nearby was carefully tilled and Dryden caught an occasional glimpse of livestock.

'The raiders from Lan-Howlek have attacked Morvran's settlement six times in the past year,' said Pryderi, cupping his hands to his lips and giving a loud 'halloo'. There was an immediate barking of dogs and figures began to scurry about. Pryderi stood up in his stirrups and waved his hand to attract attention. Then he started forward and Dryden followed him.

'It is best to forewarn them of visitors for any visitor here could be hostile,' the young man said over his shoulder.

'Why do they live so close to Lan-Howlek if they are in constant danger of attack?' queried Dryden. 'Why don't they move to a more protected area?'

'It is their home,' replied Pryderi simply.

'But the danger...' began Dryden.

'It is easy to see that you are not a farmer, Dryden. But Lan-Howlek was not always the source of evil and danger. It is only in recent years, since Nelferch cast her envious eyes to Lan-Kern, that we have to beware.'

A group of children had run out of the gates of the stockade, laughing and calling to Pryderi whom they apparently recognised.

Pryderi leapt from his horse, caught hold of one of the little girls and tossed her into the air, catching her as the child squealed with delight.

A handsome woman of middle-age emerged from the gate, followed by a man.

'How goes it at Dynas Dor, Pryderi?' cried the man, catching hold of the horses and leading them towards the stockade.

'All is well, Rudhyk. I have brought a friend with me on this visit,' replied Pryderi, extending a hand towards Dryden.

The woman and man exchanged a formal greeting with Dryden.

'You are an *estrennek*?' the woman, whose name was Morvran, the chieftainess of the settlement, asked.

'I am.'

'Not from Lan-Howlek?'

'From far beyond Lan-Howlek,' returned Dryden solemnly.

'A friend of Pryderi's is welcome in this place,' smiled the woman.

The horses were stabled and the gates were closed as the evening drew on. Dryden could see several young men at work with the animals in the stockade and it appeared that several families lived within its confines. There were, he later discovered, eight families, comprising some forty people in Morvran's settlement. The settlement was one of the richest in that part of the country and could even send its surplus stocks to Dynas Dor as a contribution to the taxes that were levied throughout Lan-Kern. Morvran's husband, Rudhyk, was a ruddy-faced farmer. When the raids started, it was Morvran who had been elected chieftainess because of her organisational ability. Her quiet, confident leadership had repelled attack after attack by Lan-Howlek raiders so that the settlement could boast that not one had fallen to Nelferch-an-Gwargh.

The settlement, like all townships in Lan-Kern, possessed a special hostel for visitors. The law of hospitality was a sacred thing among the people and no stranger who sought sanctuary was ever turned away or denied food. Pryderi and Dryden were allowed to wash and relax before being invited to the evening meal with Morvran and Rudhyk.

Dryden liked Morvran at once. She was a strong-minded woman with quiet green eyes and the mind of a general; she ran her settlement with a stern discipline, knowing precisely her strengths and weaknesses, and where every member of the community was at any one time, down to the smallest infant. But, in spite of the rigours of siege life, she had a ready smile and would appreciate a good tale or a humourous song. In her the spirit of the settlement was strong: they would survive the raids from Lan-Howlek and that survival was never questioned.

'One day evil must perish,' observed Morvran. 'The old witch of Lan-Howlek must wither and die as all creation dies to make way for the new. A new age of peace will soon be upon us.'

Rudhyk, her husband, was a soft spoken man; a man who knew the soil as well as he knew his own strong brown hands. He spoke of it as another might speak of the woman he loved. He seldom spoke but when he did it was to make a telling contribution to the conversation.

Dryden greatly enjoyed the evening spent with these people and he learnt much from them. What particularly fascinated him were their tales of past ages, tales which reminded Dryden so keenly of the folklore of his own world. Could history repeat itself, he wondered. Could the rise and fall of man be traced in some great circle in which there was really no progression? Could civilisations rise and destroy themselves and rise again? And, if so, how many times must man repeat that same process, blindly groping upwards from savagery?

He was still pondering the problem when he went to bed in the guest house while Pryderi and Morvran were left to talk of the plan for the forthcoming winter defences. But, once alone, the smiling face of Kigva swam before his eyes and banished his heavier thoughts without a struggle. Dryden sighed miserably. He had spent a brief week at Dynas Dor in her exuberant company. She had a strong will and insisted that Dryden escort her during that week so she could learn of the strange country from which he came.

At first Dryden felt nervous of the brooding menace of Teyrnon; but Teyrnon began to avoid their company and Dryden felt happy and at ease, alone with Kigva or with Pryderi.

'Dryden,' the girl said, shortly before he had started east with her brother,'I like you very much. I feel that you are one of my closest friends. Is it the same with you?'

Dryden had assured her it was. He would have said more but the girl's compulsive honesty and frankness held him back lest he commit some unpardonable sin against etiquette.

107

A shouting brought him out of his reverie.

'What's up?' he asked, blinking his eyes and realising by the light filtering into the room that it must be near dawn and that he had been asleep. Pryderi was already out of his bed, throwing on his clothes.

'A raid!' snapped the young man.

Dryden leapt from his bed and hauled on his clothes, following Pryderi into the yard. People were running to and fro but with purpose. The younger women were piling up buckets of water. The older women were herding the young children into the central hut while the men were hastening to the perimeter of the stockade clutching bows, arrows and spears. The gates of the stockade were on fire and it was towards these that a chain of young women were heaving their buckets.

Morvran, a longsword strapped to her waist, suddenly materialised beside them.

'A raid,' she said grimly. 'They managed to sneak up to the gates and fire them. My men counted three of them. One of them won't see Lan-Howlek again.'

Pryderi squinted towards the hills.

'Only three on a raid? That's unusual.'

Morvran nodded.

'A vanguard, I think, sent to burn down the gates for the main attack. They're out there, waiting.'

Dryden felt a shiver of anticipation run down his back and glanced at the shadowy hills. The fire at the gates had been brought under control but the major portion of the wood had been destroyed.

'Any time now,' murmured Morvran.

'They come!'

A cluster of shadowy figures on horseback were at the gates, the frenzied whinnies of the horses merging with the cries and curses of their riders as they tried to force their way through the dying flames.

The young women, those who had been putting out the fire, fell back and Morvran shouted commands to the men lining the stockade walls. Four men with bows immediately sent shower after shower of arrows towards the milling attackers. But some half dozen riders had broken through and started forward, menacing and large, the edge of the rising sun flashing against their sword blades as if they

108

were carrying sticks of fire.

Pryderi drew his sword and ran towards the nearest horseman, dodging a blow, ducking under his guard and seizing the bridle. The animal reared and unseated its rider who then scrambled to his feet, his sword swinging at the young *drewyth*. Morvran, to Dryden's surprise, had her sword in hand and was already closing in on a second attacker.

Dryden stood confused. He had a knife and a spear.

Even while he wondered what to do, Pryderi's first opponent staggered backwards with the young man's blade jutting from his bloodstained chest. But four more horsemen, yelling like furies, were bearing down on him. Something snapped in Dryden's mind. With a surge of anger he ran forward and seized the dead man's sword. It felt odd in his hand, long and cumbersome.

'No, Dryden! You are no warrior! Go back!'

It was Pryderi yelling at him.

Dryden ignored him. He moved forward, trying to quieten his racing thoughts. It was a long, long time since he had attended a fencing class. But he had won several championships and had been left with some skill in sabre fighting. Thank God he had specialised with the sabre and not the foils, for the sabre was nearer to this long slashing sword used by the warriors of Lan-Kern and Lan-Howlek.

There was no more time for thought.

A thick-set warrior had sprung from his horse and was swinging his blade to the attack. Dryden, testing the weight of his weapon, came to an *en garde* position, met his assailant's first downward stroke with a parry that caused the blades to clash and ring fiercely. Dryden felt himself stagger back a few paces under the sheer weight of the blow.

His opponent laughed savagely and pressed forward with a series of slashing blows that nearly brought Dryden off balance.

Then Dryden's mind began to function. He almost saw himself at the fencing class and heard his instructor's voice coaxing him in the French language of the fencing schools throughout the world. Parry! Attack! He sprang forward, five times his blade clashed with his opponent's blade and then, on the sixth stroke, just as Dryden had anticipated, his opponent's guard was raised for a chest blow and Dryden's blade shot upwards with all the force he could muster.

The attacker fell back, a look of amazement on his face, his chest reddening. The sword fell out of his hand and he crumpled slowly to the ground.

Before Dryden had time to consider that he had killed a man, a second assailant had leapt forward.

Dryden parried and counter-attacked, more sure of himself and his own ability and knowledge.

Somewhere in the distance a voice was crying: 'They flee! They flee!'

Dryden saw a look of panic and desperation spread across his opponent's face and he side-stepped and disengaged, allowing the warrior to take the opportunity to turn and run for his life. Dryden felt a little glad to see the man reach his horse and escape through the gate.

Morvran came up, sheathing her sword.

'Five dead,' she said, peering around. 'They've fled back, the jackals. Rudhyk, do we have any casualties?'

Rudhyk went off to enquire.

Morvran smiled at Dryden.

'*Estrennek,* you are a good swordsman. We owe you much.'

Dryden, in truth, was feeling sick. He had killed his second man. The first was the spearman of Lan-Howlek whom he had shot with a chance arrow. But this one was different. More meaningful. He gazed down at the corpse. This one he had killed with bare steel. He had been close enough to smell the man's breath, the stale sweat, feel his body heat, see the look of pain in his eyes and hear the dreadful, sickening squelch of his blade biting into the man's flesh.

Morvran seemed to understand what was passing through Dryden's mind.

'Each time we kill,' she said slowly, 'we kill a little of ourselves, for all life is sacred under Bel. Do not think, *estrennek,* that we take joy in this killing. Surely to kill the killer makes both parties wicked instead of one? Yet what is our solution? How can we defend ourselves without being forced to commit the very violence we are seeking to stop?'

Morvran sighed and turned away.

Pryderi had come up and was peering at Dryden in surprise.

'I see you are sickened by death, Dryden,' he said. 'Yet, at the same time, I see you are not a stranger to the sword. You handle it better than any man I have seen. Why, I doubt that even Teyrnon could wield the weapon as well and with such dexterity. Yet you say you are a stranger to warfare? There is a mystery here, I think.'

Dryden shook his head.

'There is no mystery, Pryderi. In my world a man could pursue the art of swordsmanship as another might play a sport. It was a method of keeping himself in a state of physical fitness, of toning the muscles, of co-ordinating the eye and hand. I used to study the sword for many years to counteract the fact that the rest of my days were spent in lazy study over books. I needed such activity as a means of relaxation.'

Pryderi's face lightened.

'Ah, this I understand, my friend. It is a custom that many of the *drewyth* follow. They practise the martial arts as a means to keep their bodies and minds healthy. Yes, this I understand. The *drewyth* never raise a weapon in anger but many would make first class swordsmen and warriors.'

His face coloured and he added in justification:

'These are hard times for the people of Lan-Kern, Dryden. As a *drewyth* I strugged a long time with my conscience before I took up the sword.' He laid his hand on Dryden's arm. 'The people are much indebted to you. We live in violent times. But, praise Bel, these times will pass.'

CHAPTER SIX

It was on the day of the feast which the people of Lan-Kern called Beltan, the Fires of Bel, when Dryden realised how deeply he had fallen in love with Kigva. The winter months had passed rapidly as Dryden sought to perfect his knowledge of the language and the culture of Lan-Kern. Pryderi and Kigva had taken on the task of his instruction and there developed an intimate relationship between the three of them. Dryden, after the first pang of regret at the knowledge that Kigva was to marry Teyrnon, had supposed his initial attraction towards the girl was some boyish emotionalism. But as he came to know her more, his feelings grew and matured. Then, as winter gave way to Spring, on the very feastday of Beltan, he realised he must speak to her or go mad.

Beltan was the day when the people celebrated the start of their new year; when the whins were in bloom across the hills and moorland, making a golden-yellow carpet whose bright yellow gorse sprang alive as the tiny whinchats added their bright yellow feathers to the spectacle of colours. This was the day when the *drewyth* offered praise to Bel, the sun and life force of the world, for having brought victory to the powers of light over those of darkness and for bringing the people to the period of the rebirth of the soil. The people greeted the rise of the sun with a paean of thanksgiving. Just before sunrise, all the fires throughout the land were extinguished, even the meanest household fire. Then, when the great orb reached its zenith, the Chief Drewyth, whom Dryden had never seen but who spent his days at Meneghy, which was the chief temple of the order, would rekindle a fire from the rays of the sun. This sacred fire would then be sent, by special runners, to all corners of Lan-Kern so that every house and village could rekindle their fires from its flames. Pryderi explained that the symbolism of this ceremony was that each household, each family, was freed from any mistakes or misdeeds committed in the past year and the lighting of the new fire denoted that each person was given a fresh start in the new year. To re-emphasise this custom, a number of cattle and other livestock from each herd were driven east to west and west to east through a circle of close set fires as a symbol of purification by fire - which was the earthly embodiment of Bel.

By the end of the day Lan-Kern was ablaze with roaring bonfires from one end to the other. During this time the people held sporting games, made music, danced and sang and enacted impromptu dramas which generally expressed stories from their mythology and folklore.

It was during the evening, while he was sitting feasting with the others in the Great Hall of Kesmur, that Dryden realised how deeply he felt about Kigva. Perhaps it was something to do with the music, its immediacy, which gave form to his inner feelings. Perhaps it was the words or the pain-saddened voice of the girl, or the wistful expression on her face as she sang. He half-closed his eyes and let himself be drugged into a pleasant state by the gentle caress of the song.

> Bitter the wind this night
> and
> black the sky
> there is a keening
> in my throat
> and the tears lie on my eyes.
> Sorrowing my heart this night
> and
> dead my soul
> and there is red-black fire
> in my mind
> for the welling of my grief.
> Scattered my thoughts this night
> and
> expressionless my tongue
> Can you tell
> the slamming door
> your heart is full of tenderness?

He sat a long while after the song was ended, after Kigva had surrendered the platform to a rowdy group who enacted the creation

113

of Lan-Kern in elaborate dance and mime. Dryden did not see them. His mind was still held captive by the beautiful figure of the girl, her slender fingers strumming at the *telyn,* the harp-shaped instrument, the gentle rise and fall of her voice merging with it, rising and falling like a soft summer breeze.

He stood up and left the feast, going to the door of the great hall unnoticed. It was as if some fate had drawn him outside at that particular time for there, standing just outside the door in the silver rays of the moon, stood Kigva.

She turned and smiled at his approach.

'It is too hot in there,' she said softly. 'And it is such a beautiful night.'

Dryden glanced at the dark blue canopy of the night sky, filled with a soft silver glow of moonlight. He felt a dryness in his throat.

'*You* are beautiful, Kigva,' he said hoarsely.

The girl threw back her head and laughed, unembarrassed.

'What?' she said, adopting a tone of seriousness. 'Are you attempting to flatter me, or do I perceive a new side to your character?'

Dryden felt his skin dry to match his tongue. He tried hard to swallow, feeling as if his stomach had erupted in a cloud of fluttering butterflies. Why was it so difficult to tell the girl how he felt?

'Kigva, I am being serious. I have realised that I am in love with you.'

The girl gave him a searching look and found something in his face to match his seriousness and make her face a mask of concern.

'Yes, Dryden,' she said softly.

Dryden moved unhappily from one foot to the other.

'I realise that you are going to marry Teyrnon,' he began awkwardly, 'but I feel I must speak to you or explode. We've been good friends, close friends these past months. Without your help I do not think I could fully adjust to this new society of yours. Only now I realise how deeply I love you.'

The girl looked up into his face and, leaning forward, squeezed his hand.

'Is your tongue carried away by *Lor* the moon; by the music; the ache in your heart for your own people? You are a stranger in a strange land, Dryden. Do you speak from need or from your heart?'

Dryden began to open his mouth but the girl held up a hand.

'Be careful how you answer.'

Dryden wiped his forehead with the back of his hand, hardly noticing that, in spite of his dry skin, his forehead was damp with perspiration.

'Kigva, I have no wish to cause you hurt. I realise Teyrnon...'

The girl smiled.

'Forget Teyrnon for the moment. It is yourself that is of concern.'

'I do love you, Kigva,' he said desperately. 'I realise that I have always done so.'

'Always?' the girl arched her eyebrows.

'Since I first saw you on the beach. Even before I saw you. When I was in my own world, before I came here, I dreamt of such a girl as you.'

Kigva shook her head slowly.

'Ah Dryden, dreams, fantasies. Perhaps you are still in a world of illusion?'

'Kigva!' the word was a gasp of pain.

'Dryden, I will be truthful with you. I do not know the meaning of this word you use - love. Friendship, I know. And tenderness. Yes, I know those feelings and I will not deny that I feel a close friendship and tenderness for you. But love. How is that defined? How is it measured?'

She smiled and shrugged.

Dryden swallowed stiffly.

'I should not have said anything,' he said with a gruffness in his voice as he tried to hide the emotional pain that pierced him. 'I knew you are to marry Teyrnon and I should have known your love was reserved for him.'

The girl turned and stood contemplating the moon's reflection in the still waters of a nearby horse-trough.

'You are a friend, Dryden, and therefore I shall tell you in all honesty that I do not speak an untruth when I say I do not know the meaning of the word love. For Teyrnon I have a great regard, respect and feelings of close friendship and tenderness. We grew up together as brother and sister. There are bonds between us. But I do not experience this romantic love which the bards are given to sing about. According to the custom of my people, I must marry soon, and who is there who is better and closer to me than Teyrnon? We do share something. But, in truth, Dryden, I am not in love... not with anyone.'

She turned and looked at him closely.

'As for you saying that you should not have told me of your feelings - that is ridiculous. You know that it is against life, against the wisdom of the creation, to suppress your feelings, to hide your emotions, to stifle what you truly think. You should speak and in speaking find wisdom. I shall always be a friend to you, Dryden. I hope you will be my friend. During these few months there has grown a bond between us. You are to me as Pryderi, my brother, is...'

A shadow fell across them.

Dryden looked up with a scowl and saw the tall, darkly handsome figure of Teyrnon leaning against the door of the great hall.

'There you are.' the warlord addressed himself directly to Kigva. 'Kesmur and the people are demanding you return and sing again.'

He appeared not to notice Dryden.

Kigva smiled and glanced at Dryden. Then she was gone, following Teyrnon back into the great hall.

For a short while Dryden stood unhappily, staring with unseeing eyes at the sparkling moon in the horse-trough.

Then the early summer months were gone, too. Dryden spent them mostly with Pryderi, travelling around Lan-Kern, talking to the people, recording their folklore, absorbing their knowledge, ever searching for some clue to the mystery of his metamorphosis. Finally Pryderi exclaimed that his knowledge had become such that he could readily pass as a native of the country. Dryden smiled and knew that Pryderi was merely flattering him for he knew that he would never be perfect in the language and a native speaker would always tell that he was an *estrennek*, that he did not really belong. But he had begun to feel more reconciled to his extraordinary fate and more at ease in this strange new world. In fact, and the thought filled him with amazement when he contemplated it, he felt more at peace with himself than ever he had done in his own world.

The one miserable cloud on his horizon was his feeling for Kigva. His avowal of love had not changed Kigva's friendship for him. Many times that summer they went hunting or lazed by the beach together, talking and exploring their friendship. And truly Dryden began to realise that Kigva was honest in her feelings: that she had not really experienced love, not for himself nor for Teyrnon. The truth was that Teyrnon was someone she was entirely familiar and at ease with, that was the main cause of her betrothal to him. Dryden tried to quell his feelings of jealousy and come to terms with the situation.

It was hard, however, to become friendly with Teyrnon. Many times Kigva had tried to get the dour-faced warlord to join their company and every time Teyrnon found an excuse. Dryden was secretly pleased, for he preferred to be alone with Kigva or to share her company with Pryderi. He supposed that the same thoughts motivated Teyrnon and Dryden could not repress a stupid feeling of annoyance each time he found that Kigva and Teyrnon had gone off alone. It was Pryderi who pointed out that Teyrnon and Dryden had many characteristics in common and that it was, perhaps, this reason why his sister found friendship in both of them. Dryden protested that Teyrnon and he were poles apart, but inwardly he knew that Pryderi was right.

Unknown to Dryden, Kigva was not oblivious to the conflict between the two men and many times she had tried to resolve her own conflicting emotions. She had grown up with Teyrnon and found a great many things she liked in his character and which were complementary to her own personality. His scowling silences and brooding countenance were only reserved for Dryden. And as for Dryden, there too, she found a great deal to like in the man, a deep, brooding man - something like Teyrnon - but also kind, gentle and with a deep concern for people. She felt that the mystery of his arrival in Lan-Kern, the strange 'otherworld' which he sometimes spoke of, held a great deal of fascination for her and perhaps blinded her a little to his faults.

By the end of the summer Teyrnon and Dryden took pains to avoid each other and when they were forced to speak, they spoke in double-edged invective. No matter how Kigva scolded them, or even refused their individual company to force a compromise, there existed a growing dislike between them. Because of Teyrnon's duties as warlord, which took him away for weeks and sometimes months to the eastern borders, the situation was not able to develop further.

117

It was at the end of the summer that Dryden realised that he had been in Lan-Kern nearly a year and the realisation of that thought appalled him. He had been living on the hospitality of the people without contributing anything in return. He was given food and clothing, a place to sleep, allowed to roam freely as he chose, often with Pryderi to outlying settlements. Considering his situation, Dryden realised that he had become a parasite on the society and the time had come, now that he knew enough of the customs and language of the people, to find some activity through which he could make some contribution to the society. He was a trained botanist but what use was a botanist in such a world as this? He had some skill with the sword but the idea of becoming a warrior, of making a profession of killing, was repugnant to him. Certainly the raids from Lan-Howlek had continued from the Spring throughout the summer months and there often came news of a settlement burnt down or individual wayfarers slain. According to Pryderi, the tactics of Nelferch's grandson, Cador, were to wear down the spirit of the people so that they would beg Kesmur to accept the demands of the witch queen.

Dryden took Pryderi aside one day and explained his dilemma.

'What work am I to do, Pryderi?' he demanded.

'The time has come as I knew it would, my friend.'

Dryden raised an eyebrow. Pryderi explained.

'The time has come to take you to Meneghy to see Mabon the Chief *Drewyth*. He will advise you.'

'He can suggest what I can do?'

'Mabon will know what you *will* do,' replied Pryderi, resorting to that mysterious inflection which Dryden had noticed that *drewyth* priests used when speaking to the people.

'Where is this Meneghy?' asked Dryden. 'It is your central temple, isn't it?'

'It is a place of refuge and retreat, a place where the *drewyth* contemplate the Oneness of the Universe and the Eternal quality of Bel the life-giver and creator. It is also a place of study and knowledge. It lies not far from Dynas Dor.'

'You call the place Meneghy - that is the word that is also used for sanctuary, isn't it? But I thought there were many such temples throughout Lan-Kern.'

'Meneghy is the most ancient of them, Dryden. It is there that the chief of our order dwells.'

'Well,' grinned Dryden, 'I shall go with you to see this Mabon if, as you say, he can sort out my problems. But why is it that I have never seen him at Dynas Dor, at the fortress of your father? After all, as Kesmur is the high chieftain, surely the chief of the *drewyth* should be in attendance on him?'

Pryderi laughed.

'You still have many things to learn about us, Dryden. Kesmur is merely the servant of the people, he carries out the wishes of the people. The chief of the *drewyth,* master of the inner circle of Bel's mysteries, does not come and go at the wishes of a mere chieftain, high or low. Chieftains go to consult him. Mabon hardly ever leaves Meneghy unless he comes to celebrate the festival of Mys-Du at Dynas Dor, the night when the Otherworld comes visible to mankind and our souls stand in the greatest need of protection. That is why you have not seen Mabon, but Mabon is all-knowing, Dryden.'

There was an emphasis in Pryderi's voice which made Dryden raise an eyebrow but he did not press the matter further.

CHAPTER SEVEN

Three days later Pryderi and Dryden rode towards the north-east
and, after a short journey, they left the lushness of the valleys
around Dynas Dor and started to move across the bleak and unlovely
tract of moorland which led to Meneghy. It was flat countryside, the
only relief being two giant hills which stood up like pyramids on the
distant skyline, rising with a distinct and dramatic force that gave
them the impression of mountains although they could scarcely be
more than a thousand feet high. The two men moved through dark
areas of bogland where they came across huge furrows in the soil
which, Pryderi explained, were where the tin streamers worked;
where a form of open cast mining was carried on from which the
smithies of Lan-Kern took their metals. On this desolate windswept
moorland stood an occasional stone hut where - so Pryderi said -
drewyth hermits retired to contemplate on nature in the barren
wilderness.

The actual journey to Meneghy took them no more than a few
hours but when the rise of the hills that marked the immediate
approach to Meneghy was reached, Dryden felt that he had travelled
into another country entirely, a country where sudden mists gusted
down across the moors and were so thick that travellers had to halt
until the winds swept them away and cleared their path again. In
emerging from such a mist, Dryden found that he and Pryderi stood
on a hillside overlooking a flat plain on which stood a complex
which he realised was Meneghy. Afterwards, he recalled that he
had been half-expecting to see something of the sort that towered
before his gaze.

In his world he had seen the great stone circles such as Stonehenge
and even the complex at Carnac in Brittany. But they were old and
worn and only hinted at their former glory. Before him, however,
stood a towering stone circle with what must have been at least one

hundred stones, arranged in a complicated series of patterns; stones that stood, not old and decaying and toppling, but in all their pristine beauty, stretching firmly upwards towards the heavens.

Again that chill feeling came to him - the feeling that instead of being precipitated into a future world, he had somehow gone backwards in time to some pre-Christian world of ancient Britain. In spite of the evidence of the ruins of London, a far-off memory now, he seriously wondered whether it were so - whether he had been propelled into the world of the past.

Before him was one great dominant stone circle, ringed by tall stones, while all around were smaller standing stones arranged in concentric circles. Even with an uninformed eye Dryden could see the stones were more than mere decorative motifs. To one side of this intricate complex of circles stood a fair sized village of traditional beehive stone huts. It was such a scene as he could imagine Stonehenge to have been long before the birth of Christ.

'You look worried, Dryden,' observed Pryderi, dismounting from his horse.

Dryden followed his example and the two walked slowly down the hill, leading their beasts.

'This worries me, Pryderi,' said Dryden, nodding towards the circles. Pryderi was the only person to whom he had confessed his entire past, of his strange journey, and Pryderi had read the truth in his eyes. 'Is this the future or is it the past?' went on Dryden. 'Have I gone forward or backwards in time?'

Pryderi smiled.

'It is neither the future nor the past, Dryden. It is only now.'

'I cannot accept your mysticism,' rejoined Dryden curtly. 'I must know.'

'Isn't the fact that it is now enough? You are always seeking, Dryden. You are always questioning. You even question your questions.'

'Do you mean that I should not question anything?'

'We can spend eternity questioning. Would it not be better to accept that this green hill is simply a green hill and nothing more?'

'But if man doesn't question how can he progress?'

'What is progression, Dryden? From what you say, your world had progressed only in the domination and destruction of its natural environment; progressed only by creating sophisticated methods of destroying both nature and man himself. Man is like a child: questioning his environment before questioning himself. What is the worth of trying to understand the things by which you are surrounded and seeking to relate to them if you have no understanding of yourself?'

'I can see your point, Pryderi, but it's very difficult for man to remain oblivious to his environment.'

'I did not say remain oblivious. As I understand it, the people of your world had many questions, yet they were entirely oblivious to nature. As much as they questioned they did not attempt to understand. All their questions were asked with one purpose - how can I dominate? How can I bend the forces of nature to my will? There was no attempt to be at one with nature, only to subvert nature and destroy her. Their destruction was inevitable.'

'I can't accept that it was wrong to question,' said Dryden.

'Perhaps one day you will see. That day is not yet,' replied Pryderi. 'The only thing that is asked of you is that you remain true to your own nature. If you feel this question important, by all means ask it. The danger lies in feeling the question important and yet not asking.'

Dryden sighed.

'Yours is a hard philosophy to follow, Pryderi.'

'The path of Bel is simple - be yourself.'

'Perhaps I'll understand one day,' Dryden shrugged. 'In the meantime I should still like to know what happened to the world I knew and whether this is my future or my past.'

'Your society has made time of great importance,' observed Pryderi as they came to the gates of Memeghy. 'There is only one time - now. Time is like a huge circle, it is repetitious. The past is the present, the present will be the future. It is all one.'

Pryderi led the way to the levelled area on which the central circle had been constructed. A few warriors stood guard here and there, a necessary precaution since the raids from Lan-Howlek, but for the most part the place was peopled by members of the *drewyth* order - elderly men who bent about their tasks, acknowledging Pryderi with a smile or a nod.

'What's the meaning of all this, Pryderi?' asked Dryden, peering around at the impressive construction. He suddenly laughed: 'A question again...is it permitted?'

'Only things injurious may not be permitted,' replied Pryderi.

'This is your temple, then? The place where you worship?'

Pryderi shook his head.

'It is not a place of worship in the sense you mean it, Dryden. It is rather a place of understanding where we learn to be at one with the world.'

'In my world there were the remains of such stone circles as these. The people thought they were for pagan religious worship where people carried out ritual human sacrifice.'

Pryderi laughed.

'People are easily deluded by their own fantasies. In these circles we chart the heavens and by the movement of the stars we can foretell the influences of nature and the Universe. We can foretell the times of the harvest, the date when a man or woman is born...'

'You mean,' began Dryden in wonder, 'all this is for astrology - fortune telling?'

'To a degree, your definition is correct. Conjunctions of stars do give people certain characteristics and one can be forewarned when times are not auspicious.'

'In my world, scientists rejected that as superstition.'

'Your world,' smiled Pryderi, 'seems to have rejected many truths in the search for the domination of Nature.'

Dryden felt a little offended for he, too, had scoffed at astrology.

'I seem to recall,' went on Pryderi, 'in one of our conversations that you said that the science of your world claimed that man's body consisted of seventy-two per cent water?'

'That's so,' frowned Dryden.

'Now is your science advanced enough to agree that the actions of *Lor* the moon governs the great tides of the seas?'

'Of course.'

'Then if *Lor* the moon can disturb whole oceans and seas, surely it can disturb the liquid of our bodies and change our rhythms and more so can the greater stars in the heavens.'

'You mean the gravitational pull of the planets can work upon our biological system?' asked Dryden, interspersing English words for the concepts he did not know.

123

Pryderi held up his hands. 'I do not know the meaning of your words but your expression says you have grasped my meaning.'

He turned and walked to the centre of the great stone circle at one end of which stood a stone cairn, a carefully built altar-like structure of grey stone.

Dryden followed him, his eyes taking in the sophistication of the complex.

'How many temples like this are there in Lan-Kern?'

'About twenty-one,' replied Pryderi, 'perhaps as many again in Lan-Howlek for they followed the same path as ourselves before they fell into darkness under Nelferch. This is our main place of enlightenment. It is here that we keep *An Kevryn*.'

'*An Kevryn?*' asked Dryden, puzzled. 'That means 'The Mystery', doesn't it?'

Pryderi pointed to the cairn. It was a small structure, three feet in height with sides sloping to a flat top, on which were carved many strange patterns. At the bottom of the stone was a small cavity.

'That is *An Kevryn*.'

Dryden bent down and peered into the cavity. Inside was a small, shiny black metal box, about nine inches by six inches by three inches high. His heart skipped a beat as he realised that the metalwork looked like something out of his world rather than the roughly beaten metals of Lan-Kern.

'What is it?' he asked.

'It has been here for countless generations,' replied Pryderi. 'You remember me telling you our story of the Age of Destruction? There is another such tale. When this ancient civilisation came to the verge of destruction, the noblest of their philosophers came together and in that box they placed the results of their labours through the ages ... the meaning of creation, of life itself ... and the reason for their destruction. They sealed the box and placed it for safe keeping in one of their great monoliths. But the civilisation perished and, finally, when man strove to rise upwards once again, he discovered the box. In the time of our ancients, our philosophers took the box and placed it in the safekeeping of the *drewyth* with the instruction that no man should open it for no one should know the secrets of creation but creation itself. No one should know the meaning of creation or of destruction. It must forever remain a mystery - *An Kevryn,* The Mystery. It has remained in our sanctuary ever since.'

Dryden bent to the cairn and stretched out a hand.

'May I see it?'

Pryderi's hand closed fiercely on his wrist.

'No one may do so, not even I. No man may reach out to learn the secret of creation.'

Dryden saw the intensity in his face and forced a smile.

'But, Pryderi, if this is a future world, my future, then perhaps that box contains something from my world, my past, something which would tell me how my world destroyed itself and how history seems to be repeating itself so precisely once again.'

Pryderi slowly shook his head.

'It cannot be, Dryden. This must remain a mystery forever. Learn to accept and not to challenge.'

Dryden was suddenly aware of two warriors looking meaningfully in their direction. Pryderi waved them away.

Dryden stood up and sighed.

'Very well, Pryderi. I came to Lan-Kern and promised to accept your customs and ways. I don't wish to offend you. I shall keep my promise.'

Fighting down his burning curiousity, he turned away from the cairn. Pryderi watched him with a suspicious look. Dryden had given in too easily.

'Come, Pryderi, let us go and see this Mabon.'

Pryderi conducted Dryden to a large stone building and halted outside.

'This is the sanctuary of Mabon, chief of the *drewyth.*'

Somewhat unwillingly, Dryden found himself propelled into the stone building which was lit by the flickering flames of two torches burning from holders on the walls. He stood blinking in the semigloom and trying to adjust his eyes from the glare of the midday sun outside. After a while he could see that the room in which he stood was sparsely furnished, but great woven tapestries hung all round the walls.

He became aware of a raised platform at one end of the room on which was seated an old man, clad in a simple homespun white robe. He was bald, his yellow face was cracked with age, but his eyes were bright - perhaps blue - and shone with a piercing intensity.

Dryden took a few hesitant paces forward, aware that Pryderi had not followed him into the hut.

The voice was high but firm.

'You are Dryden?'

Dryden bowed his head in acknowledgement.

'I am the *estrennek*,' he responded.

'No man is a stranger in the company of man,' came the soft rebuke.

The old man motioned his head, indicating that Dryden should seat himself. Dryden sank awkwardly on the mat before the chief *drewyth*. He felt uncomfortable under the penetrating stare of the old man.

Abruptly a grin split the old man's face.

'Do not be alarmed. It is an egocentricity of mine to stare at people. I like to see beyond the superficiality of the flesh into the inner soul and mind. You are a man of complexities, Dryden. I feel you are of the sign of *Puskes* for there are, in you, two natures - the physical and the spiritual, each struggling to free itself from each other but being prevented. Is that not so?'

Dryden was taken aback.

'How did you know that I was born under the sign of Pisces the Fishes?'

He tried to remember whether he had told this to Pryderi but rebuked himself for an uncharitable thought, for surely Pryderi would not pass on such information to enable this old man to impress him?

'No, Dryden. I am not a charlatan wishing to impress you,' he said, as if reading Dryden's thoughts. 'The signs are there to be read as clearly as a man can read the nature of herbs, for when he knows the secrets of the herbs and the plants, it becomes easy to say - this plant will do such and such; that herb will do so and so. Such knowledge becomes easy. Within you I see a spirituality, you are ever seeking to learn the mysteries of mankind and help towards the improvement of their lot wherever it is possible. It is written in your soul.'

'I am impressed,' replied Dryden grudgingly.

'I do not mean you to be, anymore than if you gazed at the sky and

126

recognised the sun during the daylight or the moon at night and could name the stars in the heavens. I state what is as clear to me as the sun, the moon and the stars are as clear to you. I have studied for many years; I have become an adept at the science of the influences of the heavens upon our bodies and therefore our minds. When that study is linked to application, the intellect and intuition blend in a natural and harmonious manner. They commence to vibrate in unison and the ignorant man can then become the prophetic sage.'

Smiling, Dryden shook his head.

'I cannot accept that the rotation of planets in the sky determine man's future.'

The old man gave an answering chuckle.

'It is not as simple as that and yet it is so simple, Dryden. Perhaps you are seeking to know too much?'

Dryden shrugged.

'Frankly, Mabon, I am a scientist and not really interested in metaphysics.'

The old man wagged a forefinger of rebuke at Dryden.

'I, too, am a scientist for what is metaphysics but the science which investigates the first principles of nature, the nature of Being?'

'I seek logical explanations,' avowed Dryden.

Old Mabon inclined his head.

'Yes, Dryden, you seek too much or else you have not grasped the nature of that which you seek. You disbelieve in the science of the heavens, that which you call astrology? You seem to think that we claim that the heavens are a chart which, when read, will give up divine revelations and from which we can tell you what you will eat tomorrow or where you will sleep the day afterwards. The true observer expects nothing but the clear and concise statement of the immutable Law of Nature.

'The science is not that of fortune telling. That, we brethren of the *drewyth*, leave to the *pystryores* - the charlatans who ply their trade in the markets and fairs for a few coins. For the *drewyth* the reading of Nature's laws requires many years of study and more years of application.'

The old man paused and looked at Dryden as if summing up his ability to grasp the concept.

127

'The universe is a great orchestra, alive with a multitude of vibrations. Imagine the human body as a complex musical instrument, an instrument that not only sends out musical notes but receives and transmits them from other sources. Each vibration, each note, interacts with countless others throughout the entire Universe so that each vibration should be in accord with the whole to be in total harmony.'

Dryden showed his lack of understanding.

'It is a difficult philosophy for me to grasp,' he said.

'When the body is born and starts to breathe, it begins a series of vibrations which retain their particular polarity for the whole tenor of its earthly existence. The vibrations create notes of harmony or of discord - now higher - now lower - and so on as that body progresses through life. Its vibrations change and react when brought into contact with other such vibrations. Sometimes the vibrations are in harmony, sometimes in discord.

'And what are the greatest sources of vibration, in the universe? Why, the planets and stars. The actions and interactions and the motions of the stars upon the delicate human instrument after birth is like a finger strumming upon the strings of the *telyn*. When a planet reaches a point where it forms an unharmonious angle with the angular vibrations set in motion at birth, a magnetic discord is produced. There arises a magnetic storm which has a material effect on the instrument at its apex. The stars and planets thus influence the delicate vibrations of our bodies.

'Sometimes the influences create so low a vibration that we cannot detect it. Other times the vibration becomes so strong... throbbing pulsations which we cannot ignore. It then depends on how we understand and adjust to them as to whether we become at odds with the creation or whether we can live in harmony with it. Can we control the symphony of our existence or must we set up strident discords to the detriment or ourselves and our fellow men?'

The old man paused and smiled at Dryden's puzzled face.

'It is difficult for you to grasp these things, to understand them. You have emerged from a world which has been so obviously antagonistic to a true oneness with nature. But within you, Dryden, I see a deep longing to understand, to know, to achieve. When that longing dies within you, you will find understanding.'

'What do you mean?' Dryden frowned.

'Go now,' said the old man, as if not hearing him and as if a sudden weariness had overcome him. 'There is a turbulent struggle within you. But you will achieve calmness. Go under the peace of Bel.'

Automatically, Dryden found himself standing up and leaving. Outside he stood blinking in the bright daylight, his thoughts more confused than before.

Pryderi was waiting for him.

'I have some tasks to perform here this evening, Dryden,' he said. 'We can stay the night in the hostel and start back to Dynas Dor in the morning, unless you object.'

Dryden shook his head.

He fell in step with the young man without speaking. There were so many thoughts turning round in his mind. So many questions he should have asked the old *drewyth*. Either the people of Lan-Kern were possessed of a deep and sensitive knowledge of science and philosophy, or they had some convincing charlatans and dreamers. Dryden rubbed the back of his neck. It was difficult, so difficult, to absorb concepts which would have been ridiculed in his own world.

Well, one thing the *drewyth* was right in and that was Dryden did have a longing to know, to understand. His mind returned to the black box - *An Kevryn,* The Mystery - lying in the cairn. He still possessed a burning desire to examine it, to open it, to see whether it would explain to him the strange metamorphosis of the world; to explain whether this was his future or his past. He gave a sidelong glance at Pryderi, walking by his side. Perhaps it was to his advantage that they would have to spend the night at Meneghy. He could slip out of the hostel while Pryderi was asleep. Yes, that night he would return to the inner stone circle, to the cairn, and examine the box.

CHAPTER EIGHT

The moon stood stark and white out of the blue-black night sky. Dryden walked silently through the woods which separated the great stone circles of Meneghy from the hostel in which guests to the *drewyth* sanctuary were housed. Pryderi had not returned from his ceremony and Dryden had decided to chance things, for it was well after midnight. He had to examine the black box, *An Kevryn,* for it now symbolised to him the key to every mystery his mind tried to encompass. So he strode purposefully towards the sanctuary with a rapidly beating heart.

At a bend in the pathway, before it emerged through the woods onto the open expanse of grassland on which Meneghy had been built, Dryden paused and looked cautiously at the stone circles. The great menhirs were bathed in the pale glow of moonlight and their huge shadows created menacing pools of blackness across the plain. But within the stone circles he saw movement; the white robe of a *drewyth* going on some errand flashed in the gloom.

Dryden paused for a moment to consider the situation. It was obvious that the sanctuary was attended all day and all night. The priests studied the heavens and, of course, what better time was there than the night when the heavens hung open like some gigantic painting before their searching gaze.

He must risk it; he must look at the box. But what would happen if he was discovered defiling the *drewyth* sanctuary, going against the ancient laws? How could he fight this obsessiveness, for he had a feeling that it would mean his banishment from Lan-Kern, a place in which he had finlly achieved a sense of belonging. What of Kigva? Of Pryderi? What was important to him? His curiosity or his acceptance by the community?

A woman's scream sounded along the path, through the woods. It took Dryden several seconds to move and as he did so a second scream echoed through the night. He turned and ran swiftly back along the pathway towards the sound. About a hundred yards along it there crouched a woman holding the head of a small limp figure in her arms and crying softly.

'What's up?' cried Dryden as the woman raised a tearful face to his.

The limp figure was that of a young girl, perhaps ten years old. The child's face was screwed up in pain.

'Nader!' whispered the woman, pointing to the girl's leg.

Dryden could see some blackish discolouring in the faint gloom.

'I don't understand,' he said. 'Something has bitten her?'

'Nader!' cried the distracted woman. 'Nader!'

She suddenly made a snake-like motion with her hand and arm, raising them to resemble the head of a snake about to strike.

'A snake? A viper?' said Dryden, realising he did not know the words for the reptiles. He knew that vipers were the only poisonous snakes in this area... but then who knew what poisonous reptiles had developed in this world.

He tore a strip from his jacket and wound it around the girl's leg, seizing a piece of twig and twisting the makeshift tourniquet tight. Then he lifted the child in his arms.

'This way. We need some light.'

He hastened along the pathway towards the sanctuary and, without pausing, went directly to the huts of the *drewyth*, where he could see torches lighting the night sky. The woman stumbled, sobbing at his heels. *Drewyths*, in their white robes, looked up in surprise as Dryden hurried through their midst towards the cluster of huts. He ignored them and entered the first hut he came to without hesitation.

Inside a man sprang to his feet in astonishment. It was Pryderi.

'Dryden!' the young man exclaimed. 'I thought you might come.'

His eyes suddenly took in the moaning figure of the child in Dryden's arms and the red-eyed woman at his heels.

'What has happened?' he asked quietly.

'Nader!' sobbed the woman.

Dryden laid the child down in a circle of light thrown out by a torch. Pryderi bent his head.

'In adults the bite of the *nader* is seldom fatal but in a young child...' he shook his head slowly.

Dryden was trying to summon up an almost forgotten knowledge.

'Get me a sharp knife,' he snapped. 'And have you any salt here?'

Pryderi stared at him in amazement and then handed Dryden a knife from his belt.

'I'll get some salt,' he murmured.

Dryden plunged the knife blade into the flame of the spluttering torch and watched the blade become hot.

'Hold your daughter's arms, little mother. This is the only chance to save her, so don't worry at what I am doing.'

The woman tried to stifle her sobs and nodded.

Dryden bent over the wound and, carefully, in spite of the cries and agonised threshing of the girl's body, he prised the wound open, drawing the poison from it as best he could. Fifteen long minutes elapsed, during which time Pryderi returned with a small bag of salt. It was sea salt cured and dried by the sun. Dryden bent, sweat pouring from his brow, as he examined the wound.

'If that hasn't removed the poison, nothing will,' he whispered to Pryderi.

He dampened a handful of salt and placed it over the wound.

The child had slipped into unconsciousness.

Dryden bit his lip.

'If only I could get my hands on some lobelia, trouble is it only grows in eastern America but at least it would have counteracted the poison.'

Pryderi frowned.

'I do not know this lob.. lobelia...'

'No, I know.' Dryden's face suddenly lightened. 'Wait, do you know where we can get the bark of an ash tree...what do you call it, *onnen*, the bark of the *onnen*?'

'Some grows outside,' said Pryderi wonderingly. 'I'll fetch it.'

Dryden didn't know if it would work, indeed, he did not know whether he had remembered correctly but, in ancient times, he seemed to recall that an infusion made from the ash-bark was used to cure fevers, as an anti-periodic, a laxative and purgative. Pliny had once written that ash had a considerable reputation as a cure for snakebite. Well, there was no other medicine available, so it was worth trying. As soon as Pryderi re-entered, Dryden swiftly prepared the mixture which he forced down the child's throat. Then he put a wet salt poultice on the wound.

'Little mother,' he said, turning to the red-eyed woman. 'I have done the best I can. Some poison has reached her system but I am hoping that it will not be enough to be harmful.'

The woman raised her eyes hopefully.

'Will she die?'

'I cannot say,' replied Dryden honestly. 'She will certainly enter a fever soon. If it breaks in the morning then she will recover.'

'Few children recover from the bite of the *nader*,' said the woman, gazing down at the face of her child.

'Let your thoughts be positive, little mother,' interposed Pryderi. 'The feeling for good will be a positive action. Stay here with your child. We shall be nearby. Call us if you want us.'

Pryderi guided Dryden from the hut.

'Walk with me a while, Dryden,' he said softly.

They walked slowly towards the great stone circles. There were still members of the *drewyth* apparently making sightings of the stars through the alignment of the stones.

'I came here to wait for you tonight, Dryden,' said Pryderi.

Dryden was silent.

'When you looked at *An Kevryn*, I felt what was passing through your mind. You felt the urge to examine the box, to open it, to explore its mystery. You felt that by so doing all the mysteries that frustrate you would pass away. Is that not so?'

'You know that you are right, Pryderi,' sighed Dryden.

Pryderi led him towards the stone cairn in which *An Kevryn* reposed.

'You were on your way here, knowing that it was against our law to touch *An Kevryn*, in order to break that law?'

'I cannot deny it, Pryderi. I started out with that intention.'

'Then you encountered the woman and her child?'

'Yes. And now, it doesn't matter about the box.' Dryden spoke with some surprise as if he had just realised his feelings.

'Do you still think that the examination of *An Kevryn* would create an understanding in you and make you a better person.'

Dryden frowned.

133

'A better person? I don't really know.'

Pryderi looked at him keenly.

'The box is there, Dryden,' he said, pointing to the cairn. 'If you feel the need to examine it, do so. It is the teaching of Bel to remain true to oneself. If it is your desire, then you must fulfil it. We are alone. I shall not call the warriors who guard this place.'

Dryden hesitated as he tried to analyse his feelings. He began to realise that the box, *An Kevryn*, did not hold the fascination that it had a mere half-an-hour before. Now he had only a faint curiosity about it. It would not alter his life. But the woman and the child had altered his life. Now he had a desire to exist as he was. To be. He had found a purpose; something which he could do. Before his eyes swam the sweat stained face of the child, its features contorted in agony as he tried to wrest the poison from her limb. That was the reality. That was the now. Lan-Kern was real, important - Lan-Kern and Kigva, and Pryderi. The links of his past were suddenly severed. There was no need to *know*. He just wanted to stay, to belong, to use the little knowledge he had of plants and their nature to help people.

Pryderi watched the emotions playing across Dryden's face with a curious half-smile.

Dryden looked at him and shrugged.

'It is of no importance, not now.'

He turned abruptly and began to walk towards the hut.

A frail figure moved in the blackness of a menhir and a white arm motioned Pryderi.

The young *drewyth* moved into the shadows.

Mabon took him by the arm.

'You will find, Pryderi my son, that the longing does not die if one attempts to kill it only in the mind. He was tempted and has bravely resisted the temptation. But the longing is still written on his forehead however much he may attempt to deny it. The longing only dies within the stomach, within the emotions.'

Pryderi scowled.

'You mean that he is deceiving us; that he means to examine *An Kevryn* still?'

Mabon shook his head.

'No. He is merely deceiving himself. He is an honourable man. He believes his conscious thoughts are true; that he has resisted the

134

temptation to examine this box which means so much to him. He thinks he can resist the gnawing curiosity of his heart because he wants to be one with us. But first he must be one with himself.'

'How can that be brought about?'

Mabon tapped Pryderi lightly on the shoulder in disfavour.

'Things are not brought about, Pryderi. It is written that Dryden has been sent to us at a time of great need - both for us and for himself. His search for his being will be long and arduous, involving many painful paths - paths that are often stained with blood. And at the end there will always be *An Kevryn*. Until *An Kevryn* ceases to be, Dryden will not find his being.'

Mabon sighed.

'Go to him now, Pryderi. His soul aches for the child that lies sick.'

'Can he cure the girl?' demanded Pryderi.

The old man smiled, turned and disappeared into the blackness.

Dryden, Pryderi and the child's mother watched the little girl burning with fever through the early hours of the morning. Dryden refused to allow them to give the child anything more to drink but urged that a cold, wet cloth be used to wipe her face and moisten her lips. Finally, the exhaustion of the night caught him and he dozed in a corner. How long he dozed, he did not know. It seemed merely a matter of seconds. Then a hand was shaking him awake. It was Pryderi.

'Come and see, Dryden,' the young man whispered.

Dryden bent over the child.

The face was calm and she breathed the deep, regular breaths of a natural sleep. Dryden placed a hand on her forehead. The temperature was normal. The fever had broken. He turned to the anxious mother.

'She will be alright now,' he said.

The mother's eyes flooded with tears and she suddenly reached forward and grasped Dryden's hands and kissed them. Dryden tried to pull away in embarrassment.

'May Bel prosper you,' gasped the woman. 'Tell me, what is your name so that I may remember you?'

'My name is Dryden,' he replied.

The woman wiped her tears and frowned.

135

'That is an *estrennek* name whose syllables elude my tongue. I shall call you An Yaghus, the Healer, for I shall always remember you as the Healer who was destined to save my daughter. Bel prosper you, Yaghus. Bel prosper you.'

Pryderi, smiling, followed the embarrassed Dryden from the hut.

'Well, Yaghus, I think the woman has chosen your new name well.'

Dryden grinned sheepishly.

'I have yet to earn that name, Pryderi. But perhaps I could? Perhaps your father would let me stay in Lan-Kern and become one of his people?'

'That would be for the conclave of the inner circle of *drewyth* to decide.'

Dryden faced him eagerly.

'How can I persuade them? I could use my knowledge of herbs and plants to bring cures for people, to earn my living and no longer be beholden to them for hospitality. Perhaps I can even repay them for what they have given me all these months past. Would it be allowed?'

'All things positive and for the good are allowed, Dryden,' observed Pryderi. 'But it is not an easy step you take and you must be sure.'

'I am sure,' vowed Dryden. 'I am sure.'

CHAPTER NINE

Pryderi entered Dryden's hut and smiled self-consciously.

'Mabon and Kesmur have asked me to act as mediator,' he began hesitantly.

Dryden motioned the young *drewyth* to seat himself and then sat opposite him.

'You sound rather formal, Pryderi,' he said after a silence.

'In this matter I speak as one of the brethren of the *drewyth,* the guardians of the religion, customs and lore of our people,' replied Pryderi solemnly. 'I have been asked to answer your request - the request that you be allowed to live with us as one of the people and follow the profession of healing the sick.'

Dryden leant forward eagerly.

'Is it decided?' he asked.

Pryderi made a negative gesture and Dryden's face fell.

'In the time you have been with us you have achieved much. You have become proficient in our tongue and, though it is still obvious that you are an *estrennek,* you do not lack words by which to make yourself understood. You have constantly questioned the people and obtained a great knowledge of our history, customs and way of life. You have also displayed a great knowledge of the healing power of plants and herbs. Already there are many among us who have adopted the new name of Yaghus, the healer. It is a more fitting name.'

'The people flatter me,' returned Dryden. 'I have not justified such a name as yet.'

'The woman whose child you healed of the *nader*-bite would not say so.'

Dryden hunched his shoulders in an expressive shrug.

'But,' continued Pryderi, 'you are right. To be a healer is a position of great trust. Normally, only a *drewyth* is allowed to practise such powers. Mabon, however, has seen your ability and charted your horoscope. If you would become a healer with us then there is much you must learn and much you must unlearn. You must come to a realisation of being.'

Dryden sighed. He had not thought his simple request would meet with any difficulties.

'I'm willing to undergo any test to prove my ability,' he said. Pryderi shook his head and smiled.

'It is not your ability which is in question. Are you prepared, truly, to undergo a testing?'

'I am.'

'Tomorrow is the last day of the period of the moon we call Mys-Hedra, the start of the month of darkness, when one of the four great feastdays of our year begins. It marks the end of the harvest season and the start of the winter months. It is also the period for testing those who would aspire to office among us.'

'What sort of testing?' asked Dryden.

'Firstly,' began Pryderi, 'I must tell you that you are not obliged to undergo this testing. Should you wish to do so, you could remain here in Lan-Kern as a guest of the people under our ancient laws of hospitality for as long as you wish. By the same token, of course, you are constricted by those laws of hospitality in that you could not pursue an occupation or take part in the political, military or social life of our people except as an onlooker.'

'I know this,' interposed Dryden. 'That's why I'm willing to undergo your test, whatever it is. I have no wish to live on the charity of the people. As you know, there's no path back to my world and now I am not so sure I would wish to return. I feel more at peace here than I ever did in my world. I feel I could usefully contribute to the people's welfare with my knowledge of herbs and plants.'

'I know,' replied Pryderi. 'I know your feelings, Dryden. But wait until you have learnt the degree of the testing before you affirm your desires.'

He paused.

'At the end of the period of the moon we call Mys-Hedra comes that of the moon we call Mys-Du, the month of blackness. You have heard of our religious teaching that the soul is immortal. That we believe there is another world which exists as does this one, a world

138

where all life continues and progresses as it does in this world. When a soul dies in our world, it speeds to the Otherworld where it is reborn. When a soul dies in the Otherworld, it comes to our world and is reborn here. So it is, Dryden, that we believe our souls constantly transmigrate from one world to another, hopefully progressing in spiritual quality with each new life until they finally achieve true oneness with creation.'

'I know the belief,' affirmed Dryden.

'Do you believe in it?'

Pryderi suddenly watched Dryden closely.

'Pryderi, I'll tell you the truth,' replied Dryden. 'In all honesty I can't say that I do. But I'm willing to give consideration to the matter and to learn.'

The young *drewyth* smiled warmly.

'It could not be otherwise, Dryden. You are honest. If you had said that you believed, then I could let you progress no further. You would have lied to attain to the testing and no man can go to the test with dishonesty in his soul.'

'What is this test?'

'On the evening of the last day of Mys-Hedra, tomorrow, when the sun sets, then is the time when the Otherworld becomes visible to mankind, when all the forces of the supernatural are let loose in this world; it is a time of great spiritual vulnerability - when man stands in the greatest danger of losing his immortal soul. That is the time when the testing starts.'

'And what must I do?'

'Firstly, from sunrise tomorrow, you must fast. Then, before dusk, you will be taken to Meneghy - to a place we call *golghva a-whes,* a bath house of stone in which you sit before red hot rocks over which water is poured. This will cleanse your body of impurities. After this sweat-bath you bathe in the river. Your body is purified inside by your fast and outside by the bath.

'You are then dressed in clean, newly-made clothing, and taken to the great hill we call Skentoleth, the hill of wisdom, where a sacred circle stands. You will be placed in the stone circle and must remain there alone for three nights and two intervening days. You will eat nothing nor drink. You will have no weapons, no protection from the visitations of the Otherworld. You will be alone with your own thoughts. That is the first test; it is the greatest test of all, to face oneself. But Dryden, remember that, should you fail the test in any way, should you even leave the sacred circle before the test is ended, then such is your disgrace that you will have to leave Lan-Kern immediately and never return.'

Pryderi looked deeply into Dryden's eyes.

'But I have said before that you may refuse the test and live with us as a guest. Once started on the test there are only two endings - success or failure.'

Dryden stared for some moments at the walls of the hut, hung with tapestries of delicately woven wool.

'You said this was only the first test?'

'It is. The second test is that you be given weapons; a javelin, a sword, a knife, and, following a day of rest, on the next three nights and two intervening days, you must go alone into the forests and fend for yourself. While the first test demonstrates your spiritual strength, the second test demonstrates your physical prowess. On passing both tests it will be seen that you have the qualities to become a healer of the people.'

Dryden smiled broadly.

'The second test sounds more difficult than the first.'

'It would be wise to wait and see.'

'Have you undergone these tests, Pryderi?'

The young man nodded.

'Five years ago, before I was accepted as a postulant to the order of the *drewyth*, I had to show myself worthy.'

'Why did you become a *drewyth*, because of your father?'

Pryderi laughed.

'I notice that many aspects of our society seem to confuse you, Dryden. No man or woman in Lan-Kern does or is anything because of what their parents or relatives did or are.'

'Then why did you become a *drewyth*?' pressed Dryden.

The young man shrugged.

'Oh, it was foretold. At the time of my birth, my father Kesmur consulted Mabon. He traced my chart in the heavens and foretold that I would be a poet, a healer or a *drewyth*. I had passed from my mother's womb at the fifteenth hour of the day, the hour when Bel, the life force of the universe, dominates all other forces. Thus it seemed natural that I would grow in the service of Bel.

'It was predestined by two events in my infancy and these events later resolved me to the path I took. When I was five years of age there was a boy in Dynas Dor, a boy twice my age who became possessed by some spirits from the Otherworld, or so said the people of the town. The spirit took charge of the boy's limbs and caused him to jerk and dance about. He would also laugh and cry uncontrollably. Even when he slept the spirit would not leave his body and his body would twitch with strange dreams.'

Dryden dredged his memory.

'I have heard of such a condition. In my world we call it chorea or St. Vitus' dance.'

Pryderi paused, not understanding.

'After a time,' he continued, 'the parents of this unfortunate boy called Mabon to them and begged him to exercise his gift of healing. He ordered the boy to be confined in a prone position, neither moving nor sitting. Then he ordered that the boy was to be given meals of fish and fresh eggs in great profusion. Then six nights later Mabon went and cut young twigs and leaves from the sacred mistletoe, which we revere for its healing qualities; in fact our word for it, *ughelvar,* means 'all healing'. From these he made a beverage and administered it to the boy for a period of three moons. After the third moon the evil departed from the boy and he was well again.'

As a botanist Dryden was fully aware of the healing potential of mistletoe. It was good for epilepsy and hysteria.

Pryderi was continuing:

'Even at that young age I wanted to possess that great ability, that power to heal. Then came a second event which confirmed my path to the order of the *drewyth.* I was not much more than seven years of age. I lay asleep dreaming on my bed. In my dream I saw my father, Kesmur, but while I saw his features clearly, I perceived he had the body of a great bird. While I watched, his bird body spread out its great feathered wings and slowly my father tucked his head under one wing. For what seemed an eternity I stood watching until, with a sudden shake, Kesmur spread his wings and flew up, higher and higher until he disappeared as a black speck in the sky. I awoke screaming and so vividly did I recount my dream that Mabon was consulted.

141

'The old *drewyth* told my father that my dream was a premonition that he would fall ill but he would soon recover. And sure enough, even as Mabon said, within a few days Kesmur fell and cut his leg against a plough blade. The wound caused a fever and Mabon sat night and day by Kesmur's bedside. But even as he had foretold my father grew well again. Mabon looked kindly on me from that day, saying that I had a gift of foresight and was blessed by Bel.

'So when I was sixteen years old I went to start the education through which means I would become a *drewyth*. But, as I have told you, last year came the death of Peredur my brother and I left my lessons to take up the sword until Cador is defeated.'

There was a long silence.

'Enough of me, Dryden. I have been asked by Mabon and Kesmur to explain the testing to you and to ask you if you are prepared to undergo that testing.'

'I am,' replied Dryden without hesitation.

'Then from sunrise tomorrow you must not eat nor drink until I come to escort you to Meneghy.'

'I understand.'

Pryderi rose and made to leave, turning suddenly on the threshold and smiling: 'Success be yours.'

Then he was gone, leaving Dryden with a vague feeling of disquite. Was this testing more difficult, perhaps, than he had imagined?

CHAPTER TEN

Dryden felt a pang of unease as the black shape of Pryderi's figure disappeared down the hillside leaving him alone in the white moonlight of the ancient stone circle. For the next three nights and two intervening days he would have to remain alone and weaponless within the circle, neither eating nor drinking. When this was accomplished, the first test would be passed.

Deep within, he felt a superior amusement, the product of the upbringing he had received in the pseudo-sophisticated concrete city culture of his world. What sort of test was it, to sit on a hilltop alone for three nights and two days? Yet in spite of his amusement, he felt the unease which comes with loneliness in a strange place at dusk. Also, he was weaponless. He did not even have a fire with which to frighten away any prowling animals.

Dryden sighed deeply, feeling the coolness of the night air penetrating his lungs. But the air was fresh and invigorating, not cold. He decided to sit down, back resting against a small pillar stone, and try to sleep. Later he was surprised that he had fallen asleep so easily and into a fairly deep sleep for he was still dreaming when he woke.

It was still dark and the ground was damp with dew. The position of the moon in the sky had altered only slightly, so he guessed that he had not been asleep long. At the bottom of the hill, among the dark spruce and pines, he could hear the bark and snarl of wild animals and now and then a long, eerie howling. A wild dog? A wolf? Could wolves have returned to their former habitat in this country?

His heart lurched as he saw some black shadowy shapes slinking silently outside the boundaries of the stone circle.

Dryden came quickly to his fleet, clammy with sweat, and began to search frantically for any weapon with which to defend himself.

He succeeded in gathering a pile of stones and then sat back again, the pile before him, eyes darting hither and thither to seek out any threatening danger.

He suddenly realised that he was feeling pangs of hunger and thirst. From dawn that day he had fasted, according to the orders of Pryderi. In the afternoon, the young *drewyth* had come and escorted him to Meneghy. In the presence of Mabon he was led to a stone beehive hut which, according to Pryderi, was called the *golghva a-whes,* the sweat bath.

'By the blessings of Bel!' the old man had quavered, 'Prepare to receive the purification of your body!'

He had been stripped naked and led into the stone hut. A *drewyth* had entered and motioned him to sit against a wall. Then red hot stones were brought into the hut on metal carriers and placed one by one in a big pile in the centre, throwing out a tremendous heat that caused Dryden to start sweating immediately. The heat was so powerful that Dryden edged as far back against the wall as he could. Then the *drewyth* had shut the door of the hut and proceeded to pour cold water over the glowing rocks, so that the white steam rose, hissing and swirling, enveloping him and filling his lungs. He felt a momentary panic, felt the heat would surely kill him, felt his skin scorching, the eyelids stinging and burning.

Then, amidst the white burning vapour, he heard the *drewyth* chanting: 'Oh Bel, Creator! Bel whose life force is in all things. Bel whose essence lies in these holy rocks, breathe your white breath of purification over this man. Breathe the white breath of life so that he may be cleansed of all impurities; that he may be clean; that he may grow strong.' For half-an-hour Dryden sat with the sweat pouring off him, sat gasping in the hot vapours, while every now and then the stones were replaced with more red hot stones and more cold water was poured on them.

After half-an-hour, the *drewyth* materialised from the vapours and led Dryden out into the cool air and across to a tumbling stream.

'It is best that you plunge in quickly,' he advised.

Dryden screwed up his courage and flung himself in. The shock almost made him pass out as the cold waters met his hot flesh. Two *drewyth* were already in the stream to help him and he was led gasping and spluttering to the bank. There he was immediately towelled and given clean linen garments and a thick woollen cloak.

Old Mabon looked on in approval.

'The sweat bath has prepared you for the testing, for the ordeal of meditation and the meeting with yourself,' he said. 'Now you will go to the sacred hill of Skentoleth.'

It was Pryderi alone who had led Dryden across the dusk laden moorland towards one of the great hills that stood some miles from Meneghy. It took them some time to climb the steep hill, which was skirted by a small wood of spruce and pine. On top of this hill was a small stone circle into which Pryderi motioned Dryden. No word was exchanged between them for it was in violation of custom to hold conversation with a man following the ceremony of purification. And in that stone circle Pryderi had left Dryden, still lightheaded and dizzy, his skin tingling from the sweat bath.

The remembrance came clearly to Dryden as he sat in the darkness of the night, a nervous hand near his pile of stones, peering at the creeping shadows.

He must have dozed off, for the next thing he knew was the sound of breathing, heavy breathing, near him. With pounding heart he jumped to his feet, swaying in his weakened state. The long, low, grey figure of a wolf stood not more than ten feet away. The eyes were fixed upon him, yellow baleful eyes which seemed to gleam with an unholy aura in the soft moonlight. Panic gripped at Dryden. He grabbed a handful of stones and rushed towards the beast screaming, more in fright than with the purpose of scaring the creature. Two of his stones hit the animal and, with a yelp of fright, it turned and loped off into the night.

Shuddering nervously, Dryden returned to his stone pile, gathered more together, and then sank down by his rock, legs and arms close into his body, as if trying to emulate the womb position. It was not until dawn's grey fingers began to show that he felt his eyelids becoming heavy. His mouth was dry and his tongue felt several times too large for his mouth. There was a small pain in the pit of his stomach.

In the early morning light Dryden walked about the stone circle to see if there was anything edible growing there, mushrooms or some roots. There was nothing. It even crossed his mind to make his way, surreptitiously, down the hill to a small stream which he could now see in the distance. No. The people expected honesty in this testing and honesty they should have.

The sun came up with a warming glow, chasing away the cold and the fears of the night. By noon it had warmed the central stone, which lay altar-like on its side. Dryden stretched out on it, bathing in the life-giving rays. He closed his eyes and relaxed.

When he opened his eyes again it was cold and dark. The white crescent of the moon was just above the horizon. Dryden sat up in surprise. Could he have slept an entire day away? He felt stiff and cold. Strangely, however, the pangs of hunger were gone. Only the dry thickness of his thirst remained.

He made sure of the protection of his pile of stones and hunched himself up for warmth against the pillar stone again.

Sounds were soon reaching his ears, coming to him out of the darkness; the low cry of the wind, the whisper of the pines and spruce trees, animal sounds, rustling in the undergrowth far below him. There was the inquisitive hooting of an owl, and all the voices of nature orchestrated in the haunting chorus of life.

As he sat listening to them, Dryden suddenly became *aware*.

He became aware of what he was listening to, not just observing it as a background noise to his life. He became aware of every little animal sound, even the noise made by the grass blowing in the gentle night breeze. Slowly Dryden began to understand what he was experiencing; here, alone, on this wild hilltop, without food and without water, he was experiencing the rebirth of his senses; the natural senses which civilisation - or that which passed for civilisation - had destroyed.

He sat back and started to examine the rich prussian blue canopy of the sky, with its multitude of white sparkling dots and pin pricks, its glowing lights. He began to realise, for the first time, that the night sky was not merely blue-black with white dots - it held the entire spectrum of colour. Each star, each planet, was not merely a white glow in the heavens but, when examined closely, it was a plethora of colours; that red, this green; another orange...he stared up in wonderment. It was strange how he had not noticed such things before.

The flutter of wings suddenly distracted him and he glanced

146

up to see the cumbersome body of *ula,* the owl, go swooping by. He could hear the beat of its feathered wings against the air.

In amazement he realised how sharp his senses had become.

Gradually, sleep overcame him and he dozed. It was still black night when he awoke. For a second he wondered what had disturbed him.

Then he heard the low breathing sound. He started up. His heart began to pound like the quickening swing of a smith's hammer on the anvil. There, as on the previous night, stood the long, low grey shape of the wolf... again the eyes regarded him with their baleful yellow gleam. Its mouth was slightly open, showing ridges of sharp white teeth.

With a cry, Dryden sprang forward and threw several of his stones at the creature. Again, as on the previous night, the wolf yelped in pain as a missile struck home and it turned and sped down the hill.

For a long while Dryden sat staring into the darkness, his new found senses in total disarray. But deep within his mind a small thought was clamouring for attention. The thought grew until it burst into a multitude of questions.

For the second time the sun rose in the pale blue sky and Dryden relaxed under its warm rays. He no longer felt hungry nor did he feel the compelling thirst which had previously dominated his feelings. He felt himself gradually lulled into a deep sleep by the warmth of the sun's rays and the tranquillity which the warm blue light of the autumn day spread around him.

Time seemed to have no meaning for him any more and he was not surprised nor disturbed to see, when he opened his eyes again, that black night had once more descended. He found to his surprise that night-time no longer held any terror for him. His eyes, as he peered about, seemed as keen as they were in the light of day. What his eyes missed among the shadows, his ears made up for. He could discern the cracking of twigs under the bounding feet of a rabbit bent on some nocturnal journey. He could hear the rodents gnawing at their root diet. There was the cooing of birds as they settled on their branches for the night. He realised just how much the men of his world had shut themselves away from the natural world, had hidden themselves behind their barricades of civilisation - the concrete cities and technology with which they bent to murder nature. They had blinded themselves, deafened themselves and destroyed all sense of smell and touch. They had so far removed themselves from the beginning of their existence that they had become afraid of nature.

Fear!

Fear, unjustified and unreasoning, a nameless terror which paralyses judgement and progress. Man poisons his life with fear.

It was as if someone had opened a book before Dryden and in which he read the answers to questions long sought.

What had Pryderi said? 'Would it not be better to accept that this green hill is simply a green hill and nothing more?'

Why had he sat in fright upon this hill, his mind aquiver with all manner of self-induced fears; first fears of black shadows in the surrounding woods; fear of animals; fear of night. All were part of nature. All were creation. He should be at one with it for he was part of it and it was part of him.

He found a smile breaking over his lips.

Was this the testing? Of coming to meet oneself?

He settled back against the pillar stone and closed his eyes. He heard a slight rustle among the grasses nearby but this time his heart did not panic. He opened his eyes slowly. It was as if his mind was half-expecting to see it; yes, the same grey wolf stood not more than ten feet away. Its tongue lolled panting over the sharp white teeth, the eyes still regarded him, yellow and baleful.

There came a great calmness in Dryden. The wolf was a fellow creature; a part of the creation. He wanted nothing from it and it wanted nothing from him. There was no need to attack and destroy it. There was room for the wolf and for man in the great symphony of creation.

The animal gave a whine, as if realising his thoughts.

Dryden held out a hand.

Head hanging low and relaxed, the creature ambled towards him and nuzzled at the hand. The soft whine told Dryden that this creature had understood the change, perhaps it had been waiting for the change. Dryden felt amazement that he had never listened, truly listened, to the voices of animals before. He gently fondled the animal's head.

The wolf gave a low rumble in its throat, a rumble of contentment which, a short time ago Dryden - ensnared by a thousand years of civilisation - might have mistaken for a threatening growl. In delight, however, he now found those half-dead senses reawakened. And there, with the wolf curled up by his side - each creature seeking warmth from the other - Dryden fell into a deep and dreamless sleep.

When he awoke in the glow of the early morning sun the wolf was gone and the whole thing seemed to be a strange, mystical dream.

But one thing remained: the lesson he had learnt.

He stood up and became aware that Pryderi was climbing the hill towards him.

'Well, Dryden,' smiled the young man, 'you have passed the stipulated period on Skentoleth. Is it well?'

Dryden drew a deep breath.

'I seem to have had a strange experience...' he began.

Pryderi took him by the arm and Dryden began to realise how weak he was.

'Come; let us go back to Meneghy where you may eat and drink and tell us of your experience. Mabon can then interpret your visions.'

Two hours later Mabon sat cross-legged in his hut and smiled gently at Dryden. He had just finished recounting his experiences on Skentoleth. The old *drewyth* nodded slowly and turned to Pryderi.

'*Dasserghyans*,' he said simply.

Dryden knew it as the word for 'resurrection'.

'But what does it mean?' he asked plaintively.

'I think you know in your heart of hearts,' returned Mabon. 'It means that the testing was good, Dryden, or should we start to call you Yaghus the Healer now? Yes; the testing was good. You have started to become aware of reality, of your oneness with Nature. I emphasise the word 'started' for one experience does not produce a change but only the beginning of a change. Your path to Bel is not without difficulty. You will find Bel only when you cease to like and dislike, when you avoid picking and choosing. Acceptance is the first law - not choice. The flowers wither when we want to keep them and the weeds grow when we dislike to see them come. If you say that this is beautiful - then you must also say that that is ugly. If you say that this is good - then you must also say that that is evil.

Yet is it not all creation, is it not all nature and one under Bel?'

'I think I begin to understand,' said Dryden hesitantly.

The old man wagged a forefinger at Dryden.

'Begin to feel and not to think, like the eye that sees but cannot see itself.'

He waved a hand in dismissal.

CHAPTER ELEVEN

It was the custom at Dynas Dor to celebrate every occasion with a feast, for the people of Lan-Kern lost no opportunity to eat, drink and make merry. Kesmur himself opened his great hall to mark the passing of the first test by Dryden, who was now openly being called Yaghus the Healer by the people. There was only one person whose approbation Dryden sought. He met her on his way to the great feasting, early in the evening.

With a smile of happiness, Kigva approached him and gave him an impulsive hug which left Dryden awkward and tongue-tied.

'I am truly pleased for you, Dryden,' she began. 'No, I, too, shall call you Yaghus now. It is a fitting name. You have passed the worst of the two tests and I am happy.'

'There is still a second test, Kigva,' Dryden murmured, happy in her praise.

The girl pouted.

'Pouf! What is three nights and two days in the forests to you when you survived three weeks after your ship went down?'

The girl peered at him closely.

'You look unhappy, Yaghus. Walk with me and tell me what ails you.'

Dryden shuffled uncomfortably.

'It is the same problem, Kigva. Can't you feel it? Ever since I told you how I felt at the feast of Beltan, I have been turning on a rack. My emotions have grown in strength and not diminished. I love you.'

On impulse, Kigva leant forward and touched his cheek with her slender fingers and sighed softly.

'Poor Yaghus. But my feelings towards you have not changed. You are my dear friend and I feel for you as I feel towards my brother. Let us remain friends.'

Dryden saw a pleading in her grey eyes.

He shrugged, his face miserable.

'Come,' chided Kigva, 'you are nearly as bad as Teyrnon. He also demands this emotion called love and which, in honesty, I cannot say I feel. Teyrnon is my closest friend and companion and I am willing to share my life with him. Why must there be this mysticism called "love"?'

'Perhaps one day, Kigva,' replied Dryden, 'you will find that emotion.'

'Perhaps,' admitted the girl, frankly. 'But I have not done so yet. Surely friendship and tenderness are better emotions than a non-quantifiable mystery. Friendship is a communication between people, between equals, but love is too often an excuse for domination by one or other of two people. Love, I think, is often another word for selfishness.'

Dryden opened his mouth to protest when a figure moved in the gloom. Kigva screwed up her eyes and frowned.

'Teyrnon? Is that you?'

Dryden bit his lip as the tall figure of the warlord moved forward into the circle of light that flickered from the torches outside the great hall of Kesmur. The dark face of Teyrnon was pale and his eyes burned with a curious malignancy as they swept over Dryden. The girl smiled, oblivious to his looks.

'What were you doing in the gloom, Teyrnon,' she asked.

The face of the warlord relaxed a little as he forced a smile.

'The feast is ready. I came to find you.'

Kigva caught her arm through Teyrnon's.

'Ah yes; we must go in. But Teyrnon, you have not congratulated Yaghus yet.'

Teyrnon's smouldering eyes swept Dryden.

'Is the testing then ended?' he asked softly.

'No,' smiled the girl. 'There is only the test of the forest survival and Yaghus has already proved how adept he is at that. That will be no ordeal to him. We will soon be celebrating his adoption among our people.'

Teyrnon's mouth twisted in a sneer.

'Is there not a saying of the *drewyth* that one should not count the bushels of corn before the harvest is reaped? There are many dangers in the forest.'

'Oh, don't be silly, Teyrnon,' rebuked Kigva. 'The testing is a mere formality.'

But Dryden looked hard at the warlord, his senses uneasy. The dark, handsome face was suddenly bland. Dryden knew the man was aware of his feelings for Kigva and was jealous in spite of Kigva's decision to marry him. Ever since the feast of Beltan, whenever he had encountered Teyrnon - for it seemed the warlord went out of his way to avoid him - Dryden had experienced a deep antagonism. The fact that Teyrnon was away from Dynas Dor most of the time, guarding the settlements along Lan-Kern's eastern border, had diluted the emotional rift between them. And Dryden's own jealous feelings had distorted Teyrnon's reactions. It was not until that moment that Dryden, rising above his own feelings, suddenly felt the true weight of Teyrnon's hatred for him.

He demanded love from Kigva who was not able to give it; and in his hurt passion he had come to believe that Kigva must love Dryden and only out of duty maintained an earlier promise to marry him.

Dryden regarded the warlord through narrowed lids. A jealous man was dangerous and Dryden's own jealousy was dangerous enough.

At the door of the great hall of Kesmur Teyrnon stood aside to let Kigva pass through first. As she entered, he moved close to Dryden and gave him an artificial smile.

'I would have a care of the forests, Yaghus, as you walk among the trees alone. There are many dangerous animals abroad.'

Before Dryden could reply, Teyrnon had passed into the hall.

The meal was just ending. Mabon, the old *drewyth,* was on one of his rare visits to Dynas Dor and the young men were seizing the opportunity to question him as was the custom after a feast. It seemed that the young men wanted to hear Mabon's attitudes to Lan-Howlek. Nelferch-an-Gwargh had made several raids into Lan-Kern that summer, burning and pillaging along the eastern border. It was common talk among the people that Lan-Kern would eventually have to strike back at the scheming imperial ambitions of the witch queen. But the *drewyth* order taught pacifism, so Dryden had learnt, and insisted that must must live in peace with himself and his fellow man.

A young warrior was speaking.

'Surely, Mabon, it is right that we strike back at Nelferch and her jackals of Lan-Howlek? Surely it would be right to invade Lan-Howlek, strike back at them? Surely it would be just to exchange blow for blow?'

Mabon, seated next to Kesmur, looked at the young man. 'Is war just? Let me tell you a story handed down by the ancients. Before the Age of Destruction, it is said that there was an old religion which was widespread across the earth. This religion was supposed to teach pacifism. All the nations claimed a belief in it, so it is said. But that religion confused poverty of spirit with pacifism and taught the people that the greatest virtue was to be poor in spirit. When people are poor in spirit then the proud and haughty in spirit will oppress them. Legend has it that the majority of people who believed it virtuous to be poor in spirit were slaves to those who were proud and haughty. But eventually, inevitably, the proud and haughty destroyed one another.

'Poverty of spirit does not bring peace, my people,' the old man said. 'It is not virtue. Honesty of spirit, fullness of rightful purpose - these are virtues. I say, be true in spirit, be determined to resist and, as far as lies in your power, to prevent wrong. Do not stand quietly by when your neighbour is struck on the cheek. Neither be humble before the proud and haughty who would strike you on the cheek. If a proud and haughty man strikes you, take careful measures to prevent him striking you a second time. Do not court oppression, because they who court oppression share the crime of their oppressor.'

It was Teyrnon who asked the next question.

'Then do you say, Mabon, that we should invade Lan-Howlek and destroy Nelferch?'

The old *drewyth* gently shook his head.

'We should defend our people from Nelferch's invasions, but to enter Lan-Howlek would bring forth no solution. We would be a foreign army come to impose a solution on the people. It is for the people of Lan-Howlek to cast off the evil which enslaves them, not for us to impose solutions against their will. Though, if the people rise up and seek our aid it should not be denied them.'

Dryden was only half listening to these arguments for he sat watching Kigva and Teyrnon. Every now and then he glanced up and saw the angry black eyes of the warlord upon him. Then Mabon was smiling at him and speaking quietly, to him alone.

'A man must fight many superficial emotions before coming to the true path of Bel, Yaghus. Your path is easily charted. But your twin natures struggle against each other - that you will never lose. That is your eternal struggle. But that which makes it easy is its acceptance. I see the longing still within you. I see it burning and destructive. When you give up the longing, you will learn. The time has not yet come.'

'I don't understand,' Dryden sighed, a tone of exasperation making his voice sound querulous.

'No matter,' the other returned. 'You will not understand for a long, long time.' The old man abruptly closed his eyes and reached out a frail hand, lightly touching Dryden on the forehead.

'I see...a long, long journey. I see danger. The presence of death is your constant companion. You search for twin goals and will find only one. The search, the pursuit is the fulfillment of your longing. It is a long, long journey, indeed. But the longing will cease and you will come to know.'

Dryden opened his mouth but the old *drewyth* had turned and disappeared among the throng of guests.

CHAPTER TWELVE

The pale autumn sun shafted down through the tall trees of the forest, flickering and blinking on the leaves of the evergreens. Dryden moved cautiously along the dark woodland pathway, his feet crunching and rustling through the dank leafy carpet of the fallen verdage. He was feeling tense and nervous and his knuckles showed white where he gripped the shaft of his hunting spear. This was his second morning in the forest, the second morning of his testing in the dark woodlands.

The previous day had been almost pleasantly spent. The weather was not chill and the sun still cast a flow of warmth through the thick foliage. Pryderi and a number of enthusiastic warriors had ridden with him to the edge of the vast northern woodlands of Lan-Kern. The area, according to Pryderi, was the wildest part of the country and one which bordered to the east on the forbidding terrain of Lan-Howlek. During the three nights and the two intervening days in which Dryden had to fend for himself among the dark forest groves, he was supposed to make his way to a point in the west, marked by a giant menhir where Pryderi and his warriors would meet him; that was, if he were successful in charting his way through the forest.

Dryden had no qualms; he was aided by his experience of isolation in the forest following the sinking of the *Argo*. He found no difficulty in traversing the territory with ease, taking general bearings from the sun by day and making a more accurate reading by the night stars, which he could now read as well as any man of Lan-Kern.

It was during the first night that his nervousness began. In the early evening he became aware of a strange prickling at the base of his scalp, a sixth sense which told him that something or someone was watching him. He turned and peered into the gloom several times but saw nothing. The feeling continued and when he stopped to make camp for the night in a leafy glade by a waterfall, he felt a distressing dryness in his mouth and the conviction that he was being followed became steadfast in his mind.

It was a long time before sleep caught him; caught him in spite of his efforts to stay awake, so strong had his fear become. He dozed fitfully until the early hours and then awoke with a start as something bulky rustled in the bushes nearby.

He sprang to his feet, spear at the ready, only to curse his stupidity when a wild pig snorted out of the undergrowth and waddled to the nearby stream to drink.

Dryden breakfasted on some wild apples which grew nearby. Then he resumed his journey westwards, still tired and annoyed with himself for not resting well. For some hours he fought to shake off the feeling of being followed but towards midmorning it returned stronger than ever. Now as he moved through the dark avenues of the great forest the feeling grew stronger until he shied at every rustle of the undergrowth and started in a cold sweat at every alarmed bird which flew up from its resting place at his approach. His imagination began to conjure up all sorts of images as he pushed forward. But there was one image which kept recurring with increasing frequency. It was the dark, saturnine face of Teyrnon and his deep threatening voice: 'I would have a care of the forests, Yaghus, as you walk among the trees alone. There are many dangerous animals abroad.'

Dryden shuddered. A warning or a threat? For the most dangerous of all animals was undoubtedly man.

It had grown dark.

Dryden looked up and found himself passing through an area of forest where the tall pines and spruces grew so closely together that only a narrow pathway ran between them and their branches shielded all the light from the area. He began to hurry forward, only the scrape, scrape, scrape of his feet echoing in the strange hush of the forest. Even the slight wind through the treetops seemed to have died away and there was no birdsong to lighten the gloomy oppression.

He emerged abruptly into a small clearing and, rebuking himself for his momentary panic, paused to regain his breathing. A rustle in the leaves near his feet and the glimpse of the sleek grey shape of a viper twisting away startled him and caused him to jump sideways.

157

The jump saved his life.

A heavy war spear embedded itself into a tree nearby and quivered in the wood. Had Dryden not jumped aside, the spear would have transfixed him.

For three long seconds Dryden gazed at the weapon in stupefaction. Then a soft sound made him swing round.

At the far side of the clearing was the dark figure of Teyrnon, his face contorted in fury, his longsword drawn and his body in a half-crouch.

Dryden swallowed.

'So!' It was the only word which he could manage to utter: long, drawn-out but with a wealth of meaning.

Teyrnon moved forward slightly.

There was no need for Dryden to seek any explanation. The hate and jealousy were written in the dark warlord's face. Strangely, Dryden felt his own jealousy evaporate and a calmness filled him as he watched Teyrnon's approach. He made no move to defend himself.

'Put up your sword, Teyrnon,' he said, forcing a smile. 'There's no need for this.'

Teyrnon bared his teeth.

'You would rob me of Kigva!' he flung back bitterly. 'Even for daring to try to turn her from me you should die, *estrennek!*'

'Don't be foolish, Teyrnon. It's true I love Kigva. But she has free choice. She has chosen you, not me. Now, why should we fight?'

Teyrnon made a sudden run at Dryden, blade flashing. Dryden stepped backwards and brought up his spear, using it as a staff, and smacked up Teyrnon's swordhand, following it up by a swift blow with the blunt end of the spear shaft into Teyrnon's chest. It sent the warlord flying backwards to the ground. Dryden made no attempt to follow up his advantage but stood looking down at the furious warlord.

'Be calm, Teyrnon,' he urged. 'Be calm and consider. There's no reason for bloodshed.'

'My honour demands blood!' the man snarled, coming to his feet. 'Put down that spear, *estrennek*, and fight me equally - sword in hand.'

Dryden shook his head.

'No one has slighted your honour or Kigva's. Do you not know, man, that she prefers you, that she is to marry you?'

'I am not jealous, *estrennek*,' vowed Teyrnon. 'I fight for honour.'

He was closing in again, his sword blade making circular motions. Dryden backed away.

'Coward!' hissed Teyrnon. 'Fight me! I will not have you alive in Lan-Kern blinding Kigva's affections towards me. One of us will die today.'

For several seconds Dryden stared into the hate-filled eyes of his opponent and suddenly realised that all reason had departed from the man.

Teyrnon suddenly lunged forward.

Dryden stepped backward again, fell over a rotting branch and lost his grip on his spear. Teyrnon, with a cry of triumph, kicked the spear aside and slashed at Dryden's head. Dryden rolled out of reach of the flashing blade and scrambled to his feet, hauling his own weapon out of its scabbard.

He came to the *en garde* position and somewhere, deep in the back of his mind, he heard a voice crying, 'No; no, it is all wrong!'

But Teyrnon was rushing forward again, obviously thinking that he would win an easy victory. Pryderi had not told anyone of Dryden's agility with the longsword. Teyrnon aimed a series of powerful blows, but Dryden stood his ground and parried each vicious stroke. Teyrnon drew back, the fury undiminished, but an expression of surprise on his face.

The warlord moved in cautiously; still the offensive was his. Then he lunged forward again with a series of powerful blows. Dryden parried them with all his skill and knowledge, but such was the force of the last one that the heavy blade of Teyrnon slipped down the hilt of Dryden's sword and glanced off his forearm, leaving a gash.

The hurt of the wound reddened Dryden's mind with a surge of anger and at once his own hatred and jealousy of Teyrnon sprang forth. A savage demon overtook him and he turned on the warlord, blade swinging, until he drove the surprised man clear across the glade. Now the two men fell upon each other in deadly earnest, snorting and grunting like wild beasts as blades clashed in the gloom of the silent forest like the tolling of distant bells. Each man, as a swordsman, seemed equally matched and, in spite of half-an-hour of close combat, neither gained advantage nor broke through the guard of the other.

The pace was tiring, even for men in the peak of physical condition. The sweat poured freely from them. The strain began to show with their sluggish and heavy strokes. Several times, one or the other left his guard open as he delivered a blow but the other was too tired to spring to the advantage.

Then Teyrnon seemed to summon up hidden reserves of strength and made a swift onslaught which pushed Dryden back against a tree trunk. There was a sudden exchange of blows behind which was such strength that both weapons went flying from their numbed hands.

Teyrnon was the first to recover and sprang backwards, grabbing Dryden's discarded spear. He raised it to stomach level and, with a cry of fury, he rushed upon Dryden as he leant panting, exhausted, against the tree.

In a split second Dryden knew he faced inevitable death; saw the malignant triumph in Teyrnon's eyes; saw the sharp edge of the spear blade bearing down upon him, and knew he was lost. His eyes flickered shut as he prepared to receive the blow.

No blow came.

Instead there was a sharp cry of anguish and pain.

Dryden opened his eyes, puzzled.

Teyrnon was standing a few yards away, the spear fallen to the ground. The warlord's face was twisted in pain and fright. For a moment Dryden was at a loss to know the reason. Then he saw: from the fore-arm of the warlord protruded the shaft of an arrow.

It took a split second for Teyrnon to recover from the shock. He wrenched the arrow free and cried 'Lan-Howlek!' In one motion he swooped up his sword and started to run across the clearing. Halfway across he pulled a knife from his belt and, with his good hand, he turned and threw it at Dryden. Dryden was aware of him yelling: 'Let Lan-Howlek finish you if that does not!' And then his world exploded in stars.

A voice was calling him from far away.

He tried to open his eyes and blink. It took him several attempts but he finally succeeded.

A craggy man of thirty, with a shock of sandy yellow hair, and

160

piercing blue eyes, was bending over him, dabbing at his scalp with a damp piece of cloth. The man grinned as Dryden's eyes opened.

'Have a care, friend,' he said in concern, as Dryden attempted to sit up. 'That's a nasty blow you received. Lucky the knife that man threw turned in its flight and so only the pommel of the handle struck you.'

'Where is Teyrnon? Where is the man who threw the knife at me?' said Dryden, fighting back dizzyness.

'That was Teyrnon of Lan-Kern?'

The sandy-haired man made a face and brought forth a goatskin waterbag, offering Dryden a drink.

'He had a horse on the far side of the glade over there. Without stopping to see what had happened to you, he jumped on his horse and was away faster than *lughes* the lightning. He'll be safe in Dynas Dor by now.'

'What happened?' asked Dryden as he swallowed the refreshing cold water.

The sandy-haired man grinned.

'You know as much as I do, friend. I was walking through the forest when I heard the sound of swordfighting. When I came to the edge of the clearing I saw the dark man - Teyrnon of Lan-Kern you say? - I saw him about to run you through with a spear. As you were unarmed, it seemed the dark man was not obeying the honour code of single combat. So I loosed the arrow into his arm to stay his temper. That was when he ran, throwing his knife at you in afterthought.'

Dryden frowned.

'Why did Teyrnon cry "Lan-Howlek!" when he saw your arrow?'

The man roared with laughter.

'Because I am from Lan-Howlek.'

Dryden stared at the man before him. He was dressed simply, without a sword, but with a quiver of arrows and a bow strung on his back. He wore a few bracelets but his dress was simple. Was this one of the feared raiders of Nelferch-an-Gwargh? The man read his thoughts in his eyes and held up a hand, palm outwards.

'Have no fear, friend. My name is Cunobel of Lan-Howlek. I am a farmer. We are not all ogres, neither do we all support the witch queen and her evil grandson.'

'What are you doing in Lan-Kern?' asked Dryden, climbing to his feet. He instinctively felt he could trust the man.

'I am a farmer. I have cousins in Lan-Kern, for once our countries were one. I had bad news to bring my cousin. His sister, who returned to live in Lan-Howlek with her husband, was taken as a slave by Nelferch and now no-one knows her fate. Such things happen in my unfortunate land, man of Lan-Kern. But what name are you called?

Dryden smiled at being taken for a native of Lan-Kern.

'My name is Yaghus.'

The man, Cunobel, laughed. It seemed to come easily to him and his boisterous spirit shone through his merry eyes.

'A strange name for someone who needs healing himself,' he retorted, pointing to Dryden's cuts and bruises.

'Superficial wounds, that's all.'

'And why, Yaghus, have you incurred the enmity of the warlord of Lan-Kern?'

'A personal quarrel.'

'Ah,' smiled Cunobel. 'A woman.'

Dryden bit his lip but the frank, friendly face of the man was such that no offence could be taken.

'Well,' said the man from Lan-Howlek, swinging his waterbag on his back, 'nightfall will be here soon and I have a long way to go before then.'

Impulsively, Dryden held out his hand.

'Thank you, Cunobel. You saved my life and do not think that I am ungrateful. I will repay you one of these days. Safe journey through the forests to your home.'

Cunobel took his hand in a strong, open grasp.

'Bel prosper you. Yaghus. Should you ever need a friend in Lan-Howlek be sure to ask for Cunobel the farmer. Remember that we do not all support the ambitions of Nelferch-an-Gwargh.'

The man vanished through the trees and Dryden was alone once more.

Automatically he gathered his weapons, plus Teyrnon's knife and spear. But now Dryden was in a quandary as to what he should do. Would Teyrnon try to ambush him again? He did not think Teyrnon would lie in wait for him because the warlord had seemed sure that if his knife did not kill Dryden, there was a group of raiders from Lan-Howlek nearby who would finish the job. Teyrnon was probably racing towards Dynas Dor at that very moment thinking that Dryden was dead.

But what if Dryden turned up at Dynas Dor and accused Teyrnon, the warlord and maybe the next high chieftain, of attempting to slay him? They would ask the reason, and that reason sounded so weak. Jealousy over Kigva? But why? Teyrnon was the man whom Kigva was to marry so what cause was there for jealousy? And what would Kigva say? How would she react? More likely she would believe that Dryden had attempted the life of Teyrnon because of his own jealousy. Dryden did have some proof in his wounds and the knife and spear Teyrnon left in his flight. But was that enough?

It was a long time before he finally resolved to carry on with his task of making for the giant menhir, which marked the end of his trek through the forest, and where Pryderi said he would be waiting. Pryderi was a *drewyth* and would be able to advise him what was best to do.

Dryden pressed on through the forests and, as he analysed his feelings, he realised that his greatest fear was of Kigva not believing him: of Kigva being hurt. Jealousy was the greatest evil of all and the one which arouses the least pity in the person over whom it is caused. If Kigva felt that Dryden was accusing Teyrnon through his own jealousy of the warlord, she would come to hate him. If she accepted that Teyrnon had committed an act of treachery, an act against all the moral and ethical teachings of the society, then surely she would hate him. Whatever path, there was hatred at the end of it. With such thoughts swimming round his turbulent mind, Dryden moved slowly through the dark corridors of the forest.

It was towards midday on the appointed day when Dryden struggled up the hill towards the towering menhir and was met with excited cries by Pryderi who rode his horse down the precipitous hillside to meet him. The young man leapt from his horse and impulsively embraced Dryden, a smile on his eager face.

'Well, Yaghus, you have made it! I knew you would. Now you are truly a man of Lan-Kern and fit to tend to our people. The testing is over. Old Mabon said he read your success in the heavens and I...'

He faltered as he looked at Dryden's sombre features.

163

'This does not please you?'

'Yes, but...'

Dryden suddenly poured out the story of his encounter with Teyrnon and watched the young man's face change from amazement, to incredulity, to sheer disbelief and then to horror.

At the end of his recital, Dryden presented Teyrnon's weapons. Pryderi examined them, nodding slowly.

'They are Teyrnon's indeed. But there is no need for such evidence, the truth of what you say is written in your eyes.'

'But how can I ask anyone to believe me?'

'I believe, Yaghus,' returned Pryderi.

'But what should I do?'

'If Teyrnon has transgressed the code of our people, then he must be punished. You must rest,' he said, pointing to where he and some warriors, who called out a few congratulations to Dryden, had erected a small camp. 'I have brought a horse for you and tomorrow we will go to Meneghy and consult Mabon before going on to Dynas Dor.'

'I would rather leave Lan-Kern than bring hurt to Kigva,' Dryden said.

Pryderi raised his eyebrows.

'You would rather give her into the hands of a man who has proved himself unworthy? Teyrnon is not just another warrior, he is warlord of Lan-Kern, leader of all warriors in battle and in him reposes the collective honour of every fighting man. In him the people see the future *gwelhevyn,* the future high chieftain of Lan-Kern. How can he hold such a position when he has dishonoured the code of our people.'

Dryden hunched his shoulders and looked about him helplessly.

'I do not know, Pryderi. But I am partisan in this quarrel. I told Kigva that I loved her. She said she did not love me but was to marry Teyrnon. Wouldn't she construe my accusation as an attempt to remove Teyrnon from her favour for my own ends?'

Pryderi's brow creased in an angry frown.

'That is a risk that you should not consider. Your concern is simply a selfish one, Yaghus. You want your actions to be seen by Kigva in the best light. Yet, if you speak the truth you should not worry how your actions are interpreted.' Pryderi's face softened. 'My sister is no fool.'

164

'I would rather remain silent and forget what happened in the forest than cause her pain,' vowed Dryden.

'I know you love my sister, Yaghus,' smiled Pryderi. 'But if you remain silent, what is Teyrnon going to do? If his jealousy is so deep, and rage moves him so strongly, he will not stop until one or other of you is destroyed. No, we shall consult Mabon.'

Old Mabon's face registered no surprise as Dryden, with Pryderi's prompting, brought forth the story.

The old man sighed.

'The heavens do not lie,' he muttered when Dryden had finished. 'Much was written in Teyrnon's face when he returned this way last night. There was an anger and rage in his soul. He rides the whirlwind to self-destruction. He has gone on to Dynas Dor but he must be recalled to answer for his transgressions before the court of the *drewyth* of Meneghy. I shall summon him. The *drewyth* will decide how best he should be dealt with. That is now of no concern to you, Yaghus.'

'No concern of mine?' said Dryden in astonishment. 'How can you say that, Mabon, when if it were not for me he would not have given way to his rage? In fact, there would have been no rage to give way to. Surely the cause is mine and mine alone?'

The old man raised a forefinger.

'Yaghus, there is a lot you must come to know about the world and yourself, especially how to quieten your own ego. When a tree is struck by lightning and falls, killing the man sheltering beneath, does it lament: 'If it were not for me?' Does the lightning say: 'If it were not for me?' Does the turbulent atmosphere, which produced the lightning, cry: 'If it were not for me?' No, Yaghus, we are all part of nature, we are at one with nature, and all our actions are interdependent. No action is isolated. Return now to Dynas Dor and rest. You cannot halt the vibrations of the symphony of life.'

When they reached Dynas Dor they found most of the warriors had left that morning under the command of Teyrnon. Apparently an armed force from Lan-Howlek had entered the country to the south and was raiding and burning settlements near the border in spite of the autumn season being well advanced. It was said that Teyrnon, in hastening back to Dynas Dor, had been set upon by some raiders and wounded slightly in the forearm by one of their arrows. He had managed to escape and had insisted on leading his warriors to meet the new threat.

In spite of the crisis of the new invasion by Nelferch's warriors, who were under the personal command of the witch queen's grandson, Cador, Kesmur insisted on holding a feast to celebrate Dryden's adoption as a citizen and healer of Lan-Kern under his now commonly used name of Yaghus. Kigva was also there to congratulate him but Dryden, in his embarrassment, went out of his way to avoid her and when forced to speak to her did so in monosyllables until the girl retired with hurt in her eyes, not understanding.

For Dryden the days began to pass painfully slowly.

Pryderi tried to persuade him to reveal what had happened to his sister but Dryden stubbornly refused. At that moment Teyrnon was still a hero in the eyes of the people and only Mabon shared the dark secret with Pryderi and Dryden.

'Yaghus,' urged an exasperated Pryderi, after Kigva had passed them by, and scowlingly refused to acknowledge Dryden, reacting to his treatment of her in order to disguise her hurt. 'Yaghus, I appreciate your concern for my sister's feelings. But you would be the last to want her to live under a fiction.'

Dryden squared his jaw stubbornly.

'There is nothing to be done until Teyrnon returns from the south and goes before Mabon to answer for his actions.'

CHAPTER THIRTEEN

It was nearly two weeks before Dryden learnt that Teyrnon had returned from the border conflict and had gone to Meneghy at the direct summons of Mabon. It had been two weeks of hell for Dryden. He had encountered Kigva on three occasions and each time he had dropped his eyes before her and each time, misinterpreting his actions, she had walked by, head held high, with a smile of disdain on her pretty features. The rest of the time she took every opportunity to spend time away from Dynas Dor in order to avoid him. Dryden's wretchedness became unbearable but how could he speak, knowing what he knew of Teyrnon, the man she was to marry?

In moods of black depression, Dryden passed the days. Under Pryderi's guidance, he had obtained a hut in the township and set up a small practice under the shadow of the great hillfort, leaving the comfortable guest rooms for the first time in over a year. Now he could begin to earn his keep as a member of the community, following the art of healing.

But most of the time, in that black mood of his, Dryden simply sat by the sea shore, gazing moodily at the pounding surf breaking on the sands, wishing half-heartedly that another *Argo* would come and transport him back to his world. He tried, mostly unsuccessfully because of his lack of concentration, to hunt for herbs and plants with which to build a stock for his practice. But his mind was not on such matters. The faces of Kigva and Teyrnon revolved before his eyes until he wanted to raise his hands to his head and run - he did not much care in which direction.

A few mothers brought him ailing children; children with cuts or bruises that were easily cured. Once he was asked to examine a child with a bronchitic cough. He soothed it with wild garlic. But nothing affected him. He hardly saw his patients and moved as if in a dream.

It was Pryderi who jolted him back into reality.

Dryden was standing by the door of his hut watching a column of warriors riding up to the gates of Dynas Dor.

'Those are Teyrnon's men returning from the border,' said the young *drewyth*.

Dryden started and his eyes narrowed as he examined each figure for the familiar black-clad warrior.

'No,' said Pryderi, seeing what was in his mind. 'Teyrnon is not with them. He has gone to Meneghy to answer Mabon.

'Come, Yaghus,' chided Pryderi. 'Now is not the time for gloom. Soon the weight of responsibility will pass from your shoulders. Kigva has already confessed to me how hurt she has been by your treatment of her, how you ignore her. She thinks it is because she rejected your vow of love and that you retaliate to hurt her. Soon she will come to know how little Teyrnon loved her.'

Dryden scowled.

'On the contrary, Pryderi. Teyrnon was so consumed by his love for Kigva that he saw me as a threat. How can you say he did not love her?'

'Yaghus,' said the young man, gently, 'you will learn wisdom one day. Jealousy is the disease which slays love while pretending to keep love alive. In jealousy, my friend, there is more self-love than love. Teyrnon is concerned only for his own welfare and not for Kigva's happiness.'

Pryderi turned and started up the street. After two steps he paused.

'Come and have the midday meal with me at Dynas Dor,' he said. 'I am eating with the warriors and there might be news of what is happening with Lan-Howlek.'

With a smile and wave, Pryderi was gone.

Much to his surprise Dryden found himself seated in the great hall of Kesmur at midday, sharing a meal with Pryderi and the returned warriors. Dryden had resolved not to go up to the fortress lest he meet Kigva but he had learnt that Kigva had ridden out on a journey the evening before. Even Kesmur and the major part of his warriors were on a visit to the far west. Only Pryderi and a few men remained in attendance.

Apparently, so Dryden was informed, the two weeks' campaigning

168

in the south of the country had been exhausting. There had been several skirmishes with raiders from Lan-Howlek but there had been no sign of the large force commanded by Cador which constantly eluded them.

They had come across several villages and settlements burning but always the grandson of the witch queen managed to escape from Teyrnon's force in time. It was thought that the men of Lan-Howlek had taken many prisoners.

'They have never raided so deep nor for such a sustained campaign in our territory before,' said Gugann, who was Teyrnon's second-in-command. 'They are getting too ambitious, these jackals of the witch queen. Kesmur must give us leave to conduct a punitive raid into Lan-Howlek, perhaps against Nelferch's capital itself. If we do not strike back we will seem weak and insignificant in her eyes. Her warriors will raid us with greater forces.'

'Who is protecting the southern villages now?' asked Dryden, reluctantly interested in the problem.

'Each man stands ready to defend his own homestead,' replied Gugann. 'We spent five days without any sign of Cador's force and so concluded that he had withdrawn across the great river into Lan-Howlek again. Teyrnon commanded us to return here for a rest. But I hear he means to ask Kesmur to give him leave to raise all the tribes against Nelferch.'

Pryderi frowned.

'I say Mabon is right,' he said, 'it is no answer to invade Lan-Howlek and have every man of Lan-Howlek, aye, and women and children too, turned against us. Rather we should find out if there is any in Lan-Howlek who is prepared to lead a rising against her.'

'Bah!' grunted Gugann. 'Nelferch has been ruler of Lan-Howlek for ten years. Every insurrection against her authority has been crushed as a man might crush a plum in one hand. All those who opposed her are long dead and the rest no longer have the will or the desire to be rid of her.'

Some of the warriors muttered agreement.

Another lean warrior growled: 'Well, if Mabon has summoned Teyrnon to Meneghy in order to thwart his asking Kesmur to raise the tribes, then he will not prevail. We are behind Teyrnon to a man.'

169

Dryden caught Pryderi's eyes and stirred uncomfortably.

'Well,' sighed Pryderi, 'the decision is up to the assembly of the tribal chieftains ...'

A commotion caused them to look towards the door.

A mud streaked warrior stumbled in. He still had his sword drawn and bloodied and his face was streaked black with drying blood from a cut on the side of his head. He took a few hesitant steps towards the banquet table and then fell headlong.

Dryden was on his feet before the others and revived the man with a goblet of wine.

The wounded man coughed and blinked at the surrounding faces.

'It is Bucca of the guard at Meneghy,' whispered Gugann. 'What does it mean?'

The warrior tried to raise himself but fell back, his wandering eyes searching out Pryderi.

'Meneghy,' he whispered. 'Meneghy!'

Pryderi bent forward.

'Cador and his raiders.' whispered the man. 'They are sacking Meneghy!'

Pryderi's face went white.

'Cador has dared to attack the sanctuary of Bel?' he gasped in disbelief.

'Even now it is burning.'

'I cannot believe it, even of Cador and the men of Lan-Howlek.'

'The blood of the *drewyth* and a score of warriors give evidence to what I say,' gasped the man.

'What of *An Kevryn*,' pressed Pryderi in a hollow voice.

'I do not know, Pryderi,' replied the warrier. 'I was sent by Mabon. As I rode away, I think the men of Lan-Howlek fought their way through to the Inner Circle.'

Suddenly the man gasped and passed out with the pain of his wounds.

Already Gugann and his warriors were outside shouting for their weapons and horses.

Pryderi spared no more time for the wounded man but, snatching his longsword and shield, he was after Gugann. Dryden waved to a servant to look after the unconscious man and seized a sword and shield from a pile near the doorway and was hurrying after Pryderi.

He, too, realised the enormity of Cador's deed in daring to strike at the sacred temple of Bel, whose religion was supposedly supported by the men of Lan-Howlek as well as Lan-Kern. He found a horse in the yard at Dynas Dor and was soon speeding after the flying column of warriors led by a grim Pryderi.

It was only after a few miles that Pryderi suddenly realised that Dryden was riding in their midst.

'Yaghus!' he cried. 'This is no place for a healer. There will be bloody fighting ahead.'

Dryden grinned into the teeth of the wind.

'If there is bloody fighting ahead, Pryderi, then all the more need for a healer.'

The column of horsemen plunged on across the bleak moorland. Already, from the distant hills, their eyes could make out a thick column of smoke rising upwards into the sky.

'Meneghy!' breathed Pryderi. 'Let us hope *An Kevryn* is safe!'

Dryden realised how important it was to the *drewyth* to retain the mysterious black box, though none knew what it contained. It was of central importance to their philosophy and it contained for them a mysterious symbolism of life and death, of creation and ultimate destruction.

It was an hour before the lathered horses of the warriors thundered up to the great complex of stone circles. The huts where the *drewyth* lived were a mass of roaring flames. Bodies littered the scorched ground. Even some of the great menhirs had been pushed over and were smoke blackened. Dryden's quick kaleidoscopic impression was one of black smoke, yellow flame and red blood.

Before the gateway which led into the inner circle of Meneghy lay the body of a warrior, his clothes wet with blood. A red stained sword and shield still lay in his fierce grasp. His cloak spread around him like an awaiting burial shroud. The dark, black hair blew gently in the breeze across his hardened features. Dryden felt an odd feeling in the pit of his stomach as he gazed down on the lifeless features of Teyrnon, the warlord of Lan-Kern.

He and Pryderi slid off their horses and looked down at the dead man.

'Perhaps it is as well,' muttered Dryden. 'He died defending Meneghy from barbarians. His honour will not be besmirched now.

171

His motives remain unquestioned. I hope he finds peace in the Otherworld. He died a good death.'

'No death is a good one, Yaghus,' rebuked Pryderi, gazing down. 'But, as you say, perhaps this is for the best. May he be reborn as he would wish to live.'

Dryden cleared his throad and nodded.

It was strange, he felt, looking down at the figure of Teyrnon. In death he felt a warmth of comradeship for the man that had been denied him in life. Ah, but for that littleness of soul which is jealousy. As iron is eaten away by rust, so the jealous are consumed by their own passion.

Pryderi had already moved on towards the cairn. It was shattered. He searched within and around it, examining a body here and there, while the rest of the warriors sat on the horses, thin lipped and angry. Pryderi finally turned towards them.

'They have taken it...taken *An Kevryn*,' he said slowly.

There was an angry growl from the warriors.

The young man started to stride back to his horse. A cry of pain caused him and Dryden to turn round. A body was stirring behind a menhir. Dryden was the first to reach it. It was Mabon. His eyes were weak and watery now, the vitality gone. He caught sight of Dryden and tried to force a smile.

'Ah, Yaghus, I knew you would come but, I fear, you have come too late to heal me.'

He coughed blood.

Dryden examined the sword wounds in the man's chest, glanced at Pryderi and shook his head.

'It is written...' the old man began to speak. 'You will be the one...the seeker....find *An Kevryn*. It is your destiny. Then the longing will die.

He fell back exhausted for a moment and then his eyes fluttered open again.

'Pryderi? Is that you?'

'I am here, Mabon.'

'Cador and the raiders - they have taken Kigva.'

Dryden went cold. Pryderi's face was a mask of horror.

'Kigva? How?'

The old man forced himself to speak with a tremendous effort.

'She came last night. She learnt that Teyrnon was summoned here and came to find out why. They attacked at dawn...the raiders...many are prisoners...they took her...'

'Which way, Mabon?' said Dryden quietly. 'Which way have they gone?'

'Across the moorland...to the north-east...'

The old *drewyth* suddenly gave a cry of agony and fell backwards. Dryden felt for the heart.

He did not have to say anything.

'Bel speed his journey,' said Pryderi.

Then he was springing towards his horse closely followed by Dryden.

The column of warriors spurred after them. How long they rode, Dryden was not certain. The pace was fierce and Pryderi made no effort to slow it, despite the wheezing of their mounts and the lather flecking from their horses' muzzles. At one point they saw a white-haired farmer hiding in a field, his hayricks still ablaze, and when he saw they were men of Lan-Kern he ran forward crying to them that the raiders were only half-an-hour on the road before them and that they had twenty or more prisoners to slow them down.

Pryderi acknowledged the information with a wave of his sword, not pausing.

Within the hour the column of warriors crested a rise looking out on a long flat stretch of moorland. Across the moor some twenty or so figures were being pushed along by half a dozen men on horseback. Even from this distance, they could see that each person, male and female, was bound on a long rope which was secured to one of the horses. So strong was their rage that it did not occur to anyone until later that it was strange that there were only half a dozen raiders with the prisoners.

Pryderi had already drawn his sword and, with a wild yell of hate, spurred his mount forward. As one, Dryden and the rest of the warriors followed, swooping down on their enemies screaming meaningless war cries. Surprisingly, the warriors of Lan-Howlek made no motion to flee, outnumbered as they were. Instead, their leader motioned his men to herd their captives into a close circle and then sat quietly awaiting the onslaught of Pryderi's men.

It was Dryden who tried to yell a warning to Pryderi but the young man, overcome with battle fever, paid no heed nor did his men listen to Dryden's cries of alarm. Their own battle cries drowned out Dryden's voice.

Just before the raiders and their prisoners lay a narrow but deep depression in the moorland, perhaps it had been the pathway of a former stream long dried up. It ran in such a way that a man could ride almost on top of it before stumbling into it.

The leader of the raiders had been clever.

Suddenly from the depression, there leapt forth at least a hundred savage-faced warriors, yelling triumphantly as they urged their mounts towards Pryderi's thirty warriors. Before the men of Lan-Kern could see their danger they were engaged and surrounded by the flashing longswords of their enemies.

Dryden, who was slightly behind them in the charge, had seen the sun flashing on the blade of a hidden sword just a moment before. He gripped his longsword firmly and spurred into the melee. Two of the enemy immediately rode towards him.

He wheeled his horse on its haunches. He must try not to let his assailants get on both sides of him. One man closed in making hacking sweeps of his blade. Dryden found it easy, so very easy, to parry. The man had obviously not learnt to use his weapon correctly and Dryden found himself smiling. How ironic it was that he had taken up fencing as an exercise by which to keep fit in his old, polluted world and that art now kept him alive in this one.

Like playing a chess game, the old ability took over in Dryden's mind. He measured the moves, counter-moves, until within three calculated strokes Dryden had slashed the man's sword-arm and rendered him incapable of further battle.

He had barely time to register satisfaction when the second man came at him. A third warrior attacked from the other side. Dryden was grateful for the cumbersome shield and used it to parry the third man's rain of blows while he parried the other man with his sword. Again it seemed that the warriors of Lan-Howlek were not great swordsmen and Dryden was astonished by the comparative ease with which he despatched his second opponent. In the turmoil of the fight, the third warrior was swept away.

Dryden gave a quick glance around and saw that things were not going well for the rest of Pryderi's men. Almost half their number lay on the ground stained red with the results of the conflict. Pryderi himself, blood streaming from a gash in his cheek, was striving to instil some discipline into his warriors. But to the warriors of Lan-Kern war was a matter of individual heroism, of hot-blooded courage which was symbolized by their idealisation of single combat. Pryderi had told Dryden that in the olden days, when tribes fought against tribes, the hero of one tribe would challenge the hero of another to settle the whole dispute by means of single combat. The result of that combat would settle the entire dispute. It seemed to Dryden, if there had to be warfare, then it was infinitely more civilised to settle disputes in such a fashion than by cold, calculated, disciplined armies hewing down whole populations. At the same time, Dryden wished the high individualism of the warriors would be a little more disciplined, for a concerted attack might have carried the day even against the overwhelming numbers of Lan-Howlek's forces.

The outcome was a forgone conclusion. Dryden saw another half-dozen warriors of Lan-Kern fall within the next fifteen minutes and the remaining half dozen or so men were now hard pressed.

An idea suddenly came into his mind.

He edged his horse towards Pryderi.

The young man gave him a fierce grin.

'A futile death, Yaghus!' he yelled above the din of battle.

'No, Pryderi. It does not have to be so,' he yelled back, clenching his teeth as an enemy warrior came swinging at him. 'Try to disengage, Pryderi, and ride towards Dynas Dor. One man might make it while the others cover him. Get to Kesmur.'

Pryderi swore.

'Leave my men? Never!'

'Save your men! Ride to Kesmur! Raise an army! Raise an army and follow us to Lan-Howlek! We are doomed this way. But if you escape, we can cover you. Then you can raise the tribesmen of Lan-Kern to follow us. Remember there is more to consider than dying because it is the noble thing to do - there is the rescue of Kigva and *An Kevryn.*'

A light of understanding spread over Pryderi's features.

'You are wise, Yaghus. It is the only way. Explain it to the men.'

'We will cover you,' cried Dryden. 'Ride! Pryderi, Ride!'

Pryderi, seizing his opportunity, wheeled his horse and, crouching low over its neck, spurred away from the battle throng.

One man tried to follow but Dryden cut him from the saddle.

The other warriors of Lan-Howlek, not knowing the identity of the fugitive, let him go, clearly thinking he was a warrior deserting his comrades. Some of the remaining warriors of Lan-Kern looked startled at the fleeing figure of Pryderi. One or two looked disgusted and threw down their weapons, feeling themselves betrayed.

Now there were but four men left.

'We must cover Pryderi's escape,' hissed Dryden, as the four men closed up to face the horde of Lan-Howlek. 'He's gone to seek out Kesmur and raise the tribes.'

No further words were wasted.

Dryden felt no fear. He felt no regret either. If Kigva did not love him at least he could perish in an attempt to rescue her. The only thing he felt was a longing because he would never see her face again.

He was aware of a tall, sallow warrior riding forward with his hand upraised. The man had an angular, swarthy face with a thin, cruel mouth and black eyes. He could have been Teyrnon's brother.

'Warriors of Lan-Kern,' he began, his voice oily and untrustworthy. 'Warriors of Lan-Kern, you have fought well. But you are outnumbered. We are nearly one hundred to your four. Surrender and let us waste no further time in bloodshed.'

Gugann edged his horse forward.

'I recognise you Cador of Lan-Howlek. I am Gugann of the Red Sword. I have no understanding of this word "surrender". I have slain a score of such scum as I see before me. I do not doubt that I shall slay as many more before I start my journey to the Otherworld. But is there one man among them who would dare meet me in single combat to decide whether we go free or die? If there is, let him come forward!'

A dozen or so angry voices were raised in response to Gugann's challenge but the sallow faced man stayed them.

'Warriors of Lan-Kern, we have no time for games. Surrender or die. The choice is yours.'

Gugann gasped.

'By the light of Bel! Do you deny the right of single combat?'

'Right?' sneered Cador. 'Dead men have no rights.'

176

'Then it is better to be reborn clean in the Otherworld than live dishonoured in this one,' snarled Gugann. 'Remember your dishonour, Cador. To deny a man the right to single combat is to dishonour yourself. May that right be denied you when you call upon it and may that day be soon.'

Then, without further words, he gave a shrill battle cry and spurred his horse into the midst of the warriors of Lan-Howlek, striking out left and right.

Within a moment it was all over. The enemy warriors started to close on the others, riding their horses over Gugann's pierced body.

Dryden saw another man go down near him and then he was beset by several warriors. He parried and lunged with his sword until he lost all sense of time and place, fighting like an automaton, a red film of angry desperation before his eyes. How many he killed he did not know. All he knew was that his skills could not protect him for ever.

The end came with a sudden pain in the back of his head, the world exploded in vivid reds, yellows and flashing, fizzing colours. Then came a terrible, lonely blackness.

PART THREE
The Witch Queen

Peace between people, between communities and between states, is a great and worthy objective; peace is the only condition for the ultimate survival of mankind. But between peace and slavery lies a great divide. Is it not better to live a crowded hour of conflict in freedom than a century in peaceful servitude?

An Lyver Myr a Lan-Kern
The Great Book of Lan-Kern

CHAPTER ONE

Dryden recovered consciousness. He felt a sharp pricking in his arm and tried several times to open his eyes and focus on the cause of his discomfiture. A giant red-haired warrior was standing astride him poking at him with his sword tip. Dryden tried to struggle up but found that his hands had been securely bound in front of him. The red-haired warrior grinned and, sheathing his sword, he lifted Dryden to his feet as easily as if he had been a baby.

Dryden stood for a moment, swaying and trying to regain control of his balance. He became aware that a man sat looking down on him from the back of a horse. He pulled at the ropes that bound his hands and swore under his breath. Already he felt his hands cold and numb as the ropes bit into his flesh, restricting the circulation of the blood. The man on horseback regarded him unsympathetically, sneering at his situation.

'Well, little warrior of Lan-Kern,' he drawled in a nasal voice, 'you have led my men a pretty dance. You slew five of them before they could bring you down.'

Dryden raised his eyes and focussed on the man for the first time. It was the thin, sallow-faced man who had called upon them to surrender. His features were swarthy and ill-nourished. His eyes were pale - they could equally have been blue or grey. His hair was black and greasy. His lips were thin and cruel and a permanent sneer seemed to disfigure them into a twisting line. It seemed to Dryden that he was the very stuff of which villains were made. He tried hard to remember the name by which Gugann had called the man before he perished.

'Speak, you cur!' The burly red-haired warrior at his side brought the flat of his short sword across Dryden's shoulders, causing him to wince and stagger forward a step. 'Speak when you are addressed by Cador of Lan-Howlek!'

Dryden's eyes narrowed. Now he remembered. This was the notorious grandson of Nelferch the Witch Queen.

'So?' breathed Cador, as he watched Dryden's reaction. 'You have heard the name Cador of Lan-Howlek?'

Dryden hesitated as he felt the warrior by his side move. He was surely dead already so what mattered if he spoke truly?

'Yes,' he replied shortly. 'As I have heard of *logosen vras* - the rat; as I have heard of *lowarn* - the fox and as I have heard of *bargos* - the buzzard, I, also, have heard of Cador.'

The blow from the red haired warrior was sharp and it knocked Dryden full length on the ground.

'Shall I finish this insolent one, Cador?' Dryden heard the warrior snarl.

'Not yet,' Cador hissed. 'He must suffer for his insults. Take him and put him with the others. When we get to Lan-Howlek he will provide us with some entertainment and be a salutory warning to others that the will of Nelferch and Cador must be obeyed.'

The warrior pulled Dryden roughly to his feet. As he did so, the gaunt figure of Cador tugged his horse in a tight turn and spurred away. For a brief moment Dryden saw the small black box strapped to Cador's saddle: the small black box known as *An Kevryn* - The Mystery! Then the warrior was pushing Dryden across the moorland to where several Lan-Howlek warriors were busy securing a group of prisoners. Seven of Pryderi's warriors had been captured or surrendered during the fight and these were placed with the twenty or twenty-five prisoners that Cador had taken at Meneghy. They were all being secured on a long rope.

'Well, man of Lan-Kern, you are in for an agonising journey to the Otherworld,' sneered the red-haired warrior.

Dryden did not reply.

The warrior continued to taunt him for a while as he bound him securely to the lead rope, one end of which was secured to the pommel of a horse. Dryden recognised several of his fellow prisoners but they did not speak, there was sorrow in their eyes as they engrossed themselves in their own tragic fate.

'Yaghus!'

Dryden turned at the feminine intake of breath.

The pale face of Kigva was staring at him with red rimmed eyes.

She was bound to the rope about five feet behind him.

Dryden's heart lurched as he saw her bloodstained and torn clothing.

'Kigva! Are you hurt?'

The girl shook her head.

'A few cuts and bruises, that is all. But tell me, Yaghus, why did my brother, Pryderi, flee from the conflict? I rejoice that he is safe, but to live a coward?'

There was a catch in her throat.

'Pryderi is no coward!' averred Dryden. 'It was by design he left the battle while we covered him.' He lowered his voice. 'He has gone to seek out Kesmur, to raise the tribes so that a rescue may be made.'

Kigva lowered her head and smiled gently.

'I am content that his honour is safe.'

Dryden looked at her awkwardly.

'We rode through Meneghy...' he began.

Kigva nodded.

'I know; Teyrnon was slain before my eyes.'

There was an uncomfortable pause.

'I know,' the girl suddenly said, looking straight into Dryden's eyes. 'I was there when Mabon accused him and Teyrnon did not deny what happened. He tried to justify it by reason of the love he held for me. Love!' she laughed scornfully. 'Why is it that people think that all sins are justified in the name of this mysterious emotion - malice, deceit, treachery, perjury, indeed, any impiety in justification of which a person may say "I did it for love" and he will be forgiven.'

There was a suppressed anger in her voice.

'We shall mention that subject no more,' the girl went on firmly. 'At least I understand why you felt unable to speak to me. I am sorry I reacted as I did.'

Dryden stood in silence.

'Well,' said the girl, forcing a smile. 'At least we are still alive and we should be thankful for that much.'

There was an abrupt shouting and the warrior on horseback moved forward, hauling at the rope on which the prisoners were attached, catching a few of them unawares. Dryden was pulled forward with the rest and so unable to look back to Kigva.

181

'Are you all right, Kigva?' he called.

A warrior of Lan-Kern who was bound to the rope just in front of Dryden twisted his head round awkwardly and frowned.

'Hush, man!' he hissed. 'Have a care! Do you want to let Cador know that he has Kesmur's daughter as his hostage?'

Dryden bit his tongue as he realised the implication.

'Do not worry about me,' came Kigva's voice from behind his shoulder.

They needed all their breath for the march during the next three hours, as they stumbled and were pulled along behind the warrior on horseback. A group of other raiders formed outriders around the column of prisoners but the main body of Cador's men had apparently ridden on ahead. Dryden observed from the sun, which was now setting, that they were being marched in an easterly direction, presumably towards the border. Their path lay along stony tracks, over great empty plains whose only covering was thorny black-green gorse and here and there a lighter shade of heather, tinged with pink blooms. The only relief to this desolate landscape was the occasional grey granite rock which would suddenly thrust itself up out of the earth.

As gloom settled across the moorland, the raiders halted against a group of towering boulders and pushed their captives into a circle. Demands for food were met with laughter and a kick or cuff to the head. But two of the men did bring three buckets of water which they distributed sparsely to the prisoners.

'You will not perish for lack of two or three days food,' sneered the red-haired warrior. 'You will eat when you reach Lan-Howlek and not before. Now rest you sons and daughters of lepers. You will be on the march before sun-up.'

Dryden managed to seat himself next to Kigva on the damp earth, huddled up to the granite rocks for protection against the chill night breeze which was beginning to whisper its way through the heather-strewn moorland. On Kigva's other side sat the warrior who had warned Dryden to be silent about Kigva's identity.

'I am called Tarow,' the man introduced himself. 'I was the strongest of my tribe and therefore they named me "the bull".'

'I am...'

The man grinned.

182

'I know; you are the *estrennek* called Yaghus the Healer. I have seen you at Dynas Dor.'

Kigva suppressed a shiver.

'How cold the evening air is becoming,' she whispered.

'If it is not an impertinence,' suggested Dryden, 'Tarow and I could sit closer for warmth.'

The three snuggled against each other, backs to the granite stone.

Tarow was in his mid-forties and had been captured at Meneghy where he had been second-in-command of the guard at the sanctuary.

'What will happen to us, Tarow?' the girl asked. 'You can remember the early raids of Cador when prisoners were taken.'

'It's true,' Tarow asserted. 'I also fought with your brother Peredur on the great plain by Keresk. In those days Nelferch-an-Gwargh had not departed from the customs of the people to the extent she has today. She still abided by the code of hostages. But now,' the man shrugged. 'Now, I do not know what fate may befall us because she no longer obeys the hostage code. I have heard from the mouths of many who sought refuge in Lan-Kern that she enslaves those whom she captures in battle and makes them work for her in menial tasks.'

'But that is barbaric!' whispered the girl.

'Indeed,' agreed Tarow. 'It is said she keeps prisoners in great pens, shackled until such time as she may use them as beasts of burden to carry, to build and work.'

'But that is against all rules of civilisation.'

Dryden shook his head.

'Against the rules of your people, Kigva. But not all people have the same philosophies as you do. In my country, it was a common thing to take away a person's freedom if they transgressed the laws or if they were caught in warfare.'

The girl's eyes widened.

'You mean they were shut away from society, imprisoned in rooms?'

'Yes.'

'But how then could they redeem themselves - how could they contribute to the society and compensate it for their transgressions? If they were locked away, they would not be able to make any worthwhile recompense?'

Dryden smiled.

'My society did not see it that way. The idea was punishment, vengeance, if you will. Your society seeks compensation and rehabilitation. In my country, if a person transgressed the law, he was shut away for a period of time and then released. Each crime had different periods of imprisonment. When the period of imprisonment was served, then society considered the man had paid the price of his transgression.'

Tarow whistled softly.

'But that is ridiculous. A man locked away makes no useful contribution to society; he merely becomes bitter and more rigid in his ways and will simply transgress again. And who pays for his incarceration, his food, the upkeep of the place in which he is imprisoned and provides the people to guard him? That is a childish concept, Yaghus. How could your people be so stupid? To seek vengeance on a transgressor is an understandable human weakness, although it will not cure the person of a wrong attitude to society but merely reinforce it.'

Dryden pursed his lips.

'My society was not an ideal one, Tarow,' he admitted.

'It sounds a very primitive one,' agreed Kigva. 'And if Tarow is correct then Nelferch and her people have regressed to such barbarism and we shall be shut away and treated as beasts of burden.'

'I fear this is so,' said Tarow.

'And I fear that Cador has something else in mind for me,' mused Dryden.

Kigva looked at him quizzically.

Dryden explained about his encounter with the grandson of Nelferch.

'If this is true,' observed Tarow, 'then you have only one option, Yaghus, and that is escape. You must escape before we come to Lan-Howlek for I have heard stories of terrible crimes that Cador has committed on helpless prisoners.'

Dryden shook his head violently.

'I cannot leave you here. We must escape together. And what of *An Kevryn*? I saw that Cador has plundered it from Meneghy and has it strapped to his saddle.'

184

'That surely was a foul deed, a blasphemy that will lie heavy on his soul,' Kigva said.

'Except that he has no soul,' replied Tarow. 'But we must be practical. Our task is to escape. If there is an opportunity to seize *An Kevryn* then we must surely take it. But if it has to be left then left it must be. We can always return in force.'

'Yes,' agreed Kigva. 'Tarow is right.'

'Very well,' said Dryden. 'We must...'

There was a sharp stab of pain in his thigh. Dryden started and found the red-haired warrior glaring down at him.

'Shut up talking, cur!' he snarled. 'Do you want to die before you reach Lan-Howlek?'

He chuckled and walked on.

Tarow leant forward and whispered: 'We must look for the first suitable opportunity.'

But no opportunity presented itself. For three more days, aching with cold, fatigue and hunger, the miserable column of prisoners and their abusive, rough guards, pushed onwards across the great moorland, through the forests and then across the great river which divided Lan-Kern from Lan-Howlek. Two of the prisoners died on the way from exposure. Another three, in a desperate attempt to escape, were cut down or speared to death by the guards.

On the morning of the fourth day the column came to the edge of a grass plain on which cattle and sheep grazed. In the distance there arose from the plain a flat-topped black hill. The red-haired warrior grinned down at them and pointed at it with his sword.

'Your new home, curs, if you survive,' he said. 'Dynas Drok. The fortress of Nelferch of Lan-Howlek.'

As they marched across the plain, Dryden could see that clustered around the bottom of this great hill, on which were earthworks and fortress walls, stood stone and wooden houses which comprised a fair sized township, far bigger than Dynas Dor. Unlike Dynas Dor, this township had an outer wall, completely surrounding the buildings.

Tarow was cursing under his breath.

'It seems we are too late, Yaghus. We cannot esccape from this place.'

'There's always a way, Tarow,' replied Dryden.

Crowds of people were gathering at the gateway to the township. Dryden saw that the stone walls of the town were not very high. The main defence work was the great earthen ramparts, topped with wooden stockades and here and there a stone wall.

One thing that did strike Dryden, as they were marched into the town, was that the people who gathered to watch their entrance received them with sympathetic stares. Some dropped their eyes as if embarrassed by the sight. The only jeers that were hurled at them were from young children or a few warriors. The atmosphere of Dynas Drok contrasted strongly with the happy township of Kesmur's capital.

The prisoners were finally halted in a big square which seemed to be the focus of the township and in which stood a great stone monolith carved with strange spirals and circles.

As soon as the warriors halted them, several of the prisoners fell to their knees, exhausted. Others, including Dryden, Kigva and Tarow, stood swaying but glaring defiantly at their captors. A few moments later a body of horsemen rode down the steep incline from the great fortress and entered the square.

Dryden had no difficulty in recognising their leader as Cador. By his side rode an elderly man dressed in the robes and accoutrements of a *drewyth*. Behind rode a middle-aged woman who bore a distinct resemblance to Cador. For a moment Dryden wondered whether this was Nelferch but she was surely too young to be Cador's grandmother. They halted before the prisoners.

The red-haired warrior bowed to the woman.

'Peace and prosperity to you Logosen, daughter of Nelferch.'

'Are these the new slaves from Lan-Kern?' asked the woman, letting her black gimlet eyes run swiftly over the exhausted prisoners and setting her mouth in a replica of Cador's sneer.

'They are.'

'Then I claim a privilege to choose some body-servants from among the females before they are taken to the public pens' she drawled, nudging her horse towards the captives. 'By Bel, they are a brooding lot. Look how sullen they are.'

Cador sneered.

'That will soon be altered, mother.'

Logosen's eyes swept over the male prisoners without interest

186

and lighted on a few females. Apart from Kigva there were three other women, a young girl of not more than twenty and two older women.

'I'll take this one,' Logosen said, pointing at the young girl. 'And I'll take...'

Her black eyes settled on Kigva.

'...that one as well. Send them immediately to my quarters so my slave-mistress, Gwaun, may instruct them in their duties.'

Dryden saw Kigva tense. He turned towards her, half raising his hands as if making some defensive gesture. Tarow hissed a warning but Dryden felt the pain of something hard strike against his back and he stumbled forward, recovering himself before he fell.

The red-haired warrior scowled at him.

'So, you would display insolence before Logosen and Cador?'

Dryden saw Kigva signalling him desperately with her eyes, imploring him to remain silent.

'Ah, it is the insolent one,' came the sneering voice of Cador. Dryden looked up to where the man sat, astride his horse. 'I might have known it would be him. I am pleased to see he has survived the perils of the journey here. It would have been a shame if he had perished and our anticipated pleasure had come to nothing.'

Dryden set his chin stubbornly.

'Careful, Yaghus,' he heard Tarow whisper.

'Is the woman yours, man of Lan-Kern? came the imperious voice of Logosen. 'Is that why you rush to defend her so readily?'

Again Dryden caught sight of Kigva's face bidding him to silence. He gazed stonily ahead.

Logosen snorted in annoyance.

'The brute says nothing. Is he dumb or insolent?'

'Insolent, I fear, mother,' said Cador. 'He can talk well enough to insult the power of Lan-Howlek when he wants to. Is that not so, cur?'

Dryden watched sullenly as two warriors, at Logosen's bidding, led Kigva and her companion away towards the fortress. A balled fist crashed into the side of his head, causing him to reel backwards.

'Speak when you are spoken to, son of a bitch,' snarled the red-haired warrior.

Dryden felt the blood, warm and sticky in his mouth.

He regained his feet and, anger overcoming his fear, he spat a mouthful of blood towards Cador. It splattered over his leg.

The red-haired warrior looked on horrified, unable to move.

Then Cadow swore terribly and drew his sword, his eyes blazing like glowing coals.

'Stop, Cador!'

The voice was quiet but firm.

For a moment Cador stood in his stirrups in front of Dryden like a statue, his sword upraised above his head.

'This is a wasteful slaughter.' It was the old *drewyth* who spoke.

Cador sat for a few moments his face working in passion. Then slowly, he smiled.

'You are right, Gowlek,' he said. 'I should not kill him now. Tonight is time enough. When the sun expires this evening he will be despatched to the Otherworld in a way that will teach the people servility for five generations.'

Cador sheathed his sword and turned to the red-haired warrior.

'Separate him from the others and bring him to the fortress.'

The warrior moved forward and cut Dryden loose from the rest of the prisoners.

Cador leaned a gloating face close to Dryden.

'You will die very slowly, man of Lan-Kern. So slowly, that before the end comes you will kiss my feet and beg me to strike you down with my sword to end your suffering.'

CHAPTER TWO

Dryden was half dragged, half pushed, up the pathway which rose among the earthwork ramparts of Nelferch's great fortress. Even Dryden, conscious and fearful of danger as he was, registered inward amazement at the vastness of Dynas Drok.

It was built on top of an oblong hill, slightly curving like a bow, which rose to at least five hundred feet at its highest point. It had been artifically flattened at the top to make an enclosure of at least forty square acres. There were three sets of great earth walls or ramparts to be negotiated before arriving in this enclosure, the biggest of them rising to a hundred feet and topped with wooden stockades of twelve feet in height. These ramparts and stockades followed the natural contours of the hill while around the base of the hill ran a large ditch, its bottom covered with wooden stakes.

The path through the various gateways to the centre of the gigantic hillfort twisted and moved like a serpent until it made its way through the irregular gateways like a pathway through a maze. It was clearly designed to make any assault difficult if not impossible.

Even as Dryden was pushed roughly forward he felt an unwilling admiration for the builders of this military architecture. The walls seemed impregnable against any attack, for the attackers who managed to overcome the ditch would have to negotiate the earthwork walls which sloped at such an angle that the attackers would have to actually climb them while the defenders could stand secure behind their wooden stockades and hurl missiles down. If the first wall was breached, then there was a second and then a third.

Once on the vast flattened hilltop, a rough hewn stone wall enclosed the entire area and Dryden observed that, unlike the township below, every building here was made of stone, some rising impressively three or four stories in height. It was obvious that most of the buildings were stables and quarters for the warriors but the largest cluster of buildings, situated at the far end of the hill fortress, had palatial pretensions and this must surely be the palace of Nelferch-an-Gwargh, the Witch Queen herself?

Dryden was pushed roughly towards a squat stone building through a low doorway which opened to an anteroom where some warriors sat playing dice.

'A special prisoner of Cador,' announced Dryden's red-haired guard. 'He is to be locked in the punishment cells to await Cador's pleasure.'

Two guards caught Dryden by the arms and undid his bonds. For a moment he felt a surge of pain as the blood rushed into his numbed hands. Then they were hustling him along behind a leather-faced jailer, down some steps into a dark corridor lit by a few flickering brands. At the far end the jailer opened a door and Dryden was unceremoniously flung onto straw-strewn flagstones and the door slammed behind him.

He lay for some moments, nursing his battered and bruised body. What made him finally stir was a scurrying sound in the straw and the feeling of several tiny bodies scuttling across his legs and back. He came to his feet with a cry of disgust and saw, in the half light, half a dozen rats scampering through the cell. It was lit by the glow that filtered in through the small iron grille from the burning torches in the corridor. The cell was small, with bare walls and not even a cot for the prisoners' comfort, just damp stone walls and a stone floor covered with musty smelling damp straw.

There was one other occupant: a man, half lying, half sitting against one wall of the cell.

Dryden moved closer, squinting at the man. The figure suddenly moved and a long, low groan escaped from its lips.

'Are you alright?' asked Dryden.

'Pain...' gasped the man. 'Terrible pain...'

Dryden froze. The words were spoken in English.

'Who are you?' gasped Dryden, in the same language, the words coming rusty to his tongue after a year of speaking and thinking in the language of Lan-Kern.

The figure stiffened. A hand came up to claw imploringly at

Dryden's arm.

'I know that voice. I know you. You speak English and...I know you.'

There was certainly something familiar about the dark, shadowy figure and Dryden cursed that there was so little light. Then he remembered.

'Good God! Chief Petty Officer Royston!' he whispered.

'Yes,' gasped the man. 'Yes,' his words were garbled in agony. 'That's me. Royston. Who are...?'

'It's Dryden. Doctor Dryden.'

'Doctor?' the man paused, 'I thought you were dead.'

'And I thought you were. What happened? You rowed back to the *Argo* leaving me ashore.'

Dryden paused.

'But you're hurt, man. Can I get you anything?'

Royston started to chuckle but it ended in a rasping cough.

'Too late, doctor. Too late. They've got me. Done for. The witch, the one called Nelferch. Done for. Not long left, doctor. I know it.'

The man started to cough again.

'Stomach wound...knife. Left me here to die.'

Dryden clenched his fists.

'But why? What happened to you?'

Dryden's presence seemed to give Royston a new surge of energy for he pushed himself up, his eyes shining in the gloom.

'The *Argo* blew up. Must have been the instability of the reactor. I was just approaching her in the dinghy as she went, after I left you ashore. The blast took me clear across the bay and knocked me senseless. I came to on the beach. I don't know how I made it.'

'I thought there were no survivors.'

'There were a couple more. Green, the officer who was with us in London, or what was left of London, and young Harris, the snotty.'

'The what?' queried Dryden.

'One ringer; the sub-lieutenant. They made it to shore as well. For a while we searched the beach. We couldn't find you anywhere, which was strange. Nor could we find any other survivors. One thing we did find, washed up on the beach, was a box which must have belonged to Commander Adamson. It was his personal kit, but inside was a pistol and a couple of dozen rounds of ammunition.

It was damned useful. We shot some sort of wild pig the next day and we were able to feed ourselves for the next couple of days.'

A dim memory burned in Dryden's mind.

'I thought I heard a shot sometime during the second day. I searched but I wasn't sure. What happened then?'

Royston's narrative was interrupted by another fit of coughing.

'We decided to try to get back up country. We thought everyone was dead. We went to the river but the estuary was too wide to cross so we struck up country to the north and forded the river at a narrower spot.

'It was about a week later that I was detailed to go off and try to bag some game for the pot. I left Green and Harris and went into the forests, hoping to get another one of those wild pigs. I had the pistol and a few rounds of ammunition. I didn't take all of it because we thought it best to conserve as much as we could. Then I was attached by a crowd of wild men, men with spears and swords...they looked like extras from an Attila the Hun film. I let off a round or two which kept them at bay for a while but finally, they got me, brought me here and here I've been ever since.'

Dryden's mind was racing.

'So Green and Harris got away.'

'I've never heard of them since,' gasped the stricken naval man.

'And you've been in this cell since then?'

Royston shook his head.

'No. At first they kept pointing to my pistol and my clothes and jabbering away. I suppose they were wondering who the devil I was and, never having seen a pistol before, marvelling at it. Christ! Didn't I wish I had an M6 carbine with me? For a while they tried to question me but their language was all gibberish to me.

'Then they started to treat me well. I was kept a prisoner but in a nice apartment. I was waited on - even had women when I wanted them. And an old man, whose name I later learnt was Gowlek, came and started to teach me their language. When I had learnt sufficient, he started to question me. Of course he didn't believe me about the *Argo* or where I came from. He thought I must have been shipwrecked from some far country. The main thing was, he said, the ruler here wanted me to explain the workings of the pistol, which they had preserved. They said that I must make them similar weapons which they could use against rebellious subjects.'

The narrative was again interrupted by a paroxysm of coughing. Royston's voice was getting weaker.

'They took me to see their ruler, an old woman - vicious, ruthless old bitch,' he spat. 'She said she would give me anything I wanted if I would make them the weapons.'

He paused and tried to laugh.

'The irony of it is that I would have done so if I had the knowledge. I tell you, doctor, if I were able, I would have built them an atom bomb in order to live the life they promised. But I just didn't know how. And they didn't believe me. They cajoled and promised in the beginning; then they began to torture me. It was so bad that I pretended that I could make any weapons they wanted and would do so. I felt that it would give me an opportunity to find a way of escape. I was well treated again. I spent over six months pretending to draw up plans and search for suitable components. Then a week ago I was taken to see that hell-woman, Nelferch, who demanded to know where the weapons were. I replied that I hadn't made them. She flew into a rage, stormed at me and finally she drew a dagger and let me have it in the gut.'

He groaned in pain.

'They dragged me down here and dumped me. Left me to die. It won't be long now. I'm glad, though, I've seen you again, doctor. But I warn you to beware of Nelferch. Do what she wants. There's no way to escape. I tried but...'

The sailor gave a sudden gasp, doubled forward in agony and sank sideways to the floor, his breath coming out in a noisy exhalation.

Dryden looked down at the man sorrowfully. He checked the pulse but, as he knew it would be, it was still. He stood up and hammered loudly on the door. No one came. After a while he sat down at the far side of the cell and closed his eyes, oblivious to the scurrying of the rats.

Poor Royston. For him there had been no moral problem in answering Nelferch's request to make weapons - just a practical one. If he could have made the weapons, he would have done so and Lan-Howlek would have devastated Lan-Kern.

And what of Green and Harris? Had they survived? Where were

they now? Dryden was overcome with an unbearable yearning, a homesickness which took a long time in passing.

The cell door crashed open without warning.

The jailer and his two assistants came in and grabbed Dryden.

'Wait!' yelled Dryden. 'That man is dead.'

The jailer laughed coarsely.

'Then he can wait.'

They hustled him from the cell.

'Where are you taking me?' he demanded.

'On your journey to the Otherworld!' snapped the jailer.

He was dragged into the yard and saw the sun well down on the western horizon.

Inwardly, Dryden braced himself. Cador had said he was to be executed at sunset. So this was it. He was surprised to find himself calm. Who was it who had said that to die is as natural as to be born? Well, perhaps death was the supreme festival on the road to individual freedom but he wished that he had learnt more of life before passing into a new existence. And what of Kigva? No, he had to remain calm.

A crowd of warriors with some women and a few children, presumably workers in Nelferch's palace, had gathered by a stone platform on the highest point of the outer wall of the fortress, overlooking the township. A great bonfire had been built on the platform over which an iron gallows stood and from whose iron arms hung a metalworked basket on a chain. It was a basket big enough for a human being to stand in.

The crowd watched in silence as the guards brought Dryden forward. One or two of the warriors grinned nervously. Standing to one side, surrounded by officials and with the old *drewyth* Gowlek by his side, was Cador.

'Ah, the guest of honour,' he drawled, as Dryden was halted in front of him. 'The sun sets and your path to the Otherworld lies open. Is there anything you want to say?'

Dryden braced himself.

'A man's dying is more the survivor's affair than his own,' he said, quoting an ancient *drewyth* saying.

Cador laughed tunelessly.

'You will find that this death is very much your affair. Especially

194

when you feel the tongues of flame licking at your flesh.'

He inclined his head towards the basket.

'Hoist him up,' he ordered. 'He will burn all night for the city to see and realise that a like fate will befall them if they nurture disloyalty in their hearts.'

Dryden felt a cold sweat burst out on his brow, his inside churned with panic and horror at the idea of being burnt to death. He almost cried aloud as the guards seized him and hauled him towards the metalwork basket which was lowered to hoist him above the bonfire that was soon to be his funeral pyre. For a brief instant he struggled and then it seemed as if a voice came into his head - the voice of Mabon: It is better to die proudly when it is no longer possible to live proudly.

He squared his shoulders and allowed himself to be pushed into the basket and hauled up above the bonfire.

Cador strode forward and seized a torch from one of his warriors. 'Let this be a lesson to all who would insult and disobey the will of Nelferch of Lan-Howlek!'

He raised the torch high above his head and, grinning malignantly up at Dryden, he plunged it into the bonfire.

CHAPTER THREE

As Dryden smelled the thin wisp of smoke curling upwards from the fire, an idea flashed into his mind.

Gowlek, the *drewyth,* was standing nearby.

Dryden raised his voice.

'Gowlek!' he called urgently, using English. 'You taught Royston to speak the rudiments of your language. You must have learnt some English from him. Can you understand me?'

The effect of his words caused Gowlek's eyes to almost pop from his head. He stared up at Dryden.

'I...I speak little,' he answered.

The words were only just decipherable as English.

'I, too, am of Royston's people. I, too, have come across the sea. I, too, am possessed of the secrets of his people.'

Gowlek frowned as he tried to catch the words.

'I do not understand,' he said, lapsing back into his own language. 'You say you are an *estrennek,* a foreigner who is of the same people as Royston?'

Cador, overhearing, looked up with a scowl.

'What game is this, Gowlek?'

'This man spoke with the tongue of Royston,' observed the old *drewyth.*

'Any fool can lisp a few words.'

'Yet I could not understand the rapidity and the assortment of words he used in his speech and I spent six months trying to learn Royston's tongue.'

Gowlek turned back to Dryden.

'Tell me the name of the ship in which you came to this country?'

'It was called the *Argo.*'

'And was this ship possessed of any magical qualities?'

196

Dryden frowned. What did Gowlek mean? It suddenly struck him that Royston must have told him that the ship was a submarine.

'It was a ship that could travel under the sea,' replied Dryden.

Gowlek's face was a mask of amazement.

'It is true,' he whispered. 'He must be an *estrennek!*'

'What matters?' snapped Cador. 'Let his mysteries and witchcraft perish with his death.'

Gowlek drew himself up.

'Death cancels everything but the truth, Cador. Release him so that he may be questioned.'

Cador scowled deeply.

'It is my will that he should die for his insults.'

'It is the will of Nelferch that any *estrennek* must be captured alive and questioned so that we may solve the mystery of Royston's thunder-weapon.'

Dryden could see Cador hesitating.

'In Nelferch's name I order his release,' commanded the *drewyth,* pressing home his advantage.

Cador's face was sullen as he wheeled round and walked rapidly away.

Calmly, Gowlek signalled the warriors to swing the basket away from the bonfire, which was now beginning to blaze, its flames shooting perilously near to Dryden's feet. Within moments Dryden was standing in front of the old man who examined him keenly.

'Obviously, it is not yet your time to journey to the Otherworld,' he smiled.

Dryden grinned weakly.

'Obviously,' he echoed.

'Well, *estrennek,* what do they call you?'

'In Lan-Kern I was called Yaghus.'

The *drewyth* smiled.

'And in your own land, what then?'

'Dryden was my name.'

'Dri - dun? Alas my tongue cannot pronounce these syllables. I will call you Yaghus. Are you a healer?'

'I have a little knowledge,' admitted Dryden.

'Well, come with me, Yaghus. I will make you presentable for an audience with Nelferch the queen. She will want to question you.

Remember this: Nelferch has a third eye which sees all; should your tongue twist around the truth, she will see it. She sees into the blackness of all our souls and knows what we are thinking even before we give utterance to our thoughts.'

Dryden shrugged.

'I can only tell her what I know.'

The old man grimaced.

'That is all anyone can tell. Come.'

Dryden followed the old man towards the great stone palace, entering through a small gate which led into an inner courtyard. Off this inner courtyard, which was surrounded by a roofed terrace and reminded Dryden of a Roman villa he had once seen, were several tall wooden doors. Gowlek explained that these were the quarters of the *drewyth* of Lan-Howlek. Dryden later learnt that the *drewyth* philosophy differed greatly from Lan-Kern. Nelferch had subverted it in a pure religion with Bel as chief deity and herself as the 'spirit of Bel on earth'. Those *drewyth* who tried to maintain the old ways were swiftly killed while others, like Gowlek, decided to throw in their lot with the Witch Queen.

Having bathed and changed into clean clothes, Dryden was led through several corridors to the main palace. The room to which he was led was like a fair-sized church and just as cold and dismal. The towering, fluted columns, the curved arches and vaulted roof showed an architecture far more sophisticated than anything he had seen in Lan-Kern. There were glass windows which allowed little light to shine through. Instead the room was illuminated with several burning torches. Weird and colourful tapestries draped some of the stone walls and Dryden could see that they were very similar to the tapestries of Lan-Kern.

The room was full of people - some were obviously attendants or slaves, running hither and thither on unaccountable missions. Others stood in quiet groups, looking round morosely at each other, some appeared to be bearing petitions, others waiting to ask boons, others, with apprehensive and guilty glances, had been summoned to answer the court. And around the walls of the hall, at distances of three paces, stood sentinels armed with drawn swords and carrying shields.

Gowlek ushered Dryden through the throng towards the centre

of the hall.

'This is Nelferch's throne room and council hall,' he whispered, like some worshipper in a cathedral.

As the crowd parted to let them through, Dryden saw a dais. The only seats in the vast hall were placed on this dais. There was one large, carved mahogany chair covered in skins in a central position while, at either side, stood two less imposing seats.

Dryden immediately recognised Cador, sprawled in the left hand chair, biting his nails and scowling under his lowered brows at the gathering. In the other chair sat Logosen.

It was the central throne that caught and held Dryden's attention.

On it sat an elderly woman: wild, grey-streaked hair tumbled about her deathly pale face. She had a large, slightly hooked nose which emphasised her close-set eyes of a brilliant blue. They watched him unblinkingly as he approached. Her thin mouth was made into a vivid red gash by some artificial means. She was slightly built, even small, and her bare arms were scrawny, just bone and sinew. She wore rich garments, the embroidered work of which was certainly alien to that usually produced by Lan-Kern woman, but her jewels bore the same spirals, circles and curves of the Lan-Kern craftsmen.

She was a strange creature; a woman undoubtedly, but something more. Even as he approached, Dryden felt her presence; a feeling of power that seemed to emanate from her very body.

'Well, Gowlek,' her voice was rasping, slightly high-pitched and totally unmusical. 'Cador has informed me that you went against him before the people to save this.'

She jerked a sharp chin towards Dryden.

Gowlek bowed before her.

'Nelferch, I salute you in health and happiness,' he began. It was an automatic salute, the falsity of which was plain in the old man's forced tones. 'Perhaps,' he asked, making his voice bland, 'perhaps Cador told you why it was necessary to interrupt the execution of this man?'

Nelferch arched an eyebrow.

'You may explain your own actions.'

'Very well, my queen. The man is an *estrennek,* he is not of Lan-Kern nor of Lan-Howlek.'

A murmur went round those gathered in the hall.

199

'He came upon our shores with the other *estrennek* named Royston,' continued Gowlek. 'He speaks his language and knows from whence he came for he was of that party. His name is Dry-dun but he has lived a while among the tribes of Kesmur and there he was called Yaghus, for he has some knowledge of healing.'

Nelferch turned her cold unblinking stare on Dryden. The bright blue eyes seemed to bore into him, into his very soul, and he felt uncomfortable. He moved from one foot to the other. It was easy to believe that this old woman was possessed of some evil and mystic quality. Then he found the red gash of a mouth twisting in a smile.

'Yes,' spoke Nelferch, 'Yes, even before he speaks I can see he is an *estrennek* for no man of Lan-Howlek nor of Lan-Kern would stand so proudly in my presence and return my gaze so defiantly without falling on his knees before me. Come forward, healer.'

Dryden licked his dry lips and moved forward a few paces until he stood immediately before Nelferch's throne.

'You knew the man Ry-stun?'

Dryden frowned.

'Royston? Yes. I knew him. We sailed to this land together.'

Gowlek interrupted eagerly.

'He, too, claims they came in a ship called the *Argo* which could sail under the sea.'

Cador gave a peal of scathing laughter.

'Doubtless, Gowlek, you believe him to be some god of the Otherworld come to plague us?'

Nelferch motioned him to silence.

'Do you claim you are a god, Yaghus?' she asked, as if amused.

'No,' replied Dryden. 'I came as a voyager and was shipwrecked.'

'And in a ship that sails beneath the seas.'

'The land I come from was advanced in science. It was not magical.'

Nelferch's eyes never left his face. She sat silently for a few moments.

'Yes,' she said, half to herself, 'his eyes tell me that he is not lying. We know in See-ti, to the east, dwell men advanced in such science. It is true just as Ry-stun told the truth about this. Ry-stun, however, lied in other things and because he lied he went to the Otherworld before his allotted time.'

200

Nelferch suddenly reached behind her and brought out a pistol. She held it out to Dryden.

'Do you know the secret of this thunder-weapon?'

Dryden fought back an impulse to say that he knew all the magical secrets of his people and would destroy them all if they did not let him, Kigva and Tarow go.

Instead he shook his head.

Cador sniggered.

'Did I not say he was a liar? Ry-stun knew such things.'

'I am called Yaghus because I am a healer. I have a knowledge of the herbs and flowers, the trees and things of nature. In my land I pursued my knowledge of nature as I pursued it in Lan-Kern. It was not my role in life to destroy but to obtain knowledge. Others, such as Royston, were the warriors in my land and they used such weapons. I did not.'

Nelferch's brow creased in a frown.

'All your people do not fight then?'

'No. There are warriors in our society as there are healers; there are farmers as there are fishermen. Each man follows his calling and does not presume to follow any other.'

On an impulse Dryden reached forward and took the pistol from Nelferch's surprised grip. He broke open the weapon, trying desperately to remember how Adamson had shown him. He revolved the chamber and saw one cartridge in it. An idea developed rapidly in his mind, faster than he would work out the implications. Acting more on instinct than a true reasoning, he pushed the chamber with the bullet to the firing position, snapped the gun shut and drew back the safety catch.

'Nelferch seeks a demonstration of my calling. Thus shall I show her.' he said, raising the pistol towards the old woman.

Nelferch watched him snake-like with her bright blue unwinking eyes. She made no move. Cador pushed himself half out of his chair. He had seen the weapon in action during the capture of Royston. There was a movement from the guards but Nelferch stilled them with a glance.

Dryden raised the gun past Nelferch's thin figure until it pointed to the great window at the far end of the throne room. Then he pressed the trigger.

There was a bark from the pistol, a flash and then the window splintered into a million fragments.

For a moment no one moved; it took them several seconds before they recovered from the shock of the noise, the blast and disintegrating window. Then shouts and screams echoed round the hall.

Now Dryden lowered the pistol back to Nelferch and pointed it towards her unmoving form. For the first time her eyes left his face and became opaque with fear as they stared towards the smoking barrel. Out of the corner of his eye, Dryden could see a tall warrior moving stealthily towards him.

'Call your men back, Nelferch, or the Otherworld's gates will open and slam shut before you know it.'

She jerked her head in assent. The warrior halted.

Then Dryden smiled softly.

'I have shown you, Nelferch, that I possess a knowledge of this weapon, of how to use it. I have also shown you that you could easily have been destroyed by that power. But now I say again: I do not destroy. I am a healer. Should I want to destroy you, I would have done so. But I give you your life and only ask to live mine in peace and follow my calling.'

He suddenly broke open the pistol, useless without bullets, removed the firing pin and tossed it on the ground before the old woman.

'The weapon is now useless, as it should be to your society.'

Nelferch's eyes narrowed into slits.

Cador had jumped to his feet, blood rushing into his swarthy face and started to call the guards forward.

Nelferch motioned him to silence.

'But, my grandmother,' protested Cador, 'do not be misled by this man's lying tongue. A healer, indeed! Did I not see him slay five of my best men with his longsword?'

'My calling is to heal,' snapped Dryden, 'but if I am attacked then I shall defend myself.'

Nelferch's eyes returned to their fixed stare on Dryden's face.

'Well, Yaghus,' she said slowly. 'You are either a wise man or a cunning fool. I am prepared to allow you time to demonstrate which of these things you are.'

She turned and scowled at Cador.

'You will not hurt this man on pain of death.'

'But,' cried Cador, 'how can you be fooled by...'

Nelferch's face contorted with fury.

'I am never fooled by anyone, Cador. Remember that.'

There seemed a hidden meaning to her words which made Cador's face colour scarlet and he lapsed into a scowling silence.

Nelferch turned back to Dryden and composed her features.

'Yaghus, you shall be answerable to Gowlek the *drewyth*. You will live at the slave-pen in the city and tend to the slaves. If your healing skills can help them, then perhaps we can find you more rewarding work. In the meantime, in your rest periods, you will consult with Gowlek and tell him more of this country from which you and Ry-stun came. I would have further knowledge of it.'

She waved her hand in dismissal.

At the doorway of the great hall, Gowlek paused and wiped his brow.

'You are a strange man, Yaghus,' he said. 'Many in your position would have used that weapon to kill Nelferch and try for freedom. As Nelferch said, you must either be a wise man, wise beyond your years, or merely a cunning fool playing some strange game of chance. Do not doubt that Nelferch will find out which before long.'

Dryden shrugged indifferently.

'It is no concern of mine, Gowlek, what you or Nelferch suspect I am. I am what I am.'

'Spoken as a *drewyth*,' observed Gowlek. 'You either learnt a great deal in Lan-Kern or your own country follows the Path of Bel.'

'It is said by the *drewyth* of Lan-Kern that your people no longer follow the truth Path.'

Gowlek sighed.

'Perhaps one day we may return but...'

Dryden had turned and caught sight of a familiar figure coming along the passageway carrying a pitcher of water.

'Kigva!' he whispered.

The girl started and raised her eyes. As she saw Dryden she gave a soft cry of recognition.

'Yaghus! I heard that you had been slain twice over!'

Dryden laughed.

'Yet I am still alive.'

'And unshackled,' observed the girl.

Gowlek gave a discreet cough and walked on several paces. Dryden lowered his voice to a whisper.

'I have been given the task of healer to the slaves in the city. This *drewyth*,' he pointed to Gowlek, who stood just out of earshot, 'is conducting me to the slave-pens now.'

He paused.

'And you? Are you alright?'

'I am one of Logosen's body servants,' Kigva answered with a shudder. 'She is a vain and cruel woman, but at least my duties are not arduous.'

'Well, I shall have some comparative freedom by Nelferch's own orders,' said Dryden. 'As soon as I have seen how things are here, I will devise some means of escape.'

'The people of Lan-Kern will come soon,' said Kigva solemnly. 'By now my father Kesmur must have received the news and Pryderi and he will raise the tribes. They will be marching towards Lan-Howlek. We will be freed soon.'

'Have you seen anything of *An Kevryn?*' asked Dryden, suddenly remembering he had not seen it in the throne-room and wondering why Nelferch was not displaying what should be her greatest trophy.

Kigva shook her head.

'I think Cador still has it and may not have informed his grandmother.'

Gowlek coughed loudly.

Dryden reached forward and took Kigva's hand.

'Stay safe and be in peace, Kigva,' he said. 'If there is a way, I shall come for you. I shall not leave Dynas Drok without you.'

The girl smiled gently into his eyes.

'Then stay safe, too, Yaghus.'

Gowlek made a motion of impatience and Dryden, with a quick smile at the girl, turned and followed him down the corridor.

Kigva stood and watched him disappear. She felt a curious tranquillity, knowing that the craggy faced *estrennek* would not desert her.

Remembering her errand for Logosen, she turned and immediately bumped into the evil, smiling figure of Cador, who materialised from behind a pillar and stood, hands on hips, looking at the girl.

'Well, well, my mother's new slave girl. Kigva the daughter of Kesmur, is it not so?'

Kigva paled.

'You heard?' she whispered, fear clutching at her heart.

'I heard,' affirmed Cador. 'How interesting that the daughter of the ruler of Lan-Kern is now but a slave in my mother's household. What would Kesmur give to regain his daughter? Or, indeed, what would Nelferch, my grandmother, do to the daughter of her ancient enemy?'

Cador let his eyes sweep slowly over the girl's lithe body.

'Well, perhaps this is something we can discuss later in more depth, if you like. Yes, we will discuss the matter in my chambers later tonight.'

CHAPTER FOUR

Gowlek led Dryden through the deserted streets of the township. The slave pens were at the far side of the town, where the perimeter walls ran close to a forest. They were in an oval piece of land, enclosed by thick stone walls on which guards patrolled. Dryden could see their shadowy forms, carrying bows and walking past the numerous flaming torches on the walls. Gowlek conducted him to a high wooden gate set in the wall and called to the slave overseer to be admitted in Nelferch's name.

Dryden saw that there was a group of stone buildings inside the wall which seemed to house guards and prisoners alike.

A big, grossly built man, carrying a sword and a whip came forward and saluted Gowlek.

'Greetings, Lowarn,' said the *drewyth*.

'And what brings Gowlek to the slave pens?' asked the man, giving Dryden a look of dislike.

'This man,' said Gowlek, indicating Dryden, 'is an *estrennek*, a stranger to our land. He is called Yaghus, for he has some knowledge of healing. It is the will of Nelferch that he tend the slaves for a while, looking after their ills. He is a prisoner but is not to be put to work with the rest of the slaves. He may have the freedom of the slave pens and no more. Neither is he to be ill treated or in any way abused. Nelferch wishes this to be so. Is that understood?'

The fat man, Lowarn, nodded.

Gowlek turned to Dryden.

'I shall leave you now, Yaghus,' he said. 'We will soon see what you really are: a wise man or cunning fool.'

The *drewyth* was gone through the gates without another word.

'So, *estrennek*,' the fat man sneered, 'you're a healer, are you? Well, there is plenty to be healed around here.'

'Where shall I sleep?' asked Dryden.

'Take your pick,' the man smiled, waving his whip towards the huts. Then he pointed: 'That hut is less crowded than others.'

'And where might I obtain herbs for my remedies, if I am to be healer here?'

'You are only allowed freedom within the confines of these walls,' snapped Lowarn.

'Then how can I carry out my task without herbs.'

'A wench comes once a day to feed the slaves in that hut. You can tell her what you want and she will find them for you.'

He turned and sauntered off to the guardhouse.

For a moment Dryden stood in indecision and then entered the hut which the man had pointed out to him.

The first thing that registered was the stench; the horrible, sickly sweet stench of confined humanity. It made his stomach heave and for a moment he felt tempted to leave the building. Inside the hut were about thirty men, chained by long lengths of metal to a central pole. Most of them were lying down, while others sat, knees to chins, hunched in postures of despair.

Two burning torches cast a smoky light upon the scene.

Dryden took a hesitant step among them.

No one took any notice of him, perhaps mistaking him for a guard. Then: 'Yaghus!'

Dryden squinted in the gloom.

One of the chained men was waving to him.

'Yaghus! It's me - Tarow!'

Dryden moved forward to the stocky Lan-Kern warrior. Tarow gripped his hand.

'I thought you would be dead now for sure,' the man said wonderingly. 'What happened? Is,' he lowered his voice, 'is Kigva safe.'

'For the time being,' Dryden briefly told him what had happened.

'And what is the situation here? Is there any chance of escape?

'Escape?'

A harsh voice cut into the conversation. It came from a sandy-haired man lying face downwards next to Tarow. The man had turned his head and was looking up at them.

Dryden started in astonishment.

'Why, it's Cunobel!'

The sandy-haired man screwed up his eyes and searched his memory.

'By Bel's fire - Yaghus! We meet again.'

Tarow looked on in surprise.

'Cunobel saved my life once, in the forests,' explained Dryden. Then turning to the Lan-Howlek farmer he asked with concern: 'What's brought you here?'

'A long story, Yaghus,' replied the man with a grimace of pain. 'One that would be too long in the telling. Did I not say that not everyone in Lan-Howlek supported Nelferch-an-Gwargh?'

'Are you in pain?'

Cunobel nodded.

'You ask about escape? Look at my back, then you will know what happens to people who try to escape.'

Dryden bent forward and peered at the man's back. The sight made him flinch. It was a mass of open weals; blood and clothing were matted together.

'That was made by the whip of the overseer, Lowarn. And that is the fate of the person who tries to escape.'

Dryden examined Cunobel's back more closely.

'Well, Nelferch has asked me to heal her slaves,' he said. 'I'd best begin on you.'

The man groaned.

'The overseer said a girl comes to feed us and that she could bring me herbs,' said Dryden. 'Do you know when she comes?'

Tarow shrugged but Cunobel nodded.

'Not until sun-up, Yaghus.'

'Then in the meantime I'll get some water to bathe your back,' he said. 'Tomorrow I'll ask this girl to bring some herbs for a proper dressing.'

He went out of the hut for, outside, beyond the reach of the chained men, was a trough fed by a well. Dryden picked up a leather bucket and filled it.

'What are you doing?' snapped a voice.

It was Lowarn.

'It was Nelferch's order that I tend to the health of the slaves. A man in there may die unless I tend his back.'

Lowarn spat.

208

'You mean that scum Cunobel? He got what he deserved. No one escapes from here, remember that, Yaghus.'

'Unless he is tended to, he may yet escape from here,' replied Dryden looking the fat overseer steadily in the eyes.

Lowarn's eyes narrowed.

'What do you mean, *estrennek*?'

'He may have the ultimate escape to the Otherworld.'

'Very well, *estrennek*. Tend the man. But he must go to the tin fields with the rest of them come sun-up.'

Dryden did not bother to argue but turned back into the hut with the bucket of water.

Cunobel was still lying on his stomach. As Dryden knelt down the man looked up.

'I hope the people of Lan-Kern were justified in calling you "the healer" because I am in urgent need of the art.'

Dryden bade him to be silent and commenced gently bathing the man's back, removing the clots of blood and matted cloth.

'Lowarn said something just now about slaves going out to the tin fields in the morning.'

Cunobel nodded through the pain.

'Each morning groups of us are led to certain areas by the granite rocks to the south of the town. From the earth and the streams, tin is extracted by streaming. Other slaves work the copper mines or the iron fields and so the smithies of Lan-Howlek are supplied with much metal to make weapons for Nelferch's armies.'

Dryden continued his task and then sat back.

'There now, Cunobel. Your back is cleansed. But tomorrow I must apply dressing to ease the pain and heal the wounds.'

Cunobel gave a snort of laughter.

'You should not have bothered, Yaghus. I know the rules of the slave pens. I shall be forced to the tin fields tomorrow. Each slave is worked until he dies. I shall die tomorrow.'

CHAPTER FIVE

At dawn there was a stir by the main gates of the slave-pens.
Dryden crossed to the doorway of the hut and peered out. Several
women were entering bearing baskets of bread and fruit. Dryden
had learnt that each woman was alloted one hut to serve and they
were chosen for this task because some relative had been sentenced
to incarceration among the slaves.

Cunobel, who had passed the night in a fever, tried to smile as
Dryden returned from the door.

'This hut is tended by Berlewen,' he said. 'Her father was a great
smithy in Dynas Drok at one time. When Nelferch embarked on her
war to conquer Lan-Kern, he said it was an immoral war and refused
to forge weapons for her warriors. He spoke out several times against
her. The end was inevitable. He and his wife were taken to the slave-
pens and perished. Berlewen was ordered to support and feed thirty
of us slaves for three years to expiate her father's so-called crimes.'

Dryden gave Cunobel a cup of water.

Tarow was stirring from his sleep.

'Is it time to go to the tin-fields?' he yawned.

Cunobel sighed.

'I will not last a day in the tin-fields, I know it.'

'They can't take you before your wounds have healed,' said Dryden
emphatically.

Cunobel gave a rueful laugh.

'You do not know them, Yaghus. Ah, here is Berlewen.'

Dryden turned as a young girl, scarcely out of her teens, entered
the hut. She placed her baskets where the chained slaves could help
themselves to the bread and fruit and came straight to Cunobel's
side, a look of anxiety creasing her pretty features.

To say that Berlewen was a striking beauty would have been

an understatement. Even Dryden, who now measured all women's physical attributes by the yardstick of Kigva, felt sheer admiration for her perfect features. At the same time, Berlewen's beauty was not the earthy dark beauty of Kigva but an ethereal, fair beauty that seemed unreal. The pale face was angular, yet at the same time possessing a softness of form, the eyes green, the hair a wispy brown. In all, there was some meditative quality about the face, as if it held the knowledge and wisdom of countless generations, and the girl seemed to emit an aura of tranquillity, of peace.

She bent over Cunobel.

'They told me you had been recaptured, Cunobel,' she said in a voice that was soft yet full of resonance. 'I willed that you would survive the ordeal of punishment.'

Cunobel smiled and reached for her hand. Dryden felt the magnetism that the two shared; a deep bond of feeling that none could separate.

'Berlewen, this is Yaghus of Lan-Kern. He and Tarow were among the new captives that were brought in yesterday morning. But Yaghus has won the enmity of Cador.'

Berlewen raised her green eyes to Dryden.

'If you have won the enmity of Cador then you must beware,' she said with concern. 'No man wins Cador's hatred and lives long.'

Dryden grinned.

'He has tried to kill me twice already but was unsuccessful. Nelferch intervened.'

The girl's eyes widened in surprise.

'Nelferch?'

'Yes,' interposed Cunobel. 'She sentenced Yaghus to tend to the health of the slaves. Praise Bel she did. He tended my back through the night and kept me from delirium. If it were not for him, I should be in the Otherworld or at least preparing my passage.'

'Then, Yaghus, I am your friend before Bel,' said the girl with a sincerity of feeling that made Dryden feel awkward.

'But the end is not yet, Berlewen,' he said, 'I must have herbs to cure Cunobel's back. The slavemaster...'

'The overseer? The pig called Lowarn?'

'Yes. He said he would give you permission to find herbs for my remedies.'

211

'This I am very willing to do, Yaghus. What manner of herbs do you need?'

'I would like some clusters of burnet but I do not know what it is called in your language,' said Dryden. 'It grows in moist soil, in low sheltered valleys, in round clusters of small purplish flowers. When it is laid on a wound it staunches bleeding and heals it rapidly.'

The girl's face lightened.

'I think I know this flower, Yaghus. But I am not sure where it can be obtained.'

'If it can't be found, fetch me the leaves and young bark of the oak tree, the tree you call *derowen*.'

'The sacred tree of the *drewyth*?'

'Is it against custom?' queried Dryden.

'No,' replied Berlewen. 'But I did not know the tree had any healing properties.'

'The young bark and leaves, made into a poultice, will also act to staunch bleeding and heal open wounds,' said Dryden. 'Nature provides mankind with every healing agent.'

The girl smiled and turned back to Cunobel.

'Rest well, Cunobel. I must go now.'

Dryden walked with her to the door.

'Could you also bring me some leaves of the cowslip?'

'I will try,' said the girl, puzzled.

'When can you come back?'

'As soon as I have found the herbs you need.'

Dryden watched her stride quickly to the gate.

A few minutes later the guards were shouting in harsh voices.

'Slaves to assemble outside. Outside scum!'

Cunobel struggled to rise to his feet, grunting with pain.

'Lie still!' snapped Dryden. 'Do you want your wounds to open immediately?'

'But Lowarn will not accept this. He works his slaves to death.'

'He has to deal with me first,' returned Dryden shortly. He was beginning to possess a belief in his own indestructability for he had chanced death and survived too many times in this new world not to stand up for the life of another.

Tarow looked worried.

'Have a care, Yaghus. Lowarn is an evil man.'

212

A throaty chuckle made them look towards the door.

Lowarn was standing there, his fleshy face wreathed in amusement. He motioned to a second guard to start unlocking the prisoners' chains and herd them outside.

'Evil, eh? he sneered at Tarow. 'You will pay for your impudence and learn how to talk of your betters.'

Tarow stood like a statue, eyes fixed in front of him. In the one day he had been a slave under Lowarn he had learned the value of speaking only in answer to a direct question.

'Outside!' snapped the slave overseer, jerking his heavy jowls towards the door.

Tarow cast an anxious glance at Dryden but obeyed.

'And now, healer,' sneered the fat man, 'I hear you have been busy already. Why,' his eyes fell on Cunobel, still lying as Dryden had told him to. 'Why, if it isn't the would-be escaper. The one-time farmer who thought he could disobey the rightful ruler. Why are you still lying in here, slave? You should be in the tin fields. Out!'

Cunobel flinched as the overseer raised his whip.

Dryden swiftly moved between them and looked steadily into Lowarn's eyes.

'Unless this man rests for two days at least, you will kill him. His wounds have to heal.'

Lowarn gave a snort of laughter.

'He is dead already, Yaghus,' he gloated. 'When a man is sentenced to become a slave there is only one escape for him: to the Otherworld.'

'Nevertheless,' insisted Dryden, 'he must remain here for two days so that I may heal his back.'

Lowarn stared in disbelief.

'You dare to insist?'

He opened his mouth and started laughing, laughing so hard that he ended in a paroxysm of coughing.

Cunobel tried to get to his feet.

'It would be best if I tried to make it to the tin-fields, Yaghus,' he gasped through his pain.

'Remain where you are, Cunobel,' said Dryden quietly.

Lowarn's red-rimmed eyes sought Dryden's in anger.

'You, too, can have a dose of the whip if you want it, healer,'

213

he snarled.

'Nelferch told me to tend to the wounds and illness of the slaves, not preside over their burials,' replied Dryden evenly. 'It is Nelferch's will that her slaves be healed.'

A shadow of doubt crossed Lowarn's features.

'I am overseer of slaves here,' he said.

'Nelferch is queen of Lan-Howlek,' observed Dryden.

'My methods have not been questioned before. Not by a slave. And you are as much a slave as they are.'

'That is not so,' Dryden said. 'Did you not listen to the orders that Gowlek gave you last night.'

'He is right, Lowarn,' said a quiet voice at the doorway.

Gowlek the *drewyth* stood surveying the tableau.

Lowarn scowled and swore.

'So slaves are now to be pampered, Gowlek?'

'Men are not irreplaceable, Lowarn,' the old man said. 'How many slaves have died within the past moon? Nelferch would be angry at losing so many able-bodied men who can build, forge and mine for her just because her overseer is a sadist. How can Lan-Howlek grow great and strong without slaves?'

Lowarn spat disgustedly.

'They are only slaves, Gowlek. They should expect to die.'

'Do you ill-treat your horse?' asked the *drewyth*. 'Yes, I suppose you do. A horse to you is merely a beast of burden to take you here and there. You have no understanding beyond that.'

'What else is there to understand about horses?' sneered Lowarn. 'Besides, what have horses to do with slaves?'

Gowlek heaved a sigh.

'Go, Lowarn. Go tend to your slaves and may Bel pity them. Leave this man and Yaghus and make sure this man does not work for two days. Do you understand me?'

Lowarn scowled and hurried from the hut without another word.

Gowlek came forward and eyed Dryden through narrowed lids.

'A wise man? A brave man? Or a cunning fool?' he mused. 'I wonder, Yaghus, I wonder. You may be defiant once too often.'

He glanced at Cunobel, then back to Dryden, and turned, following Lowarn from the hut.

Dryden squatted down by Cunobel and wiped the sweat from

the man's brow.

Cunobel shook his head wonderingly.

'Yaghus, you have saved my life twice over.'

'It is Nelferch's will,' grinned Dryden.

'You are a healer, Yaghus. A healer is more worthy than a host of warriors. It is so easy to kill, but to heal a man, to preserve a human life in the midst of so much hostility and chance, that is perhaps as great a miracle as creating life.'

'Not so,' replied Dryden. 'If my knowledge helps, why should I withhold it? It is no miracle that I have that knowledge; it is just that I have been given the good fortune to obtain it.'

Not long afterwards Berlewen returned. She brought the bark and leaves of the oak tree which Dryden, using a plate and a wooden spoon as a mortar and pestle, compressed with water into a paste which he spread over Cunobel's lacerated back. Then he gathered up the cowslip leaves, pressed the wrinkled and veined leaves into some water, and boiled the mixture to make a tea.

Berlewen watched in fascinated silence.

'The juice of the cowslip is an effective painkiller and sedative,' explained Dryden. 'If one takes a cupful, the mixture will ensure a restful sleep, at the same time as sedating the nerves from pain.'

The girl smiled.

'You are truly a healer.'

'Simply a man with a little knowledge,' replied Dryden as he coaxed Cunobel to drink the liquid.

'I feel that Bel has ordained your coming,' the girl said, her green mystical eyes on Cunobel who was already sinking into a deep sleep. 'Will he be alright?'

'If I can prevent Lowarn from working him for the next two days. That will give the poultice time to close the wounds so they will not open again at the slightest movement. In two days time he will be well enough.'

Dryden paused.

'You love him?'

The girl nodded without any false modesty. 'We met before my father was taken and my mother...before Cunobel was outlawed.'

'Cunobel told me why your father and mother were enslaved.'

'Yes; he knew the secret of smelting bronze, of working the

metals. For refusing to put his knowledge at the disposal of Nelferch and her warriors, my father was sentenced to the copper mines. My mother was taken at the same time to work in the tin fields and I was ordered to feed the slaves for three years. That is no hardship, for I would willingly feed them all to alleviate their suffering.'

The girl paused and a slightly bitter look crossed her face.

'Soon after his enslavement, my father fell, perhaps he was pushed, down a mine shaft. My mother, who was not strong, died after a week under the lash of the overseer of slaves.'

Dryden moved uncomfortably.

'I'm sorry,' he said, inadequately.

'Bringing food to the slaves has become my salvation, especially since Cunobel was captured.'

'Why was that?'

'One day, only a few weeks ago, it was discovered that he had been to Lan-Kern on a visit to some cousin. Already some relatives had been executed or sentenced to the slave-pens for disloyalty to Nelferch. So Blyth, who is captain of Nelferch's guard, had Cunobel's parents executed on the spot and Cunobel was taken to the slave-pens. They said he was a spy of Kesmur of Lan-Kern.'

'What hope is there for Lan-Howlek under this despot?' asked Dryden.

The girl's eyes flashed.

'Every hope, Yaghus. The people of Lan-Howlek live under the dictatorship of Nelferch because they think she is stronger than they are. But no ruler can be stronger than the will of the people. The people must find the backbone to stand up and say "no more!" to this tyrant; they must take back the power to themselves and so diffuse it that they can live in peace again.'

'But will this happen?'

'The bracken is dry and waiting under the feet of Nelferch. A fire needs only a spark to ignite it. With every evil deed she and her followers do, there arises the greater chance of a blaze that will destroy all traces of her evil.'

'Are there many people in Lan-Howlek of the same mind as you, Berlewen.'

The girl smiled.

'There are many who do not yet know their mind, who have

yet to articulate the passions that rage within them.'

She turned towards him and searched his face carefully.

'Tell me of yourself, Yaghus. Your accent and appearance speak not of Lan-Kern to me. Are you an *estrennek*?'

'I am...from another place.'

'Tell me of it.'

To his surprise, Dryden found he told the girl of his coming to Lan-Kern, of Kigva, of his decision to settle, of his testing, of Cador's raid and his capture. Also, he told her of the capture of the black box known as *An Kevryn* and its significance to the people of Lan-Kern and Mabon's prophecy that he would search for it and find it.

Berlewen reached out and took Dryden's hands in hers, holding them palm upwards, her eyes scanning their lines.

'Ah, Yaghus, your hands tell me much. I see many dangers, death will be your companion for a long, long time. Yet in the end you will triumph.'

'And Kigva?'

The girl frowned.

'I see ultimate happiness, but whether this means with Kigva or with another, I am not permitted to see. One thing is certain, you will be separated for a considerable time and you will have to undertake many strange journeys. Yes, I see this. You will not find the one you love for a long time and your journeys will have two goals which, finally, shall be the same goal. That may be the search for your beloved and for *An Kevryn*.'

Dryden smiled, not fully accepting that the future could be read in the palm of a human hand.

'Can you see no more?'

'No more than it would be wise to tell,' replied Berlewen mysteriously.

'Surely if you are possessed of this gift, to read the future in the hands of people, then you should know if the yoke of Nelferch will be lifted from your people?'

'Oh, yes. This I know,' replied the girl softly, with lowered lids. 'It will come. It will come soon. You are the sign that foretells it.'

'Me?' asked Dryden in astonishment.

'Yes, a stranger from another place, possessing the powers of healing. But you must not press me further on this, Yaghus.'

Dryden gave the girl an indulgent smile.

'Well, you will know if Cunobel and you will survive and prosper,' he said jokingly. 'And I am sure you shall.'

To his surprise, tears welled in the girl's eyes and streamed down her face.

'Oh, no, Yaghus. That will not happen. Death shall sever us before we have really come to know each other. But my curse is that I am not able to read all the signs and to interpret correctly whether it be my death or Cunobel's, I have no knowledge.'

CHAPTER SIX

On the evening of the third day, after Cunobel had spent a day at work in the tin fields and felt only a little discomfort from his back, Dryden announced his intention of escaping. Cunobel and Tarow reacted with horror but Berlewen, who had brought the evening meal, nodded her head as if she knew what had been on Dryden's mind for the last few days.

'It is not worth it, Yaghus,' objected Cunobel. 'Why risk a lacerated back or even worse for a few moments of freedom?'

'The place is too well guarded,' said Tarow. 'We are held too firmly by our chains.'

'You are but I'm not,' Dryden pointed out. 'I have the freedom to move about the slave pen.'

'You will never succeed,' said Cunobel.

It was Berlewen who interposed and rebuked Cunobel.

'You did not take that advice when you tried your escape, Cunobel.'

'I know better now. I have learned my lesson.'

'Perhaps you have not learned the right lesson,' commanded Berlewen. 'Let us listen to what Yaghus has to say.'

Dryden leant forward.

'For the past few days I've wandered around the compound here. I've nursed a few bruises and cuts and generally pursued the duties which are expected of me but I've kept my eyes open. I believe it is possible to escape over the wall. I don't have any fetters to restrict me. At night there are enough shadows, in spite of the burning torches, to scale the wall and get to the other side before the guards spot me.'

'I made my escape at the tin fields,' admitted Cunobel. 'Perhaps you might have a better chance from here.'

'But what about the sentries?' asked Tarow. 'They have regular

219

beats along the top of the wall.'

'And that's their weakness. I can time my escape so I can scale the wall - it's only twice as high as a man - before they spot me. I'll wait until the sentries are at their furthest and then start my climb. It would take me a few seconds to pass over.'

Tarow smiled.

'Aye, a warrior must seize any chance, however slim. I wish you well in this, Yaghus. May we be together again in freedom soon.'

Dryden felt touched by Tarow's obvious friendship.

'Had you better not tell them the purpose of your escape?' smiled Berlewen.

Cunobel turned and frowned.

'Purpose?'

'You do not think that Yaghus does this only out of self-interest, Cunobel?' admonished Berlewen. 'I see his reason written in his hand and in his heart.'

Cunobel returned his gaze to Dryden.

'Have you a reason, Yaghus?'

'The people of Lan-Howlek lie under an evil tyrant; they want to be free. This much I have learnt since my stay here.'

'That is so,' replied Cunobel.

'Do the people of Lan-Kern know this? Or do they tar all people of Lan-Howlek with the same brush as they tar Nelferch? Already, at this moment, Kesmur of Lan-Kern and his son, Pryderi, may be leading an army against Lan-Howlek. They think the people will support Nelferch. But if one of us escapes and tells Kesmur and Pryderi what is really happening here, then their army can be halted and a new stratagem arranged. With them supporting, perhaps a resistance movement to Nelferch can be fostered and made strong. If I can get a force together, it would not take too many to attack the slave pens and release you all. That would form the nucleus of an army to resist Nelferch.'

'What else is in your plan, Yaghus?' asked Tarow.

'After I escape from here, I shall make my way into the hillfort...'

Cunobel started.

'Into Dynas Drok?'

'Yes. I plan to get inside and rescue Kigva, who is now a body servant to Logosen.'

'But this is madness!' cried Cunobel. 'You may just be able to make your escape from here but to attempt to enter Dynas Drok, which was built to withstand whole armies, that is sheer madness!'

'A single man might get in where whole armies might not,' Berlewen pointed out.

'What then?' asked Tarow.

'If I can get Kigva safely out of Dynas Drok, I will make my way to Berlewen's house, if I may. It will be dangerous but we shall need shelter for the rest of the night in the town.'

'Would it not be better to get away into the forests immediately?'

'No. As soon as our escape is discovered, it will be thought that we will be heading towards the great river into Lan-Kern and Nelferch will send warriors to cut us off.'

'So?'

'After we leave Berlewen's house I have a plan. But that plan I shall keep to myself.'

'That is wise,' agreed Berlewen. 'If one man knows only one man can betray.'

'If all goes well,' went on Dryden, 'I could be back here within ten days and then the fight against Nelferch will really start.'

A guard entered and scowled at Berlewen.

'You are a long time feeding the slaves this evening,' he said suspiciously.

Berlewen gathered up her baskets.

'I am leaving now.'

She turned back to Dryden.

'You will settle the wager tomorrow,' she said in a tone of annoyance. 'My house does have two great chimney stacks. Ask Cunobel, he knows where my house is.'

Dryden recognised her message and nodded acknowledgment.

The guard stood aside to let her pass and then he frowned into the hut.

'You'd best rest, scum. You'll need it in the morning.'

'When will you make your bid?' whispered Cunobel.

'Soon after midnight. I shall try to rest until then.'

With a sigh, Dryden turned on his back and closed his eyes.

CHAPTER SEVEN

Kigva stirred uneasily in her sleep.

In her dream some dark serpent had trapped her in a corner of a room. The serpent was edging closer and closer and, try as she would, she could not open her mouth to cry out for help. Closer still and closer came the twisting body of the creature, unwinking blue eyes fixed intently upon her. Twisting its sinewy body around her legs.

Kigva jerked awake, sweat standing out on her forehead.

Gwaun, the elderly slave mistress of Logosen, was sitting at the foot of her bed, a bony hand stroking her foot.

'What do you want?' Kigva demanded of the old woman.

The ancient face before her creased in a parody of a smile.

'Gently, my pretty-pretty,' cackled Gwaun asthmatically. 'Gently. I have been sent to fetch you.'

Shivering, Kigva stumbled from her bed.

'What does Logosen want of me at this time of night?' she asked wonderingly.

'You'll see, my pretty-pretty,' chuckled the toothless harridan. 'Quickly now, you do not want to keep your mistress waiting.'

Kigva followed the old woman down the corridor and up the stone steps which led towards the apartments of Nelferch and her family, through corridors watched by armed warriors who made lewd comments as she hurried by them.

Halfway down one corridor, the old woman turned abruptly left. Kigva paused.

'Wait!' she cried. 'That is not the way to Logosen's bedchamber.'

The old woman smiled.

'Who said we should find Logosen in her bedchamber?'

Puzzled, Kigva followed her.

After turning down several corridors, she came to a heavy wooden door and knocked. Then, without waiting for an answer, she threw it open.

'In here, my pretty-pretty. In here,' she wheezed.

Cautiously, Kigva entered.

No sooner was she across the threshold than the door was thrown to by the old woman, who was cackling with amusement. Kigva wheeled around and grabbed for the door but the woman had thrown the bolts from the outside. The girl turned like an animal at bay and looked around the room. It was a bedchamber of some kind but, by the look of the dust and debris, it was one that had not been used for some time.

'Do not be afraid, Kigva of Lan-Kern,' said a voice, triumphant and gloating. 'Did I not say that we should discuss further the matter of your identity and whether it was worth revealing to my grandmother, Nelferch?'

Kigva started. The sallow-faced figure of Cador emerged from the shadows. She felt a moment of panic and then squared her shoulders. A long silence passed between them.

'You do not say anything, Kigva,' mused Cador. 'That is not friendly, is it? Ah, but then you are probably annoyed. I did promise to see you three days ago and during that time Nelferch has kept me busy with affairs of state. I crave your indulgence but, as you see, we are together now.'

He took a step forward.

Kigva sprang back, her face distorted with fear and hate.

'Touch me, Cador, and I will find a way to kill you,' she hissed.

Cador slapped a hand against his thigh and laughed.

'By Bel's light! I like spirit in a girl. Now, enough nonsense. If you submit willingly, I shall keep the secret of your identity from Nelferch. But if you do not submit, I shall take you anyway and afterwards...... afterwards Nelferch shall know that you are the daughter of her enemy, Kesmur of Lan-Kern.'

Out of the corner of her eye, Kigva saw that there was a window to the chamber, a large one. She suddenly turned and, dodging Cador's outstretched arms, raced towards it. At the edge she hesitated. It was four stories straight down to a stone courtyard. Cador was behind her in a trice; a hand gripped her wrist painfully. Then she opened her mouth in a piercing scream.

Cador jerked the girl back, almost tearing her arm from its socket, and threw her across the room, sending her crashing against a couch.

'Bitch of Lan-Kern,' he hissed. 'I will force you to submit!'

Dryden awoke with a dry feeling in his mouth. Tarow was nudging him gently.

'It is past midnight, Yaghus,' he whispered.

Dryden stood up and silently shook Tarow's outstretched hand. Cunobel was still fast asleep and Dryden smiled and shook his head when Tarow made a motion to wake him. He moved silently to the door of the hut, turned with a hand raised in farewell, and slipped out into the black night. The moon and stars were hidden by thick cloud. The conditions were ideal.

He moved swiftly along the wall of the hut, keeping well within its shadow, until he was facing the outer perimeter wall which rose to a height of twelve feet. The wall was made of thick blocks of stone without the benefit of mortar and, to an unfettered man, would be easy to scale. Dryden could see the shadows of the patrolling guards passing to and fro. He would have to judge the time it took the sentries to pass the spot where he stood and return again.

A soft, thick voice chuckled in his ear.

'Are you thinking of leaving us so soon, Yaghus?'

The bulky figure of Lowarn the overseer moved out of the shadows of the hut wall.

'You should have been more skilful in concealing yourself, Yaghus,' the fat overseer gloated. 'Now you will have to be punished.'

Dryden saw him uncurling his whip from his shoulder.

He moved suddenly, swiftly, his body obeying some primeval instinct of survival.

One hand grasped the slack, fleshy throat, while the other snatched the whip from the overseer's grip. Lowarn's hands came up pawing and strong. His breath was making strangled noises in his throat. Dryden knew that he could not hold on much longer and once he released his hold, Lowarn's shouts would bring the entire guard to exact retribution.

A cold fury seized Dryden as he struggled with the man. He felt the tough leather thong of the whip beneath his hand, and almost

224

automatically, he twisted it around the fleshy neck, taking it with both hands and pulling it tight before the scream escaped from Lowarn's mouth. The hands began to claw desperately, fiercely. The big man sunk to the ground with Dryden on top of him, pulling and straining until the body was still.

The horrible, sick sweaty smell of the body beneath him, the nearness of it, its warm flesh, made Dryden's stomach heave and the bile come into his mouth.

Dryden's mind was a whirl of anguish. To have killed a man in such a fashion - to have killed in cold blood... He turned and vomited in the shadow of the hut. Evil though Lowarn had been, his death would be a heavy burden to bear.

For some moments he squatted there in the shadow of the hut. Then he managed to pull himself together. It was necessary, he told himself. He had to rescue Kigva, he had to bring help to this poor benighted country. But it was Morvran's words which echoed in his mind: 'Each time we kill, we kill a little of ourselves for all life is sacred under Bel.'

Trying to suppress his distaste, Dryden took the man's cloak and unwrapped the whip, coiling it in his hand. Then, watching his chance, he hurried to the perimeter wall. The guards were some yards away. He swiftly clambered up, crouched a moment on the top of the wall and then let himself gently down the other side. Within a few moments he had entered the shelter of the streets of the town and there were no sounds of alarm or pursuit.

He found the main street of the town without any difficulty. It was fairly empty and dark but he kept close to the shadows of the buildings. In this fashion he came to the main square, in which stood the giant menhir by which Logosen and Cador had inspected the captives on their arrival at Dynas Drok. Hiding in the shadow of a hut's doorway, he examined the pathway which zig-zagged upwards through the gigantic ramparts of Nelferch's fortress. He looked at the three tiers of ramparts and the wooden stockades, the patrols and sentinels, with a sinking feeling. How could he get into the fortress and find Kigva?

The sound of horses caused him to press back into the shadows.

About twenty warriors, several carrying burning torches, rode swiftly up to the first gate, exchanged a password and were let through. Dryden watched them enviously as they trotted up the path, through the intricate defence system and disappeared through the final gateway into the great fortress itself.

A new sound caught his ear: the creak and rattle of wagons being pulled by tired horses. He peered into the gloom. A line of wagons was heading towards the square through the street in which he sheltered.

He pressed backwards as the leading wagon passed by. It was piled high with straw and went straight across the square towards the fortress gates.

'Halt!' sang out a voice. 'What do you want?'

'We want to enter, what else?' snapped a tired voice. 'These are the wagons from the eastern villages bearing the tribute that we were ordered to pay by Nelferch. Here is fodder and grain, the results of our harvest. Small though that harvest was.'

A guard stepped forward, his torch held high and inspected the wagon.

'How many wagons are there?'

'Nine,' replied the first driver. 'They are coming up behind me.'

'Your wagons were expected yesterday. Why are you so late?'

'We were attacked by a pack of wolves as we came through the forest. It delayed us,' said the man in a querulous tone.

The guard stepped backwards and waved the driver on.

'Right. You can go up.'

Dryden watched as the first and second wagons rumbled through the gate. He turned and saw the rest coming down the darkened street. He waited until the fifth wagon had passed, piled high with hay bales, and then ran out behind it, hoisted himself onto the tailboard and burrowed in among the bales.

Holding his breath, Dryden felt the wagon lumber its way through the gates and start up the steep incline, through the fortifications, twisting and turning, until it suddenly levelled off and Dryden knew, with a sigh of relief, that he was within the stone walls of the great hill fortress.

'Leave your wagon over by the wall,' a voice was saying to the driver. 'We don't want you to unload in the darkness. Put your wagons over there and come to the fire. There's a pot of hot mead for you.'

226

Dryden felt the wagon stop and waited ten minutes before he pulled his way out of the straw and clambered over the back of the wagon. He peered quickly around and saw that no one was near. The tails of the wagons were parked against the wall of the fortress away from the bright fires around which he could see warriors and the wagoners sitting together.

He brushed the straw from the cloak he had taken from Lowarn and which contained a brooch symbol of Nelferch's guard and drew it closely around his shoulders, one hand still gripping the leather whip.

He slipped along the wall until he found a dark patch of courtyard and then he started to walk swiftly and purposefully towards the stone buildings of Nelferch's palace.

Two young warriors suddenly appeared, strolling casually with their hands lightly resting on their sword hilts. They gave him a brief glance.

Dryden walked on with a gruff: 'Bel greet your awakening.'

'And yours,' replied one of the men.

Dryden hurried on into the blackness. He avoided the main doorway to Nelferch's palace, which was well lit and guarded, and turned along a side wall. It was so dark that he was forced to feel his way along it. Then he reached a familiar side entrance. It was the small gateway that led into the quarters of Gowlek the *drewyth*. He passed through this darkened courtyard and through a small arch into an inner courtyard. Here he paused, wondering how best to find out where the quarters of Logosen's body servants were. He was about to make a move when a woman's scream, long and loud, froze him to the spot. It came from an upper window overlooking the courtyard.

It was Kigva's voice!

'Bitch of Lan-Kern,' hissed Cador. 'I will force you to submit!'

Kigva lay on the couch, stunned by her fall, as Cador walked slowly towards her.

As he bent over her, there was a scuffling from beyond the window and a figure suddenly swung through. Cador turned with a curse on his lips. It took a split second for the figure to recover its balance and then, or so it appeared to Kigva's half-stunned mind, a black snake suddenly wrapped itself around Cador's face, sending him screaming and twisting into a corner.

Kigva pushed herself up from the couch as recognition dawned in her eyes.

'Yaghus!'

Dryden unloosened the whip which he had lashed at Cador's face.

'Has he hurt you, Kigva?' he said, a snarl in his voice.

'No, no.' replied Kigva, seeing murder in his eyes.

Dryden's face softened and he smiled down at the girl.

'I have come for you as I promised.'

Cador was crouching in a corner, groaning and holding his hands to the bloody welt made by the whip across his cheeks.

Eyes hardening again, Dryden walked to him.

'You deserve a long, slow death, Cador,' he hissed.

The grandson of Nelferch whimpered before him.

Dryden felt sickened. He raised the heavy leather pommel of the whip and brought it crashing down on the man's head. Cador fell into a senseless heap.

'That will keep him quiet while we escape,' Dryden said.

'But how?' gasped Kigva. 'How can we escape? And how did you get here? It is four floors down to the courtyard.'

Dryden grinned.

'One question at a time, Kigva. I was in the courtyard trying to find your quarters when you screamed and I saw you struggling for a brief moment at the window. Under this window is a small ledge which runs along the building to where a series of steps have been cut in the wall. I don't know for what purpose they are used, perhaps an escape route in case of fire. But they enabled me to scale the wall in a few moments. We can return that way.'

'Bel smiles on us, Yaghus,' sighed the girl.

Dryden started to the window and then paused, frowning.

'Have you seen anything of *An Kevryn*? Does it lie within easy reach?'

Kigva shook her head.

'I don't know. No one has talked about it in my hearing.'

Dryden looked at the inert body of Cador and bit his lip.

'A pity I knocked him out. He could have told us where it is. The last I saw of it was just after my capture and Cador had it tied to his saddle.'

'We cannot do much about it now,' said Kigva. 'If we spend more time searching for it, he will recover and sound the alarm.'

'You're right,' said Dryden. Without a backward look at the unconscious man, he led Kigva out onto the narrow ledge and eased himself along the wall of the building. She followed close behind. It was not difficult to find the jutting stone steps which led down the side of the building and into the courtyard.

'Which way now, Yaghus?' whispered Kigva.

'Through that arch over there,' replied Dryden. 'That leads to the main compound of the fortress. From there we'll have to find a way through the gates into the town and then I know a safe house for the night.'

Taking the girl by the hand and keeping close to the shadows of the wall, Dryden moved stealthily towards the archway which led out of the small palace courtyard.

A match suddenly blazed in his face. A torch was lit and blinded them for a moment.

When Dryden looked again, six armed guards with levelled bows stood around him and the girl. Before him, hands on hips, and a cruel smile twisting her mouth, stood Nelferch-an-Gwargh and beside her stood Gowlek.

'You have good eyes, Blyth,' observed Nelferch, speaking to the guard captain.

Blyth grinned as his bow covered Dryden.

'They grow sharp in your service, my queen,' the man replied.

Nelferch turned to Dryden, her unblinking eyes seeking his.

'At first I could not believe it when my captain, Blyth, said the *estrennek* had managed to enter the fortress. You are a man of exceptional foolishness, Yaghus. Now I learn that you have murdered Lowarn, my slave overseer, strangling him to death. For a healer you seem adept at taking life, Yaghus.'

'I have less blood on my hands than you have on one finger nail,' returned Dryden hotly.

The old woman croaked with laughter.

'Yes, I daresay. But then I do not pretend to be a healer.'

Dryden and the girl stood silent.

A cry, half of rage, half of pain, came to their ears. Cador was leaning from the window calling for help.

Nelferch looked up, frowning.

'Blyth, go up and see what that idiot is doing.'

Within a few moments Blyth had returned with Cador, his face disfigured by a terrible red welt.

A few words were exchanged with Nelferch.

'Well, well,' said the woman, her cold, staring eyes seeking out Kigva. 'We have an honoured guest in our midst.' Then she turned back to Dryden. 'Did I not say that we would soon find out whether you were a wise man or a cunning fool? Well, now we have discovered the truth. You have played your last game and now you can hear the sentence of Nelferch. At sun-up you will be led into the forest, to *Esethva a Mernans* - the place of execution, and there you will make a meal for the *gourgath*. There is no appeal this time. No last minute reprieve. This time, you will die.'

The final words were a snarl.

'And as for this bitch of Lan-Kern, this spawn of Kesmur - well, I shall see to her later. In the meantime she can return to Gwaun's control and can continue as a body servant to Logosen. But, Yaghus, in your dying moments think on this: the best fate that lies in store for her is that she is turned over to the guards for their sport. The worst fate, I shall leave to your imagination. Take them away.'

'But, grandmother,' it was Cador's whine. 'This man has done me a great hurt. See what he has done to my face. I should have the right to kill him in my own way.'

Nelferch almost spat at the man.

'You! You can only kill when backed by warriors to protect you from your victims. You will leave the killing to the *gourgath*. That is my decision. Now go and get your face dressed. At dawn you can leave with my troops to quell the rebellion among the northern villages.'

Cador hesitated as if he would disobey her.

Nelferch turned like a tigress.

'What?' The word was a near scream.

Cador backed away from her.

'I am going,' he said in a surly voice. He turned, walked by Dryden and, before anyone could stop him, punched him in the face.

Nelferch scowled after her grandson with murder in her eyes.

'Blyth,' she snapped, to the captain of the guard. 'You have charge of the prisoner, Yaghus. Make sure my grandson does not interfere with your duty. My sentence is to be carried out to the letter.'

Blyth motioned the guards to secure Dryden while two more hauled the struggling and weeping form of Kigva away.

Gowlek the *drewyth,* who had stood a silent spectator to the proceedings, shook his head sorrowfully at Dryden.

'Alas, Yaghus,' he said slowly. 'Alas, there is no appeal from the *gourgath.* A pity. I feel we could have learnt many things from you. A pity.'

Dryden shrugged his shoulders.

'Tell me one thing, old man: what is the *gourgath?*'

The old *drewyth* shook his head sorrowfully.

'Why, the *gourgath* is the *gourgath.* There is no reprieve.'

He turned and was gone, leaving Blyth and his comrades pushing Dryden towards the cells.

CHAPTER EIGHT

Just after dawn, Blyth and a detachment of guards came for Dryden. One of the guards was Dryden's red-haired antagonist who had commanded the captives on their journey from Lan-Kern. He seemed to take a sadistic joy in Dryden's predicament but was kept subdued by the presence of Blyth who, after Cador, was the most powerful man in Lan-Howlek.

They marched Dryden out of the hillfort, down through the fortifications and through the deserted streets of the still sleeping township. It took them half an hour to push through the forest pathways and into an area of red leafed trees, yellow flowering shrubs and other botanical oddities which Dryden remembered from the strange voyage of the *Argo*. They had evidently entered an area where the strange plant mutations had taken a strong hold.

Abruptly they were in a clearing; a small glade. The first thing that Dryden noticed was a strange animal smell pervading the area. Then, more chilling, was the fact that the glade was strewn with bones, a smashed profusion of bones...human bones.

'What is this place?' gasped Dryden.

Blyth grinned.

'*Esethva a Mernans,* the place of death,' he replied.

Quickly and silently, the guards led him to a thick tree stump, about twelve feet high. It served as an outsized stake and it was to this that Dryden was securely bound, hands stretched behind the stump, ropes securing his body and legs so that only his head could move. During the entire operation, the guards were constantly peering round with wide, frightened eyes.

Blyth inspected their work with satisfaction.

Then he ordered his men away. He was turning after them when Dryden called to him.

'At least you can tell me what this *gourgath* is, Blyth.'

232

Blyth turned and hesitated.

A roar of some beast, a roar which sounded remarkably like the snarling, throaty bark of a lion, erupted from the jungle.

Blyth paled.

'You will find out, Yaghus,' he said and disappeared through the undergrowth.

For a few moments Dryden struggled vainly with his bonds. They were professionally tied and tight.

Then he noticed some bushes to one side of the glade moving as if they concealed some animal. Dryden tensed himself. The bushes suddenly swayed apart and the beast - the *gourgath* - stepped boldly forward into the clearing.

For a moment Dryden could not believe his eyes.

The beast had descended from a species of lion: it bore all the characteristics of that great cat. But it had mutated itself into twice the normal size of a lion, with a sleek, glossy black hide, and terrible staring eyes of yellow, which seemed to be living coals within its flat black head. The mouth was cavernous but what was most frightening were the two great sabre teeth which curved from its upper jaws.

It stood, almost level with Dryden's chest, its great black rope of a tail swinging, a low grumbling echoing from deep within its chest. It expected and was given human food by the evil queen of Lan-Howlek. And now it advanced upon Dryden's bound and helpless form; advanced so close that Dryden could feel the hot breath against his skin.

Gowlek had said there was no reprieve.

Dryden closed his eyes and waited for the end to come.

Berlewen shook Tarow awake roughly.

'Tarow, I do not have much time,' she whispered urgently.

The stocky warrior rubbed his eyes. He could see the early morning light filtering through the hut door.

'Berlewen! You are early with the food.'

'I have news of Yaghus.'

'Yaghus?'

Cunobel was now awake and sitting up.

Berlewen turned towards him with sad eyes.

'Yes. He was caught. Both he and the girl Kigva - before they could get out of Dynas Drok. Kigva was taken back to Logosen's slave quarters.'

'Was Yaghus slain?' asked Tarow quietly.

'No, at least not yet,' replied the girl. 'I was on my way here with food as usual when I saw the captain of the guards, Blyth, with an escort walking through the forest to the place of execution. Yaghus was a prisoner with them. They were taking him to the *gourgath*!'

Tarow frowned.

'What is this *gourgath*?'

Cunobel explained in an empty voice.

'With Yaghus dead, there is no chance of escape.'

Berlewen shook her head: 'There is a way for brave people. Look hard at this loaf. It is the best I can do for you. If you are successful come to my house. It was once my father's smithy and the tools of his trade still hang outside to mark it.'

She bent forward and squeezed Cunobel's arm.

'Bel make you successful.'

She turned swiftly as she heard the approach of the guard.

'Come on, woman. You have had time to distribute the food,' snarled the man.

Berlewen forced a smile.

'I have finished.'

Cunobel waited until the guard had gone and then tore at the loaf. Inside was a small piece of pointed iron and a dagger. Seizing the small piece of iron he twisted it in the padlock which chained him to the centre pole of the hut. He twisted the pointed piece until there came a sharp click. Cunobel opened Tarow's leg-iron in a moment. Now the other slaves were sitting up and imploring Cunobel and Tarow to release them.

Cunobel held up his hand for silence. He placed a finger against his lips and motioned Tarow to get near the door of the hut.

Silently he threw him the knife and then raised his voice.

'Guard!'

A moment later the man entered the hut, peering round inquisitively.

Tarow's arm went out, gripping the man's throat and cutting off his windpipe. The dagger hit once, twice and the man sank silently to the ground.

234

Swiftly, Tarow grabbed the keys on the man's belt and released the rest of the slaves. He held up a hand.

'Listen, men, if we are to escape then we must have discipline. There can be only one leader.'

He turned and looked expectantly at Cunobel.

For a second Cunobel hesitated.

'There is only one way to get out of here, my friends,' he said. 'Over the nearest wall and among the forest trees before the guards can pick us off with their arrows. Some may fall as we rush the wall but the majority of us should be able to get away. We have one thing working for us - the element of surprise.'

The men nodded eagerly.

'We are with you, Cunobel. A quick death is better than a living death,' said one man and the others murmured in agreement.

'Very well,' nodded Cunobel. 'Tarow and I will lead the way. No noise. Just follow.'

Cunobel went to the door of the hut.

They had hit upon a lucky period. The guards were about to change and had left their posts along the walls and made their way to the guard house at the gates of the compound. The new guard had not yet gathered and most of them were still adjusting their equipment.

Cunobel turned back to the expectant faces behind him.

'Ready?'

There was a low chorus of assent.

'Now!'

The slaves erupted out of their hut and streamed towards the perimeter wall. So swiftly and so silently did they move that the leaders were on top of the wall before a guard saw them and raised a hoarse cry of alarm. The guards raced to firing positions, many fumbling with their bows while others, forgetting them, drew their swords and ran vainly towards the escaping men.

Three of the slaves were cut down as they tried to clamber over the walls, arrows piercing their backs. Two more fell dead on top of the wall and yet another received an arrow in his neck as he made to jump down on the far side.

But the main body of slaves had disappeared among the tall, red-leafed trees as the guards raced up the walls to fire after them.

Deep within the forest, Cunobel, Tarow and the surviving slaves paused for breath. Many of them were laughing with relief. It had been so simple.

Cunobel spoke.

'It is little use escaping from Nelferch's slave-pens merely to live out our lives in fear and outlawry. I believe we have escaped for a purpose and that purpose is to regain the freedom and peace of the people of Lan-Howlek.'

The slaves looked at each other dubiously.

Cunobel's eyes burned with a fierce intensity.

'Are you slaves still or free men? Gather sticks, staves, any weapon you can find and follow me. Those who so wish may go their own way.'

'Where are we going?' demanded one man.

'To rescue one to whom we owe our freedom,' replied Cunobel tersely.

Tarow smiled widely.

'We will follow you, Cunobel!'

The others took up the cry.

CHAPTER NINE

Dryden closed his eyes and braced himself for the end.

The beast was growling, a soft menacing rasp from deep within its cavernous jaws.

With a startling abruptness the low growl of the beast turned to a sharp, high-pitched bark of anger.

The great cat was crouching a few feet away, its thick tail lashing from side to side. Its massive head was held low against its mighty sinewed shoulders. It was staring past Dryden, its baleful yellow eyes unwinking on a spot on the far side of the glade.

A large stone shot by Dryden's bound form and hit the beast over one eye.

The *gourgath* retreated a few feet and snarled again, its teeth bared and grinding. Dryden tried to turn his head to see what dared to menace this great cat, but he was too securely bound.

A chorus of human cries and yells erupted behind him and a shower of sticks and stones came cascading by him to strike at the mighty beast. For a moment or two, the *gourgath* stood its ground, snarling defiance at its antagonists. Then, with a final roar of rage, it turned and loped off into the surrounding forest.

The sweat stood out on Dryden's face and his heart beat rapidly.

Then the smiling face of Cunobel was before him. Other men, too, surrounded him and willing hands undid his bonds. And there was Tarow thumping him on the back. Dryden suddenly felt weak.

'Well, Yaghus,' said Cunobel, 'we were not too late.'

Dryden stood rubbing his wrists and staring around him at the men whom he had last seen standing dejected in manacles in the slave-pen.

'What happened?'

Cunobel grinned happily.

'We freed ourselves, with help from Berlewen. How simple it was.

We could have done it before. We finally realised who it was who bound us. We, ourselves. We were the ones who had truly bound ourselves by thinking ourselves weak and Nelferch and her spawn strong.'

Cunobel took Dryden's hand and grasped it.

'You taught us this, Yaghus.'

Dryden smilingly shook his head.

'You taught yourselves.'

'Cunobel,' a stocky man came forward. 'Nelferch's warriors are still armed and strong. We should leave this place of death before they come to see why the *gourgath* is not eating.'

Cunobel nodded.

'We must find some shelter and form a plan.'

'Hide in this forest?' asked one man, a look of apprehension on his pale face as he stared at the surrounding darkness of the trees.

'No,' replied Cunobel. 'That is exactly what Nelferch would think we will do. No. We shall go back to town. We know enough sympathetic people to hide us in groups of two's and three's.'

'Back? But Nelferch's warriors...?'

'Would not think nor suspect that we would dare return to the township,' interrupted Cunobel. 'Yaghus, Tarow and I will go to the house of Berlewen. The rest of you have friends and relatives who will hide you. Disperse among the houses. Tonight, at midnight, send one man from each house to Berlewen's house to form a council of action so we may decide how we can fight Nelferch.'

There was an uneasy muttering but they assented and moved into the woods.

Dryden, Cunobel and Tarow ran through the forest and came to the perimeter of the township, at a spot not far from the slave pen. The place seemed quiet and deserted. But on the sloping path down Dynas Drok they could see columns of horsemen leaving the great fortress.

'Nelferch is sending her warriors out in search of us,' smiled Cunobel. 'If we had tried to stay in the forest, they would soon have found us.'

'Hush!' whispered Tarow. 'Horsemen are coming this way.'

The three men sank back into the shelter of the undergrowth. A troop of warriors cantered by, grim-faced and purposeful.

Cunobel motioned the others to follow and, keeping low, they ran towards the wall of the town and in a thrice were over. Keeping to the shelter of the buildings, they worked their way along several side streets until they came to a cul-de-sac. Cunobel motioned with his hand to a wall, about six feet high, on the opposite side of the road. The three men ran towards it, leaping upwards and scrambling over the stones. They fell together into a courtyard on the other side. Dryden was the first to rise to his feet, wincing at the scratches on his arms and legs. As he raised his head, he saw a shadowy figure standing in the back porch of a building facing the yard.

A female voice cracked with apprehension.

'Who is there?'

It was Cunobel who answered.

'Berlewen, it is me.'

Berlewen flew from the shadow of the door into Cunobel's arms, happiness and tears mixed on her face. Dryden and Tarow waited while Cunobel and Berlewen embraced. Then the girl turned, smiling at them, and impulsively kissed them on the cheeks.

'The warriors of Nelferch said they had already captured you and that Yaghus was dead.'

Cunobel laughed shortly.

'We all know that the warriors of Nelferch are liars.'

The girl gave a swift look around.

'Come, take shelter in the cellar.'

Below Berlewen's circular stone house was a fairly large room lined with stone and lit by a burning torch. The three men soon found themselves sitting with bowls of hot stew and telling Berlewen their story.

'What do you plan to do now?' asked the girl.

'I am going to carry out Yaghus' plan,' said Cunobel. 'We must start the revolution against Nelferch from Dynas Drok itself. There are just over twenty of us and more will join soon.'

'How is Nelferch to be deposed?' asked the girl.

'Her force must be answered with force. I would not have said that a month or so ago. I followed the path of Bel the peaceful. Now I say, we must strike back.'

'What do you say, Yaghus?' asked Berlewen.

'I agree with Cunobel,' said Dryden. 'My plan was to escape with

239

Kigva and get to Kesmur and Pryderi before they invade Lan-Howlek. They must be stopped from an invasion which will make the ordinary people blind to their real enemies. Nelferch will use the excuse of an invasion to stir up national hatred against Lan-Kern.'

'But if a revolt were started in Lan-Howlek itself, then Kesmur and Pryderi could stand by to give support.'

Berlewen nodded slowly.

'I am in this venture with you. Nelferch has usurped the ancient laws of our people for too long. She has imprisoned and killed those who have opposed her. She has girded the people for war, against its desire to be at peace. You cannot reason with Nelferch in peace. She must be overthrown by force.'

At midnight seven men gathered in the house of Berlewen. Apart from Dryden, Cunobel and Tarow, there were four men who had been elected by the former slaves to represent them on the council of action. It was left to Cunobel to outline the proposal that the former slaves try to depose Nelferch by force, forming the nucleus of an insurgent group. Three of the others nodded their approval but a fourth, a lean-faced man, held up his hand.

'We may agree on principles, my friends,' he said gruffly, 'but principles and practicalities are different matters. Fight, you say. I agree, for I have suffered as much as most people under Nelferch's despotism. But with what? We have scarcely a dozen weapons between us.'

'There is enough to start,' growled Tarow.

'Tarow is right,' interposed Cunobel. 'Let your enemy supply you with the weapons. With our few weapons we can ambush the warriors of Nelferch, in ones and twos or in small bands, taking their weapons and gradually building up our armoury. Then, eventually, we can take her fortress.'

There was a muttered assent.

The lean-faced man shrugged. 'A good strategy, Cunobel. But while we are attacking Nelferch's warriors, what will they be doing? They will surely hunt us down?'

It was Berlewen who stood up, her pale face animated.

'You must come and go like shadows in the night. Until the time when you are ready to strike, you must stay hidden, appearing only now and then to ambush, collect your weapons and disappear again.

You must strike a chill fear into the hearts of Nelferch and her warriors until they become scared to go to sleep at night in their own fortress for fear of waking with knife at their throats. You will be an army of ghosts. They will not know where you will strike next.'

'But Nelferch will search the town and countryside for us,' pointed out the lean-faced man.

'She will do so in vain,' asserted Berlewen. 'Your greatest weapon is the support of the people. Remember that they are on your side for you are the people of Lan-Howlek. Nelferch is an usurper, a traitor, who can only hold her rule through force and fear. When a people are ruled by fear it becomes necessary to bring about the change to abate it. The people will support you; hide you; be your eyes and ears against Nelferch and her movements.'

The lean-faced man sighed.

'We seem agreed on the means, we agree on the method. We know we are against Nelferch. We seek to overthrow the usurper. But, my friends, what are we for? Even the people will not support a man against a tyrant unless they know he is not merely another tyrant.'

Tarow grunted.

'Friend of the lean face,' he said slowly. 'I do not know your name. But I now name you Gwaf, for you cast a winter's shadow on these proceedings.'

There was a ripple of laughter for the name meant 'winter'.

Gwaf waved his hand.

'Jests do not answer questions, Tarow. I repeat, we know what we are against. What are we for?'

Cunobel rose to his feet and surveyed the group.

'I will tell you. You may disagree. It is your right. It is right, too, that our friend - Gwaf - should question what we are for. We are certainly agreed to rise against Nelferch and all she stands for. But with what do we replace her rule?'

'Let us return to the old ways,' interrupted Gwaf. 'Let us elect our leader and let the most worthy be chosen.'

'Indeed,' agreed Cunobel. 'The people should choose as they did in the days before Nelferch usurped the power. But in so doing we must ensure, and safeguard, that another Nelferch cannot rise again. The fact that she could do so and use our system to abuse us is a

241

warning to us that the old system was not perfect. We must strive to bring about a more ideal society.'

It was Berlewen who, surprisingly, shook her head in disagreement.

'I know the principles which motivate your thoughts, Cunobel,' she said softly, 'and I applaud them. But the ideal society...whose ideal? And how can we force it into being by our struggle? The key to the humane society lies in the centuries of evolution of people's hearts and minds. Aye, we must struggle for it; but we cannot impose it. We must fight for it; but we cannot enforce it. If we do so we shall establish a tyranny as awful as Nelferch's. If we try to force an ideal society on people who are unprepared for it, then we will have to eliminate human weakness by annihilating humans. We can overthrow tyranny, yes; but we cannot replace tyranny with our own tyranny however benevolent we mean it to be. We must educate the people to choose for themselves.'

There was a silence and then slowly a murmur of agreement rippled around the men.

'Berlewen should lead our campaign,' cried one of the men.

Cunobel raised a hand and smiled at the girl.

'It is true,' he said, when the murmurs of assent had died down. 'In Berlewen I believe we have found the long silent voice of Lan-Howlek. Berlewen - will you lead us?'

The girl smiled shyly at the company.

'If it is the wish of you all, I shall be your voice to the people. But while I am content to be that voice, the body of the people requires a fist. Cunobel has the ability of a warrior, he should lead you in the fight.'

There was a mutter of approval.

Berlewen looked to Dryden.

'And you, Yaghus? Will you go and seek out Kesmur and Pryderi and form an alliance with them on our behalf?'

Dryden shook his head.

'If Tarow is agreeable, I would rather that he go and seek out Kesmur and Pryderi. I will admit of a selfish motive. Kigva is still imprisoned in Dynas Drok and I have sworn to rescue her.'

Tarow clapped Dryden on the back.

'Of course, Yaghus. Leave this to me for I know the countryside between here and Lan-Kern far better than you. I will ride out tomorrow night, if I can get a horse, and stop any attack Lan-Kern may be attempting.'

'Then our deliberations are concluded,' said Berlewen. 'Go back to your men and report our decisions. If by tomorrow nightfall no word has reached us of any dissent, then we shall assume that the plan is supported. Tarow will go to Kesmur and Pryderi and we shall begin our campaign.'

In ones and twos they left. Dryden prepared a bed for himself in a corner, observing with a wistful smile Berlewen and Cunobel going up to the main room deep in conversation. From the far side of the cellar Tarow's snores came softly. Dryden sighed and lay back wondering at the strange turn of fortune. What turns fate could take; now he was a healer with a revolutionary group in the heart of an enemy stronghold. And Kigva? What of Kigva? Somehow he must find a way of getting her out of the clutches of Nelferch before the harridan could carry out her threats.

Soon he was caught in a deep, dreamless sleep.

CHAPTER TEN

Nelferch's face was a mask of fury.

Gowlek the *drewyth* shuddered and lowered his gaze.

'So, Gowlek, what are you telling me? In the past seven days nearly thirty of my ablest warriors have been attacked and killed and their weapons stolen, while seventeen more have been severely wounded? By whom, Gowlek? By whom?'

'By the ...' he paused and began to stutter before her unblinking gaze.

Nelferch's face contorted, displaying her decaying teeth.

'By the people. Is that what you were going to say? By my people?'

'Nelferch,' mumbled Gowlek, 'it is said that the slaves who escaped last week have done these things.'

'Without the support of the people!' jeered Nelferch. 'They could not have done it without support. Ungrateful yelping jackals. However, I shall teach them a lesson in gratitude. I shall teach them a lesson they will never forget.'

On her seat by her mother's left hand, Logosen sighed.

'That is something which should have happened ages ago, mother,' she said, plucking an apple from a bowl of fruit by her side and biting savagely into it. 'Were I ruler I...'

Nelferch almost spat at her daughter.

'You will never be ruler here, Logosen!'

Gowlek shifted his weight uncomfortably from one foot to another.

'Shall I withdraw?' he asked hopefully.

Nelferch turned back to him with a sneer.

'No, Gowlek. Not yet. Tonight my estimable grandson, Cador, returns with his warriors from their raids on the rebellious northern settlements. When he returns, he will have my permission to burn one house in ten in the township - do you hear? One house in ten.

The families of those houses will be taken to the slave pens to work. The able-bodied young men among them can be taken to train as warriors. They can choose to die by the swords of my men immediately or by the swordsmen of Lan-Kern in the future. I'll wager they choose Lan-Kern,' she added with a sadistic chuckle.

Gowlek let his jaw hang open in horror.

'But, Nelferch,' he stammered, 'this will surely drive the people into the arms of the rebels.'

'Of what are you afraid, Gowlek?' asked the old woman.

'I fear for you, Nelferch,' whispered Gowlek, dropping his gaze.

'No; you fear for yourself, little man,' snapped Nelferch. 'You wonder lest your home be one of those that I have chosen. You fear me, not for me. Is that not so?'

Gowlek trembled for he knew that she was partly right.

'But, Nelferch,' he pressed, 'we learn that Kesmur and a force of several hundred warriors are camped on our border. Surely this will give them an excuse to invade Lan-Howlek.'

Nelferch snorted.

'Blyth has just returned from the border. Kesmur has been camped there several days. He lacks courage to invade or he would have crossed into Lan-Howlek before now. He is no threat to us. And if he is, remember I hold his daughter and will use her as a hostage.'

Gowlek bit his lip.

'But to burn one house in ten?'

'Never fear, *drewyth*,' drawled the old woman, licking her lips as they twisted into a smile. 'I will let Cador loose only if the people of the township do not stop sheltering the rebels. If, by this evening, they turn over to my warriors every slave rebel, then I shall spare them. If not, then one house in ten shall suffer. Go now, little man. Have that proclaimed in the township immediately.'

With shaking shoulders, the old *drewyth* bowed low and left Nelferch's throne room.

Logosen's shriek of laughter followed him.

'Well, mother, you know how the people will hate you now.'

Nelferch smiled cynically.

'Hate? Me?'

'They that fear you in the open will foster hatred in their burrows away from you.'

245

Nelferch chuckled in amusement.

'So long as they do fear, daughter. Their fear of me is stronger than my warriors and no emotion so effectively robs the mind of reason nor of its power to act. So let them fear me, daughter. They already call me the Witch Queen, Nelferch-an-Gwargh, because they cannot credit me with being able to fulfil my destiny without some magic power. The fools! It does not take magic for a wolf to dominate a flock of sheep.'

She drank deeply from her goblet of wine.

'And tell me, Logosen,' she suddenly said, frowning, 'what do you know of *An Kevryn,* the sacred symbol of the *drewyth* of Lan-Kern?'

Logosen raised her eyebrows in bewilderment.

'*An Kevryn?* What should I know, mother?'

'I have heard some talk from the slaves captured on Cador's last raid into Lan-Kern. They say that Cador sacked Meneghy and stole *An Kevryn.* Why has he not brought it to me? Is he hiding it himself?'

Logosen shrugged.

'Cador does not confide everything in me,' she said, a slightly querulous note in her voice.

Nelferch looked closely at her daughter.

'Obviously not,' she returned dryly as she saw genuine bewilderment and annoyance in Logosen's face. 'Very well. When Cador returns, he can explain the matter to me.'

'May Bel protect us if Cador and his cut-throats are unleashed against the township,' breathed Cunobel, as Gwaf finished reciting the proclamation which had been posted up a few hours previously in the market place.

'We must look to our own defences and not rely on Bel,' said Berlewen.

'What can we do?' asked Gwaf.

'I say attack Dynas Drok immediately.'

The words had sprung unbidden to Dryden's lips.

The others turned to stare at him in astonishment.

'Attack, Yaghus?' asked Cunobel in surprise.

Dryden's mind raced swiftly over the supportive arguments.

'Cador is marching in from the north this afternoon or late this evening. He and his men will be exhausted. Nelferch has made a mistake in issuing this proclamation before Cador and his men returned and rested. They can hardly launch an attack before dawn tomorrow.'

Gwaf leaned forward.

'But, Yaghus, Nelferch does not see them launching an attack; she sees her warriors merely moving against an unarmed citizenry, arresting them and burning their houses. The citizens have been too long under her rule to fight back. They might start tonight.'

Dryden laughed shortly. 'No, I do not think so. And thinking the people are unarmed is another mistake on the part of Nelferch. She forgets the people are fighting back already. They shelter us, they join us in ones and twos agreed, but they join us. Before Cador and his men can move against the citizens, I say we must strike first.'

Berlewen smacked one balled fist into the palm of her hand.

'Yaghus is right! We will wait one hour after Cador and his warriors have marched into Dynas Drok and then we strike!'

She turned and looked quickly at Cunobel.

'We must take the advantage, Cunobel.'

Cunobel smiled at her and signified his approval.

'But how can we storm Dynas Drok? We are only two score men at most,' interrupted Gwaf. 'What you are proposing is madness! How many warriors do you think Nelferch has inside the fortress?'

Dryden reflected.

'There is a bodyguard of fifty warriors under Blyth; then another hundred men who garrison the town.'

'And Cador,' said Gwaf, 'with perhaps another hundred warriors. And yet you suggest that our forty men, fifty at most now, attack an impregnable fortress held by two hundred and fifty trained warriors?'

Berlewen motioned Gwaf to silence.

'It must be done if our revolution is to survive,' she said softly. 'The people of Lan-Howlek are only human; do not think they will protect us once they see their homes and relatives being destroyed, however much they hate Nelferch.'

'But,' cried Gwaf, 'you yourself said the people would support us, and you were right, they do; they aid us, join us. They will remain loyal.'

247

'Loyal? Loyalty is the luxury of the people who populate storytellers' tales. In reality the people do not like to suffer the sharp pain of revolution. They would rather keep the dull pain of oppression.'

'The people will be constant!' declared Gwaf.

Berlewen let a smile play around the corners of her soft mouth.

'I wish I had your belief, my friend. But I am afraid that there is nothing in life so sure and so constant than the inconstancy of people.'

Cunobel put an arm around her waist.

'Berlewen and I are of one mind, Gwaf. As Yaghus says, we must attack, relying on our own strength to start the fight. This is not to say we despise the people and think they would betray us at the first sign of hardship. But the decision is a practical one.'

He paused and, meeting no opposition, continued;

'The time to strike is after Cador and his men return, allowing them time to take off their weaponry and rest from their march. Tarow returned to the town yesterday and is hiding in a safe house a few streets away. We will send him back to Lan-Kern to advise Kesmur and Pryderi of what we intend. We could ask that a column of warriors ride here post-haste to join our attack once it has begun and not before.'

'I agree,' nodded Dryden. 'It must not look as if this attack is a foreign invasion.'

He paused and frowned.

'What is it, Yaghus?' queried Berlewen.

'I was thinking of Kigva,' he replied. 'If attacked, Nelferch would have no compunction about using her as a hostage.'

'Perhaps she could be rescued before the attack?' suggested Berlewen.

'How?' demanded Dryden.

'Our men will dress themselves as warriors,' Cunobel said eagerly. 'We will simply march up through the main gate pretending we are reinforcements sent to aid Cador against the rebels. We can say that we have come from some eastern town. I do not think we will be opposed until we are at the main gate: then it will be our task to hold open the gates while the warriors of Lan-Kern ride in and help us.'

'It is a good plan,' agreed Dryden, 'but how does it help in the rescue of Kigva? While the warriors of Lan-Kern are riding through the ramparts, Nelferch could seize Kigva and use her as a hostage.'

Cunobel shook his head.

'Just before our men march up to the main gate, the evening collection of refuse is made. An old man named Gwarnyans takes his donkey and cart into Dynas Drok to collect the rubbish from Nelferch's kitchens. The guards never look in it. Yaghus can hide himself in there. Once inside, he will have to find Kigva and take her to safety before we commence our attack.'

Berlewen smiled.

'Of course. One man could get into the palace, find Logosen's slave quarters and hold off any attempt made by Nelferch to use the girl as a hostage.'

Dryden's eyes blazed with enthusiasm.

'I shall do it, Cunobel.'

'Very well, Yaghus. Now Gwaf and I will relay the plan to the men. You explain the situation to Tarow and send messages to Kesmur and Pryderi.'

Berlewen grasped Cunobel's hand as he turned to leave.

'I think the time has truly come, Cunobel,' she said, a suspicion of tears on her eyes.

Cunobel kissed her gently and was gone.

Berlewen raised her tear-stained eyes to Dryden and sniffed.

'Forgive me, Yaghus; we must all fulfil our destiny.'

CHAPTER ELEVEN

'Let us trust that Tarow has made it across the great river and that the men of Lan-Kern hurry quickly to our aid, or we stand no chance at all.'

It was Gwaf who spoke.

Cunobel grunted: 'Ever casting winter's gloom, Gwaf?' he hissed as he motioned the man to silence.

The four of them, Dryden, Cunobel, Berlewen and Gwaf, stood huddled in woollen cloaks to disguise the fact that underneath they were dressed in warrior's costumes and carried full weaponry. They stood in the shadow of the great menhir in the square of the town before the gates of Dynas Drok. Across the square, as they watched, came a long line of tired warriors, marching with arms at the slope, pushing a small crowd of manacled captives before them, many of whom were forced to carry large bundles which doubtless held Cador's booty. And riding on a black mare, in front of his men, came Cador, holding himself in his usual proud and arrogant manner.

'The warriors certainly appear exhausted,' muttered Dryden.

'Aye, they won't be able to carry out Nelferch's orders until they have rested from their march,' agreed Cunobel.

'In her fury for vengeance,' whispered Berlewen, 'Nelferch has made the bitterest mistake she will ever make.'

'But what if we have underestimated her mistake?' interposed Gwaf. 'What if we have made the error?'

Berlewen looked at him reprovingly.

'You always plead caution at our councils, Gwaf. Perhaps your caution is a good thing, when matched against our enthusiasm. But remember that the greatest mistake you can make is the fear of making a mistake.'

Gwaf relapsed into a hurt silence.

'Are our men ready, Berlewen?' asked Cunobel, as he watched the last of Cador's warriors tramp through the gates.

'Every man and woman is armed and knows what to do,' returned Berlewen. 'The men are ready to form up and the women will block the side streets to prevent the town guards reinforcing the fortress.'

'And you, Yaghus,' pressed Cunobel. 'Are you ready?'

Dryden nodded.

'In fifteen minutes, I climb into Gwarnyan's refuse cart. Half an hour afterwards, your attack begins.'

'Then all is ready,' approved Cunobel.

Gwaf suddenly gave one of his rare smiles.

'All seems set for victory, then. We will destroy Nelferch and her kind and punish all those who have followed her.'

'No!' Berlewen's voice was harsh.

The others turned and stared at her in astonishment.

'All victories breed hate,' explained Berlewen. 'If you take captives and put them into prisons or chain them in punishment, they will not be conquered nor will you be victorious. Nelferch and Cador and the other evil architects of this system must be punished undoubtedly. But we must bring peace to the people, for peace brings victory to both sides. We must win our enemies' esteem and show them how they have erred. In that achievement will be a lasting victory.'

Cunobel caught her hand.

'Berlewen, your wisdom shames us who strive for simple solutions. You are right. No one may be punished except Nelferch and her family, and those of her warriors, such as Blyth, who have shown zeal in persecuting the people in Nelferch's name.'

'That's all very well,' growled Gwaf, 'but what is to be done with Nelferch and the others. Shall we feed them to the *gourgath* as they fed so many of our people?'

'To inflict vengeance on the evildoer is merely to copy the wrong they have done,' replied Berlewen in rebuke. 'We can appease our consciences by calling it punishment. But let me remind you that the old ways stipulated that punishment must allow for rehabilitation. To deny the wrong-doer the means to recognise his wrong and make reparation is merely to descend to the level of an assassin.'

'But how would the old law punish Nelferch?' asked Dryden.

'In the old days a wrong-doer lost all rights of citizenship.'

'They became slaves?'

'No, no. They had physical freedom but they could not participate in the life of the community other than to work in prescribed tasks for the common welfare until they made full reparation for what they had done.'

Dryden was impressed and tried hard to suppress a grin.

'You mean that Nelferch could spend the rest of her life scrubbing the floors of a hostel for the sick or some such task?'

'That is for the people to decide,' smiled Berlewen.

Gwaf was a trifle sullen.

'Yet vengeance is a satisfying thing,' he murmured.

'As a meal is momentarily satisfying - until the next time you are taken by hunger,' observed Berlewen.

Cunobel intervened.

'It is time,' he said simply.

Dryden bade them farewell and hurried across the square to where the refuse collector, Gwarnyans, was waiting to take his donkey and cart into the fortress.

Kigva raised her eyes from her task as she knelt peeling potatoes over a large bowl.

Gwaun the harridan was leering at her.

'You are to come with me,' she cackled in her shrill voice.

'Why?' asked the girl suspiciously. 'Where are you taking me?'

She did not forget that it was Gwaun who had betrayed her to Cador before.

'You are not here to ask questions of your betters, slave,' shouted the old slave-mistress.

At the sight of the old woman's brandished ash-stick, Kigva rose sullenly to her feet.

Gwaun's lips cracked a smile.

'That's better, pretty-pretty.'

Kigva silently followed the old woman down the dark stone passages of the palace building, through the slave quarters and up the stone flagged stairway to the upper levels. She peered around nervously as the harridan led her through the great hall where Nelferch usually sat in audience with her advisers, and then on through a side door into the chambers that were usually kept private for Nelferch and her family.

The old woman finally paused before a door and knocked. Then she opened it and propelled the girl inside, cackling to herself.

Kigva stood uncertainly in the middle of the room. Her eyes wandered nervously around. Shields and arms decorated the walls and there were one or two painted murals depicting battle scenes. But the room was clearly a bedchamber and, apart from one or two chests, an occasional chair and a small table, only the great bed, covered in woollen coverlets, dominated the room.

Kigva shuddered and rubbed her upper arms apprehensively.

Crouching in the back of the stinking refuse cart, Dryden felt it swaying slowly up the twisting path, through the ramparts, and into the hill fortress. It was not long before he heard Gwarnyan's dry cough and discreet bang on the side of the cart to let him know that all was clear.

He moved silently out of the cart and found himself outside a low wall which separated the palace kitchen gardens from the main building. It was an easy climb, even in the oncoming gloom of early evening. He swung himself over the wall and dropped in a crouching position to the courtyard below. He gave a swift and cautious glance around. The courtyard was deserted and he saw a flight of wooden steps leading to an upper walkway that seemed to lead off in the direction of the main palace rooms.

Keeping as close as he could to the shadows, Dryden hurried up the stairs and started down the walkway. It divided into two after ten yards. Where to now?

A warrior came hurrying round a corner and almost collided with Dryden.

'Who are you?' he snapped, his hand reaching for his sword.

With a sinking feeling Dryden recognised the man. It was the red haired warrior who had brought him a captive from Lan-Kern.

Before he could react, the man had raised the pommel of his sword and brought it crashing down against the side of Dryden's head and Dryden fell senseless to the ground.

Kigva rubbed her upper arms in apprehension.

A dry, rasping cough made her spin round.

The figure of Cador emerged from the darkness of a recess in the room. A smile played over his face.

Kigva raised a hand to stifle a cry of horror.

'Come, come, Kigva of Lan-Kern,' Cador's voice was soft, almost sibilant. 'You are not afraid of me, besides,' his fingers traced a livid white scar on his cheek, 'besides, there is some unfinished business between us.'

Kigva's mind worked rapidly. Fear was what Cador thrived on. She must deny him that pleasure; she must show him no fear.

'Afraid?' she made her voice sound hard, but there was a brittle quality to it. 'No, Cador, I am not afraid of you. You arouse in me only feelings of revulsion.'

For a moment an angry light flashed in Cador's eyes and then died almost before she was sure it had been there.

He moved forward in easy, almost lazy movements to the small table on which a flagon of wine stood.

'At least,' he drawled, 'I arouse in you some emotion.'

'As the snake arouses emotion in the spider,' retorted Kigva.

Cador ignored her.

He poured out two goblets of wine and handed her one.

She shook her head.

Without speaking, Cador took his wine and sat down in one of the chairs, examining the girl from his cold eyes.

Kigva stood, body tensed, waiting.

'You realise your situation, Kigva?' began Cador.

'I know it well enough,' returned the girl.

'You are a slave, no longer an honoured citizen of your own miserable land. You are a slave in the household of the rulers of a mighty kingdom which will one day encompass the world.'

Kigva shuddered. Cador's face shone with belief in his vision.

'I am aware that I am a slave,' Kigva said quietly. 'There is no need to remind me of the shame of your people in allowing such a monstrous thing to happen to them. May Bel grant them wisdom to see the evil of their ways.'

Cador's body jerked, some wine spilled from his goblet onto his hand, as anger flashed into his eyes. Then it seemed as if his mind battled within for self control. Self control won and he relaxed back

254

into his seat.

'See how privileged you are, Kigva, that you may say such things to me, Cador, warlord of Lan-Howlek, and yet live.'

The girl stared straight into his eyes.

'I would rather die than live under your shame.'

Cador forced a laugh.

'That I doubt unless you are not human. No, Kigva, as I have said before, you are privileged. In fact, more privileged than any woman for I would make you my favourite.'

He leaned forward from his chair, his face reddening in the eagerness of his passion.

'I would make you my personal slave, and when I rule Lan-Howlek there would be none closer to me than you.'

Kigva stared at him, uncomprehending for a moment, and then a muddled confusion of emotions went through her.

Cador watched the expressions on her face; his eyes flinced as he saw the pity mirrored there. Anger, hatred, these he could deal with, but pity?

'May I go, Cador?' asked the girl in a cold voice.

Cador leapt to his feet, his wine spilling on the floor.

'Go?' his voice was almost a scream.

Kigva drew back several paces as Cador came forward, his eyes blazing.

'You are a mere slave, you slut!' he screamed. 'I am your master!'

The back of his hand caught Kigva a glancing blow across the side of the head, sending her spinning against the bed.

She groaned in agony and held her hands to her head.

'I offered you the greatest prize that a woman could have and you dared to say "may I go?" You dare to pity me! Me?'

The girl tried to retreat before him but the bed was behind her, catching at the back of her knees, and she fell sprawling on her back.

Then Cador was upon her. She could feel the hot palms of his hands on her body, feel their heat through her dress, feel them grasping at her breasts. His face, red with rage, was just above her. She could smell the stench of his wine-sodden breath mingling with the stale sweat of his body.

'I will make you obey me!'

His voice came as a fierce whisper and then his lips were against her neck and moving towards her mouth.

For a while she fought and resisted but he was stronger than she was and, in a moment, she knew the utter futility of fighting him. In that moment a great calmness entered her mind. She ceased struggling and her body relaxed. She felt Cador's body stiffen in bewilderment. He raised his head and looked down at her, puzzled. She returned his gaze, her pity mingled with her loathing of the man.

'You are stronger than I am, Cador,' she said simply. 'It is useless to struggle against you. I will not fight you for that affords you some sadistic pleasure. Do what you will, I cannot prevent it. But all I feel for you, and shall feel, is pity. I cannot even feel hate. There is a sadness for a man whose only claim to manhood is that he is stronger than a woman.'

Cador's open hand caught her against the side of the face.

'Bitch!' he breathed. 'You bitch! I will show you whether I am a man!'

He reached forward and tore open her tunic.

There was a thunderous knocking at the door.

Cador hesitated.

The voice of Gowlek, the *drewyth,* called urgently:

'Cador! Cador! Are you in there? Quickly! The slave rebels are attacking the fortress! Cador, we are in danger!'

The thunderous knocking was resumed.

For a moment Cador looked down at the girl, his face working in rage and desire.

He climbed off the bed and buckled on a sword.

'Do not think you have been saved,' he hissed, as Kigva watched him, unmoving on the bed. 'This will be but a short respite while I deal with those scum outside.'

He turned on his heel and was gone.

With a sinking heart Kigva heard the click of the lock as he turned the key behind him.

CHAPTER TWELVE

Dryden came to in a small room. His feet were bound together but, to his considerable surprise, his hands were free. Shaking his head, he peered at his hands in disbelief. Curiously, he looked about him. Someone had started to tie a rope around one wrist. But where were they? He was in a small room, a cell, lying on a wooden plank bed. But the door stood open. Through it came the faint cries of people and the sounds of fighting.

In a second Dryden was aware of what had happened. His captor had brought him to this cell and was in the process of binding him when Cunobel's warriors had commenced their attack. His captor must have raced out in answer to the alarm leaving his task uncompleted.

Quickly, Dryden removed the rope from his wrist and from his legs. Outside the cell door was a small guard room. On a table were his weapons. Snatching them, Dryden ran outside into the early evening gloom. Perhaps he would not be too late to save Kigva, after all?

Kigva sprang from the bed and, without much hope, went to the door and tried it. Then she turned back into the room. Her eyes flashed to the shields and weapons which decorated the walls. At least, she decided, she would be able to defend herself on Cador's return. Perhaps it was better to die than continue in slavery. Why had her father and Pryderi not attacked Nelferch's fortress long before this? Each day she had hopes of rescue and each day her hopes faded a little. What was the use of a few slaves trying to rebel? They would soon be crushed. Why had Kesmur not come?

She crossed to a wall and took down a longsword and shield. They were too big for her and she made several experimental passes before she felt comfortable with the weapons. She buckled on the sword over her right shoulder and hooked the shield onto her left. Then she saw a short javelin and picked this up and weighed it in her hand. If Cador was first through the door he would be in for a nasty surprise, she thought with a grim smile. At least he would see how well trained the women of Lan-Kern were in the art of weaponry.

She stood for a moment not sure what her next move should be. The window looked down to an inner courtyard and this time there were no steps descending down. She gave a sigh, almost like a sob, when she remembered her attempted escape with Dryden. If only he were here now; he would advise her what to do. If only she had shown him more warmth, more understanding, when he was alive. Now he was dead, dead by the claws and fangs of the *gourgath!* She would never forget how Nelferch delighted in telling her the details of his death.

'Oh, Yaghus!' she whispered aloud. 'I need your strength and wisdom now.'

Outside she could hear the faint din of battle, the clash of weapons and the shouts and screams and curses of people. She pulled her mind back to the present. So the slaves were attacking the palace? Poor courageous fools! What hope had they against Nelferch's warriors? Ah, if only Dryden were alive to advise them ... She shook herself. It was no use dwelling on what might have been.

She stared around the room, letting her eyes come to rest on the dark recess from which Cador had emerged. A sudden thought pricked at her mind. The recess was dark, hung with a few drapes and woven tapestries which covered the stone walls. It was not that deep and had Cador been standing there when Gwaun pushed her into the room she would surely have seen him. Yet he had emerged there while she was standing in the centre of the room.

She went to the recess and peered carefully round it. Then she moved aside one tapestry with the tip of her javelin. It was a blank stone wall. She moved aside another tapestry. It revealed a small wooden door. Holding her breath, Kigva put her hand on the iron ringed handle and turned. It swung open with a protesting squeak, revealing a dimly-lit circular flight of stone steps. With a smile of triumph on her lips, Kigva moved through the door onto the stairway, closing the door behind.

A shrill chuckle echoed through Cador's empty bedchamber.

Opposite the recess, on the far side of the room, a small stone block, big enough to provide a peephole, was pushed back into place with a soft grating sound. Behind the wall, Gwaun, who had been there ever since she had led Kigva into Cador's room, hunched cackling with laughter.

In the gloom of the circular stairway, Kigva was feeling her way downwards. It descended very steeply, even now she felt she must be far below ground level. Then the stairway suddenly stopped and Kigva felt the steps give way to the flat surface of a passageway. It was pitch dark but the passage was very narrow and Kigva found that she could make rapid progress along it by holding out her spear in front of her with one hand and keeping the other on the stone wall at her side.

She had not gone far before she decided that it might be a wise thing to count her strides in case she had to return that way again. She had counted four hundred paces when a faint light began to show ahead and the tunnel began to slope upwards.

She emerged in a tangle of undergrowth in the night-shrouded forest. Behind her she could still hear shouting in the direction of Dynas Drok. She decided to make for Lan-Kern but she stood hesitant and unsure of her direction. Perplexed, she stood trying to work out her position by her relationship to the fortress of Nelferch. Then she made a decision. She felt positive of her choice and with purposeful strides she set out into the dark forest.

The sounds of screams and din of battle were all around him as Dryden pushed across the main hall where Nelferch had once sat in splendour. The bodies of some palace guards who had chosen to fight lay strewn in profusion over its bloody floor.

He turned quickly into a corridor which ended in a flight of stone steps leading to an upper gallery.

He caught sight of two warriors and between them the bent back of an elderly woman. The woman was splendidly dressed and carried a short sword.

'Nelferch!'

The witch queen swung round, her eyes wide in terror.

'Bel cease from reincarnation! What is this? A shade come to haunt me at my end?'

Blyth stood by her side.

He scowled at Dryden.

'It is no shade, Nelferch. The *estrennek* must have escaped the fangs of the *gourgath*. How, I do not know. Let me finish him.'

Nelferch shook her head.

'Pylyak!' she snapped to the second warrior.

The man needed no further urging and moved swiftly forward to meet Dryden.

Pylyak was a large man, over six feet in height, and in this he obviously thought he had the advantage. Dryden waited until he estimated the man to be within range of his sword arm, which he tucked closely against his side, and then he dropped to one knee, and pushed forward, thrusting the longsword swiftly and suddenly into the man's torso, straight and hard. Pylyak dropped his sword, looked down in astonishment as the blood began to stain his tunic, and then fell without a word.

Dryden leapt over the body and raced after Nelferch and Blyth who had not waited to see the outcome of the engagement.

'Which way has the girl gone?' the old woman's querulous tones came down the corridor. 'Where has she gone? She is our only hope of making a bargain!'

She whirled as she heard Dryden racing after them.

The old witch queen gave a scream of hate and pushed herself behind Blyth's tall figure.

'Where is Kigva?' demanded Dryden.

Nelferch's eyes blazed.

'You will never find the bitch of Lan-Kern,' she cried. 'Pylyak failed me, Blyth. You will not.'

Blyth, the captain of Nelferch's guard, came snarling at Dryden, his blade flashing. Dryden managed to parry his onslaught and push him back a few feet. The man renewed the attack with such ferocity that Dryden was hard pressed to defend himself from the flickering blade. He had not had such an opponent since Teyrnon.

Nelferch, trying to take advantage of the situation, was seeking to reach the far corridor. Dryden reached out with one hand and sent a chair hurtling across the intervening space, thudding viciously against the old woman's legs and sending her collapsing in a heap, snarling.

Blyth's eyes blazed in anger and he came at Dryden with a new surge of strength.

But it was the anger which led to his downfall.

He pressed Dryden fast against a wall and raised his arm for the kill. Dryden lurched sideways and smashed the flat of his sword against the man's face. Blyth stood confused for a second and then he turned towards Dryden. The second's hesitation had been enough for Dryden to recover himself, duck under Blyth's guard and shoot his blade up between the warrior's rib cage.

Nelferch climbed to her feet, looking down at her slain guard with horror.

Dryden straightened up, his sword pointing to the floor.

'Well, Nelferch-an-Gwargh,' he said, giving her the title by which she had become detested throughout Lan-Kern and Lan-Howlek. 'Well, what witchcraft have you left in you now? Will you surrender? Will you tell me where Kigva is?'

Nelferch ignored him. She moved towards Blyth as one in a dream. Her movements reminded Dryden of a sleepwalker. Slowly she bent down and tousselled the warrior's hair in her fingers, fondling it. Tears rolled down her cheeks.

'He was my lover,' she whispered softly.

Dryden's mouth hung open at the prospect of this crazed old woman having a lover, least of all the young warrior he had just slain. Then, he shrugged, who was he to judge?

'Poor Blyth. So strong and handsome. So youthful. He carried in him my lost hopes. Ah, Blyth the Wolf.'

Dryden stirred uncomfortably.

Nelferch looked up at him with hate in her eyes.

'You are privileged, Yaghus. You have seen the weakness of Nelferch.'

'Is it a weakness to be human?'

'Only strong people must rule. I seized power because only the powerful can exercise power. The anarchy of democracy, the old laws, they must pass away. There is stability only in the strong. The seed of the oak will become an oak tree but the seed of the thorn can only be a thorn.'

Dryden gazed at her in sorrow.

The old woman dashed away her tears and glanced back to Blyth's

261

body.

'Power was pleasure,' she said slowly, 'the pleasure that sweetens the pain of life.'

'You must have been hurt very badly in your life,' observed Dryden with pity.

Nelferch's eyes flashed for a moment.

'Perhaps, Yaghus. But that is over. Blyth is over. Power is over.'

She leant forward and touched the dead warrior's face and then, without a sound, she collapsed over his body.

Dryden dropped to his knees and tried to pull her away. Something warm and sticky touched his hands. He looked down. From Nelferch's breast, just above her heart, there protruded the small bone handle of a dagger. Her right hand still clasped it so tightly that the whites of her knuckles showed.

Oddly, Dryden experienced a feeling of regret as he let Nelferch's body fall back across the corpse of her lover.

Cador hacked and hewed at his enemies with desperation. Gowlek fought by his side, fought desparately, urged on by the fear of retribution for his role in the evil regime of the witch queen. The old man was crying in a shrill whine of a voice, calling upon Bel to forgive him and show him mercy, even as he parried and thrust and hacked at his adversaries.

'We are lost, Cador,' he cried. 'The slaves are everywhere.'

Cador ignored him.

His eyes flickered to the stairway behind him. They were indeed lost. The slave-swine were pouring into the fortress. At first there had been just a handful who sought control of the gates. But then, from the township, there came swarming hundreds of people holding all manner of weapons. A curse on them! Cador had seen several of his warriors lay down their arms and go over to the slaves. Now someone was crying that Nelferch was slain. Ah, if he could reach the stairway behind him and get to his room, he might be able to escape into the forests through his secret tunnel. He might be able to take that bitch of Lan-Kern with him and make a deal. Once safely in the east he could probably find men, raise a new army and return to repay these swine for this day's work.

'It is no use, Cador,' whined old Gowlek. 'We are doomed. Let us lay down our arms.'

'Ay,' cried a slave. 'Lay down your arms and surrender! We will not harm you! By the truth of Bel!'

Cador bared his teeth.

'Losles!' he sneered, calling them a species of parasitic woodworm. *'Losles!* I fight on!

Tight-mouthed, he moved back a pace.

'No!' cried Gowlek. 'Not I! I surrender!'

The old man was beginning to drop the point of his sword when Cador suddenly seized him by the scruff of the neck and pushed him towards the slaves who, having no time to lower their own weapons, impaled the old *drewyth's* screaming body on their swords. Taking advantage of the confusion, Cador turned and raced up the stairway, reaching the door at the top before his pursuers. He passed through it and slammed and bolted it.

He raced down the corridor towards his bedchamber.

The door stood open. The room was empty. Kigva had gone.

Cador swore.

Somewhere behind him he heard a chuckle.

Turning out of the room, Cador pushed his way into the next chamber. Gwaun the harridan was backing in fear from the wall, her spy-hole open to Cador's angry stare.

For a moment Cador raised his sword, and the old woman crouched sobbing, waiting for the blow to descend.

It did not.

Instead Cador seized the old woman by the throat with his free hand and pulled her face near his.

'Woman,' he snarled, 'If you want to live you will tell me where Kigva has gone. Did Nelferch take her?'

The harridan wheezed in fright.

'No, no. Kigva has not gone with Nelferch. Nelferch is dead.'

Cador's eyes did not flicker. The feeling of remorse was alien to him.

'Then where is she?'

'She...she...'

'Out with it, old woman, or make your peace for your journey to the Otherworld.'

'She went down the tunnel behind the tapestry.'

'She found my secret passage?' asked Cador, surprised.

The harridan nodded eagerly.

A slow smile crossed Cador's face.

'Then Bel may smile on me yet.'

She turned and looked into his cold eyes and suddenly read death in them.

She felt him lift up her frail body, opened her mouth to scream but his large powerful hand was around her scrawny throat, choking her windpipe. She felt him propel her into the air, felt herself falling until she thudded aginst the stone wall and collapsed sobbing to the floor. Gwaun raised her eyes and saw him raising his sword above his head.

A door splintered further down the passageway.

Cador snarled in fury, dropped his sword and raced for his room. A quick glance behind him showed him that the insurgents were smashing down the door and would soon be in the corridor. He raced into his bedchamber, slammed the door shut and shot home the bolts. Then he seized two hunting spears and a shield from the wall, noting in passing that a shield, a sword and a javelin were missing. But before he could make any deductions from the fact, he could hear a banging on his door.

He ran to a corner of the room, dropped to his knees and swiftly lifted a stone from the floor. Beneath the stone was a dark cavity in which reposed a small black metal box. He picked it up and grinned at it.

'*An Kevryn*' he whispered.

He replaced the stone and shot a glance towards the door against which heavy blows were sounding. He picked up the box and his weapons, lifted the tapestry and was gone down the circular stairway.

CHAPTER THIRTEEN

The red-haired warrior presented his sword, hilt first, to Cunobel.
'The guard surrender,' he said simply. 'Nelferch is dead. So is
Blyth and Cador has fled. We are at your mercy.'

Cunobel solemnly took the man's sword and motioned his men to
disarm the rest of the warriors, who started to throw down their
weapons.

Gwaf clapped Cunobel on the back in a display of exuberance.
'*Lawa!*' he exclaimed. 'Praise be! And the warriors of Lan-Kern
have not yet arrived. We overthrew Nelferch by our own strength!'

'Not strength alone,' observed Cunobel. 'Right and justice were
our weapons.'

'And a good longsword to underscore the point,' chuckled Gwaf.
'Did you see the way the people joined us, with sticks and staves and
any weapon they could seize hold of. They were magnificent! At
least Berlewen was wrong to doubt the constancy of the people.'

'In this instance, yes,' agreed Cunobel. 'This time they were,
indeed, magnificent. It is not always so. But where is Berlewen?'

'I saw her go into Nelferch's throne room a few moments ago.'

A horn suddenly blared and a rider tore through the open gates of
the fortress.

'Hah!' cried Gwaf. 'It must be the arrival of the men from Lan-
Kern.'

It was Tarow, who reined up his sweating horse before them.

'Pryderi will be here instantly. I rode on ahead of the main
column.'

He stopped and looked about him in surprise.

'What? Is it over? Is the fortress ours?'

'Nelferch is dead,' affirmed Cunobel. 'Gwaf, see to Pryderi and
his men when they arrive. I'll go and look for Berlewen.'

Berlewen stood in the great hall of Nelferch's palace, her green eyes wandering sadly over the bodies of the dead and wounded.

A figure stirred behind the dais on which stood Nelferch's throne.

'Who is that?' called Berlewen, raising her sword.

The figure of a woman stepped forward. She carried herself erect.

'It is I, Logosen, daughter of Nelferch!'

The woman sat down in Nelferch's chair and stared down disdainfully.

Berlewen smiled and dropped her sword point.

'It is finished, Logosen. Your mother is dead and your son Cador has fled.'

'It is of no consequence,' sniffed Logosen. 'I am now ruler here, scum!'

Berlewen frowned. The woman was clearly not in a normal state of mind. Perhaps her head had been turned by the sight of the conflict. The girl moved forward, sheathing her sword.

'Have no fear, Logosen. Have no fear. You must come with me, now. Come away from this place. Everything will be alright now.'

She reached out to take the woman by the arm.

Abruptly, Berlewen stiffened and gasped.

A smile of evil triumph cracked across Logosen's face as she withdrew the slim and bloody knife from Berlewen's side.

Pain and bewilderment etched Berlewen's face as she sank slowly down on the floor before the mahogany chair.

'Cunobel,' she gasped. 'It is...my destiny!'

'Berlewen!'

Cunobel's voice screamed through the hall. He entered to see Berlewen's form sinking to the floor. Behind him crowded Tarow and Gwaf and half a dozen of their men. Dryden also pushed his way through. They stood frozen, like statues, at the horror of the scene.

Logosen sat oblivious on Nelferch's throne, crooning softly to herself, rocking to and fro, ignoring Berlewen's bleeding body at her feet.

Cunobel broke the spell, racing forward and seizing the dying girl in his arms. 'Berlewen! Berlewen!' he mouthed over and over again as if it were some magic formula to prevent her passing on to the

266

Otherworld.

'She dared touch me,' Logosen suddenly giggled. 'Touch *me!* And I am ruler now, you know. Remove her, she wearies me.'

Cunobel looked up through his tears at the imbecilic face above him. A hatred such as he had never known surged through him. Gently he laid Berlewen down and drew out his sword, raising it high above his head.

Dryden, Tarow and Gwaf watched in silence.

Logosen stared up at the blade which flickered and shone in the light of the torches which now lit the room. Her face creased in ugliness as she let out screech after screech of maniacal laughter.

With hate marring his features, Cunobel stretched up for the death lunge.

'No!'

Berlewen's voice was a whisper.

Cunobel hesitated but did not drop the sword.

'Cunobel,' Berlewen whispered again. 'It is not the way.'

Cunobel's sword lowered a fraction.

'Remember our words about punishment. Forgive, educate, show people the error of their ways...do not make martyrs and enemies. To kill a lunatic who knows not right from wrong makes you worse than an assassin.'

Cunobel looked down on the giggling Logosen in disgust.

'Take her away. Lock her up.'

He turned and motioned two of his men to remove the demented daughter of Nelferch and then dropped to a kneeling position by his dying love. Silently, Dryden, Tarow, Gwaf and the others formed a circle around them. Tears were in their eyes.

'Does the wound hurt, Berlewen,' asked Cunobel, a catch in his voice.

'Hurt? There is no pain in a wound received at the moment of victory.'

She sighed and closed her eyes.

'Hold my hand tightly, Cunobel. I would have loved to live a little more, to have helped you with the real task, to rebuild this land...to rebuild the morality of the people, the morality of us all.'

Cunobel clenched his teeth.

'You will. I know you will. You must live, Berlewen. I cannot achieve that task alone.'

The girl smiled gently.

'The people will help you, Cunobel.'

'I cannot do it,' declared Cunobel vehemently. 'Without you, I am nothing. Yaghus would make a better peace-maker than I.'

'Is Yaghus there? It grows too dark for me to see. Too dark...'

Dryden bent low over the girl.

'I am here, Berlewen.'

'It was foretold, Yaghus,' she smiled. 'Did you find your Kigva?'

Dryden bit his tongue.

'I *shall* find her,' he said with emphasis.

'Yes,' responded the girl. 'You shall. I feel it. Be a friend to Cunobel. Counsel him to accept the task of rebuilding Lan-Howlek. Let Tarow and Gwaf be his supports. Yes, even Gwaf, for we need caution as we need enterprise.'

She gave a little sob and some blood began to trickle from her mouth.

'Promise me...promise this, Cunobel...that Lan-Howlek will return to the old laws. The laws of our forefathers. That there will be no vengeance sought, no enmity...promise.'

'Even as you say,' whispered Cunobel.

There was a murmur of assent from those who surrounded her.

'And now a word alone with my Cunobel...'

They discreetly withdrew, leaving the sobbing Cunobel cradling the dying girl.

Dryden blinked rapidly while tears were streaming down Tarow's face unashamedly.

'She was our wisdom,' the warrior murmured, 'she led us through so much.'

A cry of anguish came from Cunobel.

Dryden moved quietly forward and felt for the pulse of the pale girl.

He shook his head.

There was a silence in the great hall. It was dawn. The bodies of the dead and wounded had been taken away and now the hall was crowded with people. Several people were seated around a large table. Among them was Cunobel, red-eyed and silent. To his left sat

268

Pryderi of Lan-Kern, representing the interests of his father Kesmur. To Cunobel's right sat Dryden, morose and unseeing. Tarow was next to him and next to him sat Gwaf who was now rising to his feet.

'It is agreed then,' he said. 'Cunobel is elected our chieftain in peace and in battle. This assembly of the free people of Lan-Howlek also agrees that a set of laws will be drawn up, codified, and committed to a place of public inspection which will be in keeping with the spirit and direction of our revolution against tyranny and evil. These laws shall be known as Berlewen's Code, for it was the spirit and wisdom of Berlewen which aided us in the dark days of Nelferch; it is her spirit and wisdom which we must now call upon to guide us through the long dawn ahead.'

There was a muttering of approval and several of those gathered banged their swords against their shields in approval.

'Cunobel! Long life to our new *Gwelhevyn!* Long life to our new chieftain!'

'You do me honour,' he said wistfully. 'That honour belongs to Berlewen for, had she been granted a longer life, she should rightly have been your *gwelhevyn.* I accept this office for her sake and for her sake I undertake to carry forward the rebuilding of Lan-Howlek, both her moral rebuilding as well as her physical rebuilding. To do this I accept the charge of drawing up a code of laws which will specify the rights of every man, every woman and child, which shall be known as Berlewen's Code. And should I usurp the powers which you grant me, you must swear that the minute, indeed the very second, that I do so, I shall cease to be your *gwelhevyn* and shall be cast out of office which I hold by your sufferance.'

Applause resounded in the room.

'Before I ask you to nominate those who you think best able to help me in this administration, I would ask for your approval or condemnation on this matter...'

He paused and looked at Pryderi.

'We have at our council table Pryderi, son of Kesmur of Lan-Kern. With Pryderi came three hundred warriors of Lan-Kern to help us overthrow the evil of Nelferch. They came not for conquest; not for plunder nor for payment. They came at the request of the people of Lan-Howlek to help them in common brotherhood. They came with no other thought of reward except seeing Lan-Howlek free and prosperous again.

'For many years Nelferch and her grandson robbed and looted in Lan-Kern. I propose that one of my first tasks is to ascertain the extent of the evil that was committed against these, our brothers, and to pay compensation in accordance with our ancient custom and law.'

There was a thunderous cry of approval.

Cunobel continued:

'The greatest sacrilege committed against Lan-Kern was the plunder of the *drewyth* sanctuary at Meneghy and the murder of Mabon the chief of all the *drewyth*. That was not a crime against Lan-Kern only but against ourselves, for we are also followers of the path of Bel and we too hold Meneghy as sacrosanct. Worse still, Cador stole the greatest wealth of our people - *An Kevryn!*'

There was an astonished gasp from the people, for only a few knew of the robbery.

'Cador's soul may never be reborn in this world or the Otherworld for so heinous was this deed,' declared Cunobel. 'Since the day when *An Kevryn* was plundered and taken away by Cador, all the sacred fires of the *drewyth* of Lan-Kern have been extinguished and will never be rekindled until the sacred relic of the age beyond the time of the Great Destruction is returned to its resting place at Meneghy. As a token of our sorrow and disgust at the evil perpetrated by a man of Lan-Howlek against the sacred symbol of life, I propose that all the sacred fires of the *drewyth* of Lan-Howlek likewise be extinguished until *An Kevryn* is found and returned. Let it symbolise the age of darkness into which we were plunged and let the recovery of *An Kevryn* symbolise our going forward into a new light.'

Again thunderous applause reverberated about the room.

'Pryderi of Lan-Kern and Yaghus the healer are soon to set forth on a search for *An Kevryn* and for Kigva of Lan-Kern, both have ...'

'Hold!'

A burly man shouldered his way through the crowd to the table dragging something after him.

'Forgive me, my *gwelhevyn*,' he said to Cunobel, 'but I have some news which must be presented to Yaghus and to Pryderi of Lan-Kern immediately.'

Cunobel looked surprised.

'What is it?'

The man pushed forward that which he had been dragging after him. It was an old woman, the harridan, who spat and scowled at the assembly.

'My *gwelhevyn,* this woman is Gwaun. She was slave-mistress to Nelferch's daughter, Logosen. She has a tale to tell you.'

The old woman spat and swore at the man who merely laughed and poked at her with the point of his sword.

'Lest you want to be skewered like a fowl for the roasting, old woman, tell Yaghus and Pryderi the tale you confessed to me.'

Gwaun scowled and then grudgingly told how Kigva had escaped from Cador's bedchamber, through the secret stairway and tunnel and how Cador, seizing the black box known as *An Kevryn,* had gone after her.

Dryden was on his feet, his face tense and white.

'Which direction would she have gone?'

The old woman shrugged and then gave a sharp cry as the warrior's sword pricked her arm.

'The tunnel leads in an eastward direction, *estrennek,*' she scowled.

Pryderi, too, was on his feet.

'But Kigva would know it was going eastward and turn around westwards for Lan-Kern.'

Gwaun sneered.

'It was well after dusk when she left. The clouds were thick in the sky and the trees of the forest grow closely. How would she know which was east and which was west?'

'Then she might have gone eastwards,' whispered Pryderi aghast.

'What lies eastward?' queried Dryden, wondering why he looked so alarmed.

Gwaun gave a hoarse cackle of a laugh.

'Why, *estrennek,* you are ignorant. To the east lies the land of the See-ti. A strange, terrifying country - a country where men fly in the bowels of great birds, birds which fly to their bidding, so great is their power. Men, perhaps gods from the Otherworld, who are able to shoot lightning bolts at their enemies.'

Dryden stared at the old woman in amazement. Was there, then, still a part in this strange new world where men flew in aeroplanes and had guns?

Pryderi looked towards Dryden with a strained face.

'If Cador was pursuing her, she might have found the way west blocked by him and gone on eastward to escape.'

'If we left now we could follow the tracks,' said Cunobel eagerly. 'I have enough woodcraft for that.'

Dryden shook his head.

'No, Cunobel, your duty is to remain here in Lan-Howlek as *gwelhevyn*. Kigva is my responsibility. I shall go after her.'

'Then I shall go with you, Yaghus,' cried Tarow.

'And I,' echoed Gwaf.

'No,' replied Dryden. 'You, also, have responsibilities. You are both needed here to help Cunobel. I must travel alone.'

'You will not,' interrupted Pryderi. 'Kigva is of my flesh. She is my sister. I have the right to go with you. We shall go together and, in finding Kigva, we may also discover Cador and *An Kevryn*.'

Dryden looked into the smiling eyes of the young *drewyth*.

'Besides, Yaghus,' the young man grinned, 'my woodcraft is better than yours.'

Dryden took Pryderi's outstretched hand.

'It is agreed,' he said.

'You are always a man of wisdom, Yaghus,' said Cunobel, shaking his head sadly. 'You are right. I, Tarow and Gwaf must remain here for the sake of the people. But part of our hearts will go with you in your quest.'

'*Gwelhevyn* of Lan-Howlek,' replied Dryden solemnly, 'those words will lend speed to our ultimate success.'

'But why not take a troop of warriors? Pryderi has three hundred with him?' asked Gwaf, as Pryderi and Dryden left the hall to prepare for their journey.

'Kigva and Cador already have twelve hours start on us which we must make up for,' replied Pryderi. 'Two men can travel more swiftly than a hundred.'

Gwaun's laughter echoed after them.

'No matter how swiftly you travel, you will not find her, nor will you find Cador and *An Kevryn*. You will not return! No one returns from the land of the See-ti. No one!'

272

More top science fiction from Magnum Books

T. J. Bass
413 3467   The Godwhale   65p

Alfred Bester
413 3467   Extro   85p

Ben Bova
417 0413   Colony   £1.35

John Brunner
413 3458   The Wrong End of Time   55p
417 0208   Traveller in Black   75p

Michael Conner
417 0512   I Am Not the Other Houdini   95p

Philip K. Dick
417 0461   Dr Futurity   85p
417 0460   The Unteleported Man   80p
413 3653   The Crack in Space   70p
417 0197   The Simulacra   75p
417 0259   The Man Who Japed   85p

David Dvorkin
417 0260   Shiny Mountain   95p
